Look 'N Up Liberation

Look 'N Up, Volume 2

Janice Carr Smith

Published by Janice Carr Smith, 2026.

This is a work of fiction. Similarities to real people, places, or events are entirely coincidental.

LOOK 'N UP LIBERATION

First edition. March 3, 2026.

ISBN: 979-8987517925

Written by Janice Carr Smith.

Table of Contents

To Elizabeth, the OWL. My powerful friend and fellow warrior.

Prologue
Last Cycle, by Jerry

I had just turned 12 when the aliens came. I was hanging out at my favorite spot by the river, enjoying my last morning of freedom before the pomegranates came ripe. Mom and Dad still hadn't found anyone to help with the harvest. Yeah, I live on a farm. We call it the 'Look 'N Up Ranch, and I'll inherit it someday.

I might inherit the Look'N Up gene, too. In every generation of my family, someone has a misplaced left eye socket that cocks up and to the left. Not just a crooked eyeball, this is something freakishly noticeable. I'm lucky. My baby blues are straight across. So's my dad's. But my Uncle Patrick and my cousin, Belinda, they've got it. So did my grampa and great-grampa, all the way back to before we came here to California from Oklahoma during the dust bowl. That's why we call this place the Look 'N Up. But the Look 'N Up means more than that. It's why Mr. Richardson plucked my great-grandparents out of that hoard of starving farm workers and gave them this farm. Like my dad, Elmer, says, "It means you pull your head out of wherever you like to tuck it and look around at the people around you. Feel them. Think about them. Consider them."

So, when this weird-looking family with green skin comes walking up the river trail and says they know all about pomegranates, (they call them kips), well, we needed the help, and, we had to ask, "How do these green people feel?" My dad hired them, and they lived in the worker's quarters next door to the house for three years. That's one cycle, where they're from.

They count time in three-year cycles, because every three years, the nimblies and bumblies attack them for three days and three nights. The nimblies come in the daytime. They're like giant dragonflies with three-foot wingspans and probes like a mosquito that suck your blood dry and poison you so you can't move. Then, at night, the bumblies come. Giant bats with horns like rhinos, only sharp like knives. The guys shave with them, if they shave at all. They rip you up and eat you in minutes, even if you're not paralyzed by the nimblies.

For all three days and nights, the men, over 15 years old, or 5 cycles, fight in the trenches in front of the Great Hall, where the women prepare food and do first aid and send supplies to the trenches on the backs of the ganeeshes. They're like elephants. They have dogs, too. They look like lavender German shepherds.

So, anyway, here comes this family down the river trail, in their green skin and raggedy clothes made of woven grass and stained with "gaa", they call it. Pomegranate juice and wine, other messes, whatever, they just wear it. And they're the Holy Family! I couldn't imagine how the others dressed, but now I know, it's pretty much the same. It was the Akashic Robe that made the old man special, and he lost it when he came through the portal.

It was Baput's twelfth birthday that day, so he's just a little bit younger than me. He's bigger though. Tall, like his dad, and bigger muscles, even though he's kind of nerdy, being the royal heir. Life is harder for everyone where they come from. They have no technology. Not even metal. Baput's dad, Valko, tripped out when he saw metal. And his Uncle Felsic, Valko's little brother, turned into an expert auto mechanic in less than a cycle. Never ever seen an engine before! He's kind of goofy, and back on Nauve he was kind of the village idiot, and the town drunk. He had a family, though. His wife and daughter were outside of the Holy Cave when the portal opened up, right when the nimblies were attacking. He doesn't know what happened to them.

Baput's mom came too. Salistar. She and my mom became BFFs. All the time talking about plants and food and kids. Salistar lost a daughter to the bumblies. And her son, older than Baput, well, he was going to be the next Akash. The Holy Man, the undisputed leader of what we call "Nauve"; a village of about a hundred people who think it's the only place in the world. Nauve is their word for home. When I asked Baput where he came from, he said "home". They didn't have a name for their village, because it's the only village there is.

Baput's brother was apprentice to his G-pa, a skinny old man with the straggly white hair and beard, sage green skin turning yellow around the wrinkles, who was the ruler of the known universe.

But then, Baput was born on First Pomegranate Day, the first day of the cycle. The day the nimblies and bumblies start their three-day attack every three years. And the day the portal opened. Being born on that most holy day meant Baput would be a special Akash, if he ascended. An Alanakash. His G-pa was pretty excited about having an Alanakash succeed him. But what about Baput's older brother?

G-pa said he fell from the top of the stairs to the holy cave, but, like I had to explain to Baput, he opened the door in the Holy Cave that was clearly labeled "Death to Open". That's where they got the stuff they were fighting the nimblies with, that ended up zapping them to another dimension; that is, to the Look 'N Up Pomegranate Ranch the Seirra Foothills of California.

They were hard workers, the best we've ever had. My dad loved them for it. We were just going to keep them a secret, keep them on the farm. Mom kept track of how much money they would have made, if we could pay them, which we couldn't because these guys were way off the books. Undocumented, unheard-of, aliens. So, she bought them stuff instead. Stuff they never dreamed of. Spoiled them rotten. I don't know what they'll do if they ever go back to Nauve, but it doesn't look like they can, not without the Net. The portal is a smooth, shiny orb that sticks out of the floor of the Holy Cave back on Nauve. They spread a net of woven metallic fibers on top of the orb and plugged it into a generator powered by a stationary bicycle. The thing started glowing and poof! Everyone in the cave ended up here on the Look 'N Up. We dug in the exact spot they landed, and we found the orb! Baput says it's just like the one on Nauve. But there was no net, and we can't find anything like it on Earth, so I guess they're stuck here.

Anyway, we all got to know each other, and became great friends, almost family. It wasn't easy. They're very different from us. Going through life thinking you're the only people in the world, the only race, the only religion, the only way of thinking, it has some pretty weird effects. They're totally primitive. They worship the moon, Kakeeche, and they call the Sun Shavarandu. That means, "the power we fear". They use the same word for technology, like the stuff G-pa, the Akash, found behind the Death Door. The stuff that opened the portal.

Baput was going to be the great Alanakash, destined to teach this moon worshipping crap to his subjects, tell 'em if there's an eclipse it's all their fault for not believing hard enough. I'm a scientist. I couldn't stand letting my best friend believe that the moon is made of a bunch of tiny people who love us and watch over us, reward and punish us. So, I taught him the truth. I had to. Whenever he and his G-pa tried to meditate, they picked up the internet in their heads. It blew their minds so bad, G-pa got pretty demented, although I think he was headed that way anyhow. Baput was floundering in a sea of data he didn't understand: Science, technology, different places and races and religions and the baggage that comes with all that. It fell to me to explain it all.

Oh, and the other thing about living in a tiny village with no otherwhere. They have a limited gene pool. They had no idea it was even a problem. It took a lot of digging, but my mom finally got a clue from Baput's mom. There's an old lady called Akira who actually gets it, we think. They all have to marry who she says, and she tries to find the one that's least related to you. She births all the babies, babbets, they call them. We think she kills the mutant ones, so nobody even knows their doomed, even if the nimblies and bumblies don't wipe them out.

So, they stayed here on the ranch for three years. The only time they left was when we were evacuated by a fire. We took them to my cockeyed Uncle Patrick's place. Baput really liked my mutant cousin, Belinda. He thinks her deformity would be an advantage on Nauve, because her eye points up and to the left, and that's the way the bumblies approach when they attack you. So, he fell in love with her, when she was ten. My Aunt Lorraine is not too happy about that. She's a Civil Engineer, and she doesn't like the way Nauvians treat their women. They are supposed to be "tethers" who serve their man's every need, and raise his children, and nothing more.

When the three-year cycle was over, it was time for the portal to open and for the nimblies and bumblies to attack. Well, the portal didn't open because we didn't have the Net. But some of the nimblies and bumblies were nesting in the Holy Cave and they made it through the portal and hibernated in a cave on the Look 'N Up for all three years, like they do on Nauve. We tried to stop them, but they headed to the County Fairgrounds during the fair. We all had to go down there and fight them, me and my dad and my cockeyed relatives and the green guys. Everybody saw us. We fought side by side with the County Sheriff.

When we had wiped out the last nimblies and bumblies on Earth, it was time for Baput's G-pa to ascend him to Alanakash, but he wouldn't do it because Baput was corrupted by me and Shavarandu.

A couple days later the Sheriff's skinhead deputy brought some friends and guns up here to the ranch to eliminate the green people. My cousin called the Sheriff and he took them away, even fired the deputy. But he told us our green friends needed to disappear, or something worse would happen.

So, they're spending this cycle at my Uncle Patrick's place, and my Aunt Lorraine is going crazy trying to keep Belinda away from Baput and his mom while working full time.

NAUVE, Passascenday
Peratha & Trillella

Bupple watched the eastern horizon gradually brighten until, at last, it hatched a pink sun into the upriver mist. The distant silhouettes of the last bumblies fluttered into it, returning to their caves on their broad bat-like wings. Bupple knew they wouldn't be back, nor would today bring more nimblies, with their bloodsucking proboscises and their buzzing wings. The three-day battle was over. Passascenday had dawned, and with it, three years of peace. He lifted the giant horn made from a ganeesh tusk, freely given, to his jowly mouth and sounded the All Clear.

The men staggered out of the trenches, hooting and jumping on each other's backs, chanting, "No more nimblies! No more bumblies!" The Grand Doors opened, and the warriors poured in, thirsty for wine, burning to share their stories.

The women bustled around the Great Hall's kitchen, rushing food out to the hungry men. Peratha sat at a chopping table all alone, staring at nothing, as if she couldn't even see them.

Her daughter, Trillella, tugged at her sleeve. "Momama, we must go *nauve* now, to the house, to get ready."

Peratha's eyes slid over to her eleventh-year daughter's and slowly came into focus. "I told you; you don't have to marry Rodan today. Otherwise, you would be at Akira's lair, dressing, seeing yourself in the looking plate." She sighed, "but Akira says you are too young." Fully back from where she'd been, she gave Trillella a reassuring peck on the cheek.

"I know, Momama." Trillella answered cheerfully, taking her hands. "But I have to bottle the desperation wine for the feast."

"Well, let's hurry then." Peratha agreed, anxious to leave.

"Momama?" the lanky, olive-skinned girl asked as they walked to their hut at the edge of the village. Her natty hair straggled in clumps across her wide brow. Purple freckles crossed the bridge of her short nose. "I have been making the wine all this cycle, since Popa disappeared." It still hurt to say it.

She still didn't understand what it meant. All she knew was it was the old Akash's fault, not her popa's. "I did good, didn't I, Momama?"

The instant Trillella mentioned it, Peratha started wandering that dark path again. *What happened to Felsic? To Salistar, Valko, Baput and the wicked old Akash who wouldn't let us into the cave because we were women and not of the Akashic line? Left us to the nimblies...*

She re-lived it again, like she had so many times, especially these last three days of the Season. A whole cycle had passed since the Akashic Family disappeared, right before her eyes. Everyone who was in the Holy Cave, including Peratha's husband Felsic, the Akash's daughter's husband's brother, only there for his muscles.

She had not actually seen it. They were in the cave, and she and Trillella were outside the only entrance. There was a loud humming, then a bright flash, and then, they were not in the cave. The old ganeesh, Heffala, had picked Trillella up with her trunk and set her on her back. Shoving Peratha gently ahead of her, she climbed the steep steps and entered the Holy Cave. There was no one there. No Felsic. No Akash to say 'no'.

They spent the three days and three nights of that Season alone in the dark. Nimblies flew by all day, and bumblies all night, headed for the Great Hall to kill their share of villagers, and back to their caves in the upriver mist. They didn't seem to notice two people and a ganeesh hiding deep in the Holy Cave, quiet as dracna.

They had enough battle rations to feed the Akashic family for three days, including Valko! Peratha knew well how much her big brother-in-law could pack away, especially during battle. At night, they slept on that strange, smooth, rounded surface under that soft, itchy blanket, Heffala's tactile trunk wrapped gently around them.

On that Passascenday, three years ago today, when the battle was over, the people had come looking for the Akash and his family. Peratha and Trillella had met them on the trail and told them the whole story. No one believed them. Being the only witnesses, she and Trillella, then eight years old and still terrified, were generously "allowed" to go back into the Holy Cave with what was left of the Council: The women's leader, Akira, and Rakta, the War Chief, who brought his son, Rakted, still armed from the battle.

Rakta and Rakted had never been in the Holy Cave before. They'd never laid eyes on the Holy Rock; that weirdly smooth, perfectly round, eerily glowing sphere that protruded from the middle of the floor. They tiptoed around, searching every inch of the cave until all that was left to search was the deep, dark tunnel in the back. Rakta peered into the darkness, "Akash?" His oddly diffident voice echoed back, then silence. He grasped his son's shoulder, searched his eyes, more terrified than his own. They stepped through the doorway together.

They were relieved to find a pair of ornate pomegranate oil lamps just inside. Hands trembling, Rakta lit them with his dim pomegranate oil torch. He gasped as the round plate of shiny material behind the flame multiplied the light to an astounding brilliance.

"Is it breen?" Rakted asked his popa in an awed whisper.

Rakta shrugged and raised the lamp before him. It pushed back the darkness, and he led his son into the unknown.

The tunnel must have been very deep, for the two warriors were in there for a long time. They came out with no one but themselves, and even they were not quite the same. Rakta said he would never enter that space again. He stared at Peratha with dark suspicion. Akira pulled Trillella aside and asked her questions in harsh whispers.

"Momama?" her daughter's persistent chatter brought Peratha back just as they reached their hut. She knew she could not fall into that abyss of despair and loneness again. There was no time for that. She had a feeling Trillella was going to need her today. What was she asking about? Oh yes, her wine.

"I don't know," Peratha finally replied. "We ladies don't drink the wine, but the men seem satisfied," Peratha responded, as if that was all that mattered.

"So, Momama, since Popa is still disappeared, do you think they will make me the wine maker today? I apprenticed under Popa since I was six, and I've been making it by myself all cycle."

"The other women helped."

"I showed them how, though. I am the master wine maker. Rakta will ascend me to winemaker today. Then I won't have to marry Rodan, ever!"

Trillella declared her unattainable dream. She might just as well have said she would ride with *Kakeeche* across the night sky.

"You are a girl! And only eleven, and silly as a kiko bird!" Peratha embraced the slim bit of a girl so she couldn't see the sadness in her face.

Trillella finished the traditionally man's work with a professional efficiency that belied her tender age and budding femininity. They changed into their least-stained sets of woven grass tunics and drawstring pants. Each grasping a handle of the heavy wooden crate full of wine jugs, they headed back to the Great Hall.

The narrow foot path through the village opened up to a wide field scarred with trenches. They caught glimpses of the young Unmarriageables, the handles of their massive wooden paddles sticking up from the ditches and swaying back and forth in time with their scraping sounds. A ganeesh waited patiently, flapping her triangular ears and using her trunk to help herself to a bag of pomegranates strapped to her side. Occasionally the wide, flat shovel end of a paddle would shoot up from the trench and dump a pile of human remains onto a trailer behind the ganeesh.

Downriver in the meadow, they could hear stone shovels scratching into packed soil, punctuated by whoops and cuss words of the young men who had already married and ascended to their crafts last cycle, as they carved this cycle's burial trench. Ganeeshes bellowed as if laughing at their crude jokes as they lifted the heavy clay pots from the deepening mass grave as fast as the men could fill them.

The Grand Doors stood wide open to the crisp fall air, after three days of sheltering the stench of pomegranate-soaked vegans, elephants and purple, pointy-eared dogs. Peratha and Trillella entered, a bit late for the preparations, but they *did* bring the only wine. Desperation Wine was a Passascenday tradition. The dregs of last season, mixed with precisely so much of the under-ripe pomegranates picked before First Pomegranate Day, before the nimblies and bumblies came, to make enough of the harsh cocktail to supply the revelers through the Passascenday celebrations of death, ascension and matrimony.

Tamaya

After nine years and three betrothals, Tamaya was, at last, a bride. She stared into the full-size looking plate in Akira's antechamber, where the brides prepared. She couldn't resist running her finger down the eerily smooth surface. She'd learned at school that it was made from the largest piece of breen there was, hammered paper-thin by the Old Ones. The shiny, malleable metal was rare and precious, and Akira's looking plate was reserved only for women, only once, on the most important day of their lives.

The mirror reflected every line in brutal detail. Tamaya saw huge dark eyes, long legs, hair a rich, thick, straight black and a distinctly high forehead the color of the thick moss that grew on the north sides of the trees deep in the forest.

She wore a special gown woven of something much finer and more delicate than the usual *yalinar*. Softer and lighter, too. It was a gift from Bazu's Momama, Ritamay. Now, Ritamay wove her share of the squares that were stored communally and used by all the women for making or repairing clothes for their families. But she wasn't known for weaving anything exceptional, like this intricate textile of tiny threads that floated on Tamaya's shoulders like a cloud and glowed silver-white like Kakeeche. Ritamay swore to Kakeeche, the revered moon-beings, that she had worked on this gown in secret for years, preparing it for Bazu's wedding day. That would have been for Cinnabon.

Poor Cinnabon, the only other girl left eligible to marry into the Akashic line, rendered 'unmarriageable' as the superior Tamaya occupied its last available site. Right now, Cinnabon would be slaving in the Great Hall, helping to prepare the Passascenday Feast, or maybe she was on the battlefield, scraping pieces of dead warriors out of the trenches. When she was done with her menial task, she would march at the back of the increasingly long line of unfortunate women into that dark tunnel to spend the rest of her life in the Lair with Akira and her strings. Tamaya shuddered. Then, in her resilient way, she found something to envy, even in that dismal fate. At least Cinnabon would have a shot at being the next Apprentice to Akira, and a far slimmer shot at ascending to Akira's place if the old lady ever passed. But Tamaya, Tether to Akash, would still be just another woman. She could never dream of ascending to Akash, or even Apprentice Akash.

Or perhaps Cinnabon would be held in reserve, in case something happened to Tamaya. Or in case the rest of the Akashic family somehow reappeared. They had simply disappeared, according to Felsic's wife and daughter, three years ago on last First Pomegranate Day. No one knew why, or how, or if they would ever be seen again. For three years, Akira had been working her mysterious strings, trying to heal the hole the premier family had left in the Breeding Matrix.

For the last three days, the men had battled the nimblies by day and the bumblies by night. Each cycle, the Great Battle cost many young lives. But the losses had been worse this cycle, and last cycle, without the guidance of the Akash and his Tether. Now it was Passascenday. The battle was over, for another three years. Time to bury the dead. Time for the boys to ascend and the girls to marry and life to go on. Time for Bazu, the Akash's distant cousin's nephew, to ascend to Akash and marry Tamaya, his Tether.

Tamaya caressed the rare, billowing fabric around her shoulders. She treasured it more than she did her husband-to-be, even though he would be the supreme ruler of the known universe.

She looked at her own face, a slightly distant, slightly sad look of two-times lost love in her eyes. *Perfect.* She let her eyes return to their normal look, the one with the repressed anger of a caged animal.

Akira was coming. She could hear her waddling down the hall wheezing and gurgling as she so often did these days. She was so old! And besides, she lived in this semi-subterranean quarters. Wooden walls against bare rock and dirt. *The girls say those walls have mold colonies that date back to the Old Ones,* Tamaya remembered, jerking her hand away from the old wooden dressing table.

When she looked in the mirror again, Akira was in the frame. Her thick mop of wavy lavender hair invaded her deeply lined, lime-colored face.

"Are you ready?" she asked, but not impatiently. "You have been prepared since your eleventh year." She answered her own question.

"Was I prepared then?" Tamaya asked coldly, not caring if she angered the old lady.

"Prepared, yes. Ready, no. A girl like Salistar would have been ready, but you were not. You are not like other girls."

That again. "So I've heard." Tamaya replied, surprised at her own impudence. What did they mean? Did they think she was slow? *Downudara?*

She had waited all her life to be married to an Akash, to be his Tether. To tend to his worldly needs while he meditated, head in the sky, searching some invisible place for some great wisdom that would save them all from the nimblies and bumblies. It was an honor to be the Tether. To take care of such an important man, and in a small part, help make great things happen. And of course, you get to bear him a son and raise him to adulthood to be the next Akash. What girl would not be overjoyed? You got special lessons at school, like reading and writing in Old Akashic. The other girls didn't learn that. Even the boys didn't, except the Apprentice Akash.

"I could have done it. I am as smart as Salistar. Smarter, even." Tamaya quipped again, fully expecting a rebuke this time, for insulting the Akashic Tether.

Akira surprised her with a rare smile. "Exactly," she responded cryptically. "I would not have let it happen. You were much too young. But I knew Batuk would never ascend to Akash."

The young woman narrowed her eyes at the ancient one, who laughed out loud. "Oh, no, My Dear! I didn't have anything to do with the death of your first betrothed. But I knew it would happen."

"You foresaw it?" Tamaya asked, envying the old woman's mystical powers.

"You could say that," the old lady responded drolly. Rolling her eyes, she wondered why people always thought that foreseeing the obvious, logical consequences of things was some kind of magical prophesy. The younger heir, Baput, was superior. Born on First Pomegranate Day, he wouldn't be a normal Akash if he ascended. He would be an *Alanakash*. And the old Akash had been babbling in Council about finding a door in the Holy Cave that was marked 'Death to Open'.

Tamaya looked back to her reflection. "Now I'm too old. Twenty."

"No. You're just right. It is he that is too young."

Tamaya sagged in front of the mirror. Bazu. Frail, skinny, timid Bazu. Grandson of some ancient Akash's sister, he was the inferior product of the female line. He had been fifteen for three months now. Three Kakeeche cycles older than Baput, Tamaya's second betrothed. But he seemed younger. He was *much* smaller.

"I've seen you near the Holy Cave." Akira mused, grasping Tamaya's loose hair and twisting it into a bun. "The poor brokenhearted tether-to-be!" She held the bun to the top of Tamaya's head, looked sideways into the mirror. "But you weren't looking for Baput, were you. No. You were no different than the rest of us. Like Rakta and Bazu and me, too." She dropped the hair, re-combed it briskly. "You want to see that *Shavarandu*! We all do!"

"Even you, Akira?"

"That is why I'm here. I have special orders for you. I talked to Rakta about it. The War Chief and I are all that is left of the Council, and he agrees. You see, Bazu must devote all his time to his studies."

"To learn the Akashic breathing and meditation? The ancient rites and rituals?"

Akira grasped the girl's hands in hers and inspected her nails. She dabbed a brush into a bottle of concentrated pomegranate gaa and dotted the bride's short, pragmatic fingernails. "Of course. All that. That is exactly what you are to say to any busybody so bold as to ask." She rolled her lavender eyes, then turned to the dressing table to refill her brush. When she turned back with the dripping instrument, she seized on Tamaya's eyes with her own. "But really, Bazu is to find out what the old Akash had in that cave and how it works. He has been in there, with Rakta, getting nowhere. When he is full Akash, he is to live in the Holy Cave and work all the time on studying the Shavarandu!"

Tamaya gasped at the blasphemy, coming from a woman of the Akashic line! A woman almost as holy as the Akash, but only to the women. Ears still ringing from the shock, the next thing Akira said sank in slowly. "You will live there as well, and tend to his needs."

So now, not only am I tether to that squinty little twig, but I must live in the Holy Cave, without the conveniences of a hut in the village? Tamaya kept her complaints to herself.

"You remember how to write and read in Old Akashic?" The old lady penetrated her horror.

"Yes, of course."

"I hear there are ancient texts in there. You are to read them to Bazu and teach him how to read for himself."

Tamaya was dreading this marriage, which would be a reality within the hour.

"Tamaya." Akira said suddenly, as if the conversation had just begun. "I want you to report to me. Every week, we will meet privately, because you are Tether to Akash."

"Salistar didn't..." Tamaya argued.

Akira ignored the girl's sneer and went on. "You will tell me what you find, what Bazu finds. You will tell me what the ancient books say."

This final stab from the wrinkled old woman burst the bubble of numb horror that surrounded Tamaya's head. She watched Akira blow on her finished nails as her unexpected future unfolded. *I have a secret mission! I will know things no one else knows.* She smiled at the tiny, intricate spiral pattern that now decked the small surfaces of her nails.

The old lady rose and prepared to leave. Before she did, she leaned close to Tamaya and whispered. "You will tell me what the books say, before you read them to Bazu. I will tell you what you should pass on to the Akash, and by doing so, surely, to the War Chief."

The reflected bride now beamed with excitement, as a bride should.

Ceremonies

Death

Akira and Rakta led the solemn Procession of the Dead down the river and up into the meadow, in place of the missing Akashic Family. The immediate families of the fallen followed closely behind them. Then, the whole families. Peratha and Trillella used to walk up there with Felsic, back when they were a whole family. Now they walked in the back with the other widows and orphans. Even the Unmarriageables, the war dogs and the ganeeshes had gone ahead, having unenviable duties to perform.

With Trillella by her side, Peratha filed blindly along the well-worn path. She thought of the two young women killed by nimblies on the second day when they forgot to pack the vital pomegranate oil on the ganeesh bound for the North Trench. She sighed away a pang of guilt, then deflected. It wasn't her fault. The women's critical, if underrated, support system had unraveled without Salistar's direction.

Peratha had always been at Star's right hand, along with Rakta's Tether, Azuray. Azuray had done her best to keep it together, but Peratha had not been the same since last cycle, three years ago, when *It* happened. Azuray kept catching her gazing off at nothing, doing nothing, like she was doing now, *again*, she realized. Her eyes scanned the crowd self-consciously. No one was looking at her.

The front of the line flattened and spread out along the gaping new hole in the ground. It stank of clean meadow soil, for now. The ganeesh backed her cart to the rim of the trench. Two unmarriageable women, one on each side, pushed the trailer down so it tipped into the trench. Two dried, green husks, vaguely retaining a human shape, fluttered like feathers into the deep.

"That's Anada and Passilla huh, Mom," Trillella figured.

"Yes." Peratha replied curtly. The two foolish women had run after the galloping ganeesh, each holding a handle of the heavy wooden crate full of clay flasks of pomegranate oil, the men's only source of protein as well as wound dressing and fuel for the trench lamps. The nimblies had descended upon them despite the cloud of dust they had surely hoped would obscure them. The ganeesh's skin was too tough to penetrate, but the women were pierced and sucked dry in a relatively leisurely mid-season nimbly feast. They left their wizened shadows to be buried in this cycle's trench.

Loose bones rattled out of the trailer next. All that was left of the men, Dubbel, Zelnor, Lopak, and his son, Lopar, and the two boys who had died in their first battle, their betrothed wives remaining unmarried, perhaps forever. *Polan, and dear little Talbas.* Peratha mourned. *He was barely fifteen. I used to watch him, when he was a babbet,* Peratha recalled tenderly, then abruptly turned savage. *But not Rodan, of course. It's always the good ones, the kind ones...*

Peratha watched the sparse remains being lowered into the pit and tearfully covered with pomegranate seeds, one handful at a time, by Akira and Rakta, followed by the family members of the fallen. With each handful of pomegranate seeds lovingly offered, each of the bereaved spoke the names of all who had fallen in that battle, not just their own. Thus, the names were recited over and over until they joined with those who had fallen in the cycles before, in the eternal flow of being and intelligence that was The Plane.

The ganeesh dipped her trunk into a clay barrel of water, turned and shot it down the tilted trailer bed while the women scrubbed and the people sang a dirge. When the trailer was clean, the women removed their gore-soaked clothes and tossed them into the trench. They ran naked into the forest to cleanse themselves in their secret women's spring. No one watched them go.

The ganeeshes and young men began backfilling the trench with soil, forever covering the loved ones and a sacrificial portion of the year's pomegranate harvest. So ended the Death Ceremony. Maintaining the same precise order, the procession reversed its way and returned down the hill and up the river to the Great Hall.

Ascension

Peratha and Trillella sat down quietly in the back row of seats with the rest of the widows and orphans. Akira'a unmarriageables buzzed around, never sitting, always serving, providing drinks and snacks throughout the ceremony. The proud families of the participants sat in the front rows, to watch their sons and brothers, fifteen or older, ascend to their crafts and marry their betrotheds, carefully selected by Akira.

From that humble back row, Peratha and Trillella watched as Bazu, the skinny, squinting, sniveling distant nephew of the Akash Who Disappeared with His Family ascend to the highest office in the village with absolutely no Akashic training.

"Bazu, son of Gazu, grandson of Gazak, who was descended from Sylasan, sister of Bazan..." Akira droned the unsatisfactory lineage at the dismal looking crowd. She launched into the litany:

"I hereby extend to you the Sacred Longstick and the Holy Seed.
All the power, all the knowledge of the Akash, I pass to you by way of the Sacred Longstick."

She couldn't help but shake her head slightly as Rakta shoved a straight, six-foot long stick carved and decked with stone beads and kiko feathers into the boy's frail, fumbling hand.

"I pass the responsibility of seeing us all into the future
by way of the Holy Seed,"

Akira recited with a blatant eye roll. The revered woman draped a new woven necklace over the boy's head. She didn't even have to reach up to do it. It held four pomegranate seeds from exactly a cycle ago. She had gathered them then, just in case the unthinkable happened and the Akashic family did not reappear. She stepped back and finished the litany.

"Having given all he had, The Akash withdraws and relinquishes his power. He has returned to the stars."

Akira looked down on the weak, trembling specimen like a hawk regarding a mouse, but without the respect. They said his inadequacy was because he was from the female side of the Akashic line. *They* said. Gossips who didn't know what they talked about. Superstitious old women. It was based on the common assumption that women couldn't meditate their way to the Akashic Plane. Akira knew that wasn't true.

It had never made sense to her. Didn't it take both a woman and a man to make a person? Salistar was daughter of Akash, so her sons were of the female line. Only one generation of female line, true, but her sons were extra-large, healthy, smart, fine young men, like their Popa. *But they are gone. First Batuk, the older one, killed at the Holy Cave under intriguing circumstances known only to Badon, my brother, the Akash who Disappeared. And now Baput, who would be ascending to Akash and marrying Tamaya today if he and the entire Akashic family hadn't vanished into nothingness a cycle ago, according to those two sitting in the back row.* She fixed her gaze right into Peratha's eyes, then slid them, knifelike, across her heart to the transfixed eyes of her daughter. Trillella squirmed uncomfortably.

Now it was time for Bazu to say his part of the litany, but he didn't even know the words! Rakta shoved him forward, where he cringed before the crowd. Warriors surrounded the stage, blocking the view. A few of the men in the back, already enjoying Trillella's pomegranate wine, baulked and bawled, but the women just cowered quietly. Even Bazu's Momama in the front row accepted the blocked view stoically.

With Rakta literally prodding him and Akira feeding him the lines in a raspy whisper, Bazu recited the Akashic Oath.

"The Akashic Power is a manifestation of the Akashic Plane.
It is not a manifestation of me. I am only its conduit.
The wisdom and power of the Akashic Plane is for all the people.
I will never use the power selfishly.
I shall serve all the people equally.
I shall speak nothing but the truth.
I shall be kind at all times to all people.
I shall pursue wisdom diligently, every day of my life,
for the good of all the people.
Empathy shall be my guide when ministering to even the least of my people.
I accept the awesome responsibility of knowing the wisdom and wielding the power of the Akashic Plane.
I accept the Sacred Longstick of the past Akash, which contains his wave form, what he was and what he knew and what he continues to be.
I accept the responsibility of the Holy Seed, to see us all into the future."

The jarring ceremony was followed by a cringing, amateurish performance while Bazu struggled through the ascension ceremony for three young warriors, Samard with his longstick, Maffoon the darter, and lastly, the Clubber, Rodan. The almost-eighteenth year bully stared down at his frail new Akash, daring him to refuse his tardy ascension.

All three were ascended without a hitch, with lines hissed, sometimes repeatedly, by the burley War Chief. Bazu reached up with his longstick to gently touch the shoulder of each boy he ascended. He was grateful they kneeled so respectfully, because when they stood, even the smallest one, Samard, dwarfed him ridiculously.

The men's clumsy display finally drew to an end. The ascended boys lined up behind the War Chief for the short march to the dining tables at the back of the room where most of them only had time for a quick snack and a final sip of wine as single men. They would avoid getting gaa stains on their brand-new suits of woven yalinar, at least until after. Then they would march out the back door, stop at the stinking boors, parade around the outside of the Great Hall and back in through the Grand Doors, climb back up the steps to the stage and marry the only girl they'd ever dared look at, if they were smart.

But not yet. Several men armed with empty wine jugs dared block the path of the War Chief as he stepped down from the stage. He glanced side to side for his warriors, but they stood where they were, as if joined with these rowdy sots!

"Wine." Nowie demanded simply.

"What about it?" Rakta tried to thrust past the man, whose breath reeked of the harsh, under-fermented brew.

"You did not ascend a winemaker!" Lowie roared. "Who will make the wine if Felsic is still," he closed his fist and opened it, fingers flying apart as he made a popping sound with his tongue.

Akira waddled halfway down the stage stairs and whispered in Rakta's ear.

Growling, Rakta shrugged her off, sent the ascended boys on their way, and climbed back up the stairs, Akira at his heels.

He banged the butt of his longstick on the wooden platform for attention. It resonated like a bass drum. The crowd milled around the line of boys headed for the tables, offering rowdy congratulations.

"Wine!" the aging War Chief bellowed. The crowd silenced and turned to face him.

"Wine is a waste of men. It dulls the senses. It will destroy a young mind who knows not how to resist, or extinguish and old mind that is too tired and hurt to resist. I continue to resist."

Deep, angry grumbles rippled through pockets of the crowd. Rakta's eyes probed each cluster of men, warriors all, at least during the Season. "I understand," he softened. "Some men require it, and we need all of our men at their peaks. If that takes wine, so be it."

He leaned over and exchanged whispers with Akira. Trillella was on the edge of her seat, gaping at the stage. Peratha watched only her daughter, waiting to catch her when she fell.

"So, my Warriors, has the wine been adequate this past cycle, since Felsic..." He mimicked Lowie's gesture, even popped his tongue, although it seemed beneath his dignity. Three years and still no one had a word to describe what had happened to the Akashic family, much less an explanation.

The men roared their approval. Trillella jumped to her feet. Her dream was coming true! Peratha reached out to steady her.

Rakta pointed his knotty finger right at the vibrating girl. "This young girl. Felsic's daughter, Trill, um..." Akira whispered again. "Trillella has made the wine this cycle, and it has been adequate. So..."

"Should I go up there?" Trillella squeaked to her Momama.

Peratha shook her head violently, grasping her slender hand a bit too hard.

The War Chief continued his unprecedented proclamation. "Since this girl child can do it, it shall no longer be considered an artisan craft. It shall hereafter be considered mere woman's work, like weaving squares and cooking food and whatever else women do." He swatted the air dismissively.

A helpless hiss arose here and there, but it didn't dare catch on. "The girl will teach all you women what Felsic taught her. The tether of each household shall make the wine for that household. My tether, Azuray, need not, for I do not touch the wicked stuff. Dulls the senses, I tell you!" he stormed off the stage and hurried, this time unresisted, to the food tables.

Marriage

Shielding her shattered daughter from the evil eyes cast their way by the other women, Peratha had Trillella settled down in time for the first wedding. They stared breathlessly as Tamaya emerged. Her thick, shiny dark purple-black hair cascaded down her back, straight, with just the hint of a spring. Her long, verdant green legs, tiny waist and wiry arms were draped in a stunning gown of shimmery white fabric. The edges of the half-pomegranate rinds that cupped her pert young breasts peeked out from the plunging neckline.

"What is she wearing?" Trillella wondered in a whisper.

Peratha shushed her, then couldn't resist. She whispered back, "I hear Ritamay made it. But I've seen her squares. She's not that good a weaver."

"Bazu's Momama? But how? It's all one piece. There's no squares."

Peratha squinted at the faraway stage. "Your eyes are better than mine."

"What is it made of?"

"I've never seen anything like it." The other women in the back row wondered in hushed voices.

"I've seen it before." Trillella whispered back.

Peratha smiled indulgently. The girl said fanciful things like that sometimes. Peratha understood. She had done the same thing as a girl, to make herself feel special.

Akira performed the marriage ceremony flawlessly, skillfully, like she had hundreds of times.

Peratha found herself crying silent tears, although she didn't understand why. Perhaps it was the finality of it. Baput's betrothed was married to another. It meant the Akashic Family was no more. Including Felsic.

Akira presented Tamaya with a new Akashic Tether's Rolling Pin, the old one having disappeared with Salistar, the last Akashic Tether.

"It's too rough." Trillella noticed. "How can she roll anything smooth with that?"

"I can't see that girl rolling anything anyway," Peratha muttered coldly.

Bazu and Tamaya moved off the left side of the stage, while the other grooms lined up on the right.

"Momama!" Trillella cried out, much too loud.

Leaving her dismal train of thought to run off the cliff behind her, Peratha whirled to where her daughter's trembling hand pointed. Rodan stood on the stage with the grooms! The brash, oversized boy pushed the smaller boys out of his way. Not only was he big for his age, but Rodan was a *Nobby.* Not quite fifteen last First Pomegranate Day, he had come up in a class of boys up to three years younger than him. Now he shared his ascension with these little punks, while the other boys his age had married their betrotheds and ascended to their crafts three years before.

A confused hope dared arise in Peratha's weary breast. *He will be married to someone else, not Trillella! But then, what of Trillella?* Hope sank.

A cool hand squeezed Peratha's shoulder. Startled, she peeled her eyes away from the bully on stage and found her old childhood friend, Aoti, standing by her side. Her dense, wavy hair was cut short and fading to lavender. Peratha hadn't seen much of Aoti since she was declared unmarriageable and took the long walk down that dark hall to Akira's underground lair. *Twenty-four years ago!* Peratha was stunned to realize. *She looks so old! I thought her life was easy. She has no family to tend, to lose! Maybe I look old, too.* The thought tucked Peratha comfortably into her depression.

"Come with me. Akira must speak with you," Aoti hissed formally.

Trillella stared bug-eyed at the strange old woman.

"Leave the girl," Aoti ordered.

Peratha patted Trillella's shoulder firmly and followed Aoti into the Council's meeting room where Akira waited, perched like a raptor in her heavy wooden chair. Aoti slipped out, closing the door behind her, leaving Peratha to face the women's ruler alone.

Akira pointed at Peratha with a slim finger with a short, pointy nail and thin crepey skin. Peratha understood the signal and knelt before the spooky old lady, who got right to the point.

"Peratha, you shall marry Rodan today. Right now."

Peratha's head shot up from the submissive bowed position. "But, Felsic!" She was shocked to hear herself argue! She knew as well as anyone that Akira's decisions in these matters were absolute.

"You know Felsic is defective. He was almost downudara. Gave you a downudara son, remember?"

Peratha felt hot blood rush through her neck, flooding her cheeks and rising to her brow. Of course she remembered her little Felkin, so sweet and gentle in his perpetual innocence. Ignoring the insult, she dared to shoot back. "You say Felsic *is*, then you say Felsic *was*. Is he alive or dead, Akira?"

Akira simply shrugged. A cruel smile crossed her wrinkled face.

Peratha remained on her knees, but continued to question her ruler with a courage she didn't know she had. "If you don't know if my husband lives, how can you marry me to another?"

Akira swatted the air, impatiently. She had weddings to perform. "They are dead. All dead. That is why we waited all last cycle before ascending that, *Bazu*," she spat the name, "and to marry you off to a better man before it is too late for you to bear a quality child."

Peratha stayed firm. What did she have to lose? If Felsic was dead, there was only one thing that mattered any more. "Trillella is fine," she growled defensively.

Akira rolled her eyes to the heavily beamed ceiling and back to the fuming but still kneeling woman before her. "She is OK for a girl. A bit homely."

"But if Rodan marries me, what happens to her?"

Akira leaned forward savagely in her elaborately carved chair. "She is from Felsic. Felsic is, *was*, defective. His line will be cut."

Peratha jumped to her feet. Her legs shook and her voice trembled, exposing her bold defiance as the terror it really was. Even so, she had to fight. "Cut Felsic's line? Why? Felsic is not the smartest man in the village, but he is kind and gentle and he loves me and Trillella."

"You will have a good son with Rodan, before you are too old. You will do your wifely duties and bear him a son."

"But Rodan is betrothed to Trillella! What about my daughter?" Peratha asked again, dreading that long underground tunnel that had swallowed Aoti.

"She is only eleven. She can stay with you for another cycle. With Rodan as *popa*, not husband. Do you hear me, Peratha? Only you and he. Understand? You are responsible to make sure."

"But how? He's a brute! And what of Trillella, next cycle?"

"We will see. Now get out there." The door opened and Aoti reappeared, reaching for Peratha's elbow.

Peratha jerked away. "I'm not dressed." She whined through hysterical tears.

"You had all that hoopla last time. Just go out there. Now!" The old woman ordered.

Aoti escorted Peratha to the right side of stage where a gaggle of much younger brides waited. Two more unmarriageables came to flank Akira as she rose stiffly from the hard chair and prepared for her grand entrance.

The Wasting

Akira settled noisily into the padded seat in her private chambers deep in the Lair, alone at last. She shook her wrinkled head slowly. The marriages were always a chore, but this Passascenday, they had been particularly exhausting.

Peratha would be better now. The boy was too young, and a brute, but he was strong. His parents were a good match. Not like Felsic the *hibudara*, unauthorized offspring, of the forbidden union between his wayward mother and Felpen, the winemaker. Felsic could make wine and fight in the trenches and keep a wife and children. He was not a fully helpless downudara like his son had been. But he was dim enough to be the only adult in the village who didn't know he wasn't Valko's full brother. They'd even named him after his real Popa, made him his apprentice, and still that simpleton thought he was Valdor's son! A smirk started to catch on Akira's weary face, only to disappear as her mind wandered to more pressing matters.

The Akashic pair! She breathed an involuntary moan. Bazu was even weaker than his Popa, Gazeed, who was descended from Sylasan, sister of the Akash Bazan, many generations ago. Since Sylasan was sister to Akash, Akira and the Akira before her had bred her descendants to non-Akashic people. After all those births and deaths, their line still had the physical weakness of the typical Akash, but without the mental powers. *Or perhaps they just lack training?* Akira hoped desperately, wondering again, *who will train the new Akash?*

She shifted uncomfortably, crossed her legs, winced and uncrossed them. *Wed to Tamaya, Pindross's daughter.* Was it a good match? Intelligent and sensitive, Pindross the *Rasta*-Maker painted portraits of the people and their events, or had, until he lost his sight. Now people said he painted nothing but nonsense. He kept those rantings in his hut where Akira had never been, of course. The Pind thread was one of the few that hadn't crossed the Akashic line, at least not in the direct and intimate way that too many did. Now they would be forever joined. That had been her plan all along, to marry her to a strong, well-bred son of Salistar and Valko. That seemed worth it. But the fateful step seemed wasted on Bazu. *Bazu is even weaker than his Popa, and it's not because he is from the female line, like they say. It is because of The Wasting!*

Akira sighed a sigh that seemed too old even for her considerable years. No one saw. She was alone her chambers. Alone in the dark. Alone in her knowledge of The Wasting, as she had named it. Her neck creaked when she looked straight up at the tangled mess of multicolored threads hanging from the ceiling above her. An ugly knot clotted the center. A few lines spread out toward the sides, with only a few threads daring to reach out and touch them, cross them. The Breeding Matrix hung over Akira's head like a giant spider web of doom.

Her student, Edijay, didn't understand, or didn't believe. *My third apprentice. The other two died of old age without ever understanding! I've spent so many years! If only there was someone with an intelligent mind who could see what I see. Perhaps Tamaya. She was a bright student. She has that high forehead that speaks of intelligence, like that young Baput had, or has...* She stood abruptly as if trying to get away from herself. *I had such hopes for that pairing!*

She began her habitual pacing. *Yes, I believe Tamaya is capable of understanding. But can I trust her?*

With that thought, she waddled to the looking plate. She fought a cattail tassel through her knotted hair, donned her robe once again, and prepared for one last ceremony. Pushing the door open with a long, slow creak, she called, "Come in, Edijay."

With little ceremony, Edijay would ascend to be Akira's third, and hopefully final, apprentice.

Wedding night

Tamaya's legs ached from being spread so wide for so long. Her thighs were soaked with sweat that made her bare skin stick to the tough, wrinkled hide. The occasional hairs tickled her annoyingly. The ganeesh was so slow! She could have run to the Holy Cave in the time it took for Bazu to even get mounted on the elaborate seat that towered behind her. The Akashic Saddle swayed sickeningly from one side to the other as the elephant picked its way along the trail. Bazu squeaked and whined with every step. No

Akash had ever fallen from this perch, but there was always a first time. Most Akashes had the wisdom, or the nerve, to sit still.

The dolomite spire of the Holy Cave poked through the eternal upriver mists ahead, its wide entrance gaping above them like the mouth of a hungry giant. The stone stairs, hewn out of the very rock of the cave by the Old Ones at the beginning of the world, loomed steep and narrow.

Tamaya had never been inside. Now she would live there. She knew the ganeesh could climb the stairs, but with Bazu perched up there on that silly chair, squirming and screaming? A smile came out to play on Tamaya's lips. She hunkered down close to the animal's stinking neck, hoping for an exciting, and possibly amusing, end to this already miserable marriage.

Rakta clicked his tongue, and the elephant stopped gently at the foot of the stairs. Bazu sighed with relief, Tamaya with disappointment. Rakta reached up gallantly to help her down, grasping her around her slim waist for just an instant. Then he turned to help his two warriors unload the squeaky Akash, who wriggled noisily between them until he reached the ground. He reached out to circle Samard with his arms, but the young warrior took a quick step back, leaving his Akash to hug the ground instead.

"Come," the War Chief ordered, starting up the stairs. Tamaya followed eagerly, leaving her husband to collect himself and his dignity from the snickering soldiers. They stopped on the porch at the top of the stairs. On their right was a steep drop off, where one, such as Batuk, Tamaya's first betrothed, could easily fall to one's death. Tamaya shuddered. Turning away from that dark place, she found a view like none she had ever seen. She could see all the way to the river, glinting between the willows of the dense riparian forest. Upriver, the blue-tinged mist went on forever, just like people said.

She looked down at Bazu. He got to his feet and dusted himself off, apparently glad the soldiers were ignoring him as they busied themselves unloading the ganeesh. He didn't look up to see Tamaya and Rakta staring down at him, sharing a smile.

Tamaya's brother, Pindrad, dashed up the stairs ahead of the Akash, his long, black hair flying behind him. Tamaya hadn't seen him in the procession. He must have walked behind them. "What are you doing here?" she asked her younger sibling who was already married and ascended to his role as Rasta Maker, the village artist.

"I am your Guard," he answered simply. "A man from the tether's family," he grinned, "who else?"

Tamaya blocked the stairs, shot a wicked glance at Rakta, then whirled on her brother. "You are no soldier! You're an artist."

"Valko was a woodworker," Pindrad quipped back.

"He was a monster. No one would attack the Akash with him around." Bazu wheezed, having managed to get himself up the stairs unnoticed. No one saw how many times he had tripped and slipped, or stopped for breath. "I am to be guarded by an artist?"

"He kills his share." Rakta confirmed Pindrad's manhood. "Who would attack the mighty and wise Akash?" he roared to the small group of young soldiers below, as if issuing an invitation. Bazu ducked into the cave.

Tamaya followed, like a tether should. So, this was the Holy Cave. There was the Holy Rock. Smooth and round, sticking right up out of the stone floor. Her robe tingled on her shoulders. It was so comfortable she had forgotten she was wearing it. Now it itched, and she wanted to shed it, but all she had underneath was her pomegranate-skin bikini and that show was to be for Bazu only, not for these *real* men who busily went about the task of setting up their household. Clearly woman's work, but non-Akashic women weren't allowed in the Holy Cave, except her, the Tether. This inconvenient household was her responsibility. She should be helping these men, directing them. What did men know about setting up a household? What did she know? Little more than they did, actually.

They set oil lamps in a dark recess and laid a sleeping cushion on the floor there, double wide. They brought in two large clay pots for water and filled them with lighter bags of tightly woven fabric, carried from the river by two men in two trips. *Will they do that every day?* Tamaya wondered. There were smaller clay pots for *bee* and *boo*. *Who is going to empty those for us?* Tamaya wondered some more.

The men unpacked the food next. Three days' worth of battle rations, like the men ate in the trenches. *Is that a joke?* Tamaya mused defensively, hiding her gratitude, even from herself. She was no cook. And there was no kitchen. Would they continue to provide all this?

I am Tether. It is the Tether's job to care for the Akash while he sits on his cushion wandering the Plane in his mind. Make his children and care for them, too. She cringed at the thought, then sighed with resignation. *It has been my fate since my birth. Yet I am as poorly equipped for my job as Bazu is for his. With no one to teach me, just like him.* For the first time, Tamaya almost wished she had listened when her momama had tried to teach her to cook. But she never did. She always said 'no' and ran outside to play. It was too late now. Momama had been dead for a long time.

The household, such as it was, was set up without the Tether's assistance or supervision. The men made their exit, bowing ridiculously at the bony little man who had removed his Akashic robe and now wore the same woven grass tunic and pants everyone else wore.

Rakta was the last to leave. He bowed grandly at the Akash. He did not look ridiculous, despite the bald spot on top of his head. It looked like a grassy hummock in the middle of a dark swamp, and Tamaya had never noticed it before. Then he turned and bowed just as grandly to her, the Akashic Tether. Tamaya felt a thrill rise in her heart and spread through her blood, lifting her, just for an instant. Then he was gone.

The Akash's slim belly bobbed in and out with every wheezing breath as he watched Rakta lead the ganeesh away toward the village, the warriors marching behind in tight formation.

Pindrad stayed behind on the porch, standing guard.

"Go home to your family, Pindrad" the Tether ordered her younger brother. "It's our wedding night. You are right, my Akash. We must have a better guard. He has a family. He can't stay here and guard us all the time." She addressed her husband respectfully. He ignored her. He disappeared into the dark tunnel behind the rock.

Tamaya dismissed her brother with a wave of her hand and crept silently after Bazu. At the entrance to the tunnel, on her left, the cave rock was different. It shined dully, reflecting the light from a lamp Bazu had just lit. Tamaya gasped, brought her hand to her mouth. The lamp was so bright! And the tunnel was full of stuff she had never seen before. Stuff she couldn't have described. Shiny stuff in all different shapes and sizes hung on the walls or sat weightily on the floor. Was it the forbidden Shavarandu?

Further back, both walls were lined with shelves of books and scrolls that went on into the darkness. There was a trickling sound on her left that made her want to pee. It drew her eyes back to that strange plate in the cave wall. She ran her fingers over it, squinting in the dimness of Bazu's shadow. It was letters! Old Akashic. It said "Death to Open".

Death to Open. Tamaya's hand froze and her head spun while her world realigned. When it stopped, it all made sense. *The old Akash said Batuk fell from the porch, but that was right before he started spending all his time here in the Holy Cave, working on some weapon to fight the nimblies and bumblies. They used something they found behind this door, and that rock, but it made the Akash and his whole family disappear...* Her gown was itching like crazy. She threw it off.

Bazu emerged from the tunnel, a book in his hand. She blocked his way in her pomegranate-skin bikini, a half for each breast and three halves for the bottom, one in front and two in back, held together by thongs of gaa-stained grass.

Forced to stop, Bazu stood before her, fully clothed, arms at his sides, book in one hand. "What are you doing?"

"It is our wedding night. I will pleasure you now," Tamaya volunteered awkwardly.

Bazu's eyes found the book in his hand without seeming to even register what they must have at least glimpsed along the way. "If you want to pleasure me, read me these books. Here, start with this one."

Council of Two

The next morning, Akira and Rakta arrived at the Great Hall at the same time, he with his pair of flanking guards, she with her apprentice, Edijay, and her chaperone, Ogala. Akira had failed to detect Ogala's deafness at birth. When it became apparent, she declared the girl unmarriageable so she couldn't spread her misfortune, and found a special use for her as chaperone. No man could see Akira alone. It was an ancient rule sent down from the Old Ones. And The Council had been only she and the War Chief for this past cycle.

The two leaders filed into the private Meeting Room, which served as a nursery during the three-siege called The Season. A sturdy wooden table surrounded by chairs occupied the center of the room. The walls were lined with wicker cribs. Their entourages remained outside, even Edijay, who fumed and craned to listen. Only Ogala was admitted, carrying a lit torch she slipped into a holder on the wall. Her job was to watch silently, staring blankly with no understanding of the significance of the Council's business. In the unlikely event there was any touching, she was supposed to report it immediately to those who waited outside. To what end, neither she nor anyone inside or outside of the room had any idea. It had never happened, and probably never would. Not between these two.

Rakta sat opposite Akira at the long central table. Ogala sat between them, watching with bored eyes. This is how the Council meetings had been for the last cycle, since the Akash had disappeared. The Council of Three had become a Council of Two. They rarely agreed, so they agreed to disagree. Akira saw to the women's issues. Rakta took charge of the men. They met only three times a year for terse exchanges of gossip and complaints. Useful information was rarely shared.

"We are still two?" Akira began, her way of asking Rakta to explain the new Akash's absence.

"Wedding night! Give him some time." Rakta laughed, wiggling his eyebrows suggestively. "The poor girl looks exhausted. Ha, ha!" he slapped his own knee in exaggerated glee.

"You have seen them?"

"Yes, I visited them this morning, just to check. They have some requests."

"Already?"

"They want a different guard. The Akash wants a warrior, not an artist."

Akira squirmed. The boy was complaining already. Surely Tamaya would be, too.

"What does he fear?"

"What *doesn't* he fear?" Rakta roared. Ogala may not have heard, but those outside surely did. The warrior guards nudged one another and giggled. Edijay scanned them up and down, her lip curled, while Rakta listed the Akash's many phobias, counting them on his thick fingers. "Lin spiders, dracna mice, his own shadow, riding the ganeesh, men, women." He drawled the last slowly, trying to imagine the fear a woman like Tamaya would inspire in a boy like that. *How had it gone?* He couldn't help but wonder. She'd had huge bags under her eyes, and she had indeed looked exhausted, but she didn't seem satiated, or even happy, and that bothered him. He shook his head to clear it. His mind usually never rested on such mundane issues, not even those of his own hut.

Akira rescued him from his wayward thoughts. "It should be a man from the Tether's immediate family, so there is no temptation."

"The old Akash had Valko, the Tether's husband. A waste of one of my best warriors, but truly a great Guard of Akash."

"That was unusual. He was married to the Tether. The Akash was her Popa. This is the normal way. The Tether's husband is the Akash. So, her brother or her Popa would be guard. But Pindross is blind, of course."

Rakta laughed out loud at the thought. "He'd walk right off that porch like the boy, Batuk, did."

Akira hushed him. "Do you have a warrior? An old retired one? One that won't be tempted by that, that woman?"

"That leaves me out." Rakta heard himself say. His eyes darted around the room. *Was that out loud* Akira's expression didn't change. Perhaps she hadn't heard. An idea sprung into the awkward pause. An idea that would distract her. "Bupple?" he suggested innocently.

A slow smile spread across Akira's face. "Of course! Poor Bupple!" Big and strong, Bupple had been truly a great warrior in his day. He had raised three skilled sons and one still survived, the lead Longstick for the North Trench. But Bupple had suffered a debilitating injury to his private parts two cycles ago when he stepped in front of a friendly spear in the heat of battle. The blow had hurt so much he'd passed out, but his mates had dragged him out of the trench and loaded him onto a travois behind the battle ganeesh.

Akira explored the domestic picture. "His tether passed away last cycle. He lives with his son and his family."

Rakta filled in the tactical angle. "All he does now is blow the Warning Blast and the All Clear. The Akash should be safe in the Great Hall at those times. And he can't..." Rakta trailed off, feeling a great weight lift off his shoulders that he hadn't known was there.

"Tamaya had another request, too." Rakta added when the strange feeling passed.

"Oh?" Akira asked, raising her eyebrows in sarcastic surprise.

"There is no way to cook in the Holy Cave. And the stairs are steep. They have to carry water all the way from the river. And who will empty their boo pots?" His voice started seriously, but morphed into a sarcastic whine the people outside were surely eating up.

Akira didn't find it amusing. *As if Tamaya would cook anyway.* She had seen this coming. She just wanted to see how the Akashic Tether was going to handle her situation. *Whine to the War Chief, who seems to fancy her a bit, that's how.* "Can Bupple carry the water?" she asked.

Rakta nodded slowly. "Water, yes. But he fought honorably and I will not order him to carry their boo. Get one of your Unmarriageables to do it."

"I will see to the food." Akira resolved. "The Tether can empty her own family's boo pots, like the Tether before her, and the Tether before her, my momama. Now, enough of this trivia. It is the last meeting of the Council of Two. Let us speak freely, and softly. Passascenday is over, and so is the time for threatening people with the Akash's return. We can no longer weave our tales of the Invisible Akash who watches us all without being seen and teaches his apprentice to do this Shavarandu at his side!

"Yes," Rakta swatted the air and replied, still too loudly. "He is recording all of your sins. When he returns on Passascenday he will punish you!" he recited the lies he and Akira had spun over the past cycle.

Akira continued the yarn. "His tether writes them down, and his guard stands ready by his side, and if get a glimpse of him, the Great Valko will strike you down!" She mocked, cackling. "Kakeeche kept turning their backs, almost every spring and fall, and even Shavarandu, the sun, turned on us twice! Right after *It* happened, and again, just a Kakeeche cycle before this Season. That kept the fear good and high, where we needed it." Her brow wrinkled along old, familiar lines. She glanced at Ogala, who showed no sign of hearing the blasphemy. She cleared it from her larynx, and plunged ahead.

"So now we have a new Akash." She raised her eyebrows expectantly. No response. She tried again, more directly. "What do you think of our new Akash?"

"No one fears him. Or respects him," was the War Chief's swift reply. "Especially the young men, and you know how troublesome they can be."

"He was raised with them," Akira mused, "as a peer."

Rakta snorted. "Peer! He was never their peer. He was always the loser, the butt of their jokes. How can they respect him, *fear* him as Akash?" His eyes sought Akira's for an answer he knew she didn't have.

"You don't help, speaking of him the way you do in front of them," she snapped, dashing his faint hope.

"They already know!" he defended. "They have seen him since childhood on the practice field, always losing and crying like a babbet, blaming everyone but himself."

Akira smiled at that. "There's hope for him yet. He sounds just like my brother, when he was a boy."

"Bazu is not a boy. He is Akash."

"So was my brother, for many cycles. Was he any different? No. But people respected him. They obeyed him. Why?"

"He was trained by Baram, the great Akash."

Akira snorted. "My Popa. Another weak, sniveling man who turned egomaniac as soon as he got the power. Where do they get that power, Rakta?" She asked in a whisper.

"They ascend." Rakta answered simply, shrugging.

"So? Someone speaks some words, and now suddenly they command the power of life and death over the entire village? Why? What gives them that power?"

"The Evil Eye?" Rakta flailed for the answer that would make her stop pecking at the foundations of his belief system.

Akira laughed out loud, almost hysterically. Ogala sat up in surprise as the revered old woman almost lost it, her hand flying up to cover her mouth. She dragged it down slowly, around the lump of her chin and along her swollen jowls. "The Evil Eye," she said calmly. "Do you believe in it?"

"Of course." Rakta choked from a dry throat. He gripped the edge of the table with both hands, his dark green knuckles almost white.

"Can Bazu do it?" she grilled him.

"Why, no, I don't think so. He is not trained."

"No. He is not," Akira agreed. "He can't even fake it! They all know." She rose to her feet and leaned over, her hands on the table, her face close to Rakta's. Her words were low and clear. "He knows no more than you or I or anyone else in the village about the mysteries of the Plane, of Kakeeche and Shavarandu and *Insitucide*. And all the people know that. How can they bring their grievances to someone who knows less than them about living?"

"The old Akash didn't either, the surly War Chief replied.

"But he knew other things. Mysteries no other man knows. All the stuff he learned from his Popa, who learned from his popa, and so on."

"No one knows those things anymore." Rakta replied slowly, as if he was just now seeing the tip of that iceberg of cultural loss.

Akira turned her head so as not to scoff directly in the War Chief's broad face. "Not even the Akash. So why will they worship him? Why will they do as he says?" she was whispering now. "He's just a weak, timid, scared kid without his robe."

"Yes, I have seen." Rakta had seen many times, including last night, and this morning.

"Everyone has seen the Akash without his robe." Akira recalled. "The children in school, the parents watching the sparring matches! The women have all seen him sniveling around the Great Hall or the garden, clinging to his momama, at twelve years old! And what is his robe made of?" Akira quizzed the warrior.

"Woven yalinar, with beads."

Akira withdrew her face then, stood straight up, eyes on the ceiling. Rakta stayed seated, looking lost. Akira leaned down again, swiftly, like a hawk diving on a mouse. The warrior drew back and stood, knocking his chair over behind him. Ogala squeaked and got up, too, headed for the door to tell the others.

"Fear, you idiot!" Akira raged out loud, right in his face. "Fear and awe and respect for someone who can melt your mind with his, just by looking at you. Fear of a man who can make Kakeeche turn their backs on us, make the moon go dark before our eyes if we don't believe as he says. The sun, even, if he gets angry enough! A man who can see into the future, and tell us our fate, and tell the young ones what will befall them if they follow the evil path of Shavarandu. A man who will be believed without question. Obeyed without argument. Because he knows things no one else knows. That is what the Akashic Robe is made of! Superior knowledge and the fear that it inspires. Bazu has neither. He has no power."

Rakta gazed at the door where the deaf girl stood, her hand trembling on the latch. It was already true. He had seen it in the ranks this past cycle. Men argued with their superiors, questioned their orders like never before, with disastrous results. Casualties had been particularly high this Season. And yesterday's wine rebellion had been so unprecedented, he'd seen Pindrad sketching furiously.

He turned to face his co-leader for the last time as Council of Two. "The magic is broken," he whispered solemnly. "If the Akashic power is gone, so is our power."

Delivery

Jenevan shook a little as she approached Akira's Lair, wondering why she had been summoned. Pindrad had come home last night all upset. *He said Tamaya dismissed him, said he couldn't be Guard of Akash and stay at the Holy Cave all day and night because he had to be nauve for me and Pindren and his blind popa, Pindross.* Jenevan had been surprised at her sister-in-law's sudden compassion, and she was grateful for it, although she doubted its motivation. Had Akira overruled the decision? She wondered.

She turned to Hebert, the large male German shepherd at her heel. His deep purple muzzle and ears contrasted sharply with the rest of him, a pale lavender, a bit darker and courser along his backbone and all the way down his long, bushy tail. "Sit," she ordered. The dog obeyed instantly. "Stay," she told him, stepping past him with complete assurance.

She passed through the ornately carved façade that decked the outermost chamber of the Lair of the Unmarriageables. Her eyes adjusted slowly to the dim light.

Akira was waiting. Jenevan breathed in sharply, like she'd seen a spider. She shuddered, knowing she was late.

"Sit." Akira greeted her without ceremony. She sat as quickly as her dog had.

"I have relieved your husband as Guard of Akash." She informed the trembling girl. Jenevan knew that was Rakta's decision, not Akira's, but she didn't argue. "This is better for you, yes?"

Jenevan nodded without looking up. "Yes, Akira. I have a second-year, and another on the way. Popa Pindross is blind. It would be difficult."

"I ask something else instead, from the Tether's family."

"Yes, Akira, of course, we will serve."

"There is no kitchen in the Holy Cave. No way for Tamaya to cook." She spoke seriously, but a droll smile spread across her face. Jenevan looked up then, met her eyes and smiled too, sharing the joke. The ice melted and Jenevan relaxed a bit. *Tamaya cooking? As if!* Her smile vanished when Akira's did. In those ancient eyes Jenevan saw the path before her, as if by magic, or logic.

"You will prepare meals for them, and their Guard, Bupple, a heavy eater, I understand. Twice a day, morning and evening, you will carry three cooked meals to the Great Hall. Carry them all the way up the stairs, but leave them on the porch. You may not enter, not under any circumstances, do you understand?"

"Yes, Akira," Jenevan answered absently. The last thing she was worried about was entering the Holy Cave. It was the twenty-minute walk each way up and down that rough trail, and a 30-foot climb up those stairs.

"But, how can I carry food all that way, and up those steep stairs? I am with child, Akira!" she informed proudly, as if Akira didn't already know.

"Good girl." Akira indulged. It was, after all, the young woman's primary function, and she hadn't wasted any time. Married a little more than a cycle and already working on her second.

"I fear if I carry that weight up the stairs, every day, the babbet..." She didn't dare finish the thought. "And what of Pindren? Do I take him? Leave him with my Momama? Her hut is in the opposite direction. She can't walk to my hut, and she won't ride a ganeesh since the accident. I can't leave Pindross for long, he might wander..."

Akira stood. *There it was.* It galled her to admit it, but Rakta was right. More and more, the women were questioning Akira's orders, too. Even this mousey, dutiful one. She smiled down at her prey indulgently. "What do I teach you girls, in my school?"

"Many things, Akira." Jenevan replied, suddenly meek again.

"I teach you to trust the blessings of your spirit. The special gifts Kakeeche gives you, gives everyone. We all have at least one talent. Trust it. Use it. Now go. Your work begins tomorrow morning. Bring a nice breakfast to the Akashic family and their Guard in the Holy Cave."

Akira waved her hand in the darkness and Jenevan stood. Her legs were shaking. She fled to the door. "Come!" She commanded Hebert. He took to her heel as she walked past him. All her dogs had been this way, ever since her second cycle. She trained other people's dogs for them, or really, trained the people. She provided the early training for the battle dogs, just the basic obedience training for the pups. The battle training was men's work, but she took care of all the dogs in the Great Hall during the season. No one asked her to; she just always had. She was known as the Dog Girl long before she married Pindrad. Now she was the Dog Woman.

She looked down at Hebert, her best dog yet. Her son was already cutting into her time with him. Eyes fixed on the path ahead, his broad shoulders worked under his thick, purple mane. His front legs reached out in front of him as he strode along in long, low strokes.

Of course! The thought came in a flash, as if from the Plane. *The blessings of my spirit. My talent.*

When she reached the village, she went past her hut and on to Maylar the Ganeesh Keeper's shack right behind the Great Hall to collect her son and the old baby carrier her momama had woven for him, two years ago.

"A little early for that, isn't it?" her momama asked.

"Can you make me a new one, momama?"

"What's wrong with that one?"

"This one's for Hebert now." The dog lay on his cushion, Pindren's two-year-old head bobbing up and down on his hairless belly, probably the cleanest place in the elephant-keeper's cluttered home. "Can you help me?" Jenevan asked. "I have to make a pack he can wear so he can carry meals to Tamaya and the Akash".

"And who prepares these meals?" her momama asked warily.

"I do." Jenevan announced proudly. "Akira says so. And Pindrad doesn't have to be Guard of Akash. Bupple is. I have to feed him, too."

Jenevan's momama, Latsinda, was up on her single leg, leaning on her crutch and aptly gathering long strands of dried yalinar and sinew, freely given by dogs who died accidentally or naturally, or by dead wild animals that were found before rigor spoiled their tissues. The ganeesh rarely gave of their dead. They carried their bodies off to some unknown place in the forest. Even Maylar didn't know where, and they said he could talk with the elephants.

Seven years ago, Latsinda had been riding a ganeesh along the edge of the river bank. The ground gave way and the ganeesh had fallen over the bank and landed on her side, right on Latsinda's leg. The poor ganeesh had struggled to get off of her, grinding her leg into the hard, gravel river bar. When she was freed, her leg was crushed, and Rashetta, one of Akira's Unmarriageables skilled in crude trauma surgery, had to amputate.

As she watched her Momama work, Jenevan recalled Akira's words. *We all have our special talents. Papa can talk to ganeesh like I can talk to dogs. That's why he lets me do that part of his job. But I can never ascend, and my children will take more and more of my time.*

Jeneven sighed bleakly, her eyes fixed blindly on her momama, until suddenly, she saw her as if for the first time. *She has been a momama for many years,* she realized, *and she still uses her special talent, weaving.*

All the women wove the squares of fabric stored communally in the Great Hall, and Latsinda's work was not particularly beautiful. But it was the most innovative. Tether to the ganeesh keeper, she designed and made the harnesses that secured the crucial battle rations and supplies to the huge animals with the tough skin that was impenetrable to nimbly stingers and bumbly horns.

A warm laugh bubbled up from Latsinda's generous mint bosom, startling Jenevan from her thoughts. "Big Bupple," she chortled affectionately at the thought of the clumsy boy she'd grown up with. "You will have to cook three portions for him. Maybe six. We will make an extra-large pouch and give you some of the six-man ration packs." She babbled and laughed and measured and wove until Hebert had an elaborate backpack with compartments for all the delicate clay ration packs for cooked meals, the bottles of vital pomegranate oil and juice, and pouches for fresh fruit. Latsinda even supplied the clay containers. "These must be returned by First Pomegranate Day, for battle." Admitting to their fragility with a knowing sigh, the busy one-legged woman added, "I will make some more, just in case."

The more ornate household pottery was a man's craft, with an apprentice who would ascend formally on Passascenday. But Latsinda cranked out the unglazed battle packs in her backyard kiln without decoration or ceremony, as part of her harness making job. The fragile clay battle packs were as close to disposable as anything in the village, and the numerous broken ones were reused to pave the path to the Great Hall.

Jenevan accompanied Hebert on his mission for the first week, all the way up the stairs. Her busy artist husband watched his popa and son on that temporary basis only, such things being woman's work. Soon, Hebert could leave the hut with his load, walk the trail without distraction, climb the stairs and carry the food into the Holy Cave, where dogs and ganeesh could go, but not non-Akashic women.

The Akashic Tether was harder to train. All her sister-in-law had to do was take out the containers and put the empties in their place, so the dog could carry them home. But half the time, the dog would return with an empty pack, and Jenevan would have to use more clay containers. She was running out, so she trained Hebert to refuse to leave the Holy Cave without the empties. He was quite persistent, and would follow the Akashic Tether around, staring holes into her with those soft, brown eyes until she remembered to pack the empties. Then he would leave immediately. Thus, the dog trained the Tether, and twice a day, morning and evening, Hebert carried the food to the Holy Cave for the Akash and his Tether and Guard while Jenevan stayed home with her toddler, her blind popa-in-law, her artist husband and, in a few Kakeeche cycles, her infant daughter.

EARTH, two months later

Agents

Special Agent Rita Goldsmith strode into the Cow Chow Feed Store on her platform soles. Except, she wasn't Special Agent Rita Goldsmith at the time. She was Linda Holiday, a blonde, upwardly mobile young businesswoman in a tight-fitting white pantsuit and pink satin blouse. She recognized the round, silver haired woman behind the counter from her picture in the Musik File. *That's her, Bernice Able. She co-owns this store with her husband, her son, and her daughter, Francine Musik, of the subject family.*

"Excuse me, Ma'am," Rita/Linda squeaked, humbly assertive.

The older woman smiled warmly. "What can I do you for, Hon?"

Rita hobbled to the counter, keeping her legs together. She shot a desperate look into Bernice's eyes and whispered, "May I use your restroom?"

Bernice rested her tough, unadorned hands on the counter, denim sleeves rolled up at the cuffs, exposing boney wrists. "It's generally for customers only."

"I have IBS." Rita whispered, blushing.

"You be what, Honey?"

"Irritable bowel syndrome!" Rita hissed, clenching her legs together even tighter.

With motherly kindness that cut like a razor, Bernice schooled the younger woman, "Bad tummy, eh? It gets harder as we get older, doesn't it. I wear these." She lifted her shirt a little, ran her finger along the inside of the elastic waist of her mom jeans. "Takes the pressure off." She looked back at Rita, who continued to squirm. "I wouldn't wear that color, either, if I was you."

"I know." Rita agreed quickly, as if apologizing.

Bernice rolled her eyes, then pointed behind herself, at her office. "Well, go on, then."

Across Main Street, Senior Special Agent Lewis Kramer watched the hot-shot techie kid, Agent Myron Boyd, hook up a dashboard of media along the wall of their rented storefront. The young man's chestnut hair flopped over his wire-framed glasses as he bent to plug another chord into the expanded outlet. He flashed Kramer a satisfied grin. His classically handsome cheekbones and square jaw looked cartoonish on his smooth, young face.

It had been easy to find an empty store in the sleepy downtown. There was plenty of room in the empty general store right across the street from the Cow Chow, the feed store that Musik's wife's parents owned, where their third agent now completed her mission.

A few days after the incident that somehow killed Manuel Guzman while he waited for a bus in the town's office park, members of the hate group Right Identity Doctrine, or RID, had raided the Look 'N Up Ranch and forced the local Sheriff to send the green-skinned aliens away, somewhere. Despite the Sheriff's flailing efforts to assure them nothing untoward had happened, RID had convinced the FBI they had to investigate.

The first team, Agents Nelson and Reid, had interviewed the Sheriff, then visited the high school to converse with Kate Quinlan, who had documented the event at the fairgrounds for the school paper, and seemed to have some kind of relationship with the Musik boy, Jerry. Now the new agents reviewed that interview while they waited for Agent Goldsmith.

Agent Nelson had rudely grabbed the girl's cell phone, fumbled with it, then passed it to Agent Reid. She scrolled quickly through the history, her pink painted nails flashing. "You called the Look 'N Up Ranch that night," she observed.

"Yeah. I called Jerry."

"On the land line? You have his cell number in here, why didn't you call that?"

"Jerry dropped his phone at the fairgrounds. It flew all apart, the battery went one way and the two halves of the case went two other ways. I thought it was toast, so I called his house."

"Why?" Agent Reid had inquired gently.

"To see if he got home alright."

"Why wouldn't he?" Agent Nelson growled. The vein at his greying temple throbbed visibly.

"I don't know. Those flying things? The bad ones, they killed someone! But not Jerry's. They're harmless. It was the other kid's —"

"What other kid? And where are they now? Jerry's fake ones, where are they?"

Agent Reid pressed another button on Kate's phone. "Hmmmm, what's this? Photos. Videos! Hey look! Is that a cave?" She turned the phone toward Agent Nelson.

"What are they doing?" Nelson had asked, squinting at the phone. "They're sending an old man into that little cave with a hose."

"That big guy, is he green? Is he one of the green ones?" Reid had wondered. "I can't tell with all that hair. Look! He just picked the white guy up like he was nothing and set him to the side, turned that tank on, it's turning white..."

"What's in the tank, Sweetheart?" Nelson had demanded, gripping Kate's shoulder.

"I don't know." Kate muttered through clenched teeth.

They heard the pop on the phone, loud and clear. The short video ended abruptly.

"What was that?" Nelson barked.

"What happened to that old guy?" the gentler female agent asked.

"I don't know. I left." Kate sank deep into the chair in the empty teacher conference room.

"They gassed him. He didn't come out. That's murder." Nelson accused.

The young reporter had gone cold and silent then. As he watched the recorded interview, Kramer's experience told him she was ready to break, put distance between herself and her boyfriend's family. He could see her wondering, *Are the Musiks responsible for two deaths?* Wondering why Nelson hadn't pressed a little harder, just then, he leaned back and sighed his resignation. He knew why. Because, like him, Nelson could tell she didn't know much more, and when she started talking faster and faster, spinning some yarn, he could tell that, too. The rest of the information would be completely unreliable.

"There's another way out." Kate babbled on the screen. "Down below. The old man went in and set the charge, then went on through, and out, down below. Then they blew it up."

"Why?"

"To destroy the stuff. Those drone things Jerry made, they caused so much trouble, the family decided to seal them up in that little cave and blow it shut forever."

"Destroy the evidence. Sounds guilty."

"No, they're just freaked out."

"So, they built that platform and set up all them pulleys," Nelson counted on his dark, pudgy fingers, "got that tank, we can find out what it was, young lady, sent an old guy in, seems like a lot of trouble just to get rid of some drones wrapped in plastic."

"That's all I know, officers, really. Can I have my phone back?"

"No."

Now, in the empty general store with the blacked-out windows, Agent Boyd plugged Kate's phone into his manifold and switched the monitor so an image of the platform and pulley system filled the screen. "See, there's three winches along the driveway. These two on the ends pull the thing back and forth, and the middle one lowers you to that platform. Looks like there's another winch that takes you down to the ground below."

"Well, here she is!" Kramer interrupted, greeting the uptight-looking bleach-blond businesswoman in the tight, white pantsuit who had just arrived from the Cow Chow.

"Good job, Agent Goldsmith." Kramer complemented the petite young agent without seeing the results.

"The performance of my life!" she reported proudly as she removed her disguise. "It's not a public restroom. You have to go through the office to get there. That's why she didn't want to let me use it. I implied some very stinky consequences if she didn't let me use it, right now." She smiled irresistibly. By now, she had morphed into a tough little Jewish girl from New York in a long-tailed T-shirt and black leggings, her tightly kinked black hair cut short. "I bugged the office and the phone."

Boyd plugged in the last cord and flipped a switch. Static hissed over a muted conversation in the store.

"Have you questioned the Musiks?" Goldsmith asked suddenly. "I didn't see anything in the report, except the Sheriff and those RID guys, and of course, that reporter girl." She pointed at Boyd's frozen screen.

"She's a liar. Even the Sheriff is a liar. They're all liars." Kramer declared with calm certainty. "That's why we're not going to question them. We're going to surveil them. That RID guy said one of the so-called green guys said the flying things come every three years, so we're going to watch."

"For three years?" Boyd asked quickly as he turned a dial to squelch the static.

Kramer nodded. "Job security."

A telephone rang. Kramer found himself scanning Boyd's dashboard for a simple old-fashioned land line. But he could hear the ring tone from the calling end, too. *The phone bug!* He realized.

"Something's happening." Boyd confirmed his boss's slow reaction. They heard footsteps, then the squeak of a desk chair as someone settled down heavily. The ringing stopped.

"Hello. Frankie?" They could hear the old woman's voice in the office and on the phone.

"That's her." Rita confirmed. "The mother-in-law."

"Hi Mom," a male voice replied. "I'm calling about Christmas."

"Do you know your sister isn't coming again?" The voice in the office pitched steeply. "They're going to that Patrick's again. That's three years in a row."

"Well, that's OK, Mom. Elmer's brother lives way up north. They don't see each other that often. We see Fran all the time. She's at the store three times a week."

"They were just there for Thanksgiving, too. I'd like to see my little grandson once in a while."

"Come on, Mom. We go to all his school stuff, they come over..."

"They haven't invited us up to the ranch for three years, either. How about you?"

Frank Jr. paused, counting. "Well, I guess not, come to think of it."

"I tell you, Frankie, something's wrong."

The agents exchanged a glance. Maybe something really *was* going on at that ranch, but these folks seemed to be in the dark about it.

"Maybe New Year's?" Frankie attempted.

"They're staying all the way until New Year's Day."

"Christmas Eve?"

"Oh, get this! I asked her that. She said they were driving Christmas Eve! So, I told her I heard there was going to be a big snowstorm up there on Christmas Eve, and she'd better just stay here. So, she says, 'well, we'll just leave really early. We'll beat it.' Can you believe it?" Boyd winced as the tone reached the upper limits of the audible range.

"No, Mom. I mean yes, Mom. Don't worry about it, OK? Nothing's wrong," her poor son sputtered.

"She sounds like my mom." Boyd remarked, shaking his head as the call ended uncomfortably. "Do you think the aliens are up there where they're going? The brother's place?"

Kramer was grinning from ear to ear. "I'm sure they are. But we're checking out the Look 'N Up Ranch first, and here's our chance. Who's up for working on Christmas?"

Boyd jerked to attention. "I can't. I gotta go see my mom."

"I thought you didn't like her." Rita jeered.

"I didn't say that. I just said that old lady reminded me of her. That's why I gotta spend Christmas Eve and Christmas with her, or she'll get just like that."

"The day after, then?" Rita asked eagerly. She didn't mind. Her family didn't do Christmas.

"Yeah, I can do that." Boyd agreed.

"Nobody goes anywhere the day after Christmas." Kramer agreed calmly.

"They'll be snowed in," Rita reminded them.

Christmas Eve

Flushing

"Patrick was right," Baput whispered to himself as he watched his morning stream plunge into the pool of clear water. "This green toilet is hideous." When he flushed, he flashed back to his first night at Jerry's, when he was so confused he had thought the toilet might be the portal, the way home! He tipped his head back and laughed softly.

The mirror over the sink startled him, even though he had been seeing it every day for a month now. He still wasn't used to it, or the unfamiliar image it held. Somehow, he knew he looked different. He felt different. He *was* different. An entirely different person than he'd been at the Look 'N Up. He was just Baput then, a boy. Son of Valko and Salistar, grandson of the almighty Akash of Nauve. Now he was more than his G-Pa had been. He was Alanakash, but not of Nauve. Not of the Look 'N Up Pomegranate Ranch, either. Here at Patrick's Place, being an Alanakash meant nothing. Here, he was no longer a boy, and G-Pa was gone.

He ran his fingertip over the short, thick, jet-black hairs that poked out of the green flesh above his upper lip. *That must have shown before we um, left.* He still struggled with the word. He had lived in three different places in a little more than a cycle. Yet, he still struggled with the concept of 'places'. Not nearly as much as his parents or Uncle Felsic did, though. They just couldn't get their heads around it. There were no other places on Nauve. Just the village.

He picked up the razor that lay unused on the shelf below the mirror. "You're starting to look like your Popa," Francina had told him when she gave it to him. "Felsic can show you how, if you want to. It's up to you." She had kissed him on top of his head. He must have been sitting at the time. Otherwise, she couldn't have done that. Not anymore.

He put the razor down slowly. Not yet. Not today. He might cut himself and look foolish when Jerry and Elmer and Francina came.

He staggered down the hall to his bedroom. He could still feel the difference in the marrow of his bones. It was just like their old quarters on the Look 'N Up. Baput remembered when they first saw this quarters at Patrick's place, over two years ago. But he had just met Belinda, and he was confused about new places, and he hadn't been thinking at all clearly.

The interior walls weren't up then. They had all pitched in and finished this house together. Patrick had told them as they worked that he made it just like the quarters at the Look 'N Up because he remembered the layout so well. He had lived there for a couple of years after Francina married Elmer, to "give them their privacy", but Elmer's Popa and Momama and G-Pa and G-Mama had all lived in the house then, too, so it seemed to Baput that it was Patrick who needed the privacy.

Anyway, it was the same as the old quarters, only backwards. East was west and west was east. It wasn't just the layout of the house that disoriented him. The whole village, if that's what this was, was backwards. Jerry's house had been west of the quarters. Here, Belinda's house was east of the quarters, and much further away. After a month, Baput could still feel the difference. They all did. His people were sensitive to such things.

Despite the constant mild disorientation, Baput loved it, because now he had a bedroom window that faced south. He could watch the arc of the moon, Kakeeche, as it, or they, crossed the sky. And, he had an east window. Through it, he could barely make out Belinda's bedroom light, scattered by wavering leaves and the mist of the breaking dawn.

As he turned to pick out his clothes, he stopped to admire the loft bed Francina had somehow caused to appear in this, um, location. *Beds for all of us. This elevated bed. How did she know I longed to sleep on that top bunk the whole time I was there?* He shivered at the memory of that bottom bunk where he'd slept every night with G-Pa on the floor beside him, clinging to his hand all night.

Francina had sent a beautiful extra-wide canopy bed for Momama and Popa, and an especially firm bed for Felsic that was almost like sleeping on the floor, but better for him. To everyone's surprise, he took to it the first night, after Lori Anne demonstrated it for him.

Baput slipped into the maroon sweatpants with the comfy elastic waistband and the simple, black T-shirt that Lori Anne had provided. She said she didn't want them wearing those dirty, stained, woven grass outfits in the house. Him or Momama, when she was in there to clean. She hadn't said anything about Felsic or Popa. They rarely went in Elmer's house on the Look 'N Up, except at the end, during the battle. There wouldn't be a battle next cycle, not here, anyway.

In his bedroom was an even bigger mirror, full-length, a gift from Lori Anne for each room. Baput worried for the one in Popa's room, but Momama seemed to like it. She was the only one in the family who had ever seen such a thing, in Akira's Bridal Antechamber.

Baput took an Akashic breath and confronted the incorporeal image. There was that strange young man, looking even more alien now. He looked himself up and down and smiled approvingly. He didn't mind wearing the

Earth clothes. They were much more comfortable than that itchy woven yalinar grass. But Momama had had enough of new things, not the least of which was the backwards nature of their new home.

Abandoning his faulty gyro, Baput followed his nose toward one of Momama's fried potato concoctions, minus the fresh garden vegetables. It was the end of December and Lori Anne's garden was as bare as it had been on their last visit. Lori Anne bought vegetables for them at the health food store because Francina said we were worth the extra money, whatever that meant.

He didn't see his mother in the dining room, so he peeked into the kitchen. "Momama!" he cried when he spotted Salistar teetering on a chair, wresting a cooking pot from a high shelf. He rushed into the forbidden room without thinking. "Momama, what are you doing?" He wrapped his arms around her hips and lifted her down, pot and all. She set the pot on the counter and leaned back to look up at him, her eyes searching his frantically. He swallowed her in his arms, just like his Popa did, so he didn't have to look at her pain.

"It's your popa," she muttered into his chest. "He came in the kitchen!" Her face and voice reflected the shock of this unorthodox behavior. Nauvian men did not enter kitchens. Not even Baput, the Alanakash, but here he was.

"He said it was messy. Disorganized. He said he would fix it for me. I didn't ask him to!" She grumbled her resentment, casting her eyes toward the back door, where Valko and Felsic had exited on their way to the shop. "He put all my things way up high, where I can't get them. He's so grumpy all the time, Baput. I'm afraid."

Baput let go of his mother and began bringing pans and plates down from the high shelves. Salistar filled her pot with water and set it on the stove next to the skillet of potatoes.

"Popa was always grumpy, Momama."

"He was always grumpy because of your G-pa. Now, no G-pa, and still grumpy."

"But he would never hurt anybody. You know that."

"Of course, I know." Salistar admitted softly. "I'm not afraid *of* him. I'm afraid *for* him. Felsic too. They are not happy. None of us are happy, since,

since Francina and Elmer and Jerry..." She trailed off. She clenched her fist, palm up, then opened her hand quickly, made a popping sound with her tongue. It was the sign they used to express what had happened to them, three years ago, when they arrived on Earth. But that was not what had happened to their first Earth family.

"Momama, they didn't disappear through a portal like we did. They didn't go anywhere. We did."

"I understand what happened," Salistar cut him off, shoving her cookware where it belonged, where she could find it, and reach it.

"You do?" Baput asked hopefully.

Star nodded her head vigorously. She was smiling! Baput surged with elation, then sunk abruptly into concern. Was she OK? "What, Momama?"

"This world," she raised her hands and made a ball. That surprised Baput. He didn't think she had understood any of that 'Jerry talk' about Earth being a ball, but here she went. She even reminded him of Jerry, in the weirdest split second since his fateful arrival. She turned the imaginary ball over and went on lecturing. "The world turns over every cycle. The house flipped over. The world flipped over. Even the river is flipped on its side."

"Wait, what, Momama?"

"The river. It was Nauve. It was Look 'N Up, but at Patrick's, it is on its side."

Baput's thick black eyebrows curled into a perfect wave.

Star shoved her arm forward horizontally. "River is a line, see?" She slapped the other hand flat over the fist of her extended arm. Then she rotated her arm to vertical, capped hand on top. "Now it is only a point. The river, on its side."

Baput stood speechless until it dawned on him. "The pond?"

Star nodded happily, dropped her arms and continued her lecture. "Now Patrick and Lori Anne's world is on top, and Elmer and Francina's world is below. Next cycle, it will flip over again, and Francina and Elmer will be on top, and we will see them again. You will see Jerry." She blinked her deep, dark eyes up at him sincerely.

"But remember when we were here before? Elmer and Jerry and Francina were with us. And it was mid-cycle, not even close to First Pomegranate Day." He took both her hands in his much larger ones and gazed into her deep, troubled eyes. Then he looked through the steamy doorway into the dining room. "Come sit," the Supreme Alanakash ordered his Tether.

"I must stir the potatoes. They will burn."

Baput surveyed the strain on her face, the deep furrows in her dark green brow, pre-creased from years of practice. Her cheeks were sucked in so she looked gaunt, and dark fear glowed deep inside her eyes. *Far too much stress for burning potatoes*, he thought.

"Stir," he ordered, more tenderly this time. "Then come out here and sit."

He disappeared into the dining room where he belonged. By the time his momama joined him, Baput had cleared the dining table. He left only their cups, arranged in a diamond pattern. Valko's cup, the biggest one, was on the west point. Baput's was on the east. His Momama, Salistar's, cup was to the north, and Uncle Felsic's, to the south. Salistar sat curiously.

"They are called 'places', Momama. Look." He touched his Popa's cup, oversized like everything about Valko including his thick, black hair and beard that both reached his waist, his broad feet no Earth shoes would fit, and his towering six-foot-six, three-hundred-pound presence.

"Popa's cup is the Great Hall."

Salistar cocked her head adorably, reminding Baput of the four puppies that roamed outside herded by their momama, the lavender German Shepherd-like Shastina. "It is a model, a picture. Rasta, Momama."

The familiar word from Nauve comforted her. She nodded. "Rasta," she confirmed, wondering if Pindrad had ascended to replace the village artist, Pindross, who had lost his sight.

Baput went on. "My cup, east of the Great Hall, is the Holy Cave. See, this is the river." He pulled a strip of yalinar grass from Star's weaving basket and laid it lengthwise, south of the cups. "Your cup is our home in the village, and Felsic's is the mill, down by the river. Do you understand?" He probed her nod with sincere, deep brown eyes.

He pointed to the cups in turn, faster this time. "Great Hall, a place, Mill, a place, Holy Cave, a place, home, a place. We walk here to there. If we walk from home to the Great Hall, does home fall out of the world?

No! Home is still home. Just empty for a time. Then we walk back, and it is there, waiting for us. Yes?"

Salistar nodded, the lines on her brow easing a bit. Baput plunged ahead. "Then we came to Look 'N Up. We don't yet know how, and the potatoes will surely burn if we try to discuss it. But that aside, we were at Look 'N Up, see? He reassigned the cups. Your cup, the north cup, is still our home, the quarters, in the village where Francina lives. He swapped his cup with Felsic's. "The Holy Cave, by the river, is south now. Not exactly, but, stay with me. Felsic's cup, to the east, is the sauna. It should be G-Pa's cup, but..."

"Go on." Star insisted, surprising him again. He took the west cup, his Popa's, and dragged it further west, about halfway to the edge of the table. "This is Fair Grounds. In town. You have never been, but we men have. It is far away. Too far to walk. You could, but it would take a long time. So, we rode in the back of Patrick's plumbing van to Fair Grounds, while you stayed here with Francina." He pointed to Felsic's cup, which represented the tiny sauna building where his late G-Pa had spent many hours meditating. He accepted the pang in his heart and pressed on. If he could just get Momama to understand, she could relax a little. Another pang. *How can Momama relax when she has to live with Lori Anne instead of her best friend Francina?*

He fought to stay on track. "We men went to Fair Grounds. You stayed here in the sauna. You didn't fall off the world or stop existing, not even temporarily. Now did you?"

Salistar looked worried at something far away. "I don't know. It was dark, so dark, for so long..."

"Why didn't you turn on the lights? Francina knew how."

"We were afraid. We just waited in the dark with the dogs and Elmer's gun. We," she struggled with the word, "*exist* or not exist?" She shrugged, rising from her chair.

"Momama, wait. Please." The untranslatable English word froze Salistar in her tracks. Like "Thank you", she would never get used to hearing it. But she liked it. She stayed to watch Baput draw that oversize cup as far as he could without pitching it off the table. "Then, in that same van, we all came to Patrick's. To here. Twice. Not the same as before, Momama. Not a mysterious portal."

"Shavarandu!" Salistar muttered angrily.

"Yes, Momama," the Alanakash meekly replied. "But not this time. It's just another place, far away. Too far to walk, so we rode, remember, for four Earth hours?" He leveled his eyes into hers lovingly. "You told your horrible story of Romey and Jakima, the poor lovers who were not betrothed, *both* times? We rolled in Patrick's van," he maneuvered the big cup off the table and across thin air to the back of Popa's chair and across it. He even made motor noises, like an Earth boy.

He drove the cup all the way to the back of the couch in the apparent living room, undivided from the dining room except by furniture types. "Too far to see. Too far to walk. This world is much, much bigger than Nauve. There are many villages, Momama, and so many people, you would not believe it! You just don't see them because they are far away in other places, just like we're here. But look at the table, Momama. See, I am way over here, but the Look 'N Up is still there. Francina, Jerry and Elmer are still there. They're OK! And we will see them today, when they um, *become*, here."

Salistar grasped the strand of yalinar that represented the river and held it, end up, the long leaf dangling to the floor. "Pond," she maintained. "This Patrick place is upside down. Men do woman things. Women do men things." She nodded certainly and returned to her kitchen.

Portable Trees

The electric space heater clicked and rattled and blew air across reddened coils that stank like wet ash. Valko raised the file, eyes fixed on the blade of the machete he held on his lap. He ran his thumb across it deftly, drew a drop of blood. It was plenty sharp already. He hadn't used it once since the Season. Elmer had told him not to sharpen it too much. "There'll be nothin' left of it!" he had admonished. Valko drew the file again anyway, for the umpteenth time, all the while wondering, *what for?*

The orchard here consisted of only six pomegranate, or *kip*, trees. They'd harvested and processed those few kips in the first few days after their arrival. The trees were so young, there were no limbs to prune, no bark to strip. There was nothing to make. The tools, the furnishings, Salistar's cookware, all premade out of weird Earth materials. Worst of all, there was nothing to kill, and wouldn't be. Not ever, no more. A situation his people had dreamed of since long before he was born. A guttural growl escaped with his exhale. He took a deeper swipe, sending more of the precious but useless blade flaking to the floor.

He lifted his eyes to the shop doorway where eight saplings from two different worlds clung to life in weird, flexible sacks, straining toward the grey sunlight. Four were from Nauve, born of the four Holy Seeds the Akash had worn in a woven pouch around his neck. They should have been planted in the ground at the Look 'N Up almost three years ago, but Elmer didn't want trees from another place planted among his Earth trees. He wasn't sure they would 'get along', so he'd sent the lot here, to Patrick's, along with four trees from Look 'N Up seeds, as an experiment.

Valko sighed, shook his head. Earth's *otherwheres.* Even the trees moved among them! In his world, even people didn't move so far. People stayed in the village. Trees stayed in the orchard, rooted firmly in the ground. But on Earth, he'd learned, there were many otherwheres. People routinely moved from one world to the next, and when they arrived, they were not usually welcomed. Even the trees hated trees from otherwhere, it seemed.

Now the poor things had moved again, back indoors. They had started their pathetic lives inside the greenhouse on the Look 'N Up. Here, they had lived in the orchard with the mature trees, still in those fabric bags. Yesterday, Patrick had them brought into the shop. He had said a storm was coming. Valko peered beyond the plants at the bleak sky and nodded. But who ever heard of a tree that couldn't weather a rainstorm?

He snorted and looked around Patrick's shop, smaller, and much neater, than Elmer's. There was a lathe for turning wood and metal, welding equipment, stuff for working with the pipes that carried water in and out of these Earth residences, powering wonderful things like toilets and showers and sinks and Salistar's beloved dishwasher. He and Felsic had already organized all the tools, materials and equipment neatly on the shelves. Then Valko had done the same for his wife in her new kitchen, even though he wasn't supposed to go in there. She had been quite upset about it. *Her head is still full of all that fear and nonsense her Popa, the late Akash put in there. Men not allowed in the kitchen! Kakeeche will punish us! Bah!* He bent to spit on the floor, and his eyes fell on his much smaller brother.

Felsic knelt on the spotless concrete floor, playing with a three-inch spring. He hummed jerkily as he squeezed and released, squeezed and released, slow and steady, then fast and hard. Mouth gaping slightly, he held the spring up to his eye and squeezed, let go, squeezed, let go.

Four years ago, at Nauve, Valko would have roared at him for his indignity, then laughed while his goofy little brother cowered. *My idiot little brother*, he would have thought, like everyone thought. "*He's not quite all there*" they would say.

But now, Valko knew his brother was a genius. Boss Elmer had declared him so. Valko had never known any declared geniuses before, but he knew his brother. He was finding out there was a lot more to his imbecilic actions than he had ever realized before. But without Little Truck and Big Truck and the tractor, Beulah, a lumbering, soulless ganeesh, to restore and maintain in perfect working order, what was Felsic's genius to do? Would he turn to the dark arts of Shavarandu? Or worse, fall back into the wine bottle?

Felsic picked up a small pipe that lay beside him on the floor. Valko recognized it. He had helped his brother install a little lever at the end, but Felsic wouldn't tell him why. Now Felsic dropped the spring he'd been playing with into the pipe and chased it down with that six-inch metal rod that Valko remembered notching one end of, and grinding the other to a point, all at Felsic's request.

Tools and trees forgotten, Valko watched Felsic point the pipe at the wall and pull the lever. He whooped his familiar whoop as the rod shot across the room and struck the wall, penetrating the corrugated metal and sticking there.

"Shavarandu!" Valko accused, jumping to his feet, his machete drawn.

"Not Shavarandu, Brother!" Felsic assured him brightly. "No spooky actions. Just cause and effect, multiplied by the power of Spring," he babbled, grinning maniacally.

JANICE CARR SMITH

Pon Farr

Lorraine sat up in bed and turned to face the still-reclining Patrick, who was calmly explaining the mating rituals of their new domestics. She'd been thinking about it all night, again.

"How old are the girls when they, um, mate?" she demanded.

"Whenever their betrothed comes of age," Patrick responded simply.

Lorraine swung her long legs to the side and sprung out of bed. She paced between the bed and the bathroom door in her old Star Trek Next Generation T-shirt and floral bikini panties. "The guy, you mean. What about the girl? What if she's only ten, or twelve?"

Patrick remained, although her pacing was starting to wake him up. "They try to keep them within a cycle of each other. That's three years," he explained remedially.

"I know it's three years!" she snapped. "First Pomegranate Day. Every three years. The nimblies and the bumblies come. Don't you think I know that? I just battle-engineered those suckers into oblivion!" she bragged as she gave in and entered the bathroom.

Patrick shouted after her. "We all did it, Babe. Together."

"How old is the boy?" Lorraine shouted from the bathroom.

"Who, Baput?" Patrick was getting up now.

"The boys on Nauve, when do they come of age, like you said?" Lorraine already knew this, too. She had listened to that gruesome, but oddly comforting, legend of Romey and Jakima on that long, dark ride in the back of the van with the green family that smelled like pomegranates. She just wanted to see how much Patrick knew when he had invited them to live here with them and their twelve-year-old daughter.

Patrick knew it all. He recited as he headed to the bathroom to join his wife. "On the first First Pomegranate Day after his fifteenth birthday, a boy joins the battle against the nimblies and bumblies. If he lives through the three days and nights of fighting, then he gets married the next day, on Passascenday, and he hopes to ascend from apprentice to whatever his profession will be. You know, like Baput um, didn't." He slipped past Lorraine at the sink and raised the toilet seat.

Lorraine didn't respond, perhaps because she was brushing her teeth. As soon as she finished, she whirled on Patrick, eyebrows arched up into her short red bangs.

Oh, yeah, Patrick remembered as he flushed: *She hates when I pee right in front of her like that.*

"So, the missile was active the moment it was launched." Lorraine accused. Patrick stowed his equipment and turned to face her in his unique way, right eye narrowed and leveled at her, skewed left eye gazing at the specks of mold forming at the top of the wall above the shower. He got the reference, *The Hunt for Red October*, but he didn't see how it related to the family of green-skinned alien refugees that now resided in their worker's quarters.

"What, Babe?" he asked casually, trying to brush off her apparent building fury as if it were a trick of the fluorescent light.

"Why didn't you tell me? Did you know?" She walked forward, he walked backward, right out of the bathroom.

"Did I know what?" Patrick stammered helplessly.

"That he's in heat? Pon Farr?" she shrieked, poking at him with her painted talons.

Preferring the Vulcan reference over the canine, Patrick answered calmly. "He's not in Pon Farr. He's just eligible to marry his betrothed."

Lorraine slipped out of her clothes. After seventeen years of marriage, she still stirred him. She closed the bathroom door.

She stepped into the shower and slid the foggy door closed. The water was tepid at first. It reminded her of that greasy shower stall in the shop at the Look 'N Up, where she had realized this was the only option. It was before Patrick had asked her and invited them. In that same shower, she had also recognized that it would inevitably go horribly wrong. That's why it wasn't ever going to be her idea.

She knew her fantasy of shipping the green aliens back home with the in-laws when they left after Christmas was just that. A fantasy. Those rednecks had seen to that. The reality was, they were all coming, today. A houseful. And something else was coming, too. Not Santa Clause, but a big snowstorm. Snowed in with the in-laws. Happy Holidays!

Snow Storm

"We got here just in time!" Francine declared with a grin, snowflakes clinging to her blond hair and eyelashes. She stood beside the Prius in a bright blue winter jacket, water-repellent nylon over some miraculously light, warm fiber fill. The snow and four puppies piled up around her high-top fleece-lined booties.

"We're gonna be stuck here!" was how Elmer saw it as he clambered out of the heavily tarped Toyota pickup. He stomped his work boots, kicking at the gathering snow.

Brodey bounded out behind him. He ran halfway to Shastina, then, grunting painfully, he stopped and lifted his leg before completing the reunion.

"Whooo Hooooo!" Jerry cheered as he popped out of the passenger seat of the car, wearing a parka like his mom's, but dark green. "Where's the B Man?" Fresh powder crunching under his new snow boots, he headed straight for the hesitant group on the path from the quarters. They kept looking up at the sky, just like on that first day, on the Look 'N Up Ranch. Not the good way of looking up. The scared way. The way they looked up at the flying predators who ate the green people relentlessly for three days and three nights once every three years, right at harvest time. That kind of looking up. At the snow!

"You've never seen snow before?" Jerry realized out loud. Nauve was the same place as the Look 'N Up Ranch, just another dimension. The same latitude and longitude. The only latitude and longitude their world had. They had the same climate, except they hadn't messed theirs up with fossil fuels or technology of any kind. Jerry had only seen snow at home on the Look 'N Up a couple of times in his fifteen years, and it was just a dusting, less than an inch. This stuff was already starting to stack up. *Dad might be right,* he hoped. *We're here all week anyway, and school wouldn't start for another week after that, so who cares?*

It had only been a month, but it seemed like years since he'd seen his old friends. They seemed different, somehow. Yeah, scared, like on that first day. Especially the little woman with skin the color of newly sprouted grass who trembled in the arms of Jerry's gushing mom. *Poor Salistar!* he realized, *Aunt Lorraine's not taking Mom's place, that's for sure.*

Suddenly Baput was right there in his face, the way his people did. Mom said they have 'different boundaries' than we do. Awkwardly, he punched his avocado-skinned best friend on the shoulder. "Hey, B. Have you guys ever seen snow before?" he asked again.

"Yes." Baput began with that same old word, the word he used when he was hesitant, or scared. "I've seen it a couple times in my lifetime, but never like this!" His dark brown eyes scanned the blindingly white landscape.

Jerry added one more piece of confirming data for his dimension theory. "Me too." He agreed, certain the two had seen the same two storms, on two different worlds. "Well, see, you're further north now, and higher up in the mountains" he explained, or tried to, still amazed at the difference between them. Baput's tiny world, consisting of a single village with no 'otherwhere' was impossible to imagine. Jerry and his family had tried, many times. But how hard was it for *them* to imagine *our* world, with so many places, races, and cultures? "It snows a lot here. Didn't Patrick tell you? There's a place right up the road about 50 miles, where people pay to go play in this stuff."

"I told them when we moved the baby trees into the shop, but I don't think they knew what I was talking about." Patrick greeted Jerry, his right eye looking deep into his nephew's while his left eye scanned the white sky.

Jerry's cousin Belinda stood next to him, sharing his disfigurement, her misplaced eye socket pointing up and to the left at the grownups while her right one greeted her cousin warmly.

Jerry didn't react like other people did at their odd appearance. He was used to seeing Look 'N Ups. Every generation of the Musik Family had a Look 'N Up and a Straight-Eye. The Straight-Eyes always got drafted and died without having kids, except for Jerry's dad, because they stopped the draft. Jerry's Grandpa had lived with them until a few years ago, and great-grandpa had, too, when Jerry was little. They had the deformity, as did Jerry's great-great grandpa, and *his* dad before him was in a freak show in the 1800s. They say he thought he'd get rich and famous, but he ended up more like a slave. He escaped by jumping from a circus train in the middle of the night with a midget and a hunchback. So, the legend went, anyway. It sounded more like a bad joke now, after all the family had been through since. The trip from Oklahoma, their penniless arrival in California's Salinas Valley along with every other mother's son from the dust bowl of the Midwest, all competing for the same job that wouldn't pay enough to feed them. Then their salvation, when the good Mr. Richardson decided to right one of his father's wrongs and hired them, let them stay, and finally gave them the almond orchard that was now the Look 'N Up Pomegranate Ranch.

Elmer squeezed his brother's shoulder. "Still ain't planted those three-year-olds, eh?"

"Valko says not until spring. Good thing we put them in the shop, huh?" He wiggled his uneven red eyebrows at Valko. "The older ones have seen snow before, and they were fine."

"This one's gonna be a whopper, they say." Elmer warned.

"Isn't it beautiful, guys?" Patrick maintained his positive spin. The green people looked up again, wincing and blinking. "It doesn't hurt you, unless you get too wet and cold and you can't find shelter and get warm. Speaking of that, let's get inside. You must be freezing in those grass pants and tunics. And Baput, you look great, but those sweats are gonna get all soaked. You should be wearing your jeans."

"I have just the thing!" Fran crowed, stomping to the back of the car and producing a stack of wide, rectangular packages wrapped in bright paper. "You'll have to open your presents early, right now. I got you all winter clothes. Jerry, Elmer, get the boots."

Patrick escorted the group, not into the house, but to the quarters. Salistar and Valko didn't seem to mind the unexpected, but very welcome, intrusion into their humble worker's quarters. The brand-new linoleum floors shined like the polished wood they were supposed to resemble.

They opened their snow gear and chatted casually, stiffly catching up on minor details. They all got nice parkas like Fran and Jerry's. No more grass-woven tunics lined with lumpy pomegranate rinds. They'd even found Valko a giant pair of mukluks that fit him comfortably.

By the time the gifts were open and tried on, there was already a good foot of snow outside. The Nauvians looked like mummies. "Come on, everyone!" Belinda called, her hand on the doorknob. "Let's go outside and play in the snow."

"It's a snow angel." Belinda explained as she folded her soaked leg under herself and rose clumsily to her feet. "See the wings, where I flapped my arms?"

Baput wasn't sure what an angel was. He closed his eyes and searched the iPlane. Winged people appeared, ranging from babies to warriors. "There are winged people?" he stammered, wondering why Jerry hadn't mentioned them. What place did the winged people come from?

"Not real, Bud." Jerry assured him, slapping him on the back. Then he dropped to ground and made another angel, right next to Bel's. The puppies piled on, flecking the images with not-so-little paw prints.

Valko and Felsic stood watching, bored and shivering. "Awk!" Felsic squawked as a wet ball of snow smashed into his shoulder blade. The thick fiber fill softened the blow. Elmer cackled from somewhere behind him. He whirled, just in time to catch a second snowball in the face.

Valko roared and sprang into action, always ready to defend his little brother. He quickly gathered some snow into a ball, packed it hard, and flung it full force at his assailant.

"Ow! Damn! Lighten up, there, big guy. We're just playin'!" Elmer complained, picking ice out of his ear.

Felsic slammed him this time, right in the chest, and the fight was on. Even Francine and Belinda joined in. Salistar stood by the sidelines, arms folded, like a playground monitor.

Patrick slipped away to his porch and got a couple of three-foot wide plastic saucers and some big slabs of cardboard he had stripped from some of the appliances he'd collected for the quarters. They all took turns sliding down the slope that dropped down to the orchard. Belinda gave the puppies rides, one at a time on her saucer. Six pomegranate trees spread their bare branches, making intricate patterns on the white snow.

Elmer went over to them and tried to shake the snow off. The Nauvian men followed him, and in a few minutes the drooping branches were relieved of their unaccustomed load. Elmer stood beside Patrick, watching. "See how these guys work?" he said, pointing to the three snow flurries. He swallowed hard, recalling bitterly how his year-round, live-in crew had worked the Look 'N Up Orchard, how he'd been the first with the most every harvest since their mysterious arrival, except for this past one, when they had to fight the nimblies and bumblies right at harvest time, like the green folks did every third year on Nauve. Now he'd be lucky if he could get some day labor to help with the harvest. Angrily pushing that frustration aside, his concern turned to his old crew.

"Look, these guys need work. They gotta have something to do. They'll get bored, otherwise. They're hard workers. Felsic needs vehicles he can work on. Valko likes metal. He was a woodworker on Nauve, you know."

"I thought he was a Warrior. Guard of Akash."

"Yeah, he was all that. But his Popa was a woodworker. That's the family trade. He taught him, and he made wooden tools and stuff for everybody, and guarded the Akash, and fought in the trenches during the season. All the men fight, no matter what their usual profession is."

"But Valko was a General or something, wasn't he? He led the longstick line."

"Yeah, that was unusual for someone who's not a full-time Warrior. But, he's Valko."

"He's a big guy."

"Big and smart and powerful. He earned that spot. Most men are born to their positions. Valko did more. He's ambitious, for a Nauvian. He needs something to do. So does Felsic. I brought some woodworking tools, and some automotive stuff for Felsic in my truck, carburetors to rebuild, stuff like that. I've ordered you a four-wheeler, I guess I should order a plow for it, eh? I'm gonna leave you Little Truck. Felsic loves Little Truck. I wish I could get old Beulah up here, but I don't have a trailer big enough. Maybe if you get these trees going, I'll get you guys a tractor."

"A four-wheeler, a tractor, your pickup, that's a lot of money, Elmer. I can't let you do that."

"It's their money. Three of them worked full time for three years. Fran kept track, and deducted their expenses, sometimes. There's plenty of money there, and they can't keep it without a Social Security number, and they can't take cash to the store, so we just use it to buy them stuff."

"Like the wood flooring in the house? Was that for them? Lorraine won't even let them in."

"That's so Star don't have to vacuum. You know how sensitive these guys are to vibrations. The noise would tear her apart. So, yeah, it's for them. But how's she supposed to clean if Lorraine won't let her in?"

"She can come in and clean, and cook, except she doesn't cook meat, so she just cooks her vegan stuff for her family and brings us some. So, it's just the cleaning, mostly. And I let Baput come in all the time. We talk a lot. I try to explain stuff to him. Stuff he catches out of the air, from the internet, you know, like he does? But these days, this new President..."

Elmer snorted. "I don't envy you trying to explain *that*. Jerry did most of the explaining when we had these guys. He did pretty good, too. Like, how do you explain racism to a guy who's never seen anybody who's different?"

"Well, he's seen different now."

"But he still doesn't get why we Earthlings hate people who are different."

The families were soaked clear through their brand-new water-resistant clothing. The cardboard sleds had begun to disintegrate. Tiny brown rolls of wet paper and protruding leaves of grass soon replaced the thinning snow on the slope, even though large, wet flakes continued to drift from the sky. The Nauvians no longer looked up in fear. Without a signal, the group agreed as one that the sledding session was over, and they all headed back toward the houses.

Patrick stopped on the driveway. "Now the bad news," he announced with a grin. "Lorraine will be coming home soon. We have to clear the driveway."

"I can get used to this," he muttered to himself while Felsic, Valko, Baput and Jerry made short work of shoveling the long driveway, throwing snow over the side by the shovel load while Elmer and Fran brought their loads of food, clothes and gifts into the house.

Fran had dinner all prepared, but Lorraine still wasn't home. "It's OK, Aunt Fran. We always eat without her. She comes home after and brings something with meat, just for herself. We're vegan now, like Salistar and Baput."

"Well, I just cooked a chicken."

"It's OK," Patrick interrupted. "We'll eat meat if you're cooking, right Bel?"

"Sure." Bel agreed cheerfully, tucking into the roasted bird.

"Any word on the investigation?" Patrick laid the uncomfortable subject out on the table with the half-eaten meal. They all knew what he meant. The FBI was after them.

Just after the incident at the fairgrounds, the haters from Right Identity Doctrine, or RID, had raided the Look 'N Up Ranch and forced Sheriff Dave to send the green people away, for their own good. That might have been the end of it, if the bumblies hadn't killed Manuel Guzman while he waited for a bus in the town's office park. They hadn't heard from RID since then, but Sheriff Dave said the new deputy he had fired had moved to Los Angeles and joined that hate group, in a paid position, alongside his buddy, Dirk. And they had called the FBI.

"No Agent ever talked to any of us," Elmer began.

"They talked to Kate at school. They took her cell phone," Jerry informed them.

"Did it have anything on it?" Patrick wondered.

"Just pictures from the fairgrounds. Everybody had pictures of that," Jerry assured.

"That's it, huh?" Patrick asked. "Well, they've got pictures of my van, then. If they're smart, they'll check my Plumber's License. That will give them this address. They've got to figure the Nauvians might be here. I'm surprised they haven't shown up already."

The tires spun a half turn as the Subaru broke over the top of the steep driveway onto the flat ground in front of the house.

"Mom's home!" Belinda enthused alone. Mom would be stuck with them now. A major holiday, an epic snowstorm, and family visiting. *She'll have to stay home from work for at least the next two days, won't she?*

The door flew open, caught by a sudden wind. A hooded figure stamped clingy clumps of white snow onto the doormat. Lorraine bent down, melting flakes glistening from the top of her hood. She raised a foot, rested it on the opposite thigh, and unzipped her nylon-shelled boot topped with fake fur. Then the other. At last, she pushed her hood back and removed her parka, revealing a narrow face, pointy chin, and short, copper-red hair. Her malachite-green eyes swept the crowded room impatiently, then strayed to the staircase as if looking for a way out. The sanctity of her office, or was Jerry camped out in there?

"Have some chicken, Babe," Patrick invited. "We have meat! Merry Christmas."

Lorraine glanced at the picked carcass on the table. A back, a wing and half a breast. "I had pizza at work. A little party for us stalwarts. They were going to send us home early, because of the snow, but a few of us stayed and had pizza. I have four-wheel drive."

"All-wheel drive." Elmer nitpicked.

After a brief silence, Patrick raved, "Yeah, and a work crew! You should have seen these guys shovel that driveway for you. They had it all done in no time flat."

Lorraine looked at him like he was crazy. "There was three inches of snow on there!"

"That's 'cause we were expecting you three hours ago." Elmer was the only one brave enough to say it.

"I have to go change." Lorraine excused herself and bounded gracefully up the stairs.

Christmas Day 2017

Christmas morning was still and clear with a sky so blue you could see forever and air so cold it felt like you were inhaling icicles. "Shut that window, Fran!" Elmer barked from the bed in the upstairs guest room.

"I wanted to feel it," Fran excused herself, sliding the window down.

Elmer climbed from the warm bed in his T-shirt and boxers and joined her at the window. They gazed out at a featureless expanse of white. "We're stuck here, alright," he groused.

"Merry Christmas, you old grump." Fran grabbed the back of his neck and shook it.

"Do that some more," he whispered.

Fran fingered her phone instead. "It's just the eye, I guess. Do snow storms have eyes? Anyway, there's more coming in about two hours, then all day."

"We could make a break for it right now, while it's stopped. They'll have the roads open by the time we get ready."

"Poor plow guys, have to work on Christmas."

"Boo hoo. Double-time."

"Elmer, you can't be serious. It's Christmas Day. We came all this way to be with these folks on Christmas, and the first thing you want to do is leave. We're staying until New Year's Day, and that's final. That's a whole week. The storm will be over and the roads will be clear."

"If we went right now, we could beat it," Elmer muttered at the window. "I just don't like being stuck..."

They could see the worker's quarters through the trees, a foggy edifice jutting above the drifted white icing that piled up against its east side, almost covering Baput's bedroom window.

"How do you think they feel?" Fran nodded toward the image in the window.

"Well, they're stuck here anyway. They're used to being stuck in one place," Elmer reasoned.

"Stuck. Not buried! Come on. We've got to dig them out!"

"There's a roof over the porch. They can open the door, Fran."

"Yeah, it's so full of snow it looks like it's going to collapse on them. And if they come out, they've got four feet of snow to deal with. That doesn't happen on Nauve. We've got to go over there with some shovels and dig them out, let them know everything's OK. You know how they get. Poor Salistar!"

"We just got here, and we're bailing those guys out again already. Go wake up the boy. If I'm shoveling, he's shoveling. And make a bunch of noise so Patrick gets up, too. Don't knock on their door or nothing, though. Don't wake The Dragon."

"Oh, Elmer!" she swatted his arm, pulled on some sweats and hurried noisily down the hall to Jerry's temporary room in Lorraine's home office.

Experiment

Again, the crew made amazingly short work of shoveling. They soon had a path cleared from the quarters to the house. The driveway to the shop was shoveled, too. They left the main driveway plugged, for now.

The hungry crew filed into the quarters where Fran and Star had cooked a vegan Christmas breakfast with a side of ham for the carnivores. When they'd finished, the two women kept on cooking.

"Power's out any minute. You can bet on that." Patrick had warned them. "I'm amazed it stayed on this long."

Belinda jumped in eagerly. Lorraine hadn't emerged from the house. The men sprawled in the living room, talking about pomegranates and metal, motors and guns.

Jerry tapped Baput on the shoulder and whispered, "Come on, B. I've got something for you." He turned and addressed Elmer. "Dad, I'll drive Little Truck over to the shop, OK?"

"Sure kid, we'll be right along to unload all that stuff."

"Take your time, Dad." Jerry answered, hoping the men wouldn't show up for a while. He and Baput donned their new coats and walked the shoveled path to the pickup, just as the snow began to fall again.

"What did you bring?" Baput asked as they drove to the shop.

"Wire mesh. I got one that's aluminum, and one that's steel, but it's super-fine threads. They're both light and flexible, like, you know, the net you spread out over the Holy Rock on Nauve, that made the portal open."

"Yeah, the Net." Of course Baput remembered the Net. "We can't go home without it. So, you think you found something like it?"

Jerry grinned, nodded.

Baput looked sideways at his friend and replied, "Even if it seems right, we can't tell if it works until First Pomegranate Day."

"We don't know that." Jerry argued. "Maybe it works anytime. Or maybe every year at harvest time, like, next fall."

"No," Baput shook his head, "everything is different on First Pomegranate Day, so we can't really test it for almost three years, until it's time to go."

"Oh, yeah. The Rock has to buzz, and it buzzes best on First Pomegranate Day, every three years." Jerry recalled. "And it's the nimblies thrumming their wings that makes it buzz! And we killed them all, here on Earth anyway." He looked straight ahead, pushing against the steering wheel. "That really sucks! How can we test it?"

Jerry parked the truck and got out without waiting for the answer he knew Baput didn't have. He hefted a long, heavy package from the bed and slid it to the floor. He pierced the tape with his pocket knife, then slit the box at the joint, exposing a roll of metal fabric. He unrolled it on the clean cement floor. A pair of two-foot squares of wire mesh were stacked on top of each other. The top one was made of tightly woven fine threads of steel wool. It was smooth, dark and shiny, and quite heavy for its size.

"Much too heavy," Baput stated flatly. "I told you, none of these things we saw on the iPlane are it." He dragged the heavy steel net off, exposing the dull gray aluminum one underneath.

"That one's lighter." Jerry promised, "Try that one."

"The color is better, but it's not shiny," Baput assessed as he hefted it. "Lighter, but still too heavy. If this was big enough to cover the rock it would be way too heavy. I could lift the Net with one hand and throw it over my shoulder. It would float on the air like one of your bedsheets, lighter, even. And the threads are finer. They are not smooth like this." He kneaded his empty hand. "I don't know how to say it. It's crinkly. Scratchy. Not smooth. I told you. Why did you buy these?"

"I didn't. They're free samples. I told them I'm inventing something, and if their stuff works, I'll be buying mass quantities for commercial production�" Baput's dark, confused eyes reminded him. *These guys don't get this stuff.* "Never mind. So, we think Felsic's bicycle thing was a generator, and there were wires from there to the Net, right?"

Baput nodded slowly. "To my levers first, then to the Net on the Rock. But the Rock was different that day. It rang by itself. You didn't have to hit it or anything. That only happens on First Pomegranate Day."

"Yeah, I've seen that." Jerry cut him off. "So, what did your levers do? Could you turn the current up and down, like a dimmer?"

Another blank look. Jerry went to the back wall and started rummaging around on the shelves below the workbench. "Yes!" He pulled out a small flat rectangle with a round knob on its face and wires dangling out the back. "Dimmer switch. We'll wire this in. Let's start with the aluminum one first, since the steel is too heavy."

"They are both too heavy, and not like the Net at all." Baput repeated, sitting down in Felsic's favorite chair as if on strike. He glanced into the wine bottle on the floor beside it. *Drained dry*, he noted unhappily. Felsic was drinking more again, now that he'd had to leave the Look 'N Up, along with most of his work and his best friend, Elmer, behind.

Ignoring the protest, Jerry reached into his pocket for the plugs and the short piece of copper wire he'd brought from home. Twisting wires together feverishly, he soon had a plug connected to the dimmer switch, which he connected to the square of woven aluminum with the bare copper wire. "Let's get this done while we still have power."

Baput didn't know enough to be scared when Jerry plugged his experiment into the wall. His sensitive ears picked up the hum.

"That's low, I think." Jerry turned the knob. The hum got louder. Then the joints of aluminum wire started popping as they melted, releasing their tension. Baput jumped from his chair as a different kind of "snap!" sounded. The lights went out.

"Breaker." Jerry calmly found his way to the breaker box and flipped a switch. "I expected this. That's why I wanted to do it now. If we blow the grid, they'll just think it's the storm. What's the damage?"

Baput stood over the aluminum mesh. More mush than mesh. The joints looked like liquid, although they had already hardened to an oozy-looking solid. The melting had spread along the wires between the joints. They would all have met and liquefied together if the breaker hadn't tripped when it did. As it was, there were flecks of straight wire between shapeless blobs of melted wire in a perfect grid, cooled and stuck to the floor.

"The Net was not like that." Baput declared.

"It's not First Pomegranate Day, though. Things are different then," Jerry retorted, cutting the copper wire from the molten net. He examined the dimmer switch and plug. "Looks OK." He concluded. "Amazing, huh?"

Another blank look from Baput, crossed by a slow realization. "You're not going to..."

"Yep." Jerry connected the wire to the steel mesh.

This time, Baput knew enough to back up when Jerry plugged the second grid in. He was almost outside, standing beside the support post in case he needed cover. Jerry was in up to his elbows, fooling around with electricity. *Shavarandu!* Baput hadn't even thought of it until just now. Not that he was scared. He gulped and went back inside to stand with Jerry.

The hum was louder than before. It was almost like the hum of the Rock on First Pomegranate Day. But no, not the same. The tone was different, more artificial, somehow. Baput noticed a change in the grid. "It's turning red!".

Jerry dropped the dimmer. "Ow! That sucker's hot! Uh-oh! Look! It's like a toaster!" The breaker popped again, but not before the little grid glowed red like an electric stove. "Water! No! Not water!" Jerry panicked.

The boys clung to each other and watched, open-mouthed, as the red glow slowly faded. The steel net disintegrated as it cooled, leaving a second perfect grid pattern charred into the cement of the shop floor.

Jerry found some sweeping compound and a flat-bladed shovel, which he handed to Baput. "We'll scrape up what we can and put it in the scrap metal can. Then we'll cover up the rest." He caught Baput's eye and fixed on it. "And we shall speak of this to no one. Promise."

"Promise." Baput agreed, solemnly raising his right hand.

Incorporate

"Well, it's kind of like being married," Fran explained. She was glad she'd cooked dinner early. Patrick had been right. The power had gone out shortly after the snow started again. The unlit Christmas tree brooded alone in the dark, silent living room. The Musiks sat around the dining room table, littered with scraps of prime rib roasted in the gas grill and cold apple pie topped with molten ice cream. A battery powered lantern fought back the early darkness of a socked-in midwinter evening.

Their Nauvian friends had been rescued, offered more gifts, and played with. Now they huddled around the woodstove in the quarters like forgotten toys while the Musik Family discussed their Earthly business.

"We'd be Look 'N Up Industries. It would include the orchard, the plumbing business and hopefully the feed store, too. I'm working on my folks. That way, we offset each other's losses, like a mutual fund."

"Offset each other's gains, too," Lorraine pointed out as she paced by on her wide orbit. "I don't know if I want to tie my money in with a farm. Those things fail all the time."

"We ain't failing!" Elmer defended quickly. "We just need some help. Labor, I mean, not money."

"What about water?" Lorraine countered. "This so-called drought isn't going away, you know. It's the future. What will you do when the well runs dry? And Elmer, don't tell me this snow storm means there's no global warming. It's obviously already happening. You know, the weather report didn't used to include smoke and fire."

Elmer knew that as well as Lorraine did. Water had been a major issue in the southern California foothills for a long time, and a couple of years ago his family and green-skinned crew had shown up at this very doorstep, fleeing a wildfire. He took a different tack. "If there ain't no water, we won't need plumbers, either, now will we?"

"People will always need plumbers. That's the beauty of shit. Everybody's got it, nobody wants it." Patrick offered one of his slogans.

Fran's right eyebrow dipped and wrinkled. "Then I guess the feed store would go, too. No water, no farms—"

The next generation jumped in to finish the list. "No food," Jerry began.

"No people," Bel added.

"No life!" Jerry concluded. The Look 'N Up Corporation is the least of our worries, Mom." Jerry's sincere blue eyes rendered the adults speechless. "Can I go over to the quarters and see Baput?"

"Me, too, Mom, please?" Belinda begged.

Lorraine winced. She didn't like Belinda spending too much time over there. Salistar was always teaching her their misogynistic ways. That woman had had all her self-esteem beaten out of her, no, bred out of her, from time immemorial. "To see to her man's every need, so he can be free to do great things," she jeered, then waved her hand dismissively. "Go on, my little green *tether*!"

The kids pulled on their parkas and boots and grabbed shovels from the porch, cutting the trough that ran through the snow to the worker's quarters a little deeper as they went.

Fran lifted a briefcase from the floor beside her chair and opened it on the kitchen table next to the battery powered lantern. "Well, in case the world doesn't end, what do you think?"

"I was dreaming of expanding, anyway, now that I have help," Patrick offered.

"The orchard?" Lorraine asked first, apparently unaware of her husband's dreams.

"Naw, Elmer's got that. Some kind of manufacturing. Woodworking, or iron. Valko loves metal. I've got them a TV, out in the shop. It's hooked to one of those digital TV antennas. It gets the local stations for free, like when we were kids."

"Is that how Baput does it?" Elmer wondered.

"Yeah, kind of, I guess. He picks up the internet, though. He live-streams it, somehow...." Patrick's eyes seemed to stray in two directions as he worked the physics, again.

"Doesn't it bug them?" Elmer asked. "We had to cut the satellite cable to the quarters."

"That's why it's in the shop," Patrick replied, back from his thought experiment. "But we've got a regular satellite dish here at the house, like you do. Baput picks that up, too. He says it's OK now. He's used to it. The others don't notice it."

"It was mostly G-pa we worried about. He couldn't meditate," Fran recalled.

"Yeah, well..." Lorraine began coldly.

"Anyway," Patrick regained the floor, "one of the PBS channels has shows about fixing stuff around the house, and cars, and making stuff out of wood and metal. Cooking, too, but it's not vegan, so Star wouldn't want to—"

"She could cook it for us!" Lorraine interrupted. "Maybe I'd eat here more often." She was itching to check her computer while Jerry was gone, but she couldn't. Not while they were trying to talk Patrick into some deal that would surely cost her hard-earned money. The only reliable source of income in the whole lot was hers, for working as an Engineer in someone else's company. *Now they want that income to carry them when their farm fails?*

"I'd hate to influence their diet." Patrick's mind was on the Nauvians, as usual. "But they could learn to make stuff out of wood and metal. Furniture, maybe, and wrought iron railings and yard ornaments, solar light holders, stuff like that, and we could sell them on the internet."

Elmer tightened his lips and nodded thoughtfully. "They need something to do. I was thinking we could buy Felsic some old cars, the ones without computers, and he can fix 'em up and sell 'em. Just another branch of Look 'N Up Industries."

"I don't want a bunch of old cars lying around," Lorraine complained.

"We'll do one at a time, Babe," Patrick reassured. "I won't be much help, I'm afraid. Not like you were, Bro."

"He's way past me. He quit needing me over a year ago. I don't know where he gets it. Off the Plane, I guess, like Baput. He's a genius, you know."

"But he can't work on the computer ones, like mine?" Lorraine griped.

"Maybe with time. Give him a break," Patrick defended. "A guy who can do what he does, without ever even hearing of an engine until three years ago? Those old cars are valuable. We'll just do the collectable ones. That way we won't have to do so many. You can only sell so many a year without a dealer's license."

Lorraine crossed the floor, her voice rising with every word. "They cook, but not for me. They work on cars, but not mine. If they ever make any money, it goes to the Look 'N Up. And I have to pay them?"

"The Look 'N Up will pay them." Francine offered.

"With what?"

"Corporate money. We think we can bury them better this way. They're not employees. We'll keep their books to ourselves, pay them out of our profits. After all, it looks like we're spending all that money on ourselves. Flooring, furniture, four-wheelers. I'll keep the books, just like I do for the Cow Chow."

"Your money will be separate, Babe," Patrick assured her. "You're not paying the green people a dime."

"Great. I'll just keep working so I can bail you guys out when your ship sinks. I always figured I'd have to, sooner or later." With that promise, Lorraine climbed the stairs to her office.

Meanwhile, back at the Ranch

The day after Christmas was sunny and cool, without a hint of the snowstorm that still pounded the mountains up north where the Musiks celebrated. The plain white van crept slowly past the Look 'N Up driveway and around a curve until it reached the wide spot in the road where the Musik's west orchard sat behind a crude gate made of wires and sticks. Agent Boyd shredded the primitive contraption impatiently and Agent Kramer drove into the orchard on the little-used tire tracks until the van was out of sight of the road. Then the three agents got out and looked around.

"Are you sure they're not here?" Rita wondered as she tightened the laces on her hiking boots.

"You heard the old lady. They're up north stuck in that snowstorm with the plumber," the chief reminded her.

"That's where the greenies are, too, I'll bet," Boyd added, pulling on his grey fleece hoody.

"Yeah, but those killer things came from here. This is where it all happened. Here's where we'll find the evidence." Kramer sounded sure, like he'd been thinking about it all through his lonely Christmas.

"What the�?" Boyd squeaked as he almost fell off a cliff onto the driveway. "Look! There it is! That's the platform, and the cave. This is where that girl took the pictures from." He hastily pulled binoculars out of his shoulder bag. "There are the pulleys," he pointed. "See, you run that one to swing the thing out over the hole, and that one in the middle lowers you down. Looks like they took the batteries. I was afraid of that."

"You're going down there?" Rita asked incredulously.

"We've gotta see inside that cave, don't we? We need to find the batteries, and the harness. Then you guys can run the winches and get me down there."

"Really, Boss? Should he?" Rita fretted.

"Better him than me! But let's make sure we're alone first, and see what else we can find. Bring your stuff, we're on foot from here."

They strolled along the rutted pathway through the west orchard without appreciating the perfection and vitality of the well-kept trees. They passed behind the Musik's house, then reached the shop.

"Ahah!" Agent Kramer rejoiced. "If they were making stuff out of drones, there will be something in here, for sure." All three agents rummaged through the pegboards and counter tops, the work bench and the shelves below it.

"I found them!" Boyd cried. The other two rushed to his side to see the pieces of drones and plastic monsters. Instead, they saw a milk crate that held three car batteries and a webbed harness. "The batteries for the winches. There's a key in this four-wheeler. I'm gonna run down there and install these. You guys finish up here and then come down the driveway to where I'm at, and you can run me out to the cave."

He fired up the noisy vehicle and chugged off down the driveway between the house and the worker's quarters.

"Are we sure no one's here?" Rita worried again.

"I guess we'll find out," her boss replied. He jogged down the driveway and she followed dutifully. He stopped at the intersection, looked left and right at the porches. No one came out to see the four-wheeler. "These windows are so high!" Kramer cussed softly. "Come here."

Rita, standing right next to him asked, "Sir?" He bent slightly and wrapped his arms around her legs and lifted. She squeaked in protest. He shushed her. She could see through the window into the main room of the worker's quarters; a sparsely furnished open area with no clutter, absolutely spotless.

"There's no one here," she whispered.

"Do you see anything? Any evidence?"

"There's nothing. It doesn't look like anyone lives here."

"OK." Kramer loosened his grip abruptly, letting Rita drop to the ground. "Now the house." He crossed the driveway to the main house. The windows were just as high.

"Sir, that's the Musik's house. I don't feel right peeking in the windows of real citizens. Do we have a warrant?"

"Warrant." Kramer scoffed. "Wake up, young lady. You are in the FBI. You're a spy. We look in people's windows. It's what we do. Now, come here!"

Boyd had all three winches working when Kramer and Goldsmith came walking down the driveway, devoid of evidence but assured the place was deserted. He wore the harness he'd found in the shop. He had brought his own ultra-bright LED flashlight, hoping for a chance to do some spelunking. He hooked himself up to the pulley and instructed his co-agents.

Rita ran the upper winch that whisked Boyd off the cliff into midair, and slowly, slowly out over an expanse of nothingness until he was situated directly over the platform in front of the cave. "OK, Boss. Drop me real slow," he shouted.

When he landed, Boyd examined the remains of a metal screen the Musiks had placed across the cave opening. Tatters of twisted rebar stuck out where something big had apparently forced its way out of the cave. He shuddered. The Musiks had tried to stop the attack, to their credit, but it proved they knew a lot more than they were admitting.

A frayed cable and a crisp-looking rubber hose protruded through the grate, both cut off roughly, as if in haste, or anger. Boyd thrust his flashlight into the cave; a round tunnel with tiny, squiggly stalactites on the roof. It looked a lot smaller up close, and it seemed to get even narrower as it went. Nobody could fit in there, not even a kid, or a skinny old man, like he'd seen on the girl's video. The only evidence they had, and now it didn't seem credible.

She said it went through, that the old man came out somewhere. He turned the light off. He could barely make out a dim light in the depths of the cave. It seemed to come from below. *It* does *go through! But it's way too small. How could anyone make it? And if it goes through, why go to all the trouble to make this platform? All these pulleys and stuff?* He wondered.

"Finding anything?" Kramer shouted impatiently from above.

Boyd pulled his head out and called back. "The cave goes through. It comes out down there, like the girl said." He pointed to the ground below. "But it's super tight. I don't see how..." he scratched his head, peered into the hole once more, then turned back to the pair above him. "Take the four-wheeler. Follow the trail. I'll meet you down there."

He headed for the other winch, the one that went down to the ground. He had noticed the solar battery was still attached. On his way, he spotted several patches of something grey and moldy that draped the platform and oozed through the grate. Turning back, he found some similar blotches at the cave entrance. More goo hung from the tattered rebar screen that had apparently once sealed the entrance, now bent and pushed apart by a powerful force from inside the cave. He pulled a Ziploc bag and a putty knife from his satchel and scraped some ooze from just inside the cave mouth. He took another sample from the tattered cage, and one from the platform. Then he unhooked from the upper winch, hooked onto the lower one, and dropped over the side.

He touched down on the rocky ground and unhooked the harness. He looked up at the bottom of the platform, admiring the design, and the workmanship. He surveyed the ground. Thin, grey-orange membranes coated the gravel here and there. Needle-like proboscises, angry talons, and knife-like horns lay among the molding puddles. Boyd collected samples of all the bony parts. The proboscises were long and hard enough to pierce a man to the heart. He ran the blade of one of the horns across his thumb and jerked back sharply, blood dripping. *After three months in the weather!* He realized. *These things are lethal, alright.* He looked at the molding bodies. *And organic. Real. Not drones.*

As he bagged his last talon, he heard the four-wheeler approaching. It stopped abruptly, about a hundred feet away. "Holy crap! What is this?" Kramer's voice bellowed. Boyd grabbed his pack and sprinted down the narrow, worn trail.

Kramer whistled a long, steady tone as he walked around the perfectly round, perfectly smooth orb that protruded from the ground, half-buried in the rocky alluvium of the river terrace. Rita stood back, staring with her mouth open. When Boyd arrived, he joined Kramer in his whistling and circling, leaving Agent Goldsmith to wonder if it was a guy thing, or if she'd missed that day at the Academy.

Kramer stopped on the river side of the orb and scanned the vine-covered cliff behind it.

Boyd bumped right into his back, his eyes still on the weird protrusion. He followed his boss's gaze to a haphazard pile of stones at the base of the cliff, sticking out through a gap in the curtain of vines and iced with a coating of what looked like thin concrete, or grout.

Boyd sprinted around the orb and mounted the pile of loose rocks in a single leap. He stood on top of it, under the overhang of the cliff, behind the vines. He found his flashlight again and pointed it straight up. The light found a jagged hole in a rock tube that ran along the cliff, forming the vine-covered overhang. It was the outside of that long, narrow cave.

"Here's where he came out, I guess," Boyd speculated. "So maybe the old man's not dead. Maybe they couldn't get him up there, so they sent him through from above. That's why the platform and the pulleys and stuff."

"But why? What did he do in there?" Rita wondered.

"And what the hell is this big rock?" Kramer still wanted to know. "We need a sample." He pulled a small chisel and hammer from his pack. He placed the chisel against the strangely smooth surface with the dull metallic sheen. He dropped the chisel abruptly, shaking his hand. "It's buzzing!"

Boyd was off the rock pile in a flash. Without a thought, he leapt onto the peak of the smooth sphere. "Yow! It sure is!" he gushed. Kneeling on one knee, he reached for Kramer's hammer. Kramer gave it to him.

Boyd struck the orb, hard. The buzz travelled up his arm and spread through every cell of his body, shaking them all apart, all together. His ears rang with an intensity that drowned out all his thoughts. He saw a river of colors, of infinite variety, flowing forever...

"You OK?" Rita asked anxiously. Boyd didn't answer. Rita put her hand on the rock and felt the fading buzz for herself. It was still ringing like a cosmic bell. It was the most beautiful sound Rita has ever heard.

Kramer took his hands from his ears and grabbed the hammer from Boyd's limp hand. He stubbornly realigned his chisel and struck it with the hammer. His blow lashed back, making his arm bones shake like that jackhammer he'd run for a miserable summer as a kid construction worker. He jumped to his feet and staggered around, holding his arm and cussing softly.

The ringing was louder, with a different tone that blended with the first. Shivering with pleasure, Rita touched it again, right where Kramer has chiseled it. A ripple of excited molecules ran up her arm.

Kramer cleared his throat for attention, and Rita tumbled back to Earth. Her finger still on the rock, she reported, "It's not even scratched, Chief. It didn't leave a mark at all."

Boyd let out a moan of pain, or pleasure?

"You OK?" Rita asked again.

"It's super, super hard!" Boyd said dreamily. Then suddenly, he was back. He propped himself on his elbows and gave his report, loud and clear and more confident than ever. "It's super resonant." Turning to his side he caressed the flawless surface comfortably, peering at it closely. "It's not of this Earth," he mused reverently. "Totally alien. It's got an energy all its own. And when you hit it with that hammer, it feels really, really good up here. Come on, Rita, give it a try."

Still rubbing his shoulder, Kramer overruled the excited youth. "Goldsmith, you stay offa there. Boyd, back to work. We've gotta map this place. Then you, Genius Boy, you do your thing, work your angles, figure out where we put the cameras."

Nauve, First Full Kakeeche Ceremony

The full moon rose above the upriver mist, trimming the night in silver, flocking the tall pines and frosting the roof of the Great Hall. The air was crisp, still and expectant. The Akashic shrine had been set in the center of the plaza. Its unique material reflected the moon's sacred light, making it shine almost as brightly. Effigies of a pomegranate, a ganeesh and a dog decorated the small wooden tower, glinting as they stirred in the lightest breeze. Tamaya stood behind the Akash, her mysterious gown shimmering in the moonlight, even more dazzling than the shrine.

The population stood whispering amongst themselves, waiting for the Akash to begin the First Full Kakeeche ceremony. They were decked in all-new tunics and pants of tough yalinar grass dried to a whiteness that shone weakly in the moonlight, but the effect of all that hard work was cruelly paled by Tamaya's gown.

Solemn but joyous, the ceremony was supposed to be held on the first full moon after First Pomegranate Day. That was a month ago, but Bazu hadn't been ready then. Now they were over a month into the cycle. *A very special cycle,* Bazu recalled. *What was it the old Akash said? This cycle is 1,000 cycles from the Beginning*, or was it 1,000 *years*? Bazu found he wasn't sure.

Even worse, he couldn't remember the words for the ceremony. The Akash's words were always the same. They must be written somewhere, in the Ancient Akashic books of the Old Ones. Tamaya had searched the Holy Cave in vain for a script. Finding nothing, they had put their heads together, along with Bupple and Bazu's Momama, Ritamay, to piece the longwinded incantations together from memory, but they couldn't remember all of it.

What did I expect? Bazu scolded himself. *How can an Akash ask a couple of women and an old warrior something only an Akash would know?* But he *didn't* know, and in the end, Bazu was forced to swallow his pride and take his questions to the Council, Akira and Rakta, in their private meeting that morning.

"Is this cycle 1,000 years since the beginning, or 1,000 cycles? I have always been confused about that." Bazu squeaked his confession, then gulped in a dry throat.

"We all are." Rakta admitted. He raised his eyes to Akira. Surely the ancient, venerated sister of the old Akash would know. "Which is it, anyway?" he asked her.

"Nobody knows which." Akira snapped. She lifted her clenched hand to her mouth and mumbled, "Only the Akash knows."

Bazu stepped back two steps. He scanned the room, heart fluttering, head spinning, searching, as if he'd just realized the old Akash was no more. That *he* was the Akash! "But, then..." he sputtered.

Akira's eyes focused on him like a bowman on a nimbly. "The. Akash. Knows." She said again, slowly. She raised her eyebrows.

Bazu nodded. "Yes, of course, the Akash knows." He started to bow, then caught himself. Instead, he stood tall, gathered his robe around him and strode from the conference room without admitting further ignorance.

Now, the young Akash stood majestically before the crowd in the former Akash's elaborate robe, holding his own humble longstick, decked only with a couple of kiko bird feathers his momama had provided, assuring him they were freely given. He raised his staff in his right hand and cleared his throat with a crackly cough.

He began by showing off. "Welcome to the 334th cycle," he declared. The audience murmured vague questions among themselves. "Our second thousand years!" he snapped. Still no response. The crowd still waited, as if he hadn't spoken at all. He sighed. *My cleverness is wasted on them. Is this how the wise old Akash felt? I guess I'll just stick to the script.*

"Kakeeche is, Kakeeche not" he droned, expecting them to follow. "Kakeeche whole, Kakeeche half. Kakeeche born, Kakeeche die..." He trailed off and scanned the crowd. Still, they stared, unresponsive. "Kakeeche left, Kakeeche, right?" he squeaked.

Unprecedented outbursts erupted in the crowd. "That's not the First Full Kakeeche Song!"

"That's the regular full Kakeeche song."

"The one we sing every month."

"He doesn't even know it."

"Ever be it so! Ever be it so!" the Akash insisted on finishing the routine, afraid to omit its hopeful ending. He searched his memory for the words he had heard only four times. The first time, he was just a baby. The last time was six years ago, because last cycle's ceremony had been cancelled, due to the disappearance of the Akash and his trained Apprentice, Baput.

Bazu recalled there was a short version, and a longer one the Akash used when he was angry. *The shorter the better,* Bazu figured, although he was feeling increasingly angry. The people continued to break their rapt silence, whispering among themselves, even laughing. Laughing at their Akash on this holy occasion!

He tried to take an Akashic breath, to calm himself, hoping to find the missing words on the Plane, in his head. The exact ceremony still escaped him, but the story was etched deeply. Once he found the groove, the words seemed to flow without thought.

"Each night our guardians, the Kakeeche, assemble in the sky to watch over us. They come on their own sacred schedule, always different, always the same."

"Always different, always the same." The congregation droned the refrain. Everything was as it should be.

"One night, they all come, and make a beautiful glowing ball like a giant pomegranate in the sky." Bazu recited raptly, gesturing grandly at the moon. He had their full attention now. He fell into a rhythm.

"About 14 nights later, none of them come at all. It is a terrifying night of total darkness without the Kakeeche!"

The people oohed and ahhed as if this was news. Bazu took another deep breath while he waited for them to quiet down. More words rushed into his head and he spoke them quickly, racing to reassure his poor, terrified subjects. "But they come back, the next evening, just a few make it back the first time. Right at sunset, they appear in the west. They hold hands and form a crescent on the side toward the setting sun. Each night there are more, a thicker ring, but they come up later and later each night. By the time half of the Kakeeche have come back, they do not show themselves until midnight. Then, a week later, they all assemble in their full glory, in the eastern sky, just as the sun goes down in the west. Full Kakeeche!"

"Full Kakeeche" the grateful crowd cheered. The mood lightened.

Bazu was halfway there. Now the downside: "Later and later they come, and less and less. They come up after sundown, then later into the night, until they are so late and so few you can only see a tiny sliver at dawn, before the sun. It looks like the first evening one, but the other side is illuminated.

"This First Full Kakeeche after First Pomegranate Day is the most important time for Kakeeche. The most important time for us. We have come through the battles of the Season. Our young people have ascended to their crafts and married their betrotheds. Now we see that Kakeeche still smiles upon us." He grasped his grass necklace and raised it so the pouch of seeds showed above his collar. He tried to wave his longstick, but he didn't have the balance right. The tip sagged to the stage when he extended it. A couple people laughed, but he couldn't see who it was. Definitely his classmates, but some older voices, too. "We will go on!" he reassured with diminished authority. He would get it back with this next part.

"We take great comfort in knowing Kakeeche will come in their cycle, every month the same, do we not?" Everyone shut their mouths abruptly and nodded, even the young warriors. "We must believe in Kakeeche, or they will turn their backs. We know, because every so often someone doubts Kakeeche, and Kakeeche disappears! Just like the old Akash and his family!" He'd made up that comparison on the spot. The audience broke their silence with murmurs of appreciation and wonder.

Bazu filled in the gory details of the dire warning. "The Kakeeche all assemble at Full Kakeeche, as normal. Then, group by group they turn their backs so they no longer shine on us, and the moon darkens, not over several nights as usual, but right before your eyes! Sometimes all of them, until the moon is all dark. Sometimes, if the offense is less, only some of them go dark. They have always turned back to us within hours, but someday, if there is too much disbelief, Kakeeche will go dark forever!"

The crowd inhaled in mock surprise, part of the ritual. They held their breaths for the last, most dire warning. "Shavarandu, even! The sun in the sky, giver of all life, the power we fear, Shavarandu himself, will turn his back on you if you do not believe in your mighty and wise Akash." The collective gasp arrived on cue, but the surprise was genuine. Their Akash stood on the stage, pointing right at each one of them, all at the same time, it seemed.

Rakta and Akira exchanged a glance. Tamaya shared the same stupid, shocked look as the rest of the villagers. Even the wickedly self-centered previous Akash hadn't made the threat personal. It was supposed to be, "He will turn His back on *all of us* if *we* don't believe in *Kakeeche*."

The new Akash plunged abruptly into the end of the long version. "Remember Keeldar! He did not honor his Popa, the Akash, so the Holy Keelan used the Evil Eye on him, and melted his mind. His own son! That is why you must believe in your Akash! Oh, and Kakeeche. You must believe in Kakeeche."

"Hail Kakeeche, glorious Kakeeche." The stunned people chanted, staring at the luminous orb in the sky. "They always return without fail, as long as we believe."

Like zombies, they took their positions. The Akash stood in the center, flanked by Akira and Rakta. Tamaya joined Akira on the Akash's right side and Azuray, Rakta's tether, took his hand on the Akash's left. Bazu's Momama, Ritamay, took Azuray's hand, while Bupple, the Akashic Guard, grasped Tamaya's hand timidly. The seven of them formed a crescent shape and walked in a big circle around the shrine in the middle of the plaza. Tamaya's gown billowed behind her. It didn't itch anymore. *Probably some bugs from that ganeesh*. Tamaya shuddered at the thought. But it felt fine, now. And she knew she looked spectacular, outshining even the shrine.

When they completed the circle, Tamaya's family joined them; her blind Popa's hands held tightly by Pindrad and Jenevan, who carried little Pindren on her hip. Tamaya wanted to walk beside her popa, holding his other hand. It should be her, not Jenevan. But she was Bazu's Tether now, the Akashic Tether, so she stayed in her exalted place, clutching Akira's cold hand and Bupple's fleshy, warm one.

The Pinds were joined by Rakted, Rakta's son and second in command, and his family. Around the shrine they went again. Each time, they were joined by seven more people, high-ranked warriors and artisan craftsmen with their families. The crescent thickened to a half-circle as more rows of seven joined hands to walk around the shrine, representing the moon's trip across the sky, in descending order of status, rank or experience.

The retired men whose apprentices had ascended and succeeded them ambled behind the younger men, alongside their lavender-haired tethers, if they lived. On their slow heels followed the young warriors and craftsmen who had ascended in the last two cycles with their new families. After them came the incomplete families, packed together in a knot, orphans' faces stuffed airlessly among the sweaty thighs and buttocks of their widowed momamas, seething with an anger they would always feel and never understand. At the end came the Unmarriageables, following Edijay according to their mysterious and inescapable internal pecking order. The human crescent thickened to resemble a gibbous three-quarter moon. Finally, the fourteenth time around, the whole village, all 98 people, formed a full circle under the moon. Full Kakeeche.

Trillella and Peratha had moved up a notch since Passascenday. They were a whole family again. They walked with Peratha's new husband, Rodan the Clubber, and the other new families. Peratha felt out of place among the teens and babbets, but when she looked behind her at the miserable mass of widows and fatherless children, she could almost appreciate her new life. The appearance of it, anyway. Behind closed doors it was another matter altogether.

As always, Trillella broke through her bubble of self-pity. "Momama? How can Shavarandu turn His back on just one person?"

"Shhh!" Peratha hissed quickly. Rodan walked before them with the other young warriors. He turned around and glared at his step-daughter, brandishing his biggest club at her, shaking it menacingly.

The much shorter warrior on his left, Samard the young longstickman, turned around, too, but he didn't snarl or brandish. He smiled. He turned back to his mates and nudged the boy on his left, Maffoon the Darter. "How can the Akash know how to do the Evil Eye if there was no one to teach him?" he dared ask his peers.

"He is Akash. He knows." Rodan droned the correct answer.

Maffoon thought a little harder. "There are books in the Holy Cave. All the Akashic wisdom is there."

"Books?" Samard scoffed. "Writing?" The writing these common youths knew was a mere handful of symbols. Simple, common things critical for communication and record keeping; pomegranate, nimbly, bumbly, cycle, harvest, the seasons, Shavarandu of course, all the Kakeeche phases, and the crude signs for male and female, most often used in the graphic art of teenage boys like them.

"But it's a weapon." Dubley joined them, leaning on his throwing spear. "A guy can't learn how to wield a weapon by reading a book. He needs someone to show him, to teach him. Take his hands and show him where to put them, how to hold it, when to release..."

"It's not like that," Canam, the archer, chimed in. "It's like that weapon in the cave. It shoots pure light. The light shoots out of his eyes into yours and melts your brain. Only people though. Too bad it doesn't work on nimblies and bumblies."

"How can he tell if he's doing it right?" Dubley wondered. "He'd have to kill someone to find out if he can kill someone!"

"I don't think he *can* do it," the precocious Samard concluded, as he ran into the back of Tallmon, a retired longstickman that dwarfed him. The whole line of old men in front of them had stopped walking.

"Quiet." The big man said, turning to look down at the youths.

"You kids hush, now!" the bitter widows snapped from behind them without slowing their pace. The wizened seniors on both sides squeezed the young families between them, a tough old oyster shell of tradition clamping down on a pearl of youthful wisdom.

On the fifteen time around, the first seven, the high ones who started, stopped at the altar. Their sliver, their edge of the moon, was gone now. Each time they came around, seven more people dropped away and drifted toward the food. The circle flattened until it was a half, then a waning crescent of the youngest, the lowest and the Unmarriageables, struggling unskillfully to maintain the delicate shape. When the final seven, the newest Unmarriageables, returned from orbit, the ceremony was over. The crowd dispersed, talking in small groups around the food tables.

The Akash remained on the stage and talked blithely on, as if they still listened. "Let us raise the wine to Kakeeche. The desperation wine of last year, the first wine of the new cycle. The past is past. Life continues." The

Akash recited the ceremonial toast to their distant backs. Even Tamaya and Rakta had left him. Only Bupple remained at his side, twitching anxiously toward the kegs of under-fermented wine prepared by angry, unskilled women. Trillella's wine was long gone. Bazu dropped his stiff smile. "Go!" he hissed.

Bupple bolted, leaving his mighty Akash alone.

The Lock

Handee held his measuring stick on the outside of Trillella's bedroom door while his apprentice and son, Handar, unpacked a pre-made set of blocks and slats of wood, laboriously drilled with a hand awl to receive the wooden pins that Handee would drive gently into the finished assembly with his wooden mallet.

"I assure you, Peratha, there is no Shavarandu here." The woman's fretting was already wearing on Handee's patience. This was a strange hut. There were bad vibes here. Who asked for a lock on their daughter's bedroom door? He wished Handar had stayed home and made the parts for their next project. But he had insisted on coming. He said he wanted to meet Peratha, for some strange reason. The aging fix-it man shook his head.

He raised the assembled unit in his hand, cupped to avoid dropping the parts, barely clinging together by the roughness of their wood. The pins wouldn't go in until Handar drilled the door. After all, the boy had insisted on coming. He could do the part Handee detested.

Handar cranked the handle that turned a sharped stone awl, eroding a hole through Trillella's bedroom door slowly and noisily.

"It's like the latches on the animal pens in the Great Hall." Handee carefully demonstrated the partially assembled device. "See, you push this, and this stick comes out. Very strong. You will see. But it is just your hand pushing, see?" He demonstrated again. He would have invited Peratha to try it, but she was shaking so!

More assurance was obviously needed, but he was a tinker, not a counselor of women. No man could be that. He could barely council his own wife, let alone this pitiful figure who still wore a widow's scarf over her head when she went to the village or the Great Hall, even though it had been over a cycle and no one even knew if her husband was dead or *what*. And worse, she was now remarried to that young bully, Rodan, who had been betrothed to her daughter, Trillella. He stopped short, looking at the lock, then at the bedroom door.

While Handee stepped outside to grab a tool from his cart and ponder these adult thoughts, the young apprentice completed his speech for him, having heard it many times. "Shavarandu is the power we fear. Spooky actions at a distance. It's not Shavarandu if somebody pushes it with their hand, or a ganeesh pulls it, or if the river turns it, like the mill. If the lock moved by itself, or if the cart could move with no one pulling it, if the mill wheel turned when the river was dry, that would be Shavarandu." With that, the apprentice began gouging a hole in Trillella's door jamb with a stone chisel.

Peratha's wrinkled expression didn't change. "I want no Shavarandu in this house", she uttered coldly.

Handee stepped into the icy silence. He held the assembly up to the door, on the outside. His eyebrows turned up, putting a question mark at the end of his unspoken sentence. "Strong enough to keep a young girl with no betrothed from running wild, eh?"

Fully back from wherever she went these days, Peratha snapped without thinking. "Of course not! It's for the boy! My husband!" she spat. "The lock goes on the inside, to keep him out!"

Handee's confident face fell as he gingerly removed the lock from the outside and switched it to the inside. "Do we have a bigger stick, Boy?" he whispered to his son who shook his head, mouth gaping. "We'll have to double up on this one then. It must be strong enough to keep out that monster! He was promised a young virgin and ends up with a used-up old..." Peratha's look made him almost drop the mechanism. He might as well have. He had lost all confidence in it.

"Handar," he addressed his son again, this time with an odd politeness that chilled the boy. "Get the breen. We must cover the sticks with a piece, and wrap the other piece around the lock so he can't push through where we've drilled."

"That's all the breen we have," Handar reminded him gravely.

Handee looked up from the tool bag at Felsic's poor *widow*? Lines deeply etched her sunken cheeks, permanently rilled by the erosion of too many tears. He saw plenty of widows in his line of work, fixing things around their houses that most husbands could have fixed, if they'd lived. But he had never seen such fear in a woman's eyes. Not even during the Season.

"We must double the thickness of the door. Peratha, how long until your monster, um, your husband returns?"

"I packed him a lunch. He will stay at the practice field all day, until dinnertime." Peratha answered, ashamed, but relieved. He was finally getting it!

"Boy, you stay here and hammer that breen like I told you."

"But Popa," the apprentice dared object, "surely there's a better use for our last two nuggets of breen!"

Handee ignored his son, a mere apprentice. Who was he to say what was worthy of what? Over the boy's objections, he advanced the plan. "I will get lumber to thicken the door." He hurried out the front door to his wooden cart. Lifting the two handles from the ground, he pulled the cart, rickshaw style, down the narrow lane that led into the village.

Handar was not a disobedient boy. He enjoyed the profession he would inherit. It allowed for a bit of innovation, cleverness that made a man feel good, when it worked. No one would write a song about him, but his popa enjoyed a universal respect, and even an occasional accolade. He was betrothed to a sweet girl who he rather liked, although she did not yet haunt his tenth-year dreams of fighting and flying. Handar looked forward to his future life as a Fixer. So, he obeyed his popa no matter what.

He produced a flat rock from his bag, along with a tiny pill of shiny metal. He held it up to his eye in the light that streamed through the window. Peratha had never seen anything shine like that except...

"Shavarandu!" she accused, once again.

"Just breen," the boy replied, setting the tiny pill on the flat rock. He raised a stone hammer with a short wooden handle and brought it down on the rock. "There must be lots of breen in the Holy Cave," he wondered aloud between the strikes that rung oddly to Peratha's ears. She didn't answer. But the boy was burning with desire. Not the animal kind she sought to keep out with a strong lock, but a desire much more insidious, that permeates right through such simple devices.

The opportunity opened like a chasm before him. He plunged in, blurting, "What did you see, Peratha, when you got to live in the Holy Cave for the whole Season? What was it like to live among all those amazing things?"

Peratha did not confirm or deny the legend. She didn't answer at all. She just stood silently and let the boy ask his taboo questions as he hammered the soft, wonderous metal into a thin, vaguely rectangular plate, then wrapped it around a bundle of the three thickest slats of wood he could find in his bag.

The Apprentice Fixer lifted the last tiny pill of the soft, malleable metal from his bag reverently. "Did they really kill the nimblies from the shelter of the Holy Cave as they flew by on their way to the Great Hall?" he asked, striking the pill. It instantly broadened and thinned. "How many did they kill?" another bang. "What went wrong?" Now it took two strikes with the hammer to cover the broadening surface. "Did you see what happened?" Bang, bang, the breen was much wider than the hammer now. The boy stopped banging and looked up at her. "Why do you hate Shavarandu so much, when you've seen it make the nimblies explode?"

"Shavarandu took my husband, you insensitive child!" she snapped, headed for the kitchen. Without looking back, she instructed, "I will be out back in my garden. Call me when you two are finished."

And so, Peratha found herself stuck in the garden. Each family had its own small garden, where they grew the daily table greens for their family. Larger crops that ripened all at once and required storage were grown and harvested communally in a garden that formed a courtyard in the middle of the network of uniformly crude huts. Trillella was off helping the other women harvest that communal vegetable garden right now. Peratha knew she would work harder than the other girls her age, but the other girls would exclude her and the women would deride her. They always had. She was used to it.

Peratha knew her absence in the working group did not help Trillella's status any. But she just couldn't work with those women anymore. They all said she would just stop working and stare into space for minutes at a time with a vacant look on her face. They used to get anxious and call Azuray, or even Akira if she was available, but no more. Not after Akira spat on her and told the women not to worry about her. "She is just lazy, and she feels sorry for herself." That was Akira's assessment, wisest of all the women. So, no one wanted to work with her anymore.

Peratha hadn't had the energy to start the customary dooryard garden on the cool east side of the hut, but Trillella had gone ahead and started one anyway, promising, "I'll do all the hard work, Momama. You don't have to do anything but help pick. You always loved picking, remember, Momama?" The question at the end, echoed in her too-wrinkled little face, still burned in Peratha's heart. She hated gardening now. Even picking. But still, she got down on her knees and hoisted the crude, stone, hand-held plow and broke into the crusted soil, yanking on the autumn weeds. She did it for Trill. She was stuck out here anyway.

"We're finished, Ma'am." Handee finally called from the back door as the sun crept down the western sky toward the dreaded Time of Rodan, previously known as Dinner Time with its laughter, peaceful conversation and good appetites. Peratha sighed with resignation.

"Come, let me show you," Handee instructed.

Peratha rose to her feet and wiped the knees of her woven grass pants with a mullein leaf from the garden. She stepped inside, avoiding the eyes of the handyman's son, who gladly complied.

The door had an extra layer of wood drilled and bolted with stone pegs that blended almost invisibly into the grain. Despite the smooth workmanship, it was bulky and obvious. Sure to set Rodan off.

But that was inevitable. She couldn't say anything, anyway. Not after all that lovely work. Then she saw the lock, and the reason why. Of course! The lock was embedded in the inner layer, lined with breen, with shims between the two layers to protect the lock's freedom of movement. There was no possible way to manipulate the lock from the outside.

Handee escorted her awkwardly to Trillella's bedroom doorway while Handar gathered the tools and scraps of wood. "All she has to do is push this stick here, see, and it slides into the slot on the doorway. Handar dug it nice and deep. And look how strong! Three sticks wrapped together in breen. You won't find a better lock anywhere. And no Shavarandu. I promise." He winked shyly, trying to lighten the moment. No response.

Handar scurried out the front door with his loaded bag.

"*Braykipseulum.*" Handee uttered the formal well-wish, which literally meant "good pomegranates to you". He hoisted the items that didn't fit in the bag, already collected into a neat pile by his awkward son, and showed himself out.

No payment was offered, and none was owed. No one ever paid, or even thanked a person for performing the tasks assigned to them at birth. Like all the men, Handee and his son served the village in their own specialized way, on an as-needed basis. In turn, other men would provide for *their* needs, according to each one's unique specialties. If Handee needed a new hammer, the knapper would form one out of stone and fit it to a handle made by the woodworker. The potter, the miller, the keepers of the ganeesh, the rice paddies, and the orchard all served the community according to their assigned functions.

Peratha worked the lock over and over, studying it. *Felsic could have thought of this,* she realized. *But then, if Felsic was here, there would be no need to lock Trillella's bedroom door.*

Earth, Spring, 2018
Belinda's 13th Birthday

Belinda's birthday was on Friday, but they waited until Sunday to celebrate, when Mom could be home. Why she couldn't be home on Saturday was an open question that was yet to be answered and just wasn't asked anymore, not even on a special occasion like this.

They gathered on the front porch on an unseasonably warm February morning to sing the familiar song and watch Belinda blow out the thirteen candles, unavoidably spitting on the cake.

Baput was surprised to find that the unsanitary Earth custom didn't bother him so much anymore. Maybe he was used to it. Or, maybe it was just okay because it was Belinda. "We have gifts for you, Bel!" he piped up. "Popa?"

With a shyness unbefitting the brave warrior, Valko stepped forward carrying a shaft of folded metal by his side as if it was his longstick. He thrust it gently toward the girl. "Music stand," he informed briefly. Belinda unfolded the hinged object. A vertical tray appeared at the top, tilted just enough to rest a sheet of music, with a little shelf at the bottom to secure it. It wasn't like her regular music stand. The tray where the music rested was decked with a wrought-iron G-clef. Quarter notes decked the four corners. The music sat higher, at an odd angle that fit her unusual eye position when she played her violin. She could read it with both eyes, or rather, either eye, that's how it worked, especially with close stuff.

"You made this?" Belinda asked the quiet giant, who blushed an odd mauve color and nodded vaguely. She stretched up on her tiptoes and wrapped her arms around him. She felt his chest rumbling deep inside. It didn't scare her at all. She just squeezed tighter, then let go.

Baput was waiting with a box wrapped in bright paper, in the Earth way.

Belinda unwrapped Baput's gift and reached into the bright yellow tissue paper to find a carved maple unicorn. His horn spiraled elaborately from a friendly face below a cascading mane, every hair exquisitely detailed.

His legs and flanks were intricately muscled, and he was dyed brown-purple with gaa, the indelible stain of pomegranate juice. "Oh, Baput!" Belinda spoke through tears. "My spirit animal," she choked. "You remembered."

"A freak like you." Baput warmly recalled Belinda's words from that conversation so long ago, when they had first met.

"What did you say?" Lorraine seethed.

"It's OK, Mom." Belinda silenced her mother and threw her arms around Baput in a much more casual embrace than she had given his popa. It almost seemed like she did it all the time.

"My Momama made something for you, too," Baput whispered in her ear as he held her. Reluctantly, she backed out of his arms and turned to Salistar, who handed her a rectangular package, clumsily wrapped in the same paper Baput had used.

Belinda balanced the package on the porch rail and unwrapped it carefully. She found a pale beige tunic and drawstring pants of woven yalinar grass just like the Nauvians wore. But this wasn't everyday wear. Beads decked the V-shaped collar, seeds and shells and some of Aunt Fran's beads, like the ones they'd used for Baput's Akashic Robe. "This is special," she noted breathlessly, holding the tunic up to her chest. Tears ran down her cheeks, surprising her and infuriating Lorraine.

Salistar stepped into her embrace and they enjoyed a hug that looked just as comfortable as the hug Bel and Baput had shared.

"It is special, yes," the disgustingly humble immigrant explained tenderly, as if she were talking to her own daughter. "A girl gets this when she enters her Marriage Cycle."

"Marriage Cycle?" Lorraine asked through clenched teeth. "What do you mean, *Marriage Cycle*?"

Salistar looked at her like *she* was from another planet. "She is thirteenth year now. Next Passascenday she will be fifteen. She will surely marry then, no?"

"No!" Lorraine snapped. She strode towards Salistar, finger extended as if to poke the shy little woman. She stopped short of touching, but Salistar cowered against Valko's formidable bulk as Lorraine chewed her out. "Let's get something straight, here! You are here to cook and clean and, well, babysit."

"Mom!" the thirteen-year-old defended her budding adulthood.

Lorraine rolled right over her objection. "Belinda's not yours. She will *never* be yours! I don't want her learning your backward ways, your weaving and your vegan cooking. She isn't marrying your kid at fifteen, or ever. She won't be bringing her messed-up DNA to your miserable planet to save your ignorant race. We're stuck with you until you can go back to the Look 'N Up, or back to Nauve. I don't care which. In the meantime, try to make yourselves useful. And leave my daughter alone!"

She plucked a red foil wrapped box off the table and almost threw it at Belinda. "You're not wearing that crappy grass stuff. I told you; I don't want it shedding all over the house."

"What do you care?" Bel shrieked back. "You don't clean. Salistar does!"

"It's my house! I make the payments, and don't you ever forget it." Lorraine reminded them.

"Babe!" Patrick finally found his voice. Trembling a bit, he reached for her arm, pulled her off her daughter. She shoved the shiny rectangle into Belinda's hands as she withdrew.

"Earth clothes. Stuff you can actually wear. I swear, Belinda, don't you get enough grief at school? Are you trying to be even weirder? It won't work, you know. They'll just hate even you more."

"Lorraine!" Patrick tried again.

"I wasn't going to wear it to school." Bel retorted, tearing the gaudy wrapping from the white box. A tunic and pants with an elastic waist, just like the standard Nauvian outfit, but it was made of some bright, breathable, sleek, wrinkle-free material that wouldn't shed all over the house, and was somehow Earth-approved. "I'm not wearing this, either," she declared.

Spring Planting

Felsic pushed the lever forward and the plow blade on the shiny new four-wheeler dropped to the rutted road. He drove forward slowly, pulling soil from the cut bank, removing the hard clay from between the ruts, smoothing the little used road to the rapidly expanding orchard.

Today, six months after First Pomegranate Day, Baput would plant the four seeds he carried in a woven amulet around his neck, gathered from the Look 'N Up harvest last fall when he had ascended to Akash. And, the three-year-old saplings from two worlds would at last be permanently fixed in the earth of Earth.

Patrick had always used the shorter foot path, past the empty vegetable garden and straight down the steep slope where they had ridden their sleds, to tend his six pomegranate trees along with his annual medicinal shrubs. Now the vegetable garden had been tilled and planted, and the longer, but less steep, vehicle path was becoming a road.

Felsic's inexperienced but sensitive touch extended from the neurons firing in his brain to the muscles of his arm and beyond to the clay and rocks below his blade. He somehow knew how much earth he was moving and where he was putting it, just by feel. The engine throbbed beneath his seat, pulsating warmly like a momama's heartbeat. The vibration shook him to the core, making him part of the machine, as if he were down there moving the dirt with his bare hands, but painlessly, and with super strength. He revved the engine, dug the blade in deeper, just to feel the power of making a change in the world.

The motor vibrations never bothered Felsic. The vehicles, the drills, the lathe, they made him feel strong and alive. They weren't like the vibrations of the Holy Rock. Cold and motionless, the rock's vibrations couldn't be controlled or even understood. They controlled *you.* They seeped in before you even noticed them, insidiously rearranging your soul, making you disappear to an alien otherwhere, leaving your family behind. *Peratha! Trillella!* Did they live?

He followed the switchback around the knoll and reached the flat ground at pond level. There were Valko and Baput, digging eight holes, a bit bigger and deeper than the pots. Such big holes! When they planted the four Holy Seeds each cycle on Nauve, they dug tiny holes and planted the seeds right in the ground. Kaysen the Tender and his sons would make sure the Holy Seedlings survived. They knew the future of the village depended on it. *Does the village* have *a future?* Felsic found himself straying toward the thoughts that tangled, tricked and ensnared him like a spider in its wicked web. *Do they live? Do they even exist? Did they disappear when we did? Did they end up in another place? In another world? In* this *world?* This last thought disturbed him most of all, for he now knew this wide, new world, this Earth, was not kind to green-skinned strangers.

Together, Valko, Felsic and Baput tenderly placed the little trees into the holes and tamped the soil around them. They lined up four of the empty bags in a row alongside the new trees and filled them with store-bought potting soil Patrick had provided. Baput lifted the lanyard over his head and reverently plucked the Holy Seeds from the woven pouch. Chanting an ancient rite, he planted the Holy Seeds in the waiting pots.

Salistar handed him his elaborately woven and beaded Akashic Robe. The pale yalinar grass and Francina's white beads stood out against the background of early spring green.

Baput stood in front of the new trees and recited the Litany of Hope.

"These young trees will spread their roots deep into the soil, spreading
their hope and their promise.
They promise that pomegranates will go on, and continue to feed us.
They usher us into the future,
They promise their first tiny fruit will appear on the next First
Pomegranate Day, beckoning to the nimblies and bumblies and starting
the cycle over again."

The dignified look crumbled. "Or not. No more nimblies! No more bumblies! Not ever, no more!" he chanted, thumping his longstick on the soft grass.

They all joined in the ancient, hopeful chant. Always fiction before, but now it was true. On Earth, anyway.

New Rules

The Nauvians filed into the quarters, stomping and scraping the moist, sticky soil from the corrugated soles of their new Earth boots, indispensable for digging with steel shovels. Patrick had obtained a pair of steel crampons that strapped to the bottom of Valko's mukluks for the digging jobs. Baput started to shrug his Akashic robe off of his shoulders. Suddenly he stopped and pulled it back on.

"Family," he addressed his elders formally. "I have been Akash for six months, um, I mean six Kakeeche cycles now. If we were nauve, I would be holding Council Meetings with the War Chief and Akira." The adults nodded solemnly and slipped into their chairs around the dining table, all eyes on their Akash.

"But there is no Rakta. No Akira," Felsic stated the obvious, as usual.

"We are the council now," Baput intoned.

Felsic pointed at each one of them, counting. "We are four. The Council is only three." His face fell as he scanned the group again. He pointed at his big brother. "War Chief," he declared, to Valko's snort. Salistar leapt to her feet and fled to the kitchen. Felsic pointed a trembling finger after her. "Akira," he said.

Salistar shook her head from side to side so violently her hair danced around her. "I am no Akira! I don't know what she knows." Her head stopped shaking and her voice dropped to a chilly whisper. "I don't know what she does." She disappeared into her sanctuary, knowing the men wouldn't follow.

Felsic rose to his feet. "Well, I'm sure not Akira!" he laughed stiffly. "Or war chief. Valko is War Chief, as sure as Baput is Akash. The Council is three. I will go to the shop so I can't hear your secrets."

"You will stay," the Akash ordered, loud and clear. Felsic froze for an instant, then slowly oozed back into his seat. "You shall all be in my Council. Momama?" it was more question than order.

Salistar stayed in the kitchen. She was not going to be Akira, even if her Akash ordered it so. Her behavior was unheard of on Nauve, especially from an Akashic Tether. But this was not Nauve, this was Earth. There was no Akash on Earth, and no Tethers. Just husbands and wives. Francina went against Elmer's orders sometimes. And Lori Anne! She ruled her house, no question.

Baput turned his back on the kitchen to face the two men who sat before him. "Okay. Council of Three. First order of business. I have made some new rules. First of all, you've probably already noticed, we no longer perform the Full Kakeeche chant each month."

"Why, Son?" Valko asked evenly.

"Because I'm sick of it!" Baput snapped without meaning to. He could taste the bile burning in his throat just from the thought of that repetitive monthly chant.

A racket of pots and plates hitting the floor erupted from the kitchen. Had Momama seen the last full moon setting red in penumbral eclipse when she rose to cook their breakfast just last week? She would think it was because they no longer sang the praises of the luminescent creatures who gathered each night to form the glowing orb that rode through the sky at night, watching over the good worshippers as they slept.

"Don't we believe in Kakeeche anymore?" Felsic asked boldly, then remembered he was speaking in Council. It felt just like the family sitting around the dinner table, except Baput looked different in that robe, not like Felsic's little nephew at all.

"The Akashic Litany does not include any promise to Kakeeche. And that's the next thing. The change I made when I ascended. That will be the Akashic Oath from now on. On Earth, anyway."

"What change?" Felsic asked.

"The one he did for you, Little Brother," Valko answered proudly. "Empathy shall be my guide when ministering to *all* of my people, not 'even the least' of my people. No one is 'least' anymore. We are all equally important in the eyes of our new Akash." He grasped his less-favored little brother's shoulder and squeezed firmly. "That's why you serve on this Council."

"I thought it was because you needed a third, and Salistar won't." He looked toward the kitchen, wondering how Salistar could disobey her Akash. Maybe it was because she'd always thought he was her little boy. *Now he's her Akash, her supreme and absolute ruler, to be obeyed without question. But this is Earth. Things are different on Earth. Even the Akashic Litany is different.*

Baput filled the silence with his next agenda item. He blurted it unequivocally, as if he was the Alanakash or something. "If we don't go Nauve on next First Pomegranate Day, I will marry Belinda."

Suddenly, Salistar felt an urgent need to bring refreshments into the Council meeting. She rushed in with a tray, grinning from ear to ear. The men nodded and smiled too.

"If she wants to," Baput added. The smiles faded, the heads stopped bobbing. Instead, they all furrowed their thick, dark eyebrows and looked at each other.

"But she must!" Salistar gushed, her reticence gone. "You are already fifteen. Next Passascenday, you will be eighteen. She will be fifteen, perfect for wedding. You will be getting a little old. If we are not Nauve by Passascenday, you *must* marry her. It doesn't matter what she wants, or what Lori Anne says."

"Welcome to the Council, Akira," Valko rumbled under his beard.

Falcon

The Look 'N Up Plumbing Van chugged up the driveway in low gear, pulling hard and slow, but strong. Felsic listened to Van under stress to see how she was feeling, like a heart doctor monitoring a patient on a treadmill. Van was working extra hard, because she was towing Falcon, a new patient for Doctor Felsic.

The van came to rest in front of the shop. Felsic, Baput and Valko flocked to it like a bunch of Earth guys. "Here it is," Patrick announced as he walked around the compact 1962 Ford sedan on the rented trailer. "It's a classic, according to Elmer. Should resell for a lot of money, if you can:" he pulled a little notebook out of his pocket and read from it; "do a valve job, replace the heads, timing chain, flywheel. Can you do all that?"

"Yeah. I know all that stuff. I'll need parts."

"Of course. You tell me exactly what you need, and I'll get it, but you have to tell me exactly, because I'm not like Elmer. I don't know anything about this stuff. I swear, you might as well ask Salistar."

Valko grunted ambivalently. A laugh?

"Or we'll go on line, on my computer. You can get just what you need, pick it out yourself. I'd rather support the local store, but you can't go in there. You can look up how to do stuff on the internet, um, the iPlane, too. Maybe I'll get a computer and router for the shop, show you how to look stuff up. So, can you do it?"

"Yeah." Felsic repeated.

"Okay!" Patrick addressed the group gathered around the venerated Earth object. "So, listen, guys. When it's done, and a customer comes to buy it, you can't let him see you. Any of you. You'll have to hide. Felsic, you'll go in the house and wait by the phone. If the guy has questions, I'll just say my mechanic couldn't be here, and I'll call you on my cell phone. You just answer his questions. You guys speak the same language."

"Nauvian?"

"Motor head."

St. Patrick's Day 2018

The man-sized elf costume Patrick had found on the internet was perfect for a leprechaun. It had a green vest and knickers, a pointy green hat with a feather, and a Santa-type bag made of green felt. He replaced the red ribbon sash decked with jingle bells with a green sash with shamrocks printed on it. He had even found knee socks to match. It was perfect for his routine at the annual Saint Patrick's Day Party at the Irish Club, which he'd been performing for four years now. By himself. Neither Lorraine nor Belinda had ever seen him play the part. Not until tonight. He'd finally convinced Belinda to come. He'd even found a smaller elf costume and bag for her.

"I need your help, Bel. This event's so popular, *I'm* so popular, there's more people coming than ever. You just clown around and make everyone laugh while you hand out toys to the kids."

"What do they get?" Belinda demanded, as if it were a condition of her participation.

"I don't know, cheap plastic toys. All the same, all wrapped the same. Little action figures or something."

"Great. More plastic. Not made in America, I'll bet."

"I'm sure they're not, Bel, but that's not the point. It's for the kids," he said again, as if it mattered a lot.

Belinda didn't see it. "They have Christmas. It's just like Christmas. Leprechauns don't give gifts. They go after gold."

"Aw, Bel, you're way overthinking this. It's just a little fun for the kids. You'll see. I can be quite entertaining."

She snorted, but she couldn't help smiling.

"OK, Daddy." she agreed, without really meaning it.

So, here they were. Patrick guided her to the back entrance. A plump lady with bright red cheeks greeted them with an "Ohhhh!" that you could literally read on her lips until she drew them together to give Patrick a peck on the right cheek. She pulled away, leaving a red smudge, and looked down at Belinda. Her costume matched Patrick's perfectly, including the tacky socks and errant left eye. Exactly the same!

"So, this is your daughter!" she exclaimed joyously, as if Belinda was a long-lost relative. "Just the same! Oh, my, that must be—" She broke off, caught Patrick's look, then looked back down at Belinda. "What's your name, Hon?"

"Belinda" Bel replied through her teeth.

"What a pretty name." the fat old woman crooned. Come in and have dinner." She led them through the back door into a busy kitchen. People in green sweaters, green hats, occasional green pants, were carrying aluminum foil trays of corned beef, cabbage and boiled red potatoes through the swinging doors that led to the spacious dance hall, where tables were decked with green tablecloths and adorable table arrangements made from more cheap plastic stuff by the Irish Ladies.

"Molly O'Grady," their hostess introduced herself as she guided them to the corner of the kitchen. She pulled a chair away from a table with her swollen foot. "That's me. Irish enough for ya?" She cackled at her own joke. "You sit tight. I'll get you your dinner."

When she had waddled off, Belinda scalded Patrick with a haughty, put-out look that she must have learned from her mother. "What are we, the *help*?" As soon as she heard it come out of her own mouth, her eyes dropped to the humble table.

Molly returned and shoved a steaming plate of the traditional Irish fare into her downcast view. "See you out there! Thirty minutes!" She chirped over her shoulder as she hurried back to the steam tables.

"We're a surprise," Patrick explained. "It would kind of wreck the show if they saw us ahead of time, sitting there eating with them..." He trailed off, as if something had just occurred to him.

They finished the bland meal in silence. The moment they were done, an anxious, round little man with red tufts of hair over his ears and a circular face that matched his physique approached their table. "Patrick!" he cried, extending a knobby, freckled hand. "And hello, Miss." He moved to doff his cap, but found none. "Come on, oh good, two bags, you'll need 'em. Right this way. The ladies went a little overboard this year..." He chattered as they followed him to a storeroom full of boxes of small, soft packages wrapped in dull green with more shamrocks.

Belinda rolled her eyes, but the round man didn't seem to notice. He was looking at his watch. The he turned as if wound up like that old-fashioned watch, and grabbed at the limp packages. "Come on! Load your bags. We've got five minutes!"

Conscious of Belinda's concerns, Patrick had to ask. "What are these things?"

"Little cloth leprechaun dolls. They play 'When Irish Eyes Are Smiling'. Drives ya nuts! I don't think the boys are gonna like 'em. But far be it for me to tell the ladies..." he jeered.

Empty plates clattered and rattled as Patrick and Belinda made their way to the center of the dance hall. The tables were cleared of dishes and arraigned in a square all around them, boxing them in. Folks on the inside of the square craned and twisted their bodies or simply turned their chairs around to look at them. Everyone. Looking at the two cockeyed strangers in the ridiculous clothes with their sacks full of toys that their kids would hate and yet still succeed in annoying them to tears with.

Transfixed, Belinda scanned the crowd. Thinning red hair. Blotchy swollen red noses. White, hairy bellies peeking out from under T-shirts that read "Kiss me I'm Irish". Kids with curly red locks squirming in their chairs, shoving plastic spoon handles up their noses.

"You ready?" Patrick asked, swinging his bag over his shoulder. The crowd cheered. Belinda shook her head. Patrick sent her one last glance of disappointment. Then he morphed into his character, a demented leprechaun who wants to be Santa Clause?

He handed out toys. He danced an authentic jig. He crooned Irish songs, horribly off key and butchering the lyrics with his own not-so-funny, sometimes raunchy, parodies. He spun and danced and jumped up on the chairs. He let the women stroke his cheeks or steal a kiss. He got down on his hand and knees and turned his head almost upside-down, showing a hideous display of bumpy skull, scrawny neck, pointy chin and abundant nose hairs that was far worse than his normal face. The crowd cheered and hooted and called his name, "Patrick!". The kids opened their toys. One by one, the dolls were activated, playing a tinny electronic version of the Irish tune, out of sync, over and over.

Belinda cringed in the corner behind her big green bag, trying not to be noticed. No use. Molly had not forgotten her. She sought her out, like a predator.

"Oh, there you are!" she crowed, much too loud. So much for hiding. Belinda dropped the bag. The woman approached. She towered over Bel, at probably four times her weight. Her eyes went from triumph to soft sadness just a little too quickly. "Come on. Join in the fun! Don't take us wrong, Honey. We adore your father. He loves the attention. This is a special time for him, so don't you go spoiling it, feeling sorry for yourself. Why don't you do what he does? Get out there and have fun with it. It's all good fun."

She pursed her painted lips and chirped three times, as if coaxing a small animal out from its hiding place. That was it! Belinda bolted the other way, out the door and into the van.

Patrick didn't notice until the door slammed and the cheering stopped. His crazed face straightened. He cast his straight eye around the silent crowd. "Sorry. I'll be right back," he muttered.

As he rushed for the door, he heard them.

"She takes herself too seriously"

"It's got to be hard for her."

"It's her age, poor little thing."

Patrick raced through the dim parking lot to the van. He found his daughter in the passenger seat with her arms folded across her narrow chest. When he opened the door, she turned her head away.

"Come on back in, Babe," he begged. "The fun's just beginning."

Bel turned to him and shook her head. In the dark, he was starting to look crazy again. "Take me home," she wheezed. The words were barely audible, but Patrick heard them as if she'd screamed them. He turned to someone outside. Bel couldn't see who. Probably that moon-faced Molly. "Dad!" she barked.

"Sorry." Patrick said over his shoulder to the unknown someone. He climbed in and buckled his seat belt. Bel was already belted and ready to go. Patrick didn't say a word until he had the van moving out of the back lot. "What is it, Baby?" he finally asked, annoyingly innocent.

Bel kept her arms folded and her face forward. "Dad. That was *so* Quasimodo!"

"Quasimodo." Patrick repeated the name of the Hunchback of Notre Dame coldly, and said nothing more. He let the invisible, almost-impenetrable Curtain of Silence descend between them. Good. That's just what he needed to isolate the bitter memory from Belinda's knowing. Belinda should never hear the family's version of The Hunchback of Notre Dame.

Quasimodo

It was 1999. *Nearly twenty years ago*! Patrick was surprised to realize. He and Lor had just graduated and married, and she was working for the County Public Works Department as an Engineer-In-Training, working toward her license, following her Five-Year Plan.

The Recreation Committee put on a big Millennium Party at a fancy restaurant on a Friday night in December. "Party like it's 1999" the invite suggested above the list of prices, depending on the selected entrée. No tax dollars going toward drunk public workers, no sir.

Their entrance had gone as he expected. Like college. Mostly professionals with manners and, in his experience, relatively open minds. They greeted him shyly, but kindly, struggling between looking at him and looking away. Lorraine fidgeted and hissed at his side, her red velvet dress shimmering as she squirmed.

A dashing dark-haired young man rushed magnanimously toward them. Profoundly overdressed in a three-piece suit, Patrick mistook him for a maître d'. The illusion continued when the slightly awkward youth quickly stashed his surprise at Patrick's odd countenance under a gratuitous smile and escorted them to a table where two places were labeled with their names. It shattered, however, when he sat down with them, on Lorrain's right, and grasped her forearm gently in both hands. "I didn't know your husband was..." he whispered audibly.

Patrick grinned the most hideous grin he could muster and waved his hand as if to say, "I'm right here."

The friendly brute with the perfectly even blue eyes leaned back and let go as if Patrick's fantasy punch had been real.

Lorraine leaned forward between them. "Oh, I'm sorry," she injected innocently. "Patrick, this is Steve, the Deputy County Surveyor."

"Hello, Steve." Patrick responded coldly. He reached awkwardly across Lorraine's scarlet middle, pushing to meet Steve's hand more than halfway across. Their tense handshake made them both bristle.

"Excuse me." Steve popped up from his seat. Yeah, *his* seat. Patrick checked the name tag. "Steve Kempton, Surveyor, +1".

Lorraine ordered a drink. Patrick filled up on breadsticks while they sat alone, not talking. "Eat something, Babe, if you're gonna start drinking."

Lorraine downed her gin and tonic in a single gulp. She muttered something under her breath while she wiped her mouth on her satin sleeve. Either "shut up" or "stay here." Patrick had always wondered which.

He looked over his shoulder to where she worked the room, uninhibited and alluring. The last thing she needed was a hideous freak to explain over and over. He knew. Then they would feel sorry for her, at best, want to rescue her from the monster. She'd like that. Or, give her professional breaks out of pity, she'd hate that. *Oh, they might disguise it by saying it's because she's such a trooper for sticking with me when she could have any of these guys, even the married ones, I'll bet.*

He became aware of the stares. His eye was showing, pitifully watching his wife slither her way to success on her own merits. No pity. No gratuitous sex. She was a professional, and her looks had nothing to do with it. "As if", Patrick muttered out loud. The Curtain of Silence billowed and he tightened his lips to still it, so he could return to that wonderful memory before his moans roused Belinda.

The revelers had returned to the table all together, talking and laughing. Mercifully, Steve's Plus One sat next to Lorraine, with Steve a seat away. He spent most of dinner leaning over her to talk to Lorraine, who mostly drank. 'Plus One' kept looking over at Patrick's eye, then quickly looking away. She didn't eat a bite.

After dinner the Public Works Director stood up, clanging his brandy glass with a spoon. He gave a rousing speech about how great they all were and how good infrastructure funding was going to be under Governor Grey Davis.

Patrick of 2018 hissed a scoff at that, rippling the curtain again, risking a rude "What?" from Bel. He glanced at her. She still stared out the window, arms folded, building her own Least Favorite Memory. A place to flee to, to remind her that things could always be worse. Such was the life of a Look 'N Up.

Assured of Belinda's silence, he returned to the story. *Why should I go there again?* He asked himself. But he was right at the best part, so he plunged back in.

The director finished his speech, blah, blah, blah just fine. *But why did he have to be diplomatic and open the floor to everyone? A bunch of drunks!* "Does anyone else have anything to say?" he had invited.

To Patrick's unimagined horror, Lorrain, the newest employee, stood up and cleared her gin-soaked throat. Wavering and shimmering, the scarlet serpent began.

"You're all staring at me anyway, so, I'll say it. Yeah. I married Quasimodo! I married Quasimodo!" she keened shrilly, waving her glass at Patrick, her umpteenth drink sloshing.

It was good 'ol Steve who rushed to her side when she staggered.

Patrick rose slowly, trying not to look at anyone. He took Lorraine's other side, and he and his good buddy, Surveyor Steve half-carried her outside and held her upright where she puked in the bushes.

"Can you drive?" Steve asked anxiously as the valet arrived with their old, dented Volvo.

"I don't drink," Patrick informed him haughtily.

"Yea, but, well..." Steve gestured vaguely to his own left eye.

"Do you want to see my license?" Patrick snapped as they lowered Lorraine into the passenger seat.

"No, man. Sorry. It's cool, OK?" Steve babbled as he backed away. When Patrick reached the driver's door, he looked back. Steve was gone.

Then came the Weekend of Silence. Lorraine swore she didn't remember a thing, and therefore it couldn't have happened. She found out the truth that Monday, when she walked to her cubicle under the silent stares of her co-workers. When she reached its refuge, she found the old picture of Patrick she'd put up when she first started, like everyone did. But it had drawn too many uncomfortable questions and unwelcome conversations, so she had shoved it in a drawer.

Someone remembered, and found it, and there it sat, in the middle of her desk. Stemless red roses were piled all around it, as if he was dead or something. Patrick knew this, because she told him all about it. She mostly wondered about how much all those roses cost.

Terrified by how far he'd driven while dwelling in the past century, Patrick came to, just in time. It was their exit.

"You ready?" he asked, deliberately breaking the silence. To himself, he thought, *Time to watch the scarlet serpent devour its young. Or visa versa. Or both.*

The Net

Bel stifled her anger under a pile of tear-stained stuffed animals through a Saturday night too sleepless for a girl of barely thirteen. As the drizzly morning dawned, she skillfully packed her anger and fear away where it didn't show. She had to be charming and beautiful now, for the only one outside of her family who ever saw her that way, eye or no eye. Baput was coming over to look on the internet with Dad.

He called it the iPlane and he could search it anytime he wanted, without even having a computer or a phone or anything. Just his brain. His sweet, brilliant, wise, kind brain, always working behind that high green forehead and those bottomless eyes, darker than black coffee. Belinda sighed, hoping he wouldn't find what he was looking for.

He and Dad were searching for the Net, or something like it. Something that could cover the Holy Rock and collect its vibrations into a glowing white plasma. On Nauve, they had further concentrated that energy into a laser that killed the nimblies and bumblies. But there were no more nimblies and bumblies, not on Earth, anyway. They wanted the Net for something else.

The Net opened the portal. That's how Baput and his green family got here from Nauve. They didn't mean to. They were just trying to kill the monsters that were eating their people, for three days and nights every three years. Baput figured that was the only time the portal could open. Once every three years, on First Pomegranate Day, when the monsters attacked.

If they had the Net, the portal would open two and a half years from now. Baput and his family would go home to Nauve. They didn't really want to, but it was the right thing to do. Baput's people needed their Akash.

Belinda was glad the Net got left behind on Nauve. In three years, they had never found anything like it, and that was just fine with her.

She brushed her thick, shoulder-length waves until they shined like copper. She would try that walk Mom did when she came down the stairs to greet company. Part of her beauty queen training, she did it without thinking. Belinda had to practice it.

She heard a knock, and started her planned descent. Baput entered without waiting for an answer. Mom wouldn't like that, Belinda knew. *But at least he's wearing his Earth clothes.*

Baput looked around. "Hello?" he asked, standing on the doormat. Belinda stopped on the stairs and coughed delicately. He looked up at her, and his smile drove the drizzle from the morning. "I brought breakfast, my Momama made. Then I'm going to look at the iPlane with your Popa."

Patrick emerged from the music room at the foot of the stairs. "Let's eat!" he agreed loudly. "Lorraine!" he shouted up the staircase, "Breakfast!"

To his surprise, Lorraine appeared behind Belinda, all made up perfectly for a Sunday at home with her family. She hugged a thick stack of thin, comb-bound documents to her chest. "I'll join you," she offered magnanimously, to Belinda's chagrin.

"Good." Patrick was glad to share a meal with even half of her attention. "We could use your engineering expertise," he flattered. "We're going online to look for the Net."

Belinda served the food Salistar had prepared, the usual fried potatoes, beets, yams, onions, etc. No meat, no cheese. Lorraine would want something else later, but she would get it by herself, for herself.

She won't even ask if we want any. Belinda grumbled silently, *We're vegans. We're weird, in two ways now, at least.* It seemed she had more and more in common with the green family, and less and less with her own. The thought warmed her, and she smiled.

"Thanks, Honey." Patrick acknowledged as she set his plate before him.

"Thank you." Baput still pronounced it stiffly. They didn't say thanks on Nauve. Especially not a man to his tether, the woman who was born to serve him. And the Akash was above thanking anybody anyway, if he was anything like the last one. Baput was Alanakash, even more supreme than his G-Pa, who had perished with the Nimbumblyborg, the last and only gestating mass of sleeping nimblies and bumblies on Earth. But Baput wasn't like the old Akash.

Lorraine was the one who failed to acknowledge her daughter's delivery. Instead, she ordered Baput, "So, tell us again about the Net."

Belinda's heart sank. Mom had already taken over the operation. Belinda's eye strayed to that stack of books she'd brought with her, and it was there she fixed her hopes. Work. It would get her sooner or later, the pull, the addiction. Mom would be out of their way before long. So, she just sat back and listened to the story, again, relishing each wrinkled eyebrow, the way his eyes opened wide with excitement, wonder and fear when he described that fateful First Pomegranate Day over three years ago.

"The rock was vibrating all by itself, we didn't know why at the time. The Net had a cord. We think it was a copper wire that joined it to the stationary bicycle Felsic pedaled."

"A generator," Lorraine interrupted.

"Yes." Baput continued, raising both hands above the table. He held them horizontally, palms together. His hands separated as he spoke, about twelve inches. "The Net lifted off the rock and hovered above it on a pillow of white light. Then G-pa stepped on it, pushing it down with his longstick and his feet, so it touched the rock at three points." He demonstrated, three fingertips on one hand pressing the palm of the other. "That's when the cold blankness, the unbearable pressure, the pain, it swallowed us! Everyone who was in the Holy Cave at the time, I don't know how long we were in there, but when it stopped hurting, when we could see and think again, we were on the Look 'N Up Ranch, here on Earth."

"You said the Net's really light, right?" Patrick asked.

"Yes." Baput agreed. "Light in weight, and in color. Silvery white, like Kakeeche, um, the moon. And weight? It's lighter than anything I have ever felt."

"Like a space blanket?" Lorraine ventured.

"We tried that," Patrick confessed. "We bought one, just to see how light it is."

"It was maybe a little heavier than that." Baput tried to remember. Those adorable eyebrows wrinkled again. "But it was totally different. The Net is a net, it's woven. A tight weave, like my Nauvian clothes, but still tiny gaps between the very fine threads, or wires. And not so silver. More white, like the moon."

"That single bedsheet we tried, was that lighter or heavier?"

"That was much heavier." Baput recalled their earlier session. He also recalled the experiment he and Jerry had done that Christmas. There were still scars on the shop floor, but Patrick had never said anything. Baput was sworn to secrecy. He was also bound to tell the truth, by his Akashic oath. *Does that mean don't tell a lie? Or does it mean I have to say out loud everything I know is true?*

"Jerry and I already searched for it. Many times," was Baput's only admission.

Patrick went on anyway, pacing around the kitchen table. "So, we'll weigh the space blanket and the sheet, then calculate the weight per square inch or whatever unit they use to describe wire mesh on the internet. We'll narrow our search to that range..."

"I'm coming, too!" Belinda said as she cleared the dishes. She followed Baput and Patrick into the music room where Patrick's desktop waited. Lorraine spread her work across the cleared table and opened the booklet at the top on her stack.

Earth Glasses

Lorraine methodically plowed through the stack of sub-consultant proposals on the kitchen table. This new shopping mall they were designing was already controversial. They needed help from specialists; a Traffic

Engineer and an Aesthetics Analyst. Lorraine had a say, but she had to finish reading the proposals and rating the applicants by Monday morning. Resume after resume, all the same. Success stories, every project completed on time and within budget. *Sure.* It was tedious and time consuming, and she had actual engineering to get done, too, you know. It was time best wasted at home, if her family and their "helpers" would leave her alone.

The music room door opened. Lorraine cursed silently. *Now they'll come out here and want to talk to me. Should I give up and put it away? Go upstairs? Maybe if I look like I'm concentrating real hard they'll get the hint.* She lifted a proposal booklet and held it close to her face, squinting.

Baput emerged timidly and crossed to the kitchen to get himself a glass of water. It had taken awhile to get used to, but Earth people were okay with men in the kitchen. Patrick even cooked sometimes!

"You look like my cousin, Bazu," the green teen interrupted.

"What?" Lorraine asked tersely.

"Bazu, he," Baput narrowed his eyes tightly and leaned forward, squinting, like Lorraine had. "When he looks at small things up close."

Lorraine removed her reading glasses and looked at them. "These are my old ones. I should be using my new ones. I guess I'm getting worse. All that screen time..." she trailed off, absently extending the inadequate glasses toward the boy, who took them carefully.

They looked a bit like those cardboard goggles Francina had given them to watch the eclipses, only clear, like the glasses Popa and Felsic wore when they worked with metal on the machines in the shop. But these were smaller lenses, in a thin, plastic frame. He put them on.

"Whoa!" he cried as his vision blurred, making him stagger. Lorraine suppressed a laugh.

Baput snatched the glasses off quickly and stood blinking at Lorraine. "If you have better ones, can I have these?" he asked.

"What for?" Lorraine replied. "They make your eyes worse. That's because you don't need them."

"If we ever *do* find the Net, and make the portal work, and go back to Nauve◈" Baput's eyes widened at some imagined horror. "Or maybe we could just send a package through the portal, and not go there ourselves?" He brightened at that. "Bazu needs these, I think."

"For reading?" Lorraine asked.

"Only the Akash and his tether can read," Baput replied. He inhaled sharply. "But Bazu might have to be Akash now." The realization chilled him. His cousin, Bazu, destined to be Felsic's apprentice as winemaker, serving in the Holy Cave with absolutely no training.

Lorraine wasn't concerned about Bazu. "You mean, your Momama can read but your Popa can't?"

Baput nodded. "Not Felsic either. G-Pa was teaching me, but he didn't finish."

"Your Momama can teach you."

Baput raised surprised eyes at Lorraine. "I never thought of that. I guess she could." His smile faded. "But what's the use? Nobody uses Ancient Akashic writing on Earth."

Lorraine's Sci Fi addiction kicked in. "What if you *can* go back? Your culture will be forgotten here. You and your Momama have to write it all down, for when the world is ready. Your history! Salistar can write, can't she?"

"Yes, she must write down the wisdom of the Akash as he speaks from the Plane."

"Sounds like fun!" Lorraine cheered sarcastically. "Has she been writing down his rantings since he got here? I mean, before..."

The furrow between Baput's eyebrows deepened in thought. "I don't know. I must speak with her." With that, he left Lori Anne to her work, slipping back into the music room with her old glasses.

Nauve, Spring

Nauve Glasses

Bazu and Tamaya sat across from each other on the floor of the Holy Cave. Six oil lamps surrounded them, casting their light across the opened book in a spoke-like pattern of light and shadow.

"No, it's quay, not omp," Tamaya explained, again. "See the little curly line coming out of it? That means it's a quay." She fought the urge to rip Bazu's oversized head off of his spindly neck and hurl it out of the cave. Instead, she smiled her well-rehearsed smile.

Bupple sat on the porch outside, on guard. He had learned to give the Akashic couple their privacy. Their reading sessions usually ended badly.

Bazu untangled his crossed legs. He had never been comfortable in the meditation pose that was supposed to help him reach the Akashic Plane. How could a constant, nagging pain, followed by alarming numbness, help someone concentrate? From his knees, he leaned over the book, eyes narrowed, deep lines etched along their edges. He fought to conceal the angry tears that collected behind his eyelids. They didn't help his vision any. The letters of the Old Ones, they all looked like blobs to him. He couldn't tell one from another. And how could she, a mere woman, teach the mighty Akash to read? It just wasn't right!

"Quay, omp, ba, ta, va, all the same! Why did they make them all the same? Stupid alphabet!" he exploded, hurling the ancient book across the room. It hit the floor with a spine-snapping pop, then skidded all the way to the Rock.

Tamaya ran to retrieve it.

"Leave it!" Bazu bellowed in his pitiful way. Savagely, he grabbed his rolled scroll of drawings, unfurled it and hid his face behind the broad sheets of parchment. The drawings of the weapon. Those he could see, mostly. He had spent hours looking at them every day, for months. The parts in the drawing matched the strange objects he'd had Bupple drag off the Rock and out of the way, into that dark tunnel. They were all part of the weapon, and he knew how to reassemble it when the time came.

But those stupid Akashic letters were on the plan sheets, too. He had no idea what information they held, but he was going to find out for himself. No woman was going to read those plans to him. It was too important. He was the Akash. The Akash who would bring an end to the nimblies and bumblies once and for all, without disappearing in the process. "Bring me my dinner, Woman," he ordered.

Kiko Birds

Peratha and Trillella planted the spring greens and peas in the cool, moist soil of their dooryard garden. Due to Felsic's status, Peratha and Trillella's hut was the last hut in the last row of huts on the far side of the village, furthest from the Great Hall. The garden in the back faced north, where the kip orchard grew just beyond a grassy field, and east, upriver, toward the Holy Cave and beyond it, the mist-shrouded caves of the nimblies and bumblies.

As Trillella was poking the tiny spinach seeds into the ground, she heard a familiar squabbling. She looked towards the orchard. "Kiko birds!" She jumped to her feet with delight.

Peratha stayed on her knees, tilling the garden soil with a long, split stone she held in her rough bare hand.

Trillella pointed at the female bird in the deep green top of the closest pomegranate tree. Her red and blue plumage was puffed out, blending to a luscious purple. She tilted her head from side to side, watching the male birds bob around the base of the tree. Their tufts flashed iridescent red when they faced east and blazed an even brighter blue when they turned their heads to the west. They flapped their wings and ruffled their feathers so they looked much bigger than they all knew they were. They chased each other, lunged and pecked at their challengers. Eventually, one was declared the winner, although Trillella didn't really see why. He raised his arced beak haughtily and proceeded to walk up the trunk, circling around it, higher and higher in a spiral until he neared the branch were the spectacular female waited with an impatient air. The squabbling continued below until a second male half-flew, half-jumped onto the tree trunk and began climbing, too.

The first male had to pry his eyes away from the prize to face the challenger. Clinging to the truck, he ran down head first, squeaking and squawking. The challenger screamed back, beak open wide.

The first male continued his charge, burying his head in that open beak. Was he giving up? No, he pitched his strong feathered neck and flung his rival out of the tree, sending him flapping desperately to the ground, squeaking more than squawking.

"Yay!" Trillella cried, her pack of seeds forgotten at her knees. Peratha continued to toil with her hand-tiller.

The winning bird smoothed his feathers, turned and spiraled up the trunk once again. He soon reached the branch where the female sat, looking down her beak at him. She turned her head to its sky-blue side and looked at him with one eye. Then she checked him out with the eye on the strawberry-red side. Trillella watched, unbreathing. This was the moment!

Blending to a neutral violet shade, the female kiko turned her back on the unfortunate suitor. She strutted to the end of her branch and sat, ignoring him.

Trill could see the air escape out of the male's little chest. The red and blue shoulders sagged. He flew away in shame.

"How can she do that?" Trillella wondered out loud.

"What?" Peratha grunted, wiping her sweaty hair from her face.

"A kiko bird woman can say 'no' to a man."

Another brilliantly tasseled bird stepped onto the tree and began his upward spiral. "That's the one that got thrown down!" Trillella was sure, because his feathers were still ruffled. He reached the branch unchallenged. The female assessed him, just as coldly, or so it seemed. One eye, then the other, then she turned away. But this time, she flew out of the tree and headed upriver.

The ruffled guy lost his footing and almost fell out of the tree. Flapping frantically, he got a grip on the limb, threw his weight into his wings and flew after her.

"A kiko girl can choose," Trillella whispered, stunned. She had seen the kiko mating ritual almost every year, but suddenly it didn't make sense. "Why, Momama? Why can a bird, an animal, have a choice who she marries, and a person doesn't?"

Peratha sighed and leaned back on her heels. "Life is more complicated for people."

"Why?" Trillella asked.

"Birds don't have to cook, or clean, or tend the garden or make the oil or the pomegranate wine!" Peratha regretted that last one, but... "Trillella, I declare, you are the silliest girl in the village. Where do you come up with these ideas? It's because of your Popa, I suppose."

"What about my Popa?" Trill snapped.

"Well, you know," Peratha choked, wishing she hadn't mentioned Felsic. "Your Popa was silly, remember?"

"Yeah." A slow smile spread across her wide cheeks as Trill remembered watching the Kiko birds with Popa. He didn't think they were silly.

The male had caught up, plume flashing brilliant crimson and soothing azure as he turned his head side to side, flying and talking with his new wife in the pink-tinged sky. Together they soared upriver past the Holy Cave and into the mists, where no one ever went, toward the caves of the Nimbumblyborg that went on forever, as far as anyone knew.

Library

Tamaya ventured out alone and unguarded. Bupple accompanied the Akash everywhere he went, but Tamaya didn't get a constant guard. *Because I have nothing to fear*, she supposed, tossing her head. Her long, thick mane swayed, then settled, beautifully disheveled. *Or because I'm not important,* she snorted. Skirting the village, she scurried straight to Akira's Lair for their first meeting.

She had no idea what to expect. Their arrangement was unprecedented. Salistar, the previous Akashic Tether, did not have to meet privately with Akira on a quarterly basis. The Councilor, Nemaray, provided a liaison between Akira and the women of the high-born families. The low-born had someone else, some low-born Unmarriageable, for Council. Her name escaped Tamaya. She didn't bother to search for it.

It's the books, Tamaya settled on the explanation that made her feel most important. *She wants to know what all those books say.* Her pride disintegrated when she thought of how disappointed the old lady would be.

Two of those wasted unmarriageable women with stringy muscles and short hair flanked the door in the carved wooden façade that covered the semi-subterranean Lair of the Unmarriageables. They bowed their heads slightly and opened the door for the Akashic Tether.

The dank smell brought back the recent life-changing memory. The looking plate, the precious gown like none other, the even rarer and stranger conversation with Akira. There she was, sitting in the dark, waiting. Tamaya stepped inside and the door closed behind her.

"How does it go?" Akira began, her casual words belied by her grave tone.

Tamaya didn't know where to begin. "Jenevan sends her dog with our food."

Akira nodded, raising her eyebrows expectantly. Tamaya knew that was not the matter she was here to discuss. "I had to start at the beginning. I showed him the schoolbook you gave me in tether's school, that's okay, isn't it?" she asked, suddenly afraid.

Akira chuckled. "Of course it's okay. He is the Akash."

Tamaya relaxed. "I'm trying to teach him, but he's just not getting it. He gets so mad, Akira! My teaching angers him."

"That is because you are a woman. The Akash should have taught him. Then he would have soaked it up like a sponge. His anger at being taught by his tether is making him unreceptive, blind to the wonders of the books. Have you found any manuals?"

"Manuals?"

"Yes, instructions. Someone must have written down the words to the rituals, the meanings of the signs. The stuff he needs to know to fool, um, to lead the people. He must learn to conduct a proper ceremony before Mitten, or all is lost!" Akira ranted. "You must find the books with the rituals. If he can't read, then you must read them to him, over and over until he commits every word to memory."

The order landed like a stone in Tamaya's stomach. "I looked all over for the First Kakeeche Day Ceremony, but I didn't find it, or any books with the words of ceremonies or instructions on how to, um, be an Akash."

Tamaya reached under her tunic and produced a thick volume bound in dog skin, always freely given for that sacred purpose, after a natural death.

The ancient face lit up at the sight. "Did you bring me something interesting to read?"

This is one of the newer books. One of the ones dictated to Salistar by the Akash Who Disappeared, Badon.

"Badon." Akira repeated the name with a mix of affection and disdain.

"Yes." Tamaya replied proudly. "Badon. His True Name is written in all of his books."

"And what has my brother to say to the ages?" Akira droned incuriously.

Tamaya extended the book to the knotty hand that trembled ever so slightly. "I only brought this one. They are essentially all the same, Akira! He talks of the weapon, but gives no instructions, no details of how he assembled it. All he does is rant about the law against Shavarandu. He takes one side, then the other, like he is arguing with himself. His thinking goes around and around in a circle, with no end, no conclusion. Every book the same. You'll see." See took a step back. She had not meant to speak so disrespectfully about the former Akash. She hadn't even known he was Akira's brother.

Akira didn't look upset or angry, or even surprised. She wore a resigned, frustrated look that Tamaya could see herself wearing, or she would, if she ever got in front of that looking plate again. Emboldened, Tamaya finished her thoughts. "This volume is a little different. He talks about Insitucide. He speculates about how to kill the nimblies and bumblies in their caves, while they hibernate. I think he might have found a way, but the handwriting gets worse and worse. Maybe that part was in the Akash's handwriting, as if Salistar wasn't writing for him then. I thought perhaps she had a babbet, and couldn't work?"

Akira scoffed at the ridiculous notion.

Tamaya had another thought. "Or maybe Batuk was learning to write. See the date on the front? He would have been eight years old! So smart..." she trailed off, not wanting to image what her marriage could have been, if only... She looked at Akira with undeserved pride in her first betrothed.

Akira's dark green skin glowed almost white in the dim light as the blood drained from her face to her gut. She stared at the book, open to the spot where the spine bent habitually, shaking her head as Tamaya babbled on.

"The writing gets better and better, but then it goes back to Salistar's handwriting, but the change is so gradual! It slowly turns back into her handwriting like she was the one writing the whole time. Did she hurt her hand or something, Akira? Do you remember?"

Akira was silent, her eyes fixed on something far away, or long past. Didn't she think this was important? Tamaya pressed on. "When I could read it again, he seemed to have finally made up his mind about one thing. He was against Insitucide from that time forward."

Akira snapped the book closed and looked up. She still wore that resigned look, but there was a new bitterness in the creases around her eyes, the sides of her mouth. "Are there other books?" the ancient woman wheezed, "older ones, before Badon?"

Tamaya saw a glint of something in Akira's eyes that fought her despair, a desperate hope that softened Tamaya's resentment of her supreme and ruthless ruler. It made her feel glad to bring her some good news. Glad and powerful.

"Akira, there are more books and scrolls in that tunnel than I could read in my whole life!"

Akira stared at Tamaya like she was some specter, like one of the Kakeeche creatures come to visit her personally in her Lair. "Read more. Bring me more," she babbled, scooping the air with her hands.

Tamaya beamed with power like Shavarandu Himself, until Akira popped her bubble. "The other thing, how's that going?"

The 'other thing' was not going well at all. It had been one six-month long wedding night for the Akashic couple. Nothing had changed. No interest. Tamaya had giving up trying to entice him. It only made him angry. That made her feel ugly and unappreciated after all the trouble she had gone to, keeping herself fine all those years while she waited to be married to one handsome Akash, then another. Now she was stuck with this weak, timid, unattractive insect of a man who apparently found her equally repulsive.

Akira was watching her expectantly. She stammered her answer. "He... He's not. He won't�" She couldn't speak the words.

"You must teach him that, too." Akira replied simply.

Tamaya's 21st Birthday

Tamaya arrived at her family's hut alone. It was her birthday wish to spend a night with her Popa and brother and dear sister-in-law, her nephew and newborn niece. Bazu and Bupple had walked to the village with her, then split to their own families' huts for the night.

Jenevan cooked a special dinner for her, with all her favorites, at least those that were available so early in spring. Peas, strawberries, tender greens and asparagus spears over multicolored rice arranged in colorful stacks on fired clay plates painted with lively designs by Pindross years ago, when he could see more than just the one shape that now obsessed him.

Tamaya complemented her sister-in-law's cooking. "This is lovely. So much better than those ration packs we have to eat in the Holy Cave."

Jenevan stopped short, a spoonful of berry topping poised above her Popa-in-law's plate. "It's the same food," she hissed between clenched teeth.

"But it never looks like this. It's all cold and mishmashed and jostled by a dog!"

Herbert lifted his head and woofed in quiet self-defense.

Jenevan wagged the empty spoon at the Akashic Tether and spoke slowly and precisely, the way she spoke to her little son. "To accomplish this look, the food has to be prepared where it is served!"

Tamaya caught the slam, returned it, "There are no facilities in the Holy Cave."

"Ha!" Jenevan dared laugh at her superior. "You couldn't cook even if there was. You can't even boil water for tea!"

"I am Tether to Akash!" Tamaya played her rank.

Jenevan was not daunted. "Are you?" she dared ask. "Tether to Akash is supposed to cook, and have babbets like I do. Where are your babbets, Tamaya? You're no tether! You're no better than me or anyone else."

Tamaya and the men stared at Jenevan, their mouths open, disclosing partially chewed food. Pindren gaped too, his baby teeth showing. Wendolyn wailed from her cradle.

Jenevan swept the table with the berry-soaked serving spoon, knocking her own plate onto the floor. Rice and vegetables splattered. The plate cracked, but didn't break.

Now Hebert was staring at her, too. She nodded slightly, and the dog licked up the mess, chasing the cracked plate under the table with his tongue.

Drawing Room

The dinner party was shattered. Old Pindross rose from the table and made his memorized, sightless way to his drawing room. He got along fine as long as things stayed the same. "Don't block G-Pa's path," Jenevan was always saying these days. Hebert escorted him whenever he left the hut, rubbing against one thigh or the other, steering him, another of the dog's many talents.

Tamaya followed him, leaving Jenevan to clean up her mess.

Popa's drawing room was dimly lit now. It used to enjoy the bright light from an oil chandelier with seven wicks. But the blind, retired artist had no need for that now. Pindrad had taken it into his own drawing space in the couple's crowded bedroom, wedged between Pindren's crib and Wendolyn's cradle. Tamaya didn't miss the light. It meant she didn't have to see Popa's new paintings. The ones he had done since he'd gone blind.

She could tell her Popa's mood by what he painted. He painted Momama's face mostly, round and smooth and beautiful, like Tamaya remembered it. Then he would paint over it. A hideous explosion of baby parts, chubby little arms and legs jutting from her cheeks, bald heads protruding from her forehead. Or he would paint Momama's face completely over with a hideous baby face, distorted and misshapen in some way or another. Other times, he painted beautiful faces. A child or a young man or woman, like her and her brother, but even more beautiful. Perfect, in fact. Perhaps that was how he remembered seeing his children's faces. Or maybe that's how he pictured the face of the other one. The baby brother or sister who died in childbirth, taking Momama with him or her. He had painted over Momama's portrait so many times, the thick paint sagged, threatening to shed bright globs on the floor.

Tamaya scanned the dim room, vainly hoping for something new. Pindross's finished works were stacked against the wall. His older works, the ones that portrayed real people and events of the village, were preserved in the Great Hall or long buried behind his newer works; mostly that damn spiral. Two spiraling lines that crossed each other at regular intervals to form a series of cells with stripes streaking across them. The same shape, over and over. Only he swore they were all different. Tamaya used to try and find the differences, like a game. But she had grown tired of seeing the same old painting from the blind artist. Why didn't he quit? He would speak of nothing else but his stupid spirals and the unmanly subject of childbirth.

They used to have such great talks in this very room, when Tamaya was a girl. Popa would talk to her as an adult. He would meditate, and he could see the Plane, like the Akash could. He would tell her what he had seen, and she would write it down. She was learning the Akashic letters in school. Only she got to learn them. Even Popa didn't know how to read them. But he could meditate, and it would be her job to write down what the Akash said about his visits to the Plane, so it was good practice. Popa went further, though. He taught Tamaya to meditate, so she could see the Plane for herself, even though women weren't supposed to be able to. She could, but it took too much patience. Tamaya was easily bored.

Pindross sat down on his stool in front of his easel. Another spiral painting was propped there, as if he was still working on it. Tamaya cleared her throat, trying to draw his attention before he started babbling about it. "Popa?" Her oddly timid tone got the old man's attention. He turned his faded eyes toward her.

"Yes, my daughter. Even I can see you are troubled."

"Popa, I need to talk to you about why I have no babbets."

Pindross drew back in surprise. "Me? Why me? That is between you and Akira, or your Councilor, Nemaray. These are woman's affairs."

Tamaya sighed her frustration. "I have no Councilor. I deal directly with Akira. But I can't, not for this. It is not me, Popa. It is him, the Akash. He doesn't... he won't..."

Pindross sat up tall on his perch, his eyebrows drawn up in the center of his forehead. "He won't what? Surely you don't mean... As I recall, you are a very attractive woman. Has something changed?"

"Of course not, Popa!" Tamaya snapped at the insult. "It is him. He doesn't know what to do. His Momama didn't teach him, I guess, and no Popa. Do they teach the boys in school, like they teach us girls?"

Pindross snorted. "No one has to teach a man what to do. He just knows. I cannot imagine a man not knowing, much less not *wanting* to. Unless he fancies men. Some men do, you know."

"He fancies no one. Nothing. Only those books."

"You must teach him," Pindross decided.

"He won't let me teach him." Tamaya blurted. "He's not interested at all. He just wants me to read the books to him, and teach him to read. But he can't learn that, either. Do you remember the Akashic letters? When I used to write for you?"

"Yes, I never learned them, for it was forbidden. But I remember them."

"Popa?" Tamaya's eyes burned like coals. "When you first started to lose your sight, do you think you could have told one letter from another?"

Pindross answered slowly. "They were very small. Perhaps if they were larger. But eventually, they would just be smudges, like berries cooked in a porridge."

Tamaya sighed again, her sails quickly running out of air. Teaching Bazu to read was as futile as the other thing, her other duty as Tether.

"Still," her Popa concluded, "This is a matter for Akira. You must speak to her."

Conversations with Popa used to make her feel like she could do anything she set her mind to. But that Popa was gone, and this old blind one just made her feel even more hopeless. The bottom dropped out when he reached up to trace the lines of his latest spiral with his long fingers.

"You share a birthday with someone. Gibled and Sukia's babbet was born today. Tell me, did it live? Did Sukia?"

Tamaya shrugged, irritated, then remembered he couldn't see her. "I don't know, Popa."

"I thought Tether to Akash would know."

"No, Popa. Tether to Akash knows Akashic things. Not the mundane issues of women."

Pindross pointed at a detail on the painting. Tamaya wondered how he could find his way around it, but he seemed to know what he was pointing at. "The thread is broken, right here, do you see?"

Tamaya leaned over his shoulder, her arms folded, squinting at the nauseatingly familiar spiral in the dim light.

"I cannot see it, of course, but I know you can, Tamaya." Pindross prompted.

Tamaya saw the break, but she didn't care.

"So, I was wondering if the babbet and the momama survived," Pindross asked again. Tamaya could see he was receding into his dark tunnel. Her heart clenched in her chest.

"That's a matter for Akira, Popa!" she snapped. "Why don't *you* ask Akira?"

Abruptly turning ninety degrees on his stool, Pindross faced the thick painting on the easel to his left. The latest layer had given Tamaya hope when she'd entered. It was a reasonably accurate portrait of Momama, as she recalled her. Now Popa attacked it with his brush, painting quickly and savagely, covering her face again. Tamaya watched in fascinated horror as her momama's face became a baby's face. A hideous face with taut, chartreuse skin stretched across where the nose and mouth should be, begging for air with terrified eyes.

Her flesh crawled. Popa was in a terrible mood tonight! She wrenched her eyes away from the canvas and slunk out the door into the quiet living room, where her brother sat with his family. "Good night." She muttered curtly as she crossed to her old bedroom.

"That's going to be Pindren's room after tonight," Jenevan informed her.

Tamaya's Dream

Tamaya stared at the ceiling of her childhood bedroom, tracing the familiar knots in the wood with her eyes until she found herself picking at them, looking for differences, like Popa did with his spirals. She turned away violently, thrashing beneath the covers until she lay on her side facing the wall. More wood, more knots and broken spirals. She closed her eyes and tried to ignore her infant niece, wailing constantly from her crib in the master bedroom.

The baby stopped crying at last, and Tamaya finally managed to drift off to sleep. Or did she? She was in the kitchen. A woman worked there with her rolling pin. Momama's rolling pin was a heavy marble tool, worn smooth with years of daily use. "Pop, pop!" Tamaya heard the familiar sound of pomegranate seeds yielding their essential oil to the pressure of the heavy roller, the woman adding her own weight to the effort, pressing down hard on the wide handles, pushing the weighty pin across the flat tray that kept the shocked seeds from escaping. "Pay attention, Tamaya!" Momama's voice still made her snap to attention, after all these years gone.

"Momama?" Little Tamaya asked, looking up at her almost-forgotten face. The dark apparition didn't answer. She just kept working, popping the seeds and scraping them into a bowl to be mixed with the other ingredients. Now she flopped a lump of dough onto the pan and employed the rolling pin in its normal capacity, rolling the dough into a thin crust that covered the clay baking sheet.

Lalanar! Not momama, Tamaya realized with a stab of resentment. Lalanar never asked Tamaya to help, or told her she needed to learn. She just cooked and cleaned and slept in the kitchen closet. She didn't mind. She was downudara. A bit funny looking, and mentally slow. She didn't have the capacity to perform the duties of a full life, and of course, Akira would never let her marry.

Akira had failed to detect her disability at birth, or she would have ended her then. But Lalanar's flat, rounded face and droopy eyes had taught Akira what to look for. Those with the classic mongoloid look no longer survived their births. But like Tamaya had told her Popa, she knew nothing about Akira's tedious affairs. She just knew that Lalanar had taken over after Momama died in childbirth, when Tamaya was just eight. Lalanar didn't teach. She just did the work, and Tamaya didn't have to. Teaching Tamaya was Momama's job, and Momama was gone. And when she was here, Tamaya hadn't listened. Now Lalanar served another family, since Pindrad had married Jenevan.

The figure went dark again, and changed shape. "You try." It said with Momama's voice. "You'll see. It's fun. Take it," Momama's voice taunted from the grave. She extended the rolling pin down to her little girl, but it wasn't Momama's rolling pin, worn smooth with daily use as it should be, as a matter of pride. This was the rough one that Tamaya had received at her wedding. The one Popa had carved his damned spirals into. The one Tamaya had never used. "Take it." Momama said again.

Tamaya felt the old flash of irritation in her gut. No! She didn't want to! She could think of other uses for that heavy marble shaft. To bash something, like a Clubber would. Like Sugia had done, smashing four nimblies with her rolling pin to protect her children from the rash actions of her legendary Akashic husband, Yanzoo.

Yes, it would feel better to smash something than to pop little seeds or roll flaccid dough. Not her Momama. It wasn't her fault. Obedient, unquestioning, humble, Momama just did what she was supposed to do. Make babbets and care for them and support her husband so he could spend all his time painting rastas of the events and people of the village. Momama had filled her role without question, except she had failed to teach her daughter. Like Tamaya was failing to teach Bazu. *Not my fault! Not her fault!* Tamaya railed against her own thoughts. No, she didn't want to smash Momama with the rolling pin. Certainly not Popa. Her dream-self recalled her tender feelings for her popa. She painted them over quickly with savage mental brushstrokes just as Popa had obliterated Momama's face, again and again.

Who would I smash, if I could? She speculated in the freedom of her dreams. Bazu? Too easy. Not satisfying. *Not his fault, either* she realized, feeling a new sympathy for her pathetic husband. Akira! She pictured it, raising the weighty stone sculpture, swinging it down on Akira's skull, watching her wicked brain come bubbling out through her messy lavender hair. The thought did not thrill Tamaya. It didn't even satisfy her. In fact, it put her even more on edge, like she had just lost something she badly needed.

No. Not a person. There was something else that needed smashing. Something bigger. Something that surrounded her always, surrounded the whole village, palpable, invisible and inescapable.

"Take it!" the dark apparition insisted, shaking the carved rolling pin at Tamaya. This time, she didn't point it down, but straight across. Tamaya was no longer a child, but a grown woman. And the voice was no longer Momama's. It was Akira's. "Take this when you go," Akira said in a voice that rang through Tamaya's being with an authority she was helpless to question. Yet, being Tamaya, she did.

"Go where?" the disembodied young woman in the nearby kitchen asked the specter of her ruler. "To the Great Hall?" where else would she go?

"Take this in your hand when you go." A faceless Akira insisted without a mouth, her eyes pleading like the eyes of that doomed baby Pindross had painted. The old woman took Tamaya's left hand in both of hers. They were cold as death. She used them to force Tamaya's hand around the handle of the heavy marble tool. "Hold it just like this. When you go." A great wail arose all around them then, as if all the village cried out at once.

Wendolyn was crying again. Tamaya's eyes flew open, still facing the wall of the bedroom that was no longer hers. She rolled over and threw off the stiff woven grass cover. She sat up, and her eyes fell on two loosely bound volumes of parchment on a shelf. Her first writing. *Popa's old rantings. He seemed so wise then. Was he? Or was I just a child, too enthralled to realize it was all nonsense?* She got up and stuffed the books into her bag.

She just had to get through breakfast, and then Bazu and Bupple would come for her, and she could go home to the relative comfort of the Holy Cave. Then she remembered. She was supposed to go somewhere. Where would she go? Somewhere in the village, she assumed. Even Tamaya didn't question that simple fact.

Earth, Summer 2018

TV or no TV

"Patrick, I need to ask you for something," Baput asked, blinking his deep brown eyes.

"Anything, Bud!"

I want to watch the evening news with you and Belinda. Every night at 6:00."

"Well," Patrick hesitated. "OK, if Lorraine's not home, anyway. But can't you just get it off the iPlane, in your head?"

"Yes." Baput pulled his mouth to the side, his lips tight. "But I don't understand it. It just doesn't make sense! People killing children in school. People fighting because of the color of their skin. I need someone to explain it to me, like Jerry used to."

"Did he? Wow. How? I don't think I could explain it, especially now, with this president. But, why bother yourself with Earth's troubles? This world's gone crazy, Baput! And I'm sorry to say, you're never going to be a part of it. You're going home to Nauve, as soon as we find the Net."

"I am Akash. I must learn everything I can before that day comes. Then I will take all that knowledge home to Nauve, and use it to lead my people into a new era. The second thousand cycles." He straightened, suddenly finding he was taller than Patrick.

Patrick snorted. "I don't think you should use this world as an example. There's a lot of things here we're not proud of. I'm not, anyway."

"You know about otherwhere. Now that we've been here, I don't think I can keep 'otherwhere' a secret from my people. The Akash must always tell the truth."

"I hope you can handle the concept of other cultures better than we do. We're a lousy example. And what about the rest of your family. Should they watch, too?"

"I meditated on that. If Popa sees it, he will want to fight someone. The closer to the Season we get, the more he wants to fight. If there are no nimblies and bumblies, he will want to fight men, especially the ones who attacked us at the Look 'N Up."

"See, he's already got the wrong idea about people from otherwhere, thanks to those assholes."

"He will only get worse if he watches the news."

"I suppose. But what about your momama?"

"Momama would get too upset. If she saw a bunch of first-grade babbets getting shot, she would never get over it."

"And Felsic? He could take it, couldn't he?"

Baput sighed, then smiled. "Maybe better than the others. But he's so happy now. Happier than I've ever seen him, even on Nauve. He misses Elmer terribly, but he loves working on Falcon and helping Valko with the metal stuff. I don't want to burden him. What good would it do?"

Patrick nodded thoughtfully. "You're right. It should just be you, the Akash. But you've got to remember that our ways aren't always the right way. Especially now. We're going the wrong way now. Whatever you see on there, you should teach your people to do just the opposite."

Jerry's 16th Birthday

Patrick slid his cell phone into the long pocket on the leg of his painter's jeans and came down the porch steps to join the cluster of green men gathered around the Falcon. "OK, Felsic. It's time."

"The customer?" Felsic looked up from polishing the candy apple red paint with a chamois cloth, excitement in his eyes. "They will buy Falcon," Felsic asserted proudly. His face fell. "Goodbye, Falcon."

"You know what to do, right?" Patrick asked gently, his hand on the green man's shoulder.

"I go in your hut, to the phone. You call me and I talk. I'm the mechanic, and I'm not here."

Patrick patted the shoulder. "That's right."

"And we hide?" Baput asked, looking up at his Popa.

"You get the gate, Baput. Stay out of sight until they come through, then, well, you'll know what to do."

"I will?" Baput squeaked.

"You will. Go on, now." Patrick ordered.

Baput took off running down the driveway. Felsic went into the house to wait by the phone. Patrick walked toward the quarters with Valko. "Wait a few minutes, then come back over. Bring Salistar."

"But we are hiding!" Valko protested.

"You'll see," Patrick promised to the distant clang of the gate opening.

There was no motor noise, just the crunching of gravel, as Fran's Prius climbed the driveway in electric mode and rolled to a stop alongside the Falcon. Jerry tumbled out of the back passenger seat and Baput climbed out of the other side, both grinning. Fran and Elmer joined them around the shiny sedan.

Patrick handed the key to Elmer. "Check it out." Elmer climbed in and revved the engine. "Sounds tight!" he remarked over the hearty roar of the eight cylinders.

The noise drew Valko, Salistar and Belinda from the worker's quarters. Belinda squealed and ran down the trail into Aunt Fran's open arms. Salistar followed at a dignified walk, and was soon swallowed in those warm arms as well.

Meanwhile, Patrick handed his phone to Jerry. "Take this call," he instructed cryptically.

Jerry's brow furrowed as he put the phone to his ear. One ring tone, then heavy breathing. "Is this, customer?" someone said in a strange but familiar accent.

Jerry pulled the phone from his ear and looked at the display. It said 'home' and showed the number for Uncle Patrick's land line. He could still hear the voice. "You buy Falcon?" it asked. It sounded an awful lot like Felsic.

"Felsic?" Jerry asked the phone, then dashed into the house. Both families clambered in after him, jockeying for a position with a view. Felsic sat at the phone, holding it up to his ear, wearing his most triumphant grin. Above his head, balloons and crepe paper hung from the ceiling, interspersed with gold paper letters that spelled out 'Happy Birthday, Jerry'.

"Jerry!" Felsic greeted him through the phone and through the hot air of the living room. "If I knew it was for you, I would have hopped it up!"

"That's why we didn't tell you," Fran drizzled on the parade.

"But it would be easy, Francina. I could put a four-barrel carburetor on her. Add some headers, get a lot more horsepower out of her, easy."

"No thank you," Francina insisted.

"Why not?" Felsic's elation was headed for the rocks.

"He's sixteen," Patrick offered as explanation. Felsic looked just as confused and hurt as before.

"Nascar." Elmer reminded. "Remember when we watched that car race? The crashes, the fire? Those are professional drivers. Jerry's a smart kid, but he's still a kid. Kids don't always think about the consequences before they do stuff, like driving too fast in their hopped-up cars. Nope. Eight cylinders of old-fashioned Detroit muscle is more than he needs, believe me. Thank you, Felsic. Great job." He shook Felsic's hand, then embraced him roughly.

"Goodbye, Falcon." Felsic repeated, firmly planted back on Earth.

Jerry babbled excitedly. "You'll see it sometimes. I'll bring it over. You can tune it up. It's only a four-hour drive. I can come up here all by myself on weekends, once I get my license. I'm on a learner's permit now. I'd need Mom or Dad to come with me."

"Goodbye Falcon, hello Mustang." Elmer delivered the good news. "We'll go pick it up tomorrow. We'll need a trailer. It's not running at all. Might need a new head."

"Easy." Felsic predicted. "Mustang."

"One at a time, just like I promised Lorraine," Patrick added.

"But you're giving the first one away. Does she know that?" Fran asked.

"Look 'N Up Enterprises. Not her money." Patrick replied stiffly. "Now, come on out to the shop, and check out the *real* economic engine of LOE."

The acrid smell of metallic ions hung in the sun-heated August air of Patrick's workshop. It was bigger now. An alcove had been added for a blacksmith's forge. The floor was littered with lawn ornaments; effigies of birds and bees, flowers and trees, skillfully cut from sheet metal and welded to stakes. There were solar lamp holders that looked like tulips or daisies with glowing stamins.

"We've sold a half dozen of these things on the internet," Patrick told them. "They're catching on. But here's the real moneymaker." He crossed to the wall, where several four-by-four-foot panels of wrought iron leaned in four patterns, spirals, leaves, moons and stars, and a geometric matrix of triangles and diamonds. "Porch rails. They bolt together, see? Or you can put a hinge here instead, for a gate. Bolt these feet into the floorboards or set them right into the concrete for a fence around your pool. Lots of uses. They can crank out as many as you want, in whatever pattern. These are samples, for the display."

"Display?" Elmer asked.

"The home store that I do installations for, they're selling them. They've got a display. And they've got them up on their website. They take the orders and do the shipping. That's the hard part. But I thought you could take these samples, and some posters I made, and do a display at the Cow Chow. You can take orders, and we'll find a way to ship them directly to the buyer. The shipping guys showed me how to pack them, but I'm probably going to need a forklift and a bigger truck."

"Big Truck." Felsic recalled his old friend affectionately.

"Big Truck needs Felsic." Elmer declared. "I'm thinking about a new truck for the ranch. Now that I don't have to worry about Felsic being able to work on it, I can get one of them new ones with all the computers and stuff. You know, the Air Board is going to shut all those old beaters down sooner or later, at least for commercial use. I tell you what: After harvest, I'll bring Big Truck up here, all loaded with pomegranates. These guys will need at least a truckload, just to survive."

Doggie DNA

"I can drive home, right, Dad?" Jerry didn't want to leave his friends, but the idea of driving at 70 mph down Interstate 5 for three solid hours had beckoned him all night like Christmas morning calls to a kid who's already seen the new bike.

"I'll ride with you," Elmer promised over the Nauvian breakfast Salistar had prepared.

Both vehicles sagged heavily on their axles, loaded with wrought iron porch rails and lawn ornaments to display and sell at the Cow Chow, which was evolving into something quite different from the simple feed store Fran's grandparents had started back in the forties.

"One last thing," Patrick added. "Or two, really. One for each of these lovely cars. Valko?"

Valko picked up the two grates he had propped out of view. He was learning. Earth people *liked* surprises. *It must be because they don't have to fight for their lives for three days and nights every three years.*

The latest product was about as wide as a car, with legs that supported a mesh cleverly shaped like dog paw prints. Patrick opened the Falcon's passenger side and slid the grate behind the front seat. "Dog grates. Like the police have."

"Why?" Elmer asked cautiously. Suddenly, four half-grown puppies clamored around them, followed by their mother, Shastina and a beaming Francine. Salistar and Belinda trailed in after them, looking like they were entering a funeral parlor.

"In my new car?" Jerry objected.

"We're taking the boys," Francine informed her family.

"Both of them?" Elmer objected automatically.

"Well, of course, Elmer." Fran explained belatedly. "They're almost a year old. Pretty soon, they might, you know. We have Popa Brodey, so we'll keep the boys. Shastina and the girls will stay here."

"We'll have a purple dog!" Elmer objected. "Them damned inspectors will see him."

"He's champagne. That's what they call it. I looked it up. It's a thing." Fran replied. "They're just mutts, um, off-white German shepherd and yellow Lab. Here, you and Jerry take them in the Falcon. I'll take Brodey in the Prius."

"Why don't you just fix them, and keep them all here?" Elmer beseeched his brother. "They're not inspecting you guys." Hope fled from the pale hazel eyes as the other shoe dropped in Elmer's mind. "It's Lorraine, huh? She don't want all these messy dogs," he mocked.

"That's not it." Patrick corrected. Elmer was right, but that wasn't the reason. "We can't fix them."

"Well, if the vet asks about the color, you just say what Fran just said."

"It's not that either, Elmer. Don't you get it?"

"Get what?"

With a sigh, Patrick spelled out the obvious. “If we ever find a way to make the portal work, these puppies are all going to Nauve. They need people DNA. They probably need doggie DNA, too.”

Nauve, Summer

Bad puppies

"Don't let Pindren come out," Jenevan warned her momama. It wasn't necessary. Latsinda knew the drill. She had always made Jenevan and her older brother, Maylac, wait in the hut, twitching like two Earth kids on Christmas, whenever she went to check for new puppies. Later, she started taking Maylac with her, leaving Jenevan behind with Popa trying to control her tantrum.

Maylar, who could stop a stampeding bull ganeesh with a single shouted word, had failed to contain the three-year-old girl. She had escaped and headed straight for the stalls at the back of the Great Hall.

The large doors, wide enough for two ganeesh to pass each other, stood open as usual. She heard her momama's voice, speaking to her brother in hushed tones. "Go ahead, Son. You have to. It is a part of life. It's time you learned." Her voice was tender, but with a harshness Jenevan had never heard before.

"Sit." Back in the present, Jeneven told Hebert to stay behind, too. He didn't need to see his puppies yet. She wondered what he would do if he was with her. Would he try to stop her? Like she had tried to stop Maylac that day?

She had hidden behind a bale of hay and watched with wide, innocent eyes as her big brother, half a man at eight years old, carried two helpless, newborn puppies across the stall to a trough of soiled ganeesh water. *Is he going to wash them?* she'd wondered. One in each hand, he lowered them slowly into the water, breaking through its scummy surface where bits of hay floated. "Go on, that extra-stern Momama voice urged. Maylac plunged his hands into the trough. He didn't let go of the puppies. He held them too long. *Doesn't he know they need air? He's supposed to be the Animal Keeper!*

She'd sought her most reliable refuge. "Momama!" she had cried, rushing at her much bigger brother. Kneeling at the trough, he was about her height, and his hands were occupied. She made contact and would have bowled him over if Momama hadn't grabbed her arm.

"Momama! He's killing them!" she wailed as Momama hauled her away, turning her back on the boy and his dastardly deed. Then she spanked, not the puppy-murdering Maylac, but her, Jenevan, already becoming known as the Dog Girl, who had tried to save them.

She understood now. It didn't always happen, but she had come to expect it. She heard the pups squeaking their little grunts. She opened the stall where Shanayla lay and looked into her eyes. *Sad, but not devastated,* Jenevan read in her way that made her the Dog Woman. She knelt, and Shanayla rolled over, showing her breasts. Furry nuggets dropped from them one by one, four of them. They rolled over and paddled off blindly in four different directions. Those were OK. It was the other one. The one that did not nurse or wander, but lay still, just breathing.

Shanayla hadn't moved it away from the lair. That was a good sign. Not contagious. Since that first dramatic time, her momama had taught her all about this ugly part of life, hers unofficially until there was a real apprentice again.

She picked up the still one. She looked closer, then drew back. Part of his little head was missing. There was fur, but no eye or ear on that side, and a big dent in his skull where it should all be. He did not respond to her touch, he just lay there limply, breathing heavily. She sighed. She turned her gaze up to the sturdy roof of the Great Hall, raised the puppy above her head and thanked Kakeeche silently. *Just one, and four healthy, praise Kakeeche! Take this puppy to the stars.* This last was her secret. It was probably against some rule to think puppies could go to the stars, but what difference if nobody knew? She wanted to pass the thought to her children, but she had refrained, so far, out of fear.

She carried the still puppy to the trough. She could feel Shanyla's eyes on her back. Millicent, the ganeesha, eyed her, too. "Of course I'll change the water after," she promised, "if I'm not attacked by a three-year-old." It was an old routine, a continued apology for that time long ago when she had made her momama forget to change the water. She thought of Pindren, and it hit her like a rampaging ganeesh: *That exact thing could actually happen this time!* She peeked behind the hay bales, where she had hidden as a nosy child. No Pindren.

She sighed, relieved, and a bit disappointed. Her son didn't share her talent. He played with the dogs alright, like any toddler, but he didn't show signs of the Touch. No matter. He was to be his Popa's apprentice, a rasta-maker. The third year's drawings were nonsense to her, as bad as his blind G-Pa's, but Pindrad swore he already showed a talent for contrast and composition, whatever that meant. Jenevan would have to have another boy, to make an apprentice for her popa.

She held the limp puppy in one cupped hand, thumb and forefinger locked around its tiny waist. She plunged it slowly through that tense, littered surface. No one tried to save him. He didn't even try to save himself. He struggled just a bit, with a weak resignation that made her heart shiver. Like when she was eight, and Heffala had her twins right on Passascenday.

The puppy wasn't breathing anymore. It lay limp in her hand as she grabbed a shovel and headed out the back door. She walked the well-worn trail downriver to the burial pits that were dug into the mound of soft, boggy soil overlooking the rice paddies. Trodden by the entire village each Passascenday, and by numerous unfortunate families during each cycle, the currently deserted path required no concentration. Her mind wandered back to those elephant twins.

Dambu had come first. A healthy baby boy. Right on Passascenday, while Akira was conducting the wedding ceremonies. Her family was missing everything because Heffala was having her babbet, the first ganeesh born in seven cycles, and on such an auspicious, if inconvenient, day.

"I must tell the Akash!" Popa had babbled, as excited as she'd ever seen him. "This is a most fortunate sign!" She remembered his face, so happy, and Momama's, how it changed from what Jeneven now knew was indulgence, into horror. She pointed at Heffala's swollen end. Two trunks dangled there, wrestling each other like worms.

"Three babbets!" her maniacal Popa continued his rave.

"She can't bear three!" her Momama cried, daring to place her hand gently on the elephant's tender thigh. "Not two at once, certainly."

The dual trunks flopped wildly, as if searching for something. They found Momama and wrapped around her, pulling. She screamed. Maylac rushed to her, tried to pry the trucks off of her. Popa finally joined him, taking Momama's other side. Jenevan hated remembering what she had done, stood there screaming like the helpless little girl she was. Then something changed and Momama pulled away from the ganeesh, still attached. A single babbet followed her, flowing smoothly from his horrified Momama and plopping on the floor. One ganeesh, two trunks.

Popa was beside himself then. "Twins! And two trunks on one ganeesh! On Passascenday! Aye, Kakeeche has brought good fortune on us all this cycle! Such an auspicious sign! I must get the Akash at once."

"But Popa!" Momama used to call Popa that, too, on occasions like this. "Twins are bad luck. Akira hates twins. And two trunks, Maylar, that is hibudara! Very bad luck." Momama's eyes swept the stalls with a fear Jenevan had never seen. It was different from her fear of the nimblies and bumblies, or the pragmatic respect for the size and power of the animals they handled. It was like the fear of something that wasn't real, like the Calamunga, a boogey man.

Popa turned on Momama in a new way, another new thing. "It is the Akash who interprets the signs, not Akira. This is not mere woman's business. After losing the Akashic apprentice, the people need this hope. The future rests on the meaning of this sign. I say it is a blessing!" he insisted in a savage hiss, glaring at his son and daughter, one at a time. He turned to Momama last, hissed the loudest. "I will bring the Akash, and you, Woman, will keep your superstitions to yourself!"

Neither she nor her brother had ever heard such an exchange from their usually jovial, loving parents. They flanked their Momama on either side as she attended to the newborns. The first one was already up on his feet. At Momama's nod, Maylac guided him with a gentle nudge toward Heffala's waiting breast.

Despite the doubled breathing apparatus, the second one seemed unable to get air. Momama handed a trunk to Maylac and stretched the other out straight. The boy did the same, carefully following her every move. She peered into the end of her trunk. Maylac peered into his, held it up to his cheek and shook his head. The babbet's sides quit heaving and he ceased his futile effort, just as the Akash arrived, followed by most of the village.

Popa rushed to where the doomed baby lay, right past Dambu, the first healthy ganeesh born in 21 years. He knelt and gathered the limp animal up in his arms. He hissed at Momama again, "What have you done?" he accused.

"Nothing. He couldn't breathe." She told him the truth.

The Akash poked Popa with his fancy longstick, stabbing the back of his shoulder while he knelt with the poor thing in his arms. The memory of that cold, warbling voice chilled Jenevan to this day. "What is this, you Animal Keeper?" He had sneered Popa's venerated title. Without a second look at either elephant, he broke into a rant that Jenevan, even as an eight-year-old, had found personal and irrelevant.

"I should be ascending my grandson to Akash today, yet I have buried him, and now I must ascend a bunch of low-born warriors and tenders like you, and you dare to interrupt the Ascension Ceremony to show me a dead hibudara animal?"

Already kneeling, Popa seemed to cower before the Akash, but at last he raised his head, and Jenevan had never seen tears run so freely down Popa's face before. "But my Akash, good or bad, it must be a sign. Ganeesh is Sacred. The Old Ones say we must always listen to ganeesh, for they are wise beyond our knowing."

"Yes, yes, of course." The old man snapped. "They should learn to talk, then." He snorted a lonely laugh at his own joke and finally withdrew his longstick from Popa's back. "But seriously, Maylar, even you should know. Such things are woman's matters, for Akira."

Jenevan had sought the mystical old woman then, but didn't see her anywhere in the crowd. Nemaray, the oldest unmarriageable and councilor to the high families, was there, apparently in her stead. Akira's apprentice, Edijay, was at her side, then just a pudgy six-year-old who nodded at everything Akira, or her proxy, said.

"Akira deals with humans," Nemaray snapped. Edijay nodded. "Not animals" Edijay shook her head. "You Animal Keepers take care of the animals, and leave Akira and Akash to take care of the people," she ordered. Edijay nodded one more emphatic time.

Heffala's mate, Mangu, carried the dead babbet off to the ganeesh's secret graveyard. Even Maylar didn't know where it was. They hadn't done him the honor of showing him yet, even to this day. And to this day, Popa had never held his head quite as high or laughed quite as hard, and there was something different between him and Momama. But it was hard to tell when all that happened. Momama had been right, and Popa wrong. The auspicious birth had turned out to be most inauspicious indeed, ushering in the worst cycle in the long history of the Animal Keeper's line.

Jenevan chose the last season's pit, the grave of six warriors and those two young women who had foolishly followed Millicent, the ganeesha, into battle. It was easy to dig there, and the tiny hole needed for the one little puppy wouldn't be noticed, in the rare event someone visited. Planting the pup in the mass grave somehow seemed less invasive than imposing it on an individual who had died during the cycle and occupied their own slim plot. Her eyes strayed involuntarily to one such plot, where her brother's crushed remains had been lying for these past two and a half cycles.

When the youngest ganeesha, Delena, broke through the edge of the river bank and fell to the hard rocks below, she had writhed senselessly, grinding Momama's leg into a mush that Rashetta had amputated. They say Momama had screamed like nothing they had ever heard. She screamed from the pain of her leg, and that much deeper pain that no woman should ever have to endure. Yet, so many did that it was assumed and expected. Whether consumed in the trenches by bumblies or crushed beneath a flailing ganeesh, every Momama in the village would lose at least one child, sooner or later.

The ganeesha had screamed, too. Delena had been Maylac's favorite, and she had dearly loved the Apprentice Keeper in return. Perhaps that is why she flailed so wildly, so frantic to get up. Her desperate love took Momama's leg, and crushed Maylac's chest, driving shattered ribs into his fourteen-year-old heart.

Jenevan tamped the small area of disturbed ground with the flat side of the stone shovel. Still lost in memory, she gathered her things and wandered back toward the village on the too-familiar trail. She could never separate the events of that fateful cycle. She had to play them through to the bitter end, the next Nimbly-Bumbly Season, when she was eleven and the curse struck once more.

That was when Two-Trunks' twin brother, Dambu, followed his momama, Heffala, onto the battlefield wearing only his vulnerable babbet skin, not yet impenetrable to the teeth and claws of the bumblies that circled above him. The Akash's granddaughter, equally unprotected, jumped on the young ganeesh's back, trying to stop him. She was consumed along with him. *All because Tamaya, my stuck-up sister-in-law, opened the pen without knowing or caring enough to make sure it was latched behind her,* Jenevan recalled bitterly.

She was surprised to see she was almost back to the Great Hall. *Change the ganeesh water,* she reminded herself, circling back to that original memory: when she had disrupted her momama's day and her own universe. In the fourteen years since then, she had seen all kinds; missing limbs, twins stuck together, babbets like this one whose minds just didn't seem to work, some with less obvious problems, some just plain, well, horrible. *No wonder Momama didn't want me to see. Now I understand.*

But why? People aren't born with missing parts, messed up faces... Pindross's paintings flashed before her eyes. She kicked a pinecone on the trail, kicking the image away with it. *Akira keeps the lines apart*, she recited in her head as she entered the stalls in the back of the Great Hall.

She stared into the dark water of the trough. It was far too heavy for her to empty. She would have to bucket the contaminated water outside to the family's garden, about five trips, then five more to the river and back with fresh water. She didn't ask for help. She could have asked Popa, but she felt this was her penance for some involuntary sin, past or present. Besides, she needed time to think.

Akira keeps the lines apart, she recited again. *But Akira doesn't do animals, only people. Do animals have lines?* she wondered suddenly. The fact that she hadn't thought of it before surprised her even more than the thought itself. The long, repetitive walks gave her plenty of time to do the math. It even occurred to her at one point that carrying the puppies to the river would be easier than changing the water, but something told her it was wrong. *Perhaps just one bucket of water, instead of the whole trough? But this is how Momama taught me.*

The math was inescapably simple. The solution popped up of its own accord, despite her attempts to distract herself. *If animals have lines, the ganeesh have only one. Mangu and Heffala are Momama and Popa to the sisters, Millicent and Delena, and the brothers Mandu and Manmoot. No wonder they don't...* Popa's mantra came to her unbidden. She spoke it aloud as she dipped the pail into the sluggish river. "Always listen to ganeesh, for they are wise beyond our knowing."

As she dumped the last bucket into the clean trough, the wrinkled old momama, Heffala, stepped up for a drink.

"What happens when you and Mangu get too old to make babbets?" Jeneven asked the aging ganeesha.

Fight

It was sweltering in the Death Tunnel. Bupple's coarse woven tunic and pants were drenched with sweat. Tamaya wore airy, loose-woven shorts and a sleeveless top. Bupple had already dragged the heavy copper pipes to the Rock. Now he grappled with the stationary bicycle while Tamaya coiled the copper wire that trailed from it. Bazu stood in front of the Rock, holding the plan sheet up close to his nose and squinting at the lines. His hands were shaking. He cursed his lack of control. This was so important! He shook harder, brought the plans even closer to his face. He could see nothing else.

Hebert entered the cave silently with their breakfast. He padded up to the Akash and waited, blinking his soft brown eyes. Bazu ignored him. Hebert thrust his pointy snout under the plan sheet in front of the Akash's face and pushed up, crinkling the delicate papers.

"Arrrggghhh!" Bazu dropped the plans on the dog's head, screaming with startled frustration. The bicycle clattered to the floor behind the death door. Hebert jumped back, shaking the plans off. Bazu lunged at him, keening shrilly.

Bupple rushed from the tunnel, ready to protect the Akash, Tamaya at his heels.

"What are you doing? That's our breakfast!" Tamaya yelled as Hebert spun around toward the doorway. A bottle of pomegranate oil squeezed out of its compartment and cracked open on the floor. The crash sent Hebert bolting for the door, paws slipping on the oily rock floor. He scrambled down the stairs, the harness sliding off his back, clay food packs shattering one by one on the stone steps. Tamaya stood on the porch, yelling down at the dog until he reached the ground. He kept going without looking back.

Tamaya whirled her anger at her husband. Bupple retreated to the safety of the Death Tunnel.

Hebert arrived at Pindrad's hut, panting in hysterical squeaks. The pack was in shambles, hanging from his side with only one ration box still clinging to its purchase, unopened and uneaten.

"Pindrad!" Jenevan cried.

Pindrad wiped his paintbrush and came running. His tether rarely sounded so anxious. Was something wrong with the kids? Popa? He found the panting dog with the disheveled pack.

"Something is wrong." Jenevan was sure. "Something scared him. There's something wrong at the Holy Cave. The Akash! Tamaya!" Jenevan's anxiety built as she spoke, growing from a silly concern about the dog's outfit to near-panic about his Akash and his Tether.

"I'll get Rakta," the former Guard of Akash promised, and hurried to the practice field.

He found the War Chief working with a team of first and second-cycle warriors, the top picks of each specialty; Maffoon the darter, Rodan the clubber, Dubley, famous for the quickness and accuracy of his spear, Canam the new archer, and the young upstart Samard, known for his wit, which was even quicker than his longstick. Bupple's son, Buppan, a highly respected longstick man in his own right, was their coach.

"War Chief?" Pindrad asked timidly, feeling a bit silly. "It might be nothing, but the dog that brings the food to the Holy Cave came back all upset, and the food packs had fallen off, as if there was a scuffle�"

"What about Bupple?" was the War Chief's first question.

"I don't know." Pindrad replied.

"Come on, men." Buppan summoned his team, jumping at the chance to rescue his popa.

The young warriors fell into formation and followed their leaders to the Holy Cave, speculating as they marched.

"It's probably just a gapta," Dubley guessed, easily picturing his Akash screaming like a woman about a rat.

"Or a dracna," Maffoon chucked, imagining a mouse.

"Maybe he saw his own shadow, and finally got up the courage to fight it," Samard quipped.

Rakta shushed them as they approached the bluff with the large hole high above their heads. They heard a thump, then a clatter, like something breaking, followed by the blood curdling shriek of a woman. Then there was a horrible crash that resonated like a landslide of large boulders.

Led by Rakta, the troops crept along the cave wall so they couldn't be seen from the cave. They froze in their tracks at a second piercing scream.

"Another woman? Who?" Rakta wondered in a whisper. "What woman attacks Tamaya?"

Young Samard had the answer. "No woman. That's The Tiny Akash, right, guys?"

The other young soldiers nodded their certain agreement. "That's what he does at the practice field whenever he misses."

"We've heard it all our lives, every day, growing up. That's Bazu, our Tiny Akash."

"Silence!" Rakta commanded in his battle whisper.

They slithered up the long, narrow staircase in a single line, staying low so as not to be seen by whatever monster had invaded the holy space.

When he reached the top, Rakta stood, and now he could see inside the cave. His fear melted in the heat of his anger, and something else. The floor was littered with broken pottery, and those damned pipes. The Akash was messing with the weapon!

Tamaya stood like a statue, staring across the Holy Rock at the Akash. The side of her face was drawn back in a snarl that made sharp lines across her cheek. Rakta lowered his eyes to her tight belly, heaving in and out in angry breaths. She picked up a cracked pomegranate oil vessel from the floor and raised it above her head. The dark contents ran down the inside of her arm, tracing her taught muscles as she drew the round clay vessel back, like a spearman ready to thrust, one foot in front of the other, her bare calves bulging roundly.

She hurled the oily clay missile forward with all her weight, every muscle in perfect time, right at the Akash's head. Bupple's longstick jutted swiftly from behind the Death Door just in time to save the holy skull.

The young warriors piled into the cave, pointing and hooting, drooling like dogs at the Akash's humiliation, and at his tether. The Akashic battle dissolved into a pool of embarrassment. Rakta just stood at the entrance and stared helplessly at the Akashic Tether. Sweat gleamed on her taut, bare skin as she turned to face him, a wild mixture of anger, pride and humor playing inseparably across her lips.

"Come on, Men," Rakta ordered. He spun on his heels and dashed down the stairs.

Kaysee

Trillella watched quietly as the boy rubbed her momama's shoulders and arms gently, but with a directed firmness. Trill had never seen anyone get or give a massage before. She had not seen such kindness from a male since Popa. Shaking off the comforting sadness the thought of Popa brought, she asked, "How do you know how to do that?"

"It just comes to me. Maybe it's the Plane, I don't know," Kaysee answered, running his fingertips firmly down each side of Peratha's spine. She moaned calmly, not like the moans of pain Trillella had come to know. Momama was sick all the time now. Rodan beat her almost every day, and she drank a lot of the wine Trillella made for him.

First, she had seemed helpful. "I will taste it first," she'd say, "so we know it's good enough for Rodan." Trill knew her momama's concern was not out of love or respect, but abject fear. Peratha tried the wine. She tried it often. Now, she was always drunk. Rodan beat her even more. Trillella did the cooking and the cleaning and made twice as much wine.

Covering Peratha with a sheet of soft woven grass, Kaysee rose to his feet and looked down at Trillella. She stared back unblinking like a zebkin caught raiding the garden. He extended his hand and those deer-like eyes followed it. She grasped it tentatively. Her hand was cold, and it shook. She rose awkwardly, avoiding his eyes. He knew she had heard that the Apprentice Orchard Keeper was crazy. He dropped her hand.

"Why did Aoti send you?" she asked in a whisper choked with impossible hope.

"To help her friend, your momama. But you mustn't tell anyone. Akira doesn't know." He looked toward the back door. "There are herbs right out there in your garden that can help her. You can make her a tea, and some you can moisten and place right on the wounds, the swollen places. Come. I'll show you." He almost reached for her hand again, but quickly withdrew.

He let Trillella lead the way out the back door to the garden. He could see the orchard from there, and the trail he had left through the dry grass. "Of course, the best thing for your momama would be to get out of this situation."

Trillella whirled on him. The zebkin look was gone, replaced with the frustrated savagery of a trapped bumbly. The look cracked Kaysee's heart in two, right down the middle. *What an unthinking idiot I am!* He scolded himself silently.

"I'm sorry. How can I tell you how to get out of your situation when I don't know how to get out of my own?" He picked a showy white flower on a tall stalk. "This is for headaches, or any kind of swelling. Pretty, isn't it?" he handed her the flower gallantly. "Make her a tea, with water, not wine."

Trillella took the flower without looking at it and asked, "What situation?" She knew Kaysee like she knew everyone in the village, by name, family and position. He was fifteen now, almost a man, she realized, and something unfamiliar quivered deep inside her. Next Passascenday he would marry his betrothed, Galena. The unknown thing inside filled her belly and started writhing painfully toward her heart.

And he would ascend to Tender of the Orchard, if he lived. Even in Trillella's most private thoughts she tagged all Passascenday hopes with the customary caveat, like all the people did. And, like all the people, by the tender age of eleven, she already knew why. But, what 'situation' did the Tender's Apprentice, soon to ascend to his popa's relatively cushy position, wish to escape from?

Kaysee looked a little embarrassed. "I must say it is not as dire as yours, but I, too, am not allowed to live the life I want. It's like you and your wine, remember?"

Of course she remembered. *But, he remembered, too! A boy was paying attention,* she realized, first elated, then mortified. *He remembers what Rakta said, how all the women hissed at me...*

"You were good at it." Kaysee went on, breaking into her gloom. "You liked doing it, too, didn't you?"

Trillella barely nodded.

"It made you proud." Kaysee made it sound like a good thing.

"My Popa taught me!" she replied in that defensive tone she used now whenever she spoke of Felsic.

Kaysee went on, "You did it well. All the men said so. It was important. But they wouldn't let you! Well, see, I'm the same way."

"You're a boy." Trill stated flatly.

"Yes, but I still can't do what I want to do."

"What do you want to do?" Trill asked, raising her eyes, and the flower, just a little.

He bent toward her, tried to pick up those lowered eyes with his own. "This. What I'm doing now, here, with you."

Trill met his eyes slowly, not sure what she was anticipating that thrilled her so, that made that new thing inside quiver and expand, creeping now from her heart into her throat. Whatever it was, it didn't happen. She just hung there, breathless, while he went on.

"I call it 'healing'. It just comes to me. Where to rub, what herbs to use. I don't know how I know, or why, but it works. I've seen it many times. I've helped people!"

"Shavarandu." Trill muttered coldly when she found her voice. "Don't use Shavarandu on my momama. She hates it."

"Why?"

"It made my popa disappear," she replied in a barely audible squeak.

Kaysee wanted to take her hand again, but she had turned so cold! "It's not like that." He tried to explain. "No weapon, no shooting rays, no spooky actions at a distance. It's just the way our bodies work. It's like your wine. Is that Shavarandu?"

"No!" Trill snapped, folding her arms without dropping the flower.

"You put the ingredients in the vessel and let it work. Things happen. If the balance is right the wine is good, yes?"

"Yes." Trill responded without looking at him, arms still folded.

"Did you ever make a bad batch?"

"No," Trill answered too quickly. "Well once. The first time. It was desperation wine, that first season..." she fought for control. "I couldn't remember if Popa said one handful of dregs for every handful of the under-ripe, or was it two? I couldn't remember, so I used the higher amount."

"See?" Kaysee agreed. "Out of balance."

"It sure was!" Trillella giggled, then cut it short. She felt giddy, like when Popa used to make her giggle until she couldn't stop. But this was different.

Kaysee droned on, giving her a chance to recover. "It's the same with the body. You put good things in. Kip juice, rice, beans, oil, maybe a little wine, but not too much. Remember. Balance!" He stretched his lanky but muscular arms out wide, almost like he was trying to grab Trillella, to hug her. She backed away. He brought his arms into his chest, seemingly empty, and inhaled deeply, then spoke without exhaling. "This invisible stuff all around us that we must�" He exhaled loudly. "We take it in and let it out. The red liquid that squirts from our wounds flows through our bodies like the river, carrying the things we eat, and breathe, all through our bodies to keep us alive.

"We're not just vessels to carry water around, you know. Any more than your wine vessel is a simple juice container. What comes out is different than what goes in. Same with our bodies. We eat food, drink water. What comes out?"

"Bee and boo," was Trill's simple answer.

"Why? Because our bodies change it, use it, turn it into life! But it must be in balance. Ever have a tummy ache?"

"Yes," she answered, finally lifting her head again. "Too many zazu berries."

"Out of balance. I know how to fix it. I can help people. But I cannot. I am to be the Tender of the Orchard."

"Can't you do both? Seems to me you'd have time..." Trillella meant no insult, but everyone thought the Tender job involved a lot of sitting around watching the kips grow.

"They say I cannot. I am of the Gardener Line. I would have to be in the Akashic Line to do something like that. So, they won't let me, even though it would be good for the people."

Trill struggled to keep up as the strange boy rambled on. "Anyone can be a tender. Everyone knows how. You women tend the vegetable gardens. That takes more work and skill than tending the orchard."

Trill cocked her head. Men never noticed women's work and gave credit, not even Popa. This boy was so strange!

"All the men know how to tend the orchard. But they only help during pruning or harvest, planting and cutting down. The day-to-day tending, everyone knows how, but only we Tenders do it. The rest of the men are all doing their crafts, practicing their special skills, making pots, drawing rasta, wielding the longstick." He mocked a longstick stab with an empty hand. "My only special skill is supposed to be pulling weeds and picking bugs off of leaves. Anyone can do that."

Trillella gazed toward the peaceful orchard, deep in thought, imagining. "It's kind of the same for the warriors, when you think about it."

"How? Kaysee drew back in disbelief.

"All the men fight during the Season. But the warriors, the longstick men, the darters, the clubbers," she spat that last, brutal battle position. "That's all they do all day long is practice with their weapons. I wouldn't think bashing a dumb animal over the head with a club would take so much practice. Rodan is down there on the playing field all day, every day, thank Kakeeche. I pack him battle rations and plenty of wine. We have about two hours left..." Her face flushed with a dread that completed the previous tear in the young man's heart, leaving it completely asunder.

"He throws them too, you know. He's quite good, actually." Kaysee blurted awkwardly, after a choking pause. Why? Was he defending the brute? His mind had fled back to the practice fields of his early education, where all the boys learned the basic fighting skills needed to do their fair share of killing during the Season, even those that would go on to more peaceful professions. "He throws them at the nimblies and bumblies, sometimes. He has smaller ones for throwing and larger, heavier ones for bashing. Hasn't he shown you?"

Trillella was slouching and looking down again. Her arms didn't fold, but hung down loosely, the flower dangling tentatively. "Why would he show me?" she mumbled, not caring, not wanting to talk about Rodan. Yet, Kaysee went on.

"His great-great G-Pa tried tying a tether of his own long hair to the throwing clubs, so he could get them back without leaving the trench. With all the things flying through the air in battle, arrows, darts, stones, longsticks poking up, it was a mess! The clubs fell on the men in the trenches more than they hit the beasts. So, Rodan has to remember where he throws them, and retrieve them during The Lull, hoping a half-dead nimbly doesn't jump up and poke him."

"I hope one does," Trillella whispered. She turned and stepped away, taking with her the most intelligent conversation Kaysee had ever had. *And I took it over with battle stories, like some ignorant warrior boy! Like her husband!* Not *her husband,* he remembered. *Her next-popa.*

Trillella straightened, turned back toward him. A

Shoving Rodan out of the conversation, she completed her thought. "But when the battle comes, all the men fight, just like all the men help with the harvest."

Kaysee nodded. Despite his self-admonition, the battle stories still came bubbling out, as if a young man were a kiko bird, and battle stories were his plumage. "You're right. But they practice all the time, where others don't. So, they stand out in battle. They perform great feats and save lives with their skills. And they tell their stories." He rolled his eyes. "No one wants to hear of the Tender who pulled the weed from between the toes of the cycle-young kip tree, thus saving her from being buried in its shadow and starved by its greedy roots!"

"You're like a girl, too, you know," Trillella suddenly declared, even after all that battle talk. The statement might have earned a lethal blow from Rodan. Even Popa would object to it, but he would never hit.

"No!" Kaysee protested instinctively, but he did not raise his hand or even his lip.

Trillella hurried to explain before the stunned man decided to be insulted. "All the girls are trained the same way, for the same job. Even Tether to Akash, except she learns to read and write in Old Akashic, and she does the oil, like I was going to do the wine..." she shivered at the memory, or was it at the thought of the wine she still made even though it was killing her momama and turning Rodan into an even worse horror than he was naturally.

She focused on Star's more fortunate example. "My Aunt, she made the oil. Azuray's is not as good. It spoils before next harvest."

Kaysee's wide brow furrowed. "I know. I'm worried. The oil is vital. Do you know why?" He pulled a dried pomegranate seed out of a tight little pocket in his tunic and placed it in her palm, gripping her fingers lightly. "This seed contains the oil of life! That tiny thing will grow into a great-grandmother pomegranate tree with many branches loaded with thousands of seeds just like that one. How? What is it inside there that can fill a kip tree with life, bearing even more seeds and more life, on into forever?"

He looked down into her wondering brown eyes. "The same thing that feeds sweet Trillella." All she could see was his round, ivy-colored face framed in lush black hair and etched beyond his tender years. He stepped back again, then knelt. She followed, dropping smoothly to the ground in front of him.

"But the seed is not all there is to the tree, is it?" he asked rhetorically, placing the seed on the small patch of ground between their knees. "I can't just put this seed down here on the ground and expect a tree to grow, now can I?"

"No," Trill replied, staring at the seed on the ground. "You have to give it water."

"Yes," Kaysee chuckled. "See? Anyone can be a Tender. OK, I give it water. Is it a water sack like your wine still, like your belly?" He reached across the narrow gap to squeeze her belly playfully. She pulled away without wanting to, then wished she hadn't.

He dropped the wayward hand and went on with his lecture. "No. Something happens inside that changes things. Your juice turns to wine, the seed turns into a tree, Trillella turns into a woman..." Their eyes met, naked and unabashed for the first time, and another impossible dream was born.

Earth, Harvest 2018

Sleeping Rock

"It's almost harvest time. What are you guys gonna do? Do you need help?" Patrick's image buffered a bit, then stabilized.

"You mean the guys? We can't chance it." Elmer replied, his forehead leaning into the camera. "Those a-holes from town will be here looking for them any day now. Sheriff Dave won't even tell us when. Just, 'they're coming.'"

"It's OK. I got some guys from school to help after school and on weekends." Jerry offered from over Elmer's right shoulder.

Elmer snorted. "Yeah, after school. It'll be so late, I'll have to leave the boxes full overnight, take them to the docks in the morning. I hate doing that. Never had to, before. When we had the guys, we'd have the truck full by just after noon every day." Elmer's voice pitched into a whine. "But it's OK. We'll make it. Don't you bring them down here! It's too dangerous. Maybe next year those guys will get over themselves and move on."

Patrick felt a clench in his stomach. He knew Elmer shared it. "You sound stressed there, Bro. Have you guys been using the Rock? You know, hammer it and lay on it. It's great therapy."

"We don't go out there anymore," Elmer said sternly, looking at Jerry.

"Why not?" Patrick wondered.

"The Curse," Jerry answered with a shrug, as if it were obvious.

"That pathogen in the queen's slime?" Patrick recalled. "That died with the queen, and, um, G-pa."

"Are you sure?" Francine's anxious face took over the screen.

Patrick shrugged helplessly.

Jerry squirmed with guilt. "I used to check on it sometimes. Just the Rock, Mom. I didn't go anywhere near that pile with the grout on it. I didn't ring the Rock either. I wanted to see how long it would keep buzzing on its own after First Pomegranate Day."

"Jerry! I told you to say away—" Francine scolded.

Patrick interrupted, excited. "Did it keep ringing? For how long?"

"About six months. I could hear it at first. Then, a couple of months later, I had to touch it to feel it. About three months in, I had to lay on it to feel it. Then, I needed my tuning fork to detect it. The last time, in April, I couldn't even feel it with that."

"Interesting." Patrick whispered.

"Not really," Jerry disagreed glumly. "It's dead. I don't go out there anymore. I've got school. Now that the Nauvians are gone, I can do after school stuff, like Science Club."

"Yeah!" Patrick smiled, fondly remembering the high school club his mom, the Science teacher, had founded, mostly for him.

"And I've gotta help on the farm now, too. I don't even go to the Horizontal Tree anymore. I guess I'm growing up."

Patrick disappeared from the screen, as quickly and completely as the Akashic family had disappeared from the Holy Cave on Nauve. That uncanny event didn't faze the Earth people a bit, but something did. Elmer's jaw worked silently in an empty mouth, chewing on something deep inside.

"What is it, Dear?" empathic Fran asked.

"They seen us coming out of there that day."

"Out of where?" For Francine, RID's attack on the Look 'N Up was a chaotic jumble of shock, anger, fear and an overwhelming need to protect Salistar. Elmer and the other men had showed up just on time, but Francine had forgotten where they had come from and what they had been doing.

"The Rock, Fran. There's all them tire tracks leading right to it. They know we were down there doin' something when they got here, right at the peak of harvest time. They seen the platform and all them hoses and cables going into the cave. They're gonna want to go down there."

"We can't let them see the Rock!" Jerry was on his feet, pacing.

"Why not?" Francine asked.

"It's a key to a whole other world, Mom. What if they figure out what it is and how it works? What if they invade Nauve?"

Elmer choked back a laugh. It wasn't funny, once the thought fully landed. "Military assault weapons against sticks and rocks?" Now Elmer was on his feet, too. "They'd be wiped out!" he joined Jerry, a second agitated electron orbiting the living room. "We have to hide it."

"Harvest time, and we're pruning!" Elmer griped as the chainsaw sputtered to rest. Francine and Jerry pulled the long, forked branch from one of the oldest trees and piled it on the trailer behind the four-wheeler. "We can't take any more pom wood. We're losing product. Let's go down to the river and find some willows that need cutting."

Jerry drove. Francine and Elmer rode in the trailer, keeping the bristly load in place, thorns threatening their gloved hands and heavy canvas jackets. They followed the well-worn tracks through the grass, past the old rock sauna where the Akash of Nauve had meditated until he had stumbled on a bizarre way to kill the nimblies and bumblies that also turned him into the crystalline snake that lay under that pile of cave rocks at the base of the vine-covered cliff on their right.

Jerry pulled the four-wheeler to a stop alongside the half-sphere that stuck out of the alluvium, glowing dully in the late afternoon sun.

Jerry and Fran began pulling the long, leafy branches from the trailer up onto the Holy Rock. Elmer headed down to the river with his saw and a machete in search of dense, leafy willows.

The tangled pile of brush rose before the sinking afternoon sun, spreading its shadow further and further across the rocky river terrace. Far beyond the four-by-four-foot size limit, its ten-foot diameter covered the rock without a trace.

Elmer stood back, aching legs spread, gloved hands on his hips. "There it is," he declared. "The Look 'N Up burn pile. Nothing to see here. They can come on down here all they want, as long as they don't bring the Fire Marshall."

Inspection

When the pomegranates ripened, Jerry was in school, along with the rest of the painfully part-time help. The six kids he brought home that afternoon worked OK, but they picked *all* the pomegranates, ripe and under-ripe all the same. The Nauvians would have left the under-ripes for later. They could tell instantly, without even touching them. And they would always pile them *so* carefully in the boxes.

These kids were only human. Each day, they'd strip and dump, strip and dump for about an hour. Then they'd start yacking, especially yesterday when a girl had joined them. She worked real hard, but the boys spent the whole time showing off, competing, preening and strutting.

Now it was Friday morning, and Elmer had just returned from bringing a load to the docks, after they'd sat all night. He headed into the house for a second breakfast, after dashing out the door that morning with just a muffin, in a rush to get those poor poms to the docks.

Fran greeted him with a hug and a cup of coffee, then started some sausage and eggs. "Were you first?" she asked when he reappeared from the bathroom.

"Yeah," Elmer grunted. "But not most. And not best, that's for sure."

"It's OK, Elmer. I'm sure other farmers don't make it to the docks before they close. That's why they open so early. If you bring them in right before closing, aren't they just going to sit *there* overnight?"

"That's different," Elmer insisted.

"Why?"

"Well, that's on them. I deliver perfectly ripe pomegranates picked fresh, that very day. That's the Look 'N Up way."

Fran sighed through a fond smile at his well-deserved pride. She was even prouder of the way he gave all the credit to the humble, hardworking green folks who she missed so much it hurt. *I hope they can come back soon. I hope they never find that net*, she wished selfishly. Out loud, it was, "I'll keep advertising for day labor. Maybe we'll find someone. Oh, don't forget, at the end we have to bring a load up to Patrick's. Maybe two loads, for a year's supply of Salistar's oil, and Felsic's wine. Hopefully not for insulation and shoe leather anymore."

"Naw! You got them too spoiled for that." Elmer quipped.

Fran was handing Elmer a steaming plate when the land line rang. They froze. Their eyes met. Fran put the plate down absently and turned toward the phone on the wall. Elmer rushed around the table, taking the receiver from her. They huddled close together, listening.

"Yeah." Elmer stated curtly.

"Hey, Bud. It's me. Sheriff Dave. We're here."

"Son of a—" Elmer muttered.

"Come on, now, Elmer. We agreed," the friendly voice replied, then softer, "The greenies aren't there, are they?"

"Nuh-uh. There's nobody here. All I got is a bunch of local kids after school, and they ain't here yet. So why don't you just get outta here?"

"Elmer, please come down here and open the gate. Let's get this over with. I promise, I'll keep these guys under control."

"What guys, exactly?"

"That RID guy from LA, and my good old Deputy Otto. He's RID now, too. They pay these SOBs. Can you believe it? And your old pals Ian Foster and Ted Bates."

Elmer snorted, not budging. "Yeah. Ask Ian how his harvest is going. Where does his help come from? Did you check?"

"Actually, I did, in fairness to you. They're all documented, this year. Now, please let us in. They could make me break in, you know, because of our agreement."

"Go on." Fran advised, putting his uneaten breakfast away. "Let's just get it over with."

Elmer hung up the phone. He searched Fran's eyes with his own steel grey ones. "Remember our plan. I'll lead. You bring up the rear. Keep 'em from straying." He put his hat and coat back on and trudged out the door, muttering about his Constitutional rights.

"Come on, Lassen." Fran called out the door behind him, addressing the one-year-old, purple-tinged German shepherd who galloped on the grass with his yellow lab brother. Their dad, Brodey, a senior yellow lab, lay on the couch, as usual. The two puppies clattered up the porch steps on long legs and oversized feet. The sat on the doormat, looking up at Fran expectantly, begging. She grabbed the semi-purple one by the collar. The yellow lab pup, Tobey, stuck to his heels like he never did to any human. The brothers were inseparable.

"Come on," Fran said again gently. She dropped the collar and led the pups up the unfamiliar stairs. They followed her into the previously forbidden territory without question. Fran had questions enough for all of them. *Which room do I sacrifice?* She remembered Elmer's grandpa's adage. "A dog is a dog, two dogs is half a dog, and three dog is no dog a'tall." He applied it to boys, as well. She decided on the bathroom. No carpet, no windows. "Shhh!" she warned, closing the door. She opened it again, suddenly. The puppies looked at her innocently, waiting for the game to start. She plucked the toilet paper off the holder and stuffed it in a cabinet. "Be good," she told them vainly.

By the time she was back downstairs, the inspectors were pulling up in front of the house and the quarters, just like last time. She was glad the green family wasn't here this time, or Patrick and Belinda, or especially Jerry. She had never been so afraid of losing him as that last time these four guys were here with their guns pointed. A year ago! It seemed like yesterday.

She slipped into her jacket while Brodey oozed noisily off the couch and joined her slowly, stretching and yawning. Not like last time. *Good judgement, or old age?* She wondered as they stepped out onto the porch together. Her neighbor and fellow pomegranate farmer, Ian Foster, and Elmer's softball teammate, Ted Bates, emerged from Ian's silver Dodge Ram with its monstrous grill and fully stocked gun rack. Meanwhile, that skinhead former deputy and the quiet, dull eyed soldier from the LA chapter of the Right Identity Movement arrived in the same jacked up GMC as before, now painted in desert camouflage.

Sheriff Dave brought up the rear in his patrol car. He parked behind the others while Elmer jetted around them recklessly on the four-wheeler, peppering their trucks with gravel. Fran stood on the porch, Brody still at her side, watching the men's backs as they turned to face his assault, chests puffed, shoulders higher and somehow wider, like a blowfish, or one of those frilly lizards. Elmer came to a stop in front of the parked parade and cut the engine.

"You dinged my truck, Elmer!" Ian snarled a greeting.

"You dinged my harvest pretty good." Elmer growled back, unfolding from the seat and removing his helmet. "How's yours goin' eh, Buddy?" He approached Ian with a menacing grin and extended hand. "Got lots of help, do you?"

Ian put his hands in his pockets. "We're the same as you. We got some damn hippie punks passing through, ran out of money. Bums really. Three guys and a girl?" He paused, as if inviting speculation. No one bit, so he continued his rant. "Whatever. They're full time, stay in the quarters. They work OK. Not as good as some I've had, but at least they're Americans."

Elmer had long since walked away, not really concerned. He glared at Sheriff Dave's former deputy, Rod Otto, who had been fired on this very spot for bringing these guys here last year. Now here they were again, with the Sheriff's blessing. Elmer lunged at the deputy like a bulldog on a leash.

"Elmer!" Francine cried from the porch. Brodey seconded her with a single bark, then sat down beside her.

The Sheriff turned to her and doffed his hat. "Hello, Fran," he smiled, friendly enough. She knew he'd done the best he could to help them. And this was it, the deal they'd made. Annual inspections, at harvest time, for an unspecified number of years, until these guys accepted that the green aliens were gone forever. Then they could come back. *And we'll have their help again, and their friendship.*

A stab deep in her gut made her think of Salistar. It was the smell. So faint, just a hint on the breeze, like the chill of a ghost, barely perceptible. She looked over at the quarters. Ian and Ted had flung the unlocked door open. They strutted right in, guns drawn, like they had before. But before, they had found Salistar and dragged her out of there at gunpoint. Francine couldn't bear the memory. Worse, she couldn't bear seeing those mean, sweaty men stinking up Salistar's house. Sheriff Dave stood in front of her, holding her back.

"How can you let them go in there?" she ranted at him.

"It's in the agreement Elmer signed." He reached into his back pocket.

"I read it." Fran stopped him. "You can't come in our house, though," she stated, just for the benefit of the former deputy who stood, devoid of authority, listening intently. A high-pitched yap emitted from upstairs, as if on cue.

The Sheriff's eyes strayed up the stairs. "No," he confirmed, "I can't. Come on, Otto," he growled. He was no longer the man's boss, but he followed anyway.

They left the house and followed Ian and Ted into the open, empty quarters. The place was spotless. Only Fran would have smelled it, it was so ingrained in her. Pomegranate oil, G-pa, fried potatoes, Star's house. She sighed as she entered, her heartache fully triggered.

There was no visible indication that the green people had ever been. It relieved Fran, but her heart hurt even more. How had Star done it? When had she found the time to erase every visible speck? And why?

"You happy now?" Elmer barked as Ted and Ian emerged from their trip through the empty bedrooms. They would see bunkbeds with bare, stained mattresses, OK, no erasing that sign. They called it 'gaa'. Pomegranate juice. They had spread seeds everywhere during the harvest, for drying. The green-skinned vegans' primary source of protein on Nauve, the 'kip' seeds had to last all year.

"Let's see the orchard." Ian urged.

"OK, it's out back here, we can take a shortcut, out the back door." Elmer offered.

"I ain't walking this whole orchard." Ted objected. Elmer hadn't noticed Ted's new paunch, concealed under his long jacket. The zippy center fielder had gone to pot. Or beer, more likely. Elmer knew he wasn't going to get these guys to walk.

"I'll get my jeep. It's a four-seater. Sheriff, you can ride with me, and two more, if you want."

"We'll take our own," Ian answered coldly.

"You'll follow me then," Elmer asserted. "My wife will follow you on the four-wheeler, so stay in line."

"Sounds fair," the Sheriff agreed, settling into the passenger seat of the jeep. The two trucks followed them into the east orchard. Fran brought up the rear, Brodey perched on the platform behind her.

"I'm glad they didn't take you up on the offer," Sheriff Dave remarked as they led the parade down the first row.

"Extra tire tracks," Elmer grumbled, pressing harder on the gas.

"Slow down," Dave ordered. "Take your time. Drive through all the rows, nice and slow, and listen. The story's changed. We've got to get on the same page here. We can't say it was drones anymore. There's no evidence to support it. There were plenty of horns and beaks and claws at the fairgrounds. All organic. Real animal parts. No plastic. And that scene at the office park, more horns and claws and what was left of Manuel. Definitely an animal attack."

"The bad kid with the bad drones..." Elmer tried the old story.

"No evidence for that. None. But that's good. It clears you, and your kid. It was an animal attack. Wild animals. Natural. In no way caused by humans. What they were and where they came from, that's for the biologists to figure out, and believe me, they're on it. They've run DNA tests, but they won't tell me what they found. The FBI's asking questions. Did they contact you?"

"Nope. Not a word," Elmer replied, gripping the steering wheel, his knuckles white. His chest felt empty, except for his throbbing heart.

"Watch out," Dave cautioned, "There's another shoe gonna drop here pretty soon, I'm telling you. So, here's what you say. Get it straight. They're animals. They showed up here at the ranch, and you guys were just trying to stop them. You and your, ah, helpers."

"You mean the aliens who have no right to exist because they're green?"

"Yeah, but they're not really aliens. They're from, I don't know, some weird, foreign place, like India or Pakistan. They dyed themselves green for that religious ceremony they did at the fairgrounds. They were undocumented, and they moved on after your harvest. I let them go, and let you off with a warning, and these inspections."

"Well, I want to inspect Ian's place, too."

"Come on, Elmer! You want to send his workers packing, too? I've got better things to do. I checked him, and I will check him every year, as long as he keeps wanting these fool inspections. And if I catch him, I'll bust him like I didn't bust you, because you minded your own business and he's being a pain in the ass!"

They had reached the end of the last row. Elmer drifted slowly to a stop, craned his neck to look back with a forced grin and a tentative thumbs up.

"Okay," Came the terse reply from Ian's Dodge.

Elmer accelerated across the shop driveway spitting gravel behind him. Then he slowed down and idled into the west orchard. Dave hung onto the top of the windshield as the hard leaf springs crawled over the ruts. They started at the north end, working back and forth along the rows in their little procession. "You should have seen those guys mow," Elmer reminisced wistfully as he traveled the familiar route. "Just like this. First the east, then the west. They'd cover it all, about this fast, all mowed."

Dave nodded, unimpressed.

"By hand." Elmer added. "On foot. With scythes."

That got Dave's dark eyebrows to shoot up under the bill of his Sheriff hat. They had reached the last row, which ran along the top of a cliff. An oak tree leaned out over the driveway below. A cable ran down from it to a metal gate mounted in the downhill side of the driveway. More cables went from the gate down to a platform mounted on a cliff face in front of a two-foot diameter hole. A couple cables went on into that hole. Elmer slowed to a stop.

"You ready?" Dave asked.

Elmer turned off the ignition and climbed out without answering. The two pickup trucks pulled up behind him and stopped. The four men piled out of them, talking and pointing at the contraption below.

Dave led the presentation, just the way he'd planned it. He hoped Elmer could keep up. Here came Francine on the four-wheeler. She didn't know the new story, but she was a sharp one. Dave was pretty sure she'd catch on quickly, or keep quiet.

"Here's where they came from, right Elmer? You tried to stop them?" he prompted.

"Um, yeah." Elmer had to think fast. With a conspiratorial glance toward Fran, he started his spin. "We saw them the year before. Just a few, right at harvest time. Scared the hell outa us. My workers, the um, Pakistani guys," another glance at Fran, "they said they knew what to do. They'd seen 'em before back in the old country."

"They brought them with them from the *old country*," Otto pointed out with stinging sarcasm. He wasn't buying it. He'd fought side-by-side with the green men against the flying predators, the scant, bloody remains of one Manuel Guzman at their feet. "Which was not Pakistan. Pakistanis aren't green."

"They dyed themselves." Elmer shrugged. "It's camouflage. They wear it when they fight the things. That's why they did that ceremony at the fairgrounds with the sticks and bowls and that awful noise they made. It's traditional. The noise kills some of 'em. You seen it, Deputy, I mean Mr. Otto. That noise popped the suckers, didn't it? Then they kick ass on the rest of 'em with their wooden spears."

"And a weedeater," Otto recalled. "And the white kids with the electric guitar and the violin. Were they part of the ancient rite?"

"We contributed some good old Earth, um, American technology. It worked, too. Didn't it, Otto?"

"Shooting works, too," the former Deputy pointed out.

"Yeah, and after the attack, the critters went back into their cave to hibernate, and we gassed them. That's what all that mess down there is about." He waved his arms at the elaborate setup below. "They're all dead now."

"And the green people?" Otto insisted.

"Gone. Down the road, thanks to you guys. The best workers I ever had, gone somewhere else, I guess." Elmer looked up at the grey sky, as if seeking his missing friends in the clouds. Fran put her hand on his back, felt the vibration of his seething anger mingle with her own sadness. He pulled away from her touch and crawled back into the jeep without looking at anyone. "What do you want to see now?" he asked coldly.

"I wanna go down there." Ian pointed to the river bed below the platform. "That's where you guys came from that day. You and your cockeyed brother, your kid and those green guys. That was almost a week after their little ceremony at the fairgrounds, and they were still green."

Elmer snorted a laugh. "They used grass to dye their skin. That stuff doesn't come out for a long time. They call it gaa." He couldn't resist using the Nauvian word for the indelible stains they collected with pride on their unwashable grass clothing. Fran shushed him softly. He sighed, missing them with a depth he couldn't fathom, and started the jeep.

The procession followed him across the rutted path through the grassy area, past the abandoned stone sauna without slowing to give a clue of its significance, then along the river to where the trail narrowed too much for the full-sized pickups that followed. Elmer pulled as far forward as he could, half hoping Ian or his buddy Dirk would dip a tire off the edge of the river bank and roll their fancy ride right into the drink, but no such luck. They parked on the flat spot just above the river, in front of the giant burn pile.

"What were you doing down here that day?" Ian demanded, as if it was any of his business.

"Piling brush for burning." Elmer had practiced this part. The immense burn pile provided massive evidence.

"Right at harvest time?"

"I'd already brought a load to the docks. We don't pick in the afternoon. My poms go to the docks fresh, picked that day, or at least they used to, when I had those guys. Pick a whole load by lunchtime, do other stuff the rest of the day. I tell ya, you guys don't know what you cost me. Almost seems like you can't take fair competition, eh, Ian? You're jealous, 'cause you can't find workers like that. Well, maybe that's 'cause you don't treat them right, eh? You gotta respect your helpers, no matter where they come from and what color they are."

Elmer found himself in Ian's face with his finger raised. Had he poked him? Yeah, he could still feel the cold sting on the tip of his finger where he'd jammed it into that scrawny, heartless chest. He backed off, embarrassed, but he didn't apologize.

"You got a special permit for that huge pile?" Ian shot back. "Sheriff, check his permit."

"That's not our business," Dave grumbled.

"It's the law! You're the Sheriff!" Ian insisted.

"We're not here for that!" Dave snapped. "We're looking for undocumented farm workers. That's all!"

"You had concrete stuff." Otto recalled. "A cement mixer and some empty sacks."

"We made a fire ring," Elmer explained.

"Where?" Otto asked.

Elmer smiled a wrinkled smile and gestured grandly at the burn pile. "It's under there someplace," he assured.

Council

The instant his plate was empty, Baput jumped up from the dinner table and disappeared into his bedroom. He returned fully decked in his Akashic Robe, the Sacred Longstick tightly clutched in his left hand. "It is harvest time," he announced formally, a lead-in to the fall Council meeting.

Valko grunted angrily. "Eighteen trees. Only six mature ones. The first picking took an hour."

"It won't be enough, Baput." Salistar piped up timidly. "Enough for fresh eating, for now, but not enough to put aside, or to make oil."

"Or wine," Felsic added. Back home, fermentation was the only way to preserve the nutritious juice. Like Salistar's oil, Felsic's wine was essential to the people's pomegranate-based diet, sustaining them long after fresh pomegranates were but a fond memory.

"Elmer will bring Big Truck, all full, just for us," Baput explained.

"Big Truck!" Felsic chirped his enthusiasm, more anxious to tune up his old friend than he was to start his wine.

"Is that enough?" Valko asked his wife.

Salistar shrugged helplessly.

"It's twelve boxes." Baput explained. "You've seen the boxes. They're half full, or course, so as not to crush�" He stopped abruptly as his Momama sprang from her seat and began her frantic pacing, a new habit she had discovered since they had arrived at Patrick's Place.

"I don't know how many boxes!" she scoffed. "I make the oil, the stuffing for clothes, the leather for shoes we don't need anymore. Felsic makes the wine. How many kips? Who knows? We just keep working until they are all gone." She gave Felsic a questioning look.

He nodded. He didn't know how many kips it took either. When they came in, he made wine until there were no more.

Baput raised his free right hand to his face and covered his eyes, squeezing them closed, as it to keep them from rolling out of his head. "We will see, then. If we need more, Elmer will bring a second load at the end of harvest. Then he will leave Big Truck for us to use for your metal works all year."

"I'll tune it up." Felsic promised, brightening.

"Elmer is counting on it." Baput grinned at Felsic the Auto Mechanic, a much happier man than Felsic the Wine Maker.

Baput turned to Valko, the woodworker turned metal worker. "Popa? Are the presses ready?" He knew they were. They all did. But this was Popa's chance to report his accomplishments to the Council.

Valko let the glorious opportunity pass with a grunt and a nod, then a whispered declaration, "All steel."

"Will Francina be here, when Big Truck is?" Salistar asked. Her pacing had slowed, but she had by no means settled down, clearly not comfortable as a Council member. Baput regretted putting on the robe. They could have had this conversation much more comfortably without it.

"No, Momama," he broke the news.

Salistar stopped in her tracks, right in front of him. "Why no?" she demanded.

"It's just Elmer, and he's not staying. We will unload the truck, he's bringing the forklift, then he has to go right back to Look 'N Up to finish the harvest."

"I want to tune Big Truck."

"Not this time." Baput said sternly, as if saying 'no' to a child. "At the end. After harvest, he will bring it back with another load and leave it here. Francina or Jerry will have to come then, to drive him back."

Baput's subjects stared at him silently, blank looks on their green faces, wondering why the Holy Alanakash had chosen to deny their wishes. How could he explain the long-distance comings and goings of these Earth people? He barely understood it himself.

He fingered the clasp of his robe. As beautiful as it was, as hard as Momama, Francina and Belinda, the three women who loved him, had worked on the intricate weave and the elaborate beadwork, he hated the thing. It was supposed to give him authority, so people would listen to him and obey him without question. It was supposed to be his power and his glory. But when he wore it, he couldn't even talk to his family. And they were his only subjects.

Look at them, gazing at me. Even Popa, staring up at me from his chair, looking to me for guidance, waiting for me to tell him everything is going to be alright. Momama wants Francina and Felsic wants Big Truck, as if I could just make them appear if I wanted to. So, if I don't, it's because I don't want to, because I'm just a mean old Akash like G-Pa.

He released the clasp, letting the Akashic Robe slip silently to the floor. Salistar dropped to her knees in an instant, catching it before it hit the well-swept surface. It draped across her extended arms. Baput turned and walked toward his bedroom, leaving her there, kneeling on the floor holding the shed skin of the first-year Akash as the men stared, moon-eyed, after him.

Nauve, Harvest

Man Up

"The people bow when I pass. They say 'yes, Akash' and 'no, Akash', as they should. But I can see right through it," Bazu insisted, pounding his frail fist on the table. He flinched immediately, cradling his hand in the other one as he whined what was meant to be a roar. "They don't believe in me. They don't respect me. Especially the young men. Your men, War Chief!"

He dared put his face within inches of the War Chief's, who was not much taller, but weighed almost twice as the Akash, all muscle.

Rakta was unruffled, but his indulgence was running thin. A stronger, less important man would have earned a shove or possibly a punch, but this was the Akash. Not so different from the old Akash, he realized. "They knew Bazu, the boy, their classmate," he explained. "You are no longer he. He is no more. Now you are the Mighty Akash. You have to show them."

"How?" Bazu asked glumly, his aggression already dissolving into the usual whining.

"Work with them. It is what they understand and respect. I will have Buppan and Bupple show you their tricks with the longstick. They can twirl it, and balance it. Not much good for fighting, but spectacular to watch. Most impressive. You will look like Meldan, the Warrior Akash."

Bazu made a small, incomprehensible noise. Akira rolled her eyes silently.

Rakta clasped the Akash by the shoulder, trying to reassure him. "Just Buppan and Bupple at first, while the others are doing their calisthenics. Every Quarter Moonday, you and Bupple come to the practice field and spend all morning. Once he and his son have built your skills, and your, um, confidence," he eyed Bazu up and down scornfully, "then we will re-introduce you to the men as their Warrior Akash."

Rakta beamed with pride and excitement at his own idea. The others did not share his enthusiasm.

"Bupple will be with me?" the Akash finally asked in a squeak.

"Of course! Do you think he would let his son try to usurp his prized position as Guard of Akash?"

Akira choked back a laugh, tried to make it sound like a cough. Bazu didn't seem to notice.

"Very well then," the Akash agreed stiffly. Every Quarter Moonday morning."

"Yessss!" the War Chief hissed.

First Quarter Moonday

Tamaya had never seen Bazu so animated. He had sharpened his longstick, under Bupple's infinitely patient guidance. He had even etched it with the common symbols for 'Warrior' and 'Akash'. He said he was going to the practice field to complete his Warrior Training. To Tamaya, it seemed like the most ridiculous notion the foolish boy had come up with yet, but he was excited and determined, and best of all, headed out of the cave for once. He said he would be gone all morning, every Quarter Moonday until further notice.

She felt her own excitement grow as she stood on the high stone porch watching her husband's back disappear, dwarfed by his burly guard. A whole morning by herself! No whining, no demands, no reading the endless, circular ramblings of Badon, the old Akash. She could do whatever she wanted. But she didn't know what that was. All she could think of was something someone else had told her to do. She could read more books. The older ones. She had tried to read them aloud to Bazu, but he only wanted to hear from Badon, the one who made the weapon. The one who disappeared himself and his family. She read the old books, the ones in the tunnel behind the door, to herself whenever she had the chance. They were more interesting. The thinking was clearer. Essays on compassion and empathy and fairness, about weighing decisions to come up with what was best for the most people.

She was eager to read more, but surely there was something more exciting for a young woman to do with this precious free time she'd been unintentionally granted. She was about to head back into the cave, into the depths of the Death Tunnel where hundreds of volumes of ancient writing still waited to be read, when something caught her eye.

Someone was moving through the bushes along the river, hidden like an animal. A head burst out of the willows near the foot of the stone stairs. A green bald spot right in the middle of the top glowed in the morning sun. Rakta!

"What is he doing here?" Tamaya wondered in a whisper. She ducked inside the door and ran a cattail comb through her loose hair without even realizing she was doing it. She heard him on the stairs, breathing just a little hard. Much quieter than Bazu, though he weighed a lot more.

"Meyhey!" he shouted a greeting, announcing his arrival.

Tamaya put the brush down quickly. Her heart was beating unusually fast. She unconsciously raised her right hand to her chest, as if to still it. "Rakta?" she answered with a question. "You just missed Bazu and Bupple." She tried to sound casual, as if she hadn't seen how intentional that miss had apparently been. "They went to the practice field. He says he will complete his warrior training." She tried to say it with a straight face, but it broke at the end into a choked snicker that the War Chief shared, melting the ice just a bit.

"I know," Rakta answered through a ridiculous grin, cheeks pulled wide, yellow teeth showing. "I have ordered this, to make a man of him."

Another shared snicker, then suddenly, Tamaya's humor dropped to the cold stone floor. "Well, they have gone. They are at the practice field by now," she informed him brusquely, raising her eyebrows expectantly. What did he want?

He just nodded, still wearing that creepy grin. "At Council, I said 'make a man of him, so the men will respect him'. So, I help. Akira says, 'make a man of him, so he makes babbets.' I help there, too."

Tamaya stared at his craggy Adam's apple, the way it bobbed up and down along with his voice. She couldn't look into his eyes. What was he saying? She heard her own voice asking slowly, "What do you mean, you help with babbets?"

"There are no babbets, Tamaya!" he whispered gently. "Why? It's him, isn't it? It can't possibly be you."

She brought her eyes to his. "What are you talking about?" she slapped him with her voice.

Rakta talked faster now, as if fighting his way out of a whirlpool. "You are all woman, Tamaya. Everything a woman should be, and more!"

What was he talking about? She had no babbets, didn't cook or weave. Nobody else thought she was all a woman should be.

Rakta babbled on, oblivious to her confusion. "And Bazu is nothing of what a man should be. Does he prefer men? I can arrange a companion for him, but of course he still must do his duty with his tether, like any man. The village needs babbets, Tamaya! We need more men to fight, more women to feed them and patch them up and make more of them. And the Akash! If we have learned anything from the last cycle, it is how important the Akashic succession is. It's up to you, Tamaya! The village depends on you." He stopped babbling and squirming and looked at her.

She stared back, feeling like a nimbly must feel right before it dives on its prey.

Rakta broke the gaze first, addressing the floor. "And him. It is up to him. So, I make him into a man for you. On the practice field."

Tamaya tried to speak, but she couldn't summon enough air. It was just as well. She had no words. She felt a chill prickle across her shoulders, and a burning heat deep inside. She could feel the blood in her cheeks; knew he could see her blush. Her voice came from the cold part of her. "That is hardly your concern. It is between me and Akira. You think more battle training will make him a man," she choked, covering another laugh, "Great. Fine. He told me. So, why are you here?"

"To help?" he answered helplessly.

"How?"

He met her eyes again. They shared a speechless staring contest until Tamaya awkwardly withdrew. Her head was spinning with feelings and questions and forbidden thoughts she found no way to express or expel.

"I don't even want babbets," she blurted, still not looking at him.

He drew back a step, mouth gaping. "All women want babbets," he declared, "just like all men want to make babbets." He laughed rudely, like he was chatting with his men.

"We are not all men and all women," Tamaya replied regally. "We are the Holy Akash and his Tether. You would do well to respect that, War Chief." She sneered his title, but somehow it came out like a teasing meow instead of the scornful hiss she'd intended.

"Yes, Your Highness." Rakta used the rare superlative. She felt its power like a mild electric shock. "I shall return next Quarter Moonday to um, check on his progress." He turned on his heels again, in his military way. He headed through the grand arch onto the porch. Then he turned back to her with a sly smile. "He'll be gone until just after noon, four whole hours each week. You will be here alone and unguarded. I must protect the Akashic Tether, so she can have babbets and the Akashic line will go on. I will be back next week, at your service."

He bowed, showing that bald spot again, making her feel that weird quiver in her loins, that little rush of power, again. She found herself smiling, but dropped it quickly when he stood.

"At your service, always," he pledged again, whirled again and rushed down the stairs and back into the willows.

One More Try

Tamaya stared at the page, checked the number. She was shocked to see she had read twenty pages. She didn't remember a bit of it. Something about creating illusions. It was written by the Akash before Badon. Tamaya's vague impression had been of a weak, sniveling excuse-maker like the last Akash, and the present one. He was bragging about clever ways he used to make himself look more powerful. *Must reading for Bazu, but he'll take it wrong.* Tamaya remembered thinking. *Is this what Rakta meant by 'helping'?*

That was all she remembered of the book. The rest was all about Rakta. *What was he saying? What did he want? Why did he come here, knowing Bazu and Bupple would be gone? He arranged for them to be gone! Every week, for four hours. He made that clear. He'll be back next Quarter Moonday, for four hours.* "So much for my alone time," she sighed.

She turned more pages, without remembering them, until she heard Bazu sluffing his feet on the steps, wheezing. Had it been four hours already? She didn't hear Bupple. She set the book down on the dining table and ran to greet her warrior husband.

She began with what was surely the wrong question. "Where's Bupple?"

"He's outside doing his business, for the usual hour," Bazu remarked dryly, brushing past her. "Is there food? Get me some before he gets up here and eats it all."

Tamaya knew Bupple would be gone a good hour, or more, judging from Bazu's temper. He had problems with his bowels, since his injury, but Tamaya knew he exaggerated the time it took. She'd seen him walking around down there. She understood. It was one of the few times he could get away from the Whining Akash. She unpacked the prepared food and served it on two clay platters, more elegant than the usual ration packs. She even lit a small lantern and set it on the table. She sat down across from him.

"How was your training?"

"Stop making fun of me."

"I'm not. I�"

"Read, Woman!" the Akash demanded.

"We're eating," Tamaya objected.

He glared at her, his new confidence already emerging. Had he challenged Bupple? *That poor man.* Tamaya marveled at the guard's level patience. *It must be his injury*, she was sure.

Maybe the illusion is already working! She hoped as she reached for the book she'd been reading. "You'll like this, My Akash. It's by the Akash before Badon. His Popa, Baram." She scanned the page she'd opened to, reading silently. *You gain fear and respect by performing marvels before the people. An ornately carved longstick can be used to impress, with a bit of practice. It must be a light one, not like the real ones the warriors wield.*

"Well?" Bazu prompted with his mouth full.

"Never mind," Tamaya replied, closing the book.

"Read Badon, like I told you!" Bazu demanded. "He is the only one who matters."

Tamaya felt that old irritation, but she promptly obeyed. Maybe it was better if the Akash himself wasn't in on the illusion. Maybe he had to think it was real, or it wouldn't work. Maybe she'd share this book with Rakta, when he came over next week. She opened the second-to-last Book of Badon to the page she'd marked with a maple leaf.

She read a couple of pages out loud, snatching bites between, which made the Akash most impatient. She was glad when he was finished eating. She didn't care that she wasn't. She had work to do. She stood and walked over to his chair and tilted it back so it stood on one leg. He was so light! She spun it so he faced her, then dropped it, jarring him so a little air escaped, and perhaps some food, but he re-swallowed it subtly.

"What are you doing?" he complained in his usual whine.

She straddling his lap and ran her thin finger down his surprisingly sweaty tunic. "I can already see the difference in you," she lied smoothly. She squeezed his biceps. "Ooh. You're such a big, strong man now. Why don't we try?" she touched his chest again, pressing on his sternum a bit too hard. "Your chest is so big! I can see you've been working."

"Get off me, Woman, and keep reading!"

Tamaya blinked, rebuffed. Her conquest in flames, she got up and flared back. "Akira says we should read the older Akash's books, before Badon." *Not that last one, surely*, she resolved to herself, *but maybe the older one about fairness and justice.* She searched her brain for where she'd shelved it while her husband prattled on the same old track, just like his predecessor.

"Did the older Akashes open the door to the tunnel? Did they shoot the weapon?"

"No, they didn't," she fired back. "They didn't disappear either. And none of them opened that door. Batuk did. And it killed him!" She finally aired her suspicions.

"What are you talking about?" the Wise Akash asked dumbly.

"Tamaya rushed to the entrance of the tunnel. She pointed to the letters savagely. "I told you. It says 'Death to Open'. When Batuk died, it was open. Don't you get it? Batuk opened it. Batuk, my first betrothed. If he'd lived, I'd be a woman now."

"What do you mean?"

"I'd have babbets. And we would live in a hut in the village. And he would pleasure me, like a true man is supposed to," she wailed in frustration. "There would be a strong Akashic Heir by now. Think about it, oh Wise Akash." She grabbed a torch and dashed into the Death Tunnel, completely unafraid, and pulled the next volume from the shelf. She crossed her legs, lowered to the floor, clutched the lantern close, and read silently to herself.

Full Kakeeche

The next Quarter Moonday was Full Kakeeche. The Akash and his Tether attended the ceremony at the Great Hall with the rest of the village, to sing the Full Kakeeche Song. Not the First Full Kakeeche song. That was only sung on that one special night in the three-year cycle. Tonight, they sang the ordinary Full Kakeeche Song, as they did every month on full moon. Four times it repeated, honoring the four phases of Kakeeche. After each set of four repetitions, the singers turned ninety degrees and chanted four more times, pleading to the four cardinal directions. Sixteen times in all, the monotonous chant recurred each month.

Bazu lead the singing, showing just a hint of his new confidence. It helped that he knew the song so well, having sang it sixteen times each month since he'd been able to form the words. He forgot about the crowd and just sang, a trick Buppan had suggested. It seemed to be working.

Tamaya stood by his side, turning when he turned, like a pair of carved wooden rollers on a scroll. Rakta and his wife and tether, Azuray, were on the platform too, turning with them, so they never faced each other. Still, Rakta kept shifting his eyes to steal glances at her. She knew, because her eyes were wandering, too.

At dinner they sat in the customary order, with Bazu crosswise at the head of table, Akira on one side, next to Tamaya, Rakta and Azuray on the other side. Tamaya had been looking forward to a hot meal served on a nice plate. Now she couldn't eat a bite. Rakta was right across from her. She couldn't look at him. Or not look at him. Not politely. Not like she wanted to. Every time she looked up from her plate, he would raise his lowered head just enough to peek at her with one eye. She would look away in a flash. At one point, she felt his foot touching her ankle, stroking gently up and down. She jerked her foot back, searched for Bazu. He and Akira were engrossed in comfortable-looking conversation. Relieved they hadn't seen, Tamaya couldn't help wonder what that was about. Azuray got up and started directing the servers to begin clearing the tables. Tamaya looked straight at Rakta.

"I won't come if you're not ready." He used his battle whisper, clear and distinct, but quiet.

She froze, wide-eyed as a zebkin doe. Her left eye twitched involuntarily. She knew she had to move before Bazu and Akira noticed. If this was what she thought it was, *aye Kakeeche! What would they think? What would they do?*

She shook her head, just to clear it, to break that gaze that held her.

Rakta broke it for her, looked down again. "Yes, your Highness. At your service," he uttered in his just-audible whisper, leaving Tamaya to wonder just what he had agreed to so willingly, and what else she could get.

Power

Bazu ran his forefinger over the raised letters on the plate in the door to the tunnel, again. Tamaya called it the 'Death Door', but it didn't stop his impudent tether from using it. She went in and out of the tunnel as much as he did, going through those ridiculous old books.

He carefully traced each letter, memorizing each curve, every angle. "Ta, omp?" he muttered, fingering the circle again, feeling for that little squiggle that might make it a quay. Nothing. No tail, just the strange, hard smoothness of the plate between the letters. Then another curve, a full circle again, no tail. "Omp again!" Bazu cursed. "That can't be right, two in a row. It must be a quay." But Tamaya had read this plate to him, naming the letters out loud, forming the words for him, 'DEATH TO OPEN' over and over again until he knew better than to ask her again. The words seemed to anger her, beyond the condescending annoyance she always wore when teaching her Akash to read, or trying to.

Now he knew why. *She thinks Batuk died opening this door. She thinks Batuk was a better man, and she would have been a better woman if she had him. Would she cook and clean, if she had him? Or would she trick his momama, Salistar into doing it for her?*

He had sent her and Bupple to gather firewood and whole stalks of the mullein leaves they used for wipes. He was on his own now, struggling with this limited sample, the only letters he had learned of the Alphabet of the Old Ones. And yes, sometimes they repeated. Tamaya said it wasn't an error. This plate wasn't the alphabet. It was words. Letters formed words. The smooth space between the two omps meant they were in to different words, 'to' and 'open'... "Stupid system," he whispered to the plate on the wall.

That trickling noise was driving him crazy! He could always hear it when he worked on the Death Plate, as Tamaya had come to call it. It sounded like water, but even Tamaya's sharp eyes and Bupple's persistence had failed to locate its source. It was somewhere behind the wall.

Bazu traced the nay for the umpteenth time, feeling the sharp angles at the top and bottom, all straight lines, no curves. "Nay," he recited, "Death to Op-ennn." He knew he wasn't really reading; he had it memorized. He dragged his finger to the right across the unnaturally flat surface to the ridge at the edge. He had explored it before. The ridge went all the way around the rectangular plate. This time, he ran his index finger straight over the ridge and off the plate, to the natural rock of the cave wall. Relieved, he pressed on its cold, familiar hardness. His finger penetrated the solid rock, all the way to the first knuckle. He jerked it back in surprise. It was wet!

He grabbed a torch from the wall and brought it close. Squinting, he drew his face right up to the wall, almost igniting his stringy black hair with the torch. He saw nothing but the usual blur that was edging its way into his world, a tiny bit more each day. He stared, trying desperately to focus. He saw a dull flash in the fog, like distant lightening. Then again, and again. He tried to count the interval between flashes, but it was too short, much less than a second. He could tell without counting. The tiny, dull flashes in the fog were pulsing on and off at a regular interval.

He drew his face back, brought the torch closer. From that perspective, with that lighting, he could barely make it out through the fog. A tiny wheel made of that hard, shiny material so common behind the Death Door, but so rare in the village. It flashed because it reflected the torchlight as it turned around and around, pushed by a tiny stream of water, the same way the wheel at the mill turned the giant stone grinders that made the rice into flour. Clever, but not Shavarandu. The river provided the power, rather than men, or ganeesh, or dogs. No spooky actions at a distance.

He had to use some imagination to fill in the details, piece the whole thing together. He was looking at a tiny version of the mill wheel, made of that mystifying shiny material, turned by that maddening trickle. *Why would someone bury this inside a cave wall, at the doorway to the Death Tunnel, right beside that heavy latch that doesn't work anymore?* He brought his probing finger back up and stuck it in as far as it would go.

"Do not look at Shavarandu.
He will burn your eyes.
Only cool light from Kakeeche
Can enter your mind
Think cool, kind thoughts of giving
Guided by their silver rays
Or evil thoughts from Shavarandu
Will burn your only world away."

The Kakeeche sang the chant Bazu had memorized and repeated at the start of each school day, from his second three-year cycle through his fourth, when he had graduated, a nobody with no apprenticeship.

But now he was Akash! An Akash no training. An Akash who had never truly ascended to the Akashic Plane. He knew how to meditate. He had learned in school, like all the boys. They used that Kakeeche song as a mantra.

Am I there now? he wondered. *Is this the Plane? It must be. This vision couldn't possibly be my imagination. They're all here! The whole multitude of luminous creatures who make up the moon. A full moon as plump and round as a ripe kip!* Bazu could focus on the distant object better than he could on the Akashic letters, no matter how close he held them to his feeble eyes. But he couldn't see the moon well enough to actually distinguish the individual creatures, like the teachers said they could.

He squinted, then opened his eyes wide. Something came into focus. Tiny mouths, all over the full moon, opening and closing as they sang their warning song. He couldn't begin to count them. No need. He knew there were 1,095 of them, the number of days in a cycle.

"Yes Kakeeche," he droned, in awe. "I will not look at Shavarandu."

One by one, the tiny mouths disappeared, lost in the glare that came from below them, blinding Bazu to their details, drowning out their pale silver light as a thundering voice drowned out their song. The sun, Shavarandu, was rising, right in front of the full moon like a backwards eclipse.

"Ahhh, but you do, young Akash! Every day you study the weapon. You plan to deploy it. To use it against the nimblies and bumblies as you must to save your people. You are right, Bazu, that is what you must do."

Bazu trembled to his core when Shavarandu addressed him personally. Yet, somehow, in this disembodied state he found the courage to argue with the ultimate power.

"No! You will burn my eyes. They are bad enough already."

"I shall burn the film from your eyes, so that you may see clearly."

"I must not!" Bazu insisted, temptation tugging at the Akashic robe he was suddenly wearing.

Bazu felt a hot wind as the sun sighed at him in frustration. "You must. You are Akash. The future of the people is in your hands. The Sacred Longstick and the Holy Seed! You will be the Akash who defeats the nimblies and bumblies, but you need me. You must follow me. You must complete the weapon!"

"But it made the last Akash disappear, and his apprentice. His whole family—"

"You have not completed your training, Boy!" Shavarandu mocked him, not in the soul-shaking voice of The Power We Fear, but in the raspy warble of the old Akash. It was a voice that had filled Bazu with awe all his life. But after conversing with Shavarandu, the old man's feeble voice held no power. He, Bazu, was Akash now. He lashed out with an anger he didn't know he had been holding.

"You did not train me. You didn't even think something might happen to Baput. Not even after Batuk—" He stopped short. The old Akash was gone. He heard a noise near the Holy Rock. He raised his lantern and peered that way. Two silhouettes stood on either side of the Rock, facing each other. One was small, frail and thin. The other, much larger and heavier, towered over it.

The hulk in the dark spoke. "You have trained me, G-pa. If my training is not sufficient, it is because you have failed." The voice was strong and confident, and vaguely familiar, in a distant way.

The smaller apparition replied in the voice of the old Akash. "I have taught you all I know. I know it is not enough. It is up to you to take it further. It is up to you to save us. Only you can do it, Batuk!"

"It says 'Death to Open,'" the large apprentice argued.

"Perhaps it is figurative. The death of ignorance. The beginning of a new age of light."

"Of Shavarandu!" faithful Batuk replied. "He will burn our world away!"

"How do you know?" the Akash countered.

"The chant. What they teach us in school, what *you* taught me!" Batuk seemed to be getting bigger. The Akash, shrinking. Neither seemed to see Bazu there, watching them.

Everyone knew the Old Ones forbade Shavarandu, the exploration of mysterious powers that performed spooky actions at a distance. The Old Ones were most wise. How could even the Akash question them?

Yet, old Badon did. "If Shavarandu is so evil, why did the Old Ones draw all the things?"

Bazu gasped as the old Akash rattled the oversized pages of his cherished plan sheets.

"They built them," Batuk replied. "But then they hid them behind the Death Door so we would never use them, because they learned that Shavarandu is evil, G-pa!" Batuk dared shake his fist at his mentor from across the Holy Rock.

"It is up to you, my apprentice," the old Akash repeated, swelling a bit, without approaching his grandson's size. Then he vanished, and Batuk was alone. He walked toward where Bazu stood, at the open doorway beside the shiny plate with the lettering and the tiny wheel. He walked right *into* Bazu, so they occupied the same space. Batuk didn't seem to notice Bazu, and Bazu couldn't feel Batuk's intimate presence. It made Bazu feel like *he* was the ghost.

The Death Door was closed. Bazu had never seen it that way. A heavy bar of a weird material, much heavier and harder than breen, crossed it and disappeared into the door frame beneath the lettered plate. Batuk gripped the bar and slid it slowly to the left, away from the etched plate.

A blinding white light flashed. Bazu's hair stood up, making his scalp crawl and his arms tingle. His head spun in a wide, elongated circle, like a rock in the pocket of a sling. Then, just as suddenly, Bazu could see again, as if he had just opened his eyes. There was Batuk, apparently no worse for wear. But they weren't standing at the doorway anymore. Bazu and Batuk were in the Death Tunnel. It was lit up like daylight, like Shavarandu itself! No, not that bright, not that color. Whiter and softer. Bazu had never seen the contents of the mysterious space so clearly. Objects of various hard, shiny materials littered the floor and hung on the wall in all shapes. The parts of the weapon; the long, heavy tubes, the thin, flexible wires and the contraption with the pedals, were all there, even though he and Bupple had brought them out and assembled them on the Holy Rock months ago. There were countless more shiny plates, rods and spirals of unknown origin and purpose.

The back half of the tunnel was all bookshelves, six rows of them, six shelves high. Oriented lengthwise, they disappeared in their own shadows, but Bazu had dared to venture. He knew they went all the way to the back, where the tunnel ended abruptly in a flat, smooth wall.

He could see the former apprentice clearly now. He remembered his third cousin vaguely, decked in the trappings of a small boy's idolatry. Strong, handsome Batuk would be as big as his Popa, Valko. And he would be Akash. He would be a great one, Bazu had been sure. A new Akash for his generation.

Now Batuk stood before him clad in mundane clothing, a bit disheveled, but still large and handsome and somehow commanding. But he was dead!

"How are you here?" Bazu squeaked a question at the specter.

Batuk looked up at him, as if he'd heard him. "Where else would I be?" he answered with a shrug.

"On the ground at the bottom of the stairs, smashed to pieces." Bazu answered with the story he'd been told. Batuk looked confused. Bazu tried again. "You died a long time ago. You are a star in the sky by now."

Batuk raised his eyebrows, rolled his eyes, and turned away. He lifted a strange object that hung from a hook on the wall by a long, neatly coiled string, like the one attached to that pedal contraption. The end he held had a pear-shaped bulb you could see clear through, with a tiny, delicate-looking shaft inside. Bazu had seen the object glinting in the dim torchlight with his dim eyes and even dimmer imagination. He had never given it much thought. Just another weird thing in this weird place with no explanation and no instructions. None that he could access anyway.

The thing didn't seem to bother Batuk. He grabbed it confidently and carried it to the open doorway as if he'd done it every day of the ten years since his death. He bent down to look closely at the receptacle in the door frame that had held the heavy bar that used to latch the Death Door. Below that slot were two others, much smaller, just big enough to receive the two prongs at the end of that long string. Garrick aptly unrolled the cord and plugged the lamp in.

Obscured by blinding light once again, Batuk's voice boomed like Shavarandu's. "Now do you see, Bazu? It is up to you. I didn't give up my life as Akash for nothing, you know." He was gone. The tunnel was dark.

Bazu opened his eyes. He found himself at the very end of the tunnel, between the two central bookshelves, facing the wall. He reached out and touched it, noticing how oddly flat and smooth and perfect it was, not like the rest of the cave rock. He could barely see it. The only light was a dying torch back at the entrance to the tunnel. He looked down and realized he was preparing to pee. "What am I doing?" he cried out loud, and his own voice made him squeak in terror.

He pulled himself together, so to speak, and felt his way toward the flagging orange light. Halfway there, he stopped and reached as high as he could for something that hung on the wall. Batuk had grabbed it easily, but Bazu had to stretch on his tip-toes. He pulled the lamp down and carried it to the doorway without looking at it, as if in a trance. He picked up the torch, and in its dying light, he squinted at the spot on the doorframe Batuk had shown him. He slipped the two- pronged plug into the socket and the Death Tunnel flooded with light, just like in his vision.

He heard voices, footsteps on the stairs. Bupple and Tamaya were back, at the perfect time, for once.

"Whew!" Bupple complained. "It is hot, yet I cut firewood."

"It's cold at night, Bupple. I'm sure you've noticed." Tamaya replied casually, easily. She was never that way with Bazu. "I'll get you some pomegranate juice," she offered, like a tether would.

"I have my fat to keep me warm," the retired warrior bragged.

They stopped, transfixed, at the door, staring at the light that spilled from the Death Tunnel. They could not even see its full brilliance from there, Bazu realized. Most of the light illuminated the tunnel. The wonderful, magical tunnel full of marvelous things.

"I have made a great discovery." Bazu informed them of the obvious.

"Shavarandu!" Bupple uttered, raising his axe and backing away. Tamaya went in the opposite direction, rushing forward to see more.

"No. It's like the mill. See here? The water turns a wheel!" Bazu babbled excitedly.

Tamaya was surprised Bazu had seen it. She was surprised she hadn't.

"But that's not all," the newly animated Bazu spouted, rushing fearlessly into the well-lit Death Tunnel, leaning his ear to the wall on his left. "Here! It's close. Bupple, come here. Bring your axe."

The big man gazed at the unnatural light and made a very small noise that embarrassed him. Clutching his stone axe tightly, he plodded step by step around the Holy Rock and through the Death Door into the usually dark tunnel. Each step rang through his nerves, from the ball of his foot to the hairs on his arms. Every fiber of his being screamed that this was wrong. But his Akash had ordered him to go through the Death Door into the Death Tunnel and look upon his Shavarandu.

Brightly lit, the tunnel was no less terrifying. In fact, it was worse. Now the strangely smooth surfaces of the inexplicable objects shined in the colors of fire, of the sun. Colors he had no names for, unknown in the village. He didn't even dare look upon the books and scrolls that filled the rows of shelves that went on forever, into the tunnel's relatively dark depths.

The Akash knelt on the floor, just inside the door.

"Here, Bupple," he ordered, "Strike the floor with your axe, hard, right here."

"The rock?" Bupple questioned, turning his axe around to the dull side.

"Yes!" the Akash hissed impatiently. "Hit it hard. Break right through!"

Bupple obeyed, braced for an impact that would ring his arm bones up to the shoulders and make him sore in the morning, on top of all that wood cutting. The axe broke through six inches of rock, then gave away to nothingness. He opened his eyes, fortunately. The Akash was on his knees, bending over the hole, sweeping the loosened rock away with his slim hands.

"Water!" the Akash cried. He sat up, raised his cupped hands over his head, and dumped two handfuls of cool, clear liquid over himself. "Bupple, with that one blow, you have saved yourself a lifetime of hauling water, for you and all the Guards of the future. Your name shall be sung!"

Bupple doubted he would make the legends for doing something the people would never benefit from, or even know about. But he did appreciate not having to carry the heavy, sloshing clay vessels up those unforgiving stone stairs.

His Akash had risen, and now he was staggering toward the back of the tunnel, leaning oddly left to keep his ear on the tiny underground stream. He disappeared into the darkness between the two middle shelves of books and scrolls. "Here, Bupple. Bring your axe" the Akash called. "Woman! Bring the Akashic Lamp."

"Again? Back there?" Tamaya asked. She lifted the single bulb from its holder and brought it toward the bookshelves, dragging the long cord behind her.

Trembling from the top of his head down to his numb toes, Bupple crept into the tight space between two bookshelves full of the Akashic magic of the Old Ones. His broad shoulders blocked most of the light Tamaya held, casting a terrifying, giant shadow on the floor and shelves ahead of him.

"Right here," the Akash ordered. "It might be harder. I think it's deeper, further away."

Bupple struck the solid ground, got that painful reverb he had expected the first time. He knew now to look and wait for the excited Akash to remove the broken rock before he struck again. And again. The third time it got easier. On the fourth blow he broke through to nothingness, like before. The tinkling sound was much louder. He opened his eyes.

Bazu was on his knees, pulling loose rocks aside. He raised a dripping stone above his head and turned to the uncomprehending eyes of his tether and guard. Even clever Tamaya hadn't caught on. Bupple obviously hadn't a clue.

"Downstream! It's a boor! No more going outside! I go here, and the water washes it away. Bring a stalk of mullein in here, Woman. I shall initiate the Akashic Boor."

Third Quarter Moonday

Tamaya watched the mismatched pair amble away down the river trail once again. Bazu didn't reach Bupple's shoulder with the top of his head, and he looked like a stick walking beside his guard's meaty bulk.

She pulled out the book she'd been reviewing all week, marking the passages she would read to Rakta when he came. *If* he came. She still wasn't sure *why* he would come. He didn't show up last week, but that was Full Kakeeche.

She didn't remember telling him not to come, *quite. Maybe he's just returned to his senses and dropped whatever this is,* she sighed. *His signals are so weird! I'm not a warrior! How am I supposed to know what he means?*

But there were no signals for this kind of thing. Akira decided who married whom, and that was that. Akira had to keep the lines apart.

Tamaya tried to read, but she couldn't take in any of it, except the parts that might concern Rakta. At midmorning, she slammed the book closed and stepped out onto the broad rock porch. She breathed deeply, trying to relax the knot in her gut.

She would have her precious alone time, after all. Time to read, and nothing else. She had that amazing light now, and the indoor boor she just might use, in the Akash's absence. Its constant tinkling always enticed her. She was just turning to head back inside and try it when she spotted movement in the trees below. Her heart raced and her brow furrowed so deeply it made her head ache. Here came that bald spot again. It was so obvious from up here. She wondered if he even knew he had it.

He scooched up the stairs, staying low.

"Where have you been?" she barked like an old tether. "I've been waiting. You're driving me crazy."

He was standing before her, grinning a little less creepily than last time. He moved to take her hands, thought better of it and dropped his big paws lamely in front of him. "Crazy, eh?" he sought her eyes eagerly.

Tamaya stepped back, half a step. "Annoyed," was all she would admit. "You said you would come."

Rakta's grin turned cagey. "I am a warrior by nature. You must understand. It is in a warrior's best interest to be unpredictable. Never form patterns."

"You said every quarter moon, at my service."

"You said 'no'. You weren't ready for my service. At the Great Hall, you kept looking away from me. You weren't ready."

"Ready for what?" Tamaya snapped. Her patience had run off the end of its track. What was he talking about? It couldn't possibly be what she thought it was. People just didn't do that! And she was the Akashic Tether, second highest woman in the village. And Rakta was the second highest man. And her husband, the skinny, timid kid who this was supposed to be all about, he was above them all, even Akira. No, she was sure that couldn't be it. It had to be something else.

"Did he tell you about his discovery?" she launched a decoy. Rakta took the bait, nodding like a hungry bird. "Come on, I'll show you." She strolled confidently to the tunnel entrance. Rakta didn't follow.

"Come on, right here." She beckoned the suddenly timid warrior to the dark recess behind the Holy Rock.

"I went in there once." Rakta declared, clearly implying it would be the only time. "If the Akashic boor is in there, I don't need to see it."

Tamaya hissed a scoff. "The boor is nothing. Water runs through the cave behind the wall. We take water out upstream, and he uses the boor downstream."

"Just him?"

Tamaya was surprised that Rakta had asked. Maybe it was Bupple he was concerned about. "The Akashic Boor, Rakta." She answered, rolling her the eyes. "But there's more. Watch." She found the lamp, plugged the chord into the plug at the entrance where the tiny wheel turned in the trickle, charging the capacitor. Rakta gasped hoarsely as the fearful, dark passage flooded with an oddly colored light. Rows of bookshelves holding bound volumes and rolled scrolls disappeared into the back. The front half was littered with odd objects of shiny, hard material, lying on the floor, hanging from the walls.

Rakta entered the terrible space for the second time. He didn't even think about it, he was so fascinated by the tools and weapons of Shavarandu. He seemed to even forget about Tamaya while he fondled the sharp, hard steel, admired the shine and the smoothness. Tamaya felt a familiar jealousy. No matter what man, her charms were no match for the secrets of Shavarandu.

She let him play for a while. Then, with a sigh, she turned and left him there, exploring in his rapt wonder. She went and got the book she'd intended to read to him, hoping to get his attention back, even though she didn't really want it. She returned with it, came just inside the well-lit space and leaned against the door jam, one knee bent, foot pressed against the wall. "I found this book by the Akash before Badon. It might help you with your plan to um, help, the Akash."

Rakta grunted, holding the end of another cord up to his eye, staring at the tiny slots where the prongs would go.

"It's all about illusions," Tamaya continued. "How the Akash tricks people into fearing him. It mentions the longstick training, like you're doing now. It says he should use an extra-light one."

Rakta looked at her then. He looked at the book in her hand, then down her legs to the floor, then back up to her eyes. Her innocent eyes, sincerely offering something to help him help her husband become the powerful Akash he should be, for the people. The man he should be, for her.

"Is it working?" he asked dryly.

"The boor?" she asked back, stubbornly obtuse.

He turned then toward the back of the tunnel, looked into the dark, trickling space between the bookshelves. He turned back slowly, met her eyes again and shook his head. "Is he better?" he asked cryptically.

Tamaya knew what he meant, but she still didn't get why he was asking. "No," she answered flatly, not inviting further questions. She read more of the book; tricks to look bigger, stronger. Sayings that make him sound 'smarter, but not too smart', the condescending ancient advised.

Rakta came to her side, where he could see the illustrations. He nodded vigorously, pointing at the drawings and saying things like; "good idea," "I can do that" and "Bupple can teach him that one."

The tension melted until Tamaya felt like she was talking with Bupple, or her Popa or brother. She kept reading, and soon they were talking about the part she could play in teaching Bazu some of these tricks, without telling him why.

When at last she'd finished with the relevant bits, she closed the book and turned to Rakta to hear his ideas.

He looked back, as if ready to summarize them. "I have had four strong sons. Two have even lived to adulthood," he declared his resume.

"What?" No more friendly, fraternal relationship. *We're back to* that *again*. "You're too old," she pointed out bluntly. "Send one of them."

Rakta raised his hands, waved them both. "Oh no, I assure you, I am not too old. My tether, Azuray, may be too old to bear them, but I can certainly still make them, oh yes!"

"How do you know?"

"I know I can. As for my sons, they can't. Not with you, I mean. Only I can. It must be our secret."

"Akira has approved of this?" Tamaya asked incredulously. Surely, Akira would have told her.

He whirled on his heel again, turning away from her but not leaving. He faced the depths of the tunnel. He whirled back. His face had changed radically, from flirtatious, hopeful bragging to raging lust. "Forget Akira! Akira can rot in her lair! She paired you with Bazu! How's that working?"

"Akira has to keep the lines apart!" Tamaya defended the party line with no idea if it was true, or even what it meant.

Rakta closed in, pinning her against the wall. "The Akash must have an heir. The future of the village depends on it! I will give you a strong son. You will say nothing. I will come whenever he trains, until it is done."

"Don't be too predictable, War Chief!" she snarled right back at him without trying to escape.

Rakta threw his head back and laughed. "No one will know, until they see how strong he is. Then they will know his is not the son of Bazu, but what can they say? Even Akira will be silent. She wants a strong Akashic heir more than anyone. Why do you think she gave Salistar to that big woodworker, Valko? Because he made strong sons for the Akashic line. Well, my son, our son, Tamaya, will be beautiful, flawless and strong, and Akira will hold him up and say he is the Son of Akash, the Heir and Successor of the Sacred Longstick and the Holy Seed!"

He had worked himself into an almost religious lather, like the old Akash on Passascenday. The one who knew all those theatrical tricks, taught to him by his Popa, no doubt. It looked like Rakta's line could bring some theatrical talent to the recipe, as well as his strength and health. "Who will dare say otherwise?" he concluded, suddenly looking like a small boy talking his momama out of more gup cakes.

"He will know," she countered, numbly. Her shock was the only thing keeping the full realization at bay. The unthinkable was about to happen, and she knew she wasn't going to stop it. Not that she wanted it. Or did she? She didn't know. She'd never had it.

"How will he know? What can he say?" Rakta's enthusiasm hadn't ebbed.

"He will know," she assured him, without saying why. He didn't seem to realize the totality of the Akashic failure. No matter. She plunged forward. "He will know. When the people sing his praises for making a strong, beautiful son, he will let them. But he will know."

Rakta had relaxed away from her a bit, without moving his feet. He looked a little confused. Then he looked past her to the relative darkness of the cave entrance. Tamaya unplugged the lamp. Rakta rushed past her, out of the tunnel and around the Rock.

"How long has it been?" His eyes darted around the cave, then outside, at the sky. "It's almost noon. Too late."

"How long...?" Tamaya began, still numb, not sure what he was asking.

"I won't be rushed," he declared, bringing his face close to hers. He touched her chin. "Not with you."

He took a last, lingering, look and spun away. He flowed down the stairs, keeping low, and disappeared into the willows again, just like before, leaving Tamaya more confused and anxious than ever.

No Moon Day

A week later, it was No Moon Day. Dense clouds dumped rain on the muddy ground outside. A drenched young warrior arrived at the Holy Cave with the obvious message. "No practice today. Next week, on First Quarter Moonday, if there is no rain. There can't even be a drop of rain, Buppan says."

Bupple had already told Bazu this would be the case. They had been arguing about it all morning.

"Now this upstart warrior comes," Bazu waved his new lightweight longstick at the young man, who did not quiver enough, he seemed to think. Unsatisfied, he turned back to his giant guard.

"We will do it inside the Great Hall!"

"It is forbidden." Bupple informed him.

"I am Akash." Bazu declared himself above the law.

"It is bad luck," Tamaya reminded him. "Everyone knows that."

Bazu snorted. "Women's talk. What kind of bad magic do you silly women think will happen if the Akash swings his longstick in the Great Hall?"

Tamaya shrugged. "Broken plates and pots? Maybe chairs or even tables, if the Mighty Akash is Powerful enough!" she cooed in a soothing voice.

He gathered himself and nodded sharply. "Yes, I might well be that! I do not yet fully realize my new power." He turned to the messenger boy. "Yes, tell the men I will return on next quarter moonday, if the weather is clear. It must be perfectly clear, fine weather before the Akash will rejoin you on the practice field. Perhaps next spring, when the weather is perfect. Until then, I will practice here, outside, whenever I can, with Bupple to train me. When I return, I will take over the training of the longstick-men. You be sure to tell Buppan I said so."

"Yes, Akash," the stunned young man replied breathlessly. Then he whirled on his heels, just like Rakta did, sending a sudden flash of heat to Tamaya's loins. It faded into a soft mixture of relief and disappointment as she watched the soggy messenger slog back to the village, futilely holding a floppy grass mat over his head.

Earth, Spring 2019
Reading

"Thanks for teaching me to read Old Akashic." Belinda smiled up from the papers spread out on the dining table in the quarters. Baput looked up, too, and stared at the two women with saucer-like eyes. There was a warmth between them that he had never seen between his Momama and Tamaya, his betrothed on Nauve. In fact, he realized, he had never seen them together except in the Great Hall during the three-day Season. Even then, Momama was always busy in the kitchen and Tamaya was, well, *not*.

"You will be tether to Akash," Star was explaining. "You must learn, so you can write down his thoughts as he rides the Akashic Plane." She gestured at Baput, then vaguely upward.

Belinda broke the warm gaze, turning her head so that neither eye faced them. "My Mom says I can't be that. I can't marry Baput," she reminded them softly.

Salistar rose from her seat and walked halfway around the table, into Belinda's averted view. She planted her round, green face right in front of Belinda's straight eye, eyebrows raised and lips pursed prudishly. "Since when does a girl and her momama decide such things?"

Belinda didn't flinch. She leaned in, uncomfortably close, even by Nauvian standards. "On Earth, we do."

"Your momama decides?" Star backed off a bit, eyebrows wrinkled.

"I do." Belinda clarified. "Once I'm 21, I can do whatever I want."

Salistar snorted, "You will be too old to get married by then."

"Tamaya is 21," Baput added without knowing why.

"That is because she was for your older brother, Batuk. Normally, the girl would be a little younger than you, within a cycle, if possible. Your age, Belinda, my daughter," she traced Belinda's chin with her fingertip. "Dear child. So smart! You have already mastered our alphabet. It took me many months, years, even. G-pa never finished teaching Baput." She returned to her seat and stared down at the open page. A wet droplet fell, blurring the ink.

"It's because it's like our English alphabet," Belinda said. "Each letter is a sound, and you put them together to make words. I'm used to it. I just have to learn your different letters."

"Yes," Star choked, "Read more." She turned the book to where Belinda had retaken her seat, and pointed to the page, just below the smudge.

Belinda read, haltingly, but in perfectly pronounced Nauvian. "People take great comfort in knowing Kakeeche will come in their cycle, every month the same. We must believe in Kakeeche, or they'll turn their backs on us. If anyone doubts the power and love of Kakeeche, they will turn their backs on all of us."

Baput slammed his hand down on the page, covering it completely with his oversized palm. "No Kakeeche," he declared unilaterally, in the Akashic way, with no fear in his voice.

Star's lips tightened and she looked away, mumbling. Belinda leaned forward awkwardly to hear her whisper, "Our Akash does not believe in Kakeeche."

Belinda's skewed, green eye shot lasers at Baput. "Baput! You are the Holy Akash! The High Priest! How can you not believe your own religion?" She almost shrieked, hating her own impudent tone. Salistar had taught her better. She turned to the timid foreigner, who sat, frozen.

"My son, the Holy Alanakash, rejects our faith," the statue muttered softly, but clearly.

"I do not, Momama," Baput confirmed. "I believe in the Plane. The ever-flowing force of life and death, always changing, always the same, all knowing, all one. I see the past and project the future. It guides me, not by command but by teaching. It is real, but not real. It is in my mind, my heart, my soul. That is what I believe in. That is the source of my Akashic power. Not the moon. Not a dead rock circling in space."

Salistar bowed her head and prayed in fervent Nauvian. "He who doesn't believe in Kakeeche dooms us all and dies in a most terrible way!" She looked up, her eyes dripping with fear. "Like Batuk!"

Baput was on his feet, towering over them as if he wore his robe. "No, Momama!"

Salistar sat up tall, wriggling like a snake to approach his face. "They turned their backs on us, last full Kakeeche, last week!" she accused. "All of them turned red. Then they turned all dark, right before bedtime."

"There was no eclipse..." Belinda interrupted.

"Yes, there was," Baput revealed. "Remember when we all watched the lion movie together? That was to distract you all, so you wouldn't see it."

"I saw. I stepped outside," Star insisted. "The Kakeeche were so red, so angry! After the movie, I looked again, before bed. They were all black. They had turned their backs completely." Salistar recalled, shaking as she had all that night. "I thought they would never shine on us again. I was so frightened!"

The imposing Akashic posture melted and Baput rushed to her. "Momama, why didn't you tell me?" He reached out to stroke her hair. She pulled away.

"Because it was your doing! They heard your thoughts. They can read your mind like we are reading their Holy Commands right now. I thought you would be a great Akash, but you failed, right away. You know better! You fail deliberately. You fight your fate. You are too much Jerry, too much Earth! You know Science now, Shavarandu," she jeered, sounding like G-pa. "You think you don't need Kakeeche."

"I don't." Baput's answer was cold. He sounded like G-pa, too. "I believe in the Plane. And I believe in science, which is truth. The moon is a rock that circles the Earth. The Earth circles the sun. When the paths cross, Earth casts a shadow on the full moon. But it's not real, Momama. The moon is still there. It's only a shadow."

He stood tall again, gathering himself up for a sermon, like he'd seen G-pa do. *So, this is how it feels*. "Just a shadow," he repeated. "Not somebody up in the sky telling us what to do, what to believe, rewarding us, punishing us. Earth people don't believe that."

Belinda had to correct him. "Well, actually, a lot of Earth people do believe that very thing. They call it God."

Baput rolled his eyes and paced across the room, grabbing his longstick on the way.

Salistar peered at Belinda with moist, curious eyes. Belinda continued to explain to her half-audience. "He's an old man with white hair and a long beard, kind of like G-pa. He lives in Heaven, in the sky, and he watches everything, hears everything, even your thoughts. He tells people what to do, punishes them if they're bad, just like a big Popa over all the Popas of the world."

Familiar comfort seeped into Salistar's confused eyes, suddenly eclipsed by terror. "G-pa in the sky, always watching? Hearing my thoughts?"

Baput whirled gracefully and stormed back to the table with his ornate longstick, looking even taller than before. He roared down at his subjects like a seasoned Akash.

"No, Momama! That is not what we believe."

Belinda stood, crossed to the back of Star's chair and glared at the imposing Akash. "She can believe whatever she wants. This is America. If she's comfortable believing there's somebody watching over us, why can't she? Nobody really knows what's out there until you die, and then you can't tell anybody. So, we just believe whatever we want to. Whatever gives us comfort."

"Comfort?" Baput snarled. He didn't want to yell at Belinda, or Momama either. Momama, who seemed to be melting into a pool of some thin liquid, indistinguishable from her tears. "Look at her!" he roared anyway. "A simple eclipse and she thinks the world is ending and it's all her fault! Or my fault! Or my dead brother's!" The butt of his longstick resounded on the wooden floor. "No more Kakeeche! And no God, either! Belinda, don't you teach her that anymore. She believes in the Plane, and Science, and what I tell her to believe!"

"You can't tell somebody else what to believe." Bel shot back. "Even if you *are* the Akash. If you think that, you're just as bad as your g-pa!"

Her cell phone rang. She jumped and stepped out of the tense green bubble. "Dad?"

"They're here." Patrick informed her, his voice solemn.

"Who, Dad?"

"You know. The RID guys. Call 911, Babe. Send the others to hide in the woods, like we planned."

"Baput, go to the shop and tell the guys to hide. Take Salistar with you. Hurry!" she told him, their argument forgotten.

Star had not recovered from her liquid state. She whispered palely from her seat. "I told you. It is Kakeeche, punishing us!"

Baput grabbed her shoulders, lifted her to her feet and shook her gently while he spoke to Belinda. "Do you see? She thinks Kakeeche blames her and punishes her when she's done nothing wrong. Then when men do real evil, she blames the moon!"

"Go, Baput!" Belinda ordered as she poked three numbers into her phone.

Right Identity Doctrine

Baput and Salistar leashed the three dogs and clamored out the back door. Belinda crept out the front door onto the porch, the phone at her ear. The dispatcher picked up.

"Nine one one, what is your emergency?"

Belinda described the scene that unfolded in the driveway in front of her house, her view filtered through the wavering trees. The pickup in front was now painted in desert camouflage, but she recognized it, and the two men who climbed out with rifles in their hands. That skinhead deputy from down south, and that stupid guy from that Right Identity Doctrine, RID. The rabid xenophobes had now been officially declared a hate group. Two unfamiliar pickups pulled to a stop right behind the RID guy's.

"Armed men have broken through my gate and they are attacking my father." She stated in a calm voice that seemed to come from somewhere far away, like a distant narrator. "There are three pickups. Six men. I think they're from RID."

"The hate group?"

"Yes," that calm voice replied.

"Are you, um, citizens?"

"Does it matter?" Belinda snapped, suddenly reanimating that empty voice with her whole self.

"No ma'am," the dispatcher corrected. "Just assessing the situation."

"We're mutants, Okay?" Bel fought to control her wavering voice. "We have a genetic deformity. Me and my dad. They think we're aliens. They broke in here with guns. My dad's a total pacifist. He doesn't even have a gun. You gotta help us."

"What is your location?"

Belinda recited her street address and hung up. She scrolled through her contacts and found a number she had only called once before, last year at Uncle Elmer's. Tulare County Sheriff Dave Riley. Doors slammed and four more men emerged from the other two pickups, all carrying rifles.

"Sheriff Dave?" she whispered from the doorway. "It's Belinda Musik again."

"Belinda, well, why hey, Doll!" the sheriff searched his memory. "What's going on?" his voice turned grave when he found the bitter recollection.

"Those guys are here with their guns again. They broke through the gate. My dad's talking to them, but he's all alone and he has no guns and you know how he is, Sheriff Dave. Do you remember?"

Dave remembered alright. Elmer's cockeyed little brother getting beat up in school, just for being different. Him refusing to fight, trying to defend himself with words, Elmer always coming to his rescue, or Francine. Why, he wouldn't even kill the monsters at the fairgrounds! "Where's Elmer?" he asked.

"At the Look 'N Up, I guess." Belinda reported.

Uh-oh. "You're not at the Look 'N Up?" he asked gently.

"We're at home, up north here. They found us. They're looking for the green people."

"Are they there?" Dave had to ask. He had always figured that's where they went, but Elmer wouldn't say.

Neither would Belinda. The phone went silent.

"It's okay, Doll. I won't tell anybody. I just have to know, OK?"

"Yes," Belinda whispered. "They're hiding." Sirens wailed in the distance.

"Well, honey, you're out of my jurisdiction up there."

"I know. I called 911. They're coming, but do you know the Sheriff up here in El Dorado County? I was hoping you could tell him the whole story. The made-up one, I mean."

The burley Sheriff of Tulare County inhaled a deep breath and exhaled it noisily. "Okay. I'll call the Sheriff up there and tell him the history, about how they harassed you guys before, because of your eyes."

"What about the Nauvians?" Bel asked.

"The what? Oh, you mean those Pakistani farm workers Elmer had last year? The ones who dyed themselves green for that crazy ritual at the fairgrounds? They moved on, didn't they? You guys don't have a farm up there, do you?"

"No?" Belinda answered uncertainly. Did eighteen pomegranate trees and Dad's medicinal herb constitute a farm?

"Well, why would you have farm workers then? They're long gone, to some other farm, don't you think?" Dave suggested.

"Sure," Belinda answered weakly. The men below were advancing on Patrick. He backed away from them, up the steps of his front porch. They followed, step for step.

"Listen." Dave told her firmly. "Here's what you need to do. When the Sheriff arrives and those men put their guns down, when it's safe, I want you to show yourself. I'm telling him it's about your eye, so show yourself. Be, um, sad and hurt and all that. Just be yourself. Show 'em!"

"Like last time?"

"Just like last time. But for now, you stay hidden, OK? I'll call the Sheriff."

"You don't have a warrant." Patrick argued lamely with his hands held high and his back against the closed front door of his house. "You're not even cops."

Belinda felt a stab of shame at his weakness. Another step and he'd be inviting them in! Then she felt more shame, at herself. She knew her dad wasn't weak. Patrick defended his pacifism with the courage and fidelity of a Marine.

So what if he lets them in. Baput and his family aren't in there. There would be no sign of them there, except the CD player with the recordings. Hours and hours of Baput's recollections, all the legends, stories of primitive weapons, unquestioning obedience to the Holy Akash. Stories that betrayed their profound innocence, their staggering ignorance. If Earth guys like these ever found a way through the portal, the green-skinned race would be enslaved or wiped out before they could even shut their mouths from the shock of seeing people with white skin and light hair, much less understand the conquest in the hearts of their invaders.

The sirens neared and slowed, then stopped abruptly. A vehicle crunched on the gravel driveway. The local sheriff had arrived, just in time. The four men Belinda hadn't seen before stood on the ground at the foot of the porch stairs. They turned to look at the approaching vehicle, their guns sinking slowly to their sides. On the porch, Dave's ex-Deputy, Rod Otto, and Dirk from the LA Chapter of RID kept their guns drawn on the unarmed man.

Sheriff Reed stepped out of the El Dorado County Sheriff vehicle and unfolded his lanky frame to tower above its roof. He reached in for his semiautomatic service rifle, his eyes scanning the scene. The shorter Deputy Landers popped out the other side with is handgun drawn.

"What's going on?" the Sheriff asked, almost casually.

"There are illegal aliens here." Otto reported, jamming his uncocked rifle into Patrick's ribs.

"Hold them." Sheriff Reed ordered his deputy, pointing at the four men who stood loosely at the bottom of the porch steps, looking at each other. He gained the porch in a single leap and started shoving his way to Patrick. His surprise showed clearly in his eyes, although he'd been warned. Dave Riley from Tulare County had told him the whole story.

"They're not aliens," Sheriff Riley had told him. "They're from down here. I grew up with this guy. He's got a messed-up eye. Him and his little daughter. His dad had it, and his grandpa, too. They've had a farm down here for about a hundred years. Now these nuts got the idea they're from outer space..."

"Do you live here?" Sheriff Reed asked the weird looking guy with the gun barrel stuck between his ribs.

Patrick seemed to look at the Sheriff with one eye and his assailant with the other. He nodded.

"Want to get your gun off this guy, Holmes?" the Sheriff addressed Otto with that same casual air.

Otto grunted, then stepped back, pointing his barrel straight up.

"And you, Sir?" the Sheriff asked Dirk, more politely than necessary, it seemed to Patrick, but it worked.

Dirk dropped his gun to his side and hung his head, as if he was counting the nails in the porch deck. The men on the ground stood in awkward silence, eyes wandering.

The Sheriff was there. The guns were down. So, Belinda started slowly down the trail from the quarters. One of the strangers on the ground spotted her and cried, "Look!"

Everyone looked up, to where he pointed. With the late afternoon sun behind her, Belinda's auburn hair blazed and her shadow stretched long, reaching toward them.

"What are you men so afraid of?" she asked loud and clear, and her voice sounded like the Liberty Bell pealing out from behind its imperfect face. "Are you afraid of me?" The peal turned into a disarming squeak, just in time. She walked slowly down the trail, kicking that monstrous shadow ahead of her. The men just stood there, mouths open, guns hanging limply by their sides watching her approach.

"Why do you hate us? We're not hurting anybody."

The fervent silence broke into mumbles and whispers between men who had shared a ride, each pair drawing away from the others. The hideous, pitiful child continued her advance, her questions. "How do you think I feel? I have to go to school like this." She pointed to her own face. "And your kids pick on me all the time, because you guys taught them to hate me just because I'm different. My dad, too. What's he ever done to you? He wouldn't hurt a fly. He just lives here, minding his own business, and you guys think you can come in here and push him around with your guns? Why don't you just leave us alone?"

"Poor kid."

"I didn't sign up for this."

A pair of men mumbled as they withdrew to their truck. The Sheriff watched them unload their guns and rack them.

The next pair didn't move. The taller one addressed Dirk, the apparent leader. "What about the green people?" he asked.

Belinda and Patrick exchanged a look, in their undetectable way. It spoke volumes, or rather, it indicated which volume of the anthology was The Story today. "What green people?" they said in perfect unison.

Sheriff Reed and his Deputy echoed the question with total sincerity, "what green people?"

Still on the porch steps, Dirk and Otto exchanged a look. Dirk raised his eyebrows invitingly, offering Otto the floor. He's the one who'd started all this.

Otto looked up at that narrow head on that tall uniform. His stomach clenched. He had worn a uniform like that, for just a week. *One miserable, frustrating week with that Sheriff Riley. A sympathizer, just like this guy.* Eyes at chest level, he stared at the badge he had longed to wear all his life and felt nothing but disgust.

He stepped back so he could look into those eyes up there, although he couldn't see them through those cop sunglasses. He swallowed, looked around. His two buddies, the two who hadn't left, were waiting for him to tell this cop the incredible story he'd told them. His boss, Dirk, knew it was true. He'd seen the green aliens at that farm they call the Look 'N Up. But Dirk just stood there smiling with those cold eyes of his, like he was laughing inside. And that freaky brat was standing there with her arms folded, staring right at him, or was she? He shuddered, ran his tongue around his lips, and tried, once.

"Well, see, this guy's brother has a farm down south and they had these green aliens working there last year." He scanned his audience, saw he was losing them. Even the mutants weren't letting on what they knew to be true. "They went to the fair and played music and they brought their predators with them and they attacked the fairgrounds, and then they killed a Mexican guy in the office park because they only eat green people but it was dark—"

Otto heard the familiar sound of handcuffs coming out. "You're under arrest. Breaking and entering. Assault with a deadly weapon. It's for your own good, Mister. You need help." The sheriff turned to Patrick, still pressed against his front door. "And you need a restraining order."

The Deputy collected names. Then, once again, Patrick and Belinda watched Rod Otto get loaded into a patrol car while his buddies scurried away, apologizing. Not a bit sorry, they knew. Just scared.

When the patrol car followed the two pickups down the driveway, Patrick peeled himself off the door. His wayward eye caught motion to his left. He looked there, then to the right. Felsic and Valko stepped from the trees on either side of the porch, their faces streaked with black charcoal war paint. They held Felsic's spring guns in their hands, locked and loaded with the potentially lethal darts Valko had designed.

"Aww, Guys!" Patrick whined. "I told you. I don't do violence. It's not my way. See how it all worked out without it? Great job, Babe." He and Belinda swayed back and forth in a long embrace while their racing hearts slowed. Valko walked away, shaking his hirsute head.

Lying

"Can I come in?" Baput asked from the front doorway. It was open just a crack, and all Bel could see was that broad green nose and those lush lips moving. He didn't usually ask, unless Lorraine was home.

"Of course, Silly." Belinda invited.

"Yeah, come on in." Patrick agreed in a somber tone.

Baput entered meekly. "My Popa says 'sorry' for going against your ways and bringing violence. He's a warrior. That's his way. He just couldn't let anything happen to you two."

"I know," Patrick sighed. "He didn't hurt anybody. He just backed us up. Who knows? We might have needed it. It could have gone a lot worse. But, see how we resolved it without shooting anybody?"

"By lying," Baput pointed out. "You went against my code, just like Popa broke yours."

"What lie?" Belinda asked.

"You said, 'what green people?' like you didn't know us."

"We didn't actually *say* we didn't know you," Belinda argued. "We just asked a question."

"But that's still lying, isn't it?" Baput insisted. "You indicated you didn't know us, and you do. I can't support that. Lying is against the Akashic Oath. If the Akash shouldn't do it, his people shouldn't, either."

"Your people?" Patrick mused, hoping the green boy never said that in front of Lorraine. "Look. We had to do it. We can't let them see you. You know that. It's just a little lie, and it worked. They went away, nobody got hurt. We call it a white lie."

"Because white is good?" Baput asked. "It's OK for white people to lie?"

Patrick sighed, the weight of the world's hate pressing down on his shoulders. "We're not supposed to lie, either, but we do it all the time. We all do, I think. To be totally honest, I guess I lie all the time."

"Well, if you were totally honest, you wouldn't." Baput was getting pretty clever with his English. "Why do you lie all the time?" he asked.

Patrick turned so he couldn't look at Baput or Belinda with either eye. He spoke softly, clearly, from a flat place deep inside. "To keep the peace, mostly. Just like today. Sometimes saying the truth just starts trouble."

"What if you just don't say anything?" Baput answered with the question that had been bothering him. *What does the Akashic Oath mean when it says, "Speak nothing but the truth"? What if I don't speak at all?*

"Sometimes people make you—" Patrick replied defensively.

"Like when, Dad?" Belinda interrupted.

"Well," Patrick began guardedly, "like when I tell your mom I don't mind that she's at work all the time and even when she's home, she's always in her office on her computer." He was blinking hard, making the angry tears squirt. "Leaving her little girl to be raised by an incompetent father and a bunch of aliens. No offense."

Belinda rushed to hug him again. "You're not incompetent. You're just too nice. But it's OK, Dad. Salistar keeps me in line."

Patrick leaned out of the hug to look down at her inquiringly. "She does?"

Belinda smiled up at him without any tears. "When we cook together, or weave, she tells me how to be a good tether."

Belinda turns Fourteen

"Come on, Bel!" Patrick urged. "Baput and I are going in the music room to meditate. He's working on a new chant that he hopes will get Felsic and Valko onto the Plane. He's trying it on me first. He's only got two months to work it out so he can use it for the Mitten Ceremony."

"Mitten Ceremony?" Lorraine asked without looking up from the thick, comb-bound volume she was redlining by hand on the kitchen table. "Is Salistar going to knit us all mittens now?"

"No, Mom," Belinda sneered. "It's Nauvian. It means it's halfway through the three-year cycle. Eighteen months until next First Pomegranate Day."

"Eighteen plus two, twenty months until they leave," Lorraine muttered, jotting a note in the margin. She raised her head and looked over her glasses at Belinda like a bitter old schoolteacher. "Well, what are you waiting for? I got you that nice meditation cushion for your birthday, and you had a fit about it right in front of everyone, just like last year. Okay, thirteen I expect it, but your fourteen now. You have to get a grip on your emotions, little girl. It won't get any easier, let me tell you."

"Mom. You embarrassed me in front of Star. Women don't get meditation cushions. Women don't meditate."

"Says who?" Lorraine snapped back, the book almost forgotten.

"Star doesn't. Women don't. Especially Akashic Tethers. They have to stay on the ground and take care of things while their men surf the Akashic Plane."

Lorraine pulled her glasses from her face, set them down on the open page of *Project Specifications for the Canal Street Bridge* and glared at her budding teenage daughter. "If that backwards little woman chooses to limit herself, that's her problem. My daughter doesn't say, 'I'm a woman! I can't!'" she jeered.

"That's right, Babe." Patrick agreed, squeezing his wife's shoulder. It felt like the cable of a suspension bridge. "You come, too. Come meditate with us. We have an extra cushion."

"Are you kidding?" Lorraine ducked out from under his touch. "I don't have time for that crap!"

FBI Plots

"Finally!" Agent Boyd removed his headphones and pressed a button on his growing console of devices.

"The warrant?" Special Agent Kramer asked carelessly.

"I thought we didn't need a warrant." Agent Goldsmith challenged her superior, who grunted guiltily.

"We needed it for the telemetry," Boyd explained as he rapidly entered lengthy strings of digits on his computer's keypad. "The FCC codes to transmit the videos, and audio," he winked, as if the audio was something extra-special. Dumbing it down for his dinosaur boss, he pointed at the ceiling. "All these teeny cameras I'm gonna set up can transmit right into to the sky." He redirected his finger toward his console, "and then, right there to that monitor. We can watch them in real time. Watch the farm. Watch that rock. Now we just need a chance to get out there and deploy the cameras."

"Here comes Francine Musik." Rita informed them from her post at one of the clear spots high on the blackened front window. Boyd clicked on the feed from the bug in the Cow Chow office.

"Mmmwah!" Rita gagged at the fake kissing noises Francine and her mom made. Jealous? Naw. Her mom wasn't so demonstrative, but she was real. She could almost see the beaming face that matched that excited voice.

"Mom! I got the Community Hall. Saturday, March 30, all day. We'll do a potluck, and I'll make a sheet cake that says 'Happy 50th Anniversary, Bernice and Frank."

"I'll make a big lasagna," Bernice offered.

"You'll do no such thing, Mom. It's your party. You just show up at noon. We'll have everything all set up. The whole town will be there! We'll eat a big lunch and the Hillbillies will play. You like them, right?"

"They're nice local boys. Good old fashioned country music," Bernice agreed reluctantly.

Rita could hear the smothered laugh in Fran's throat. "It's called bluegrass, Mom. We'll all dance to the Hillbillies. Then we'll open presents. It's the Golden Anniversary, you know!"

"No presents." Bernice stated adamantly.

"We'll see." Fran replied. Rita relished the sly smile in Fran's voice, found herself wondering what the big surprise gift would be.

Boyd pumped his fist. "They're finally going somewhere! March thirtieth, that's our chance!"

Mitten Ceremony

At sixteen and a half, Baput was quickly approaching his popa's grand stature. The elaborately woven Akashic Robe his momama had made for him, with help from Francina and Belinda, made him look even bigger. He stood before his few "subjects", all family members many years his senior. With the tiny orchard of eighteen young pomegranate trees behind him, they could almost imagine they were nauve, watching the Akash deliver the Mitten Ceremony. That is, until he opened his mouth. This was not like any Mitten Ceremony they'd ever heard.

"Today is Mitten," Baput declared, addressing Patrick and Belinda, who stood behind his family. Halfway between First Pomegranate Days. On this very day, one cycle ago, we dug up the Rock on the Look 'N Up Ranch. It is the same rock as the Holy Rock in the Holy Cave back on Nauve. When we dug it up last Mitten, it was silent, so we know it is silent today, and defenseless. In eighteen months, on my eighteenth birthday, it will ring again. The nimblies and bumblies will make the Holy Rock on Nauve ring, and the Rock here on Earth will ring, too. The Portal could open, but I don't believe we can return to Nauve without the soft, light net of woven wires that we laid over the top. The Net remains on Nauve. If anyone on Nauve tries to use it, to fire the weapon, they might come here, I mean, to the Look 'N Up. Maybe more nimblies and bumblies will come through. We must be prepared for this, by the end of this cycle.

"But we must also think about the past. Why did we come here to Earth? There must be a reason for such a profound event." He scanned the small crowd again, as if seeking an answer. Hearing none, he offered his own theory. "There is something Nauve lacks. Something our survival depends on." His eyes fixed on Belinda.

Patrick put his hand on her shoulder and stepped in front of her.

Baput continued. "It is called DNA. We need more people. New people. Different people. If we can ever find a net that works, we must return to Nauve with some Earth people. Preferably small children who won't rebel against our culture. There will be social change, surely, if we return to Nauve after so many years on Earth. But we, I, must control those changes and make sure they happen slowly, in a carefully managed way, not by showing up with a bunch of rebellious Earth teenagers or stubborn adults who are set in Earth ways.

"On this Mitten, your Akash orders, um, *requests* that you join with me in meditation. Lend me your psychic energies so that I can have more power to search for the answers we so vitally need to save our people.

"I'll do it!" Patrick's enthusiasm popped the solemn bubble. "Link our hard drives together and soup up the search engine. Come on, Belinda, sit down with me, right here on the grass."

"Yes!" Baput encouraged.

Valko and Felsic grunted stiffly as they folded themselves into the unaccustomed meditation pose. They had learned to meditate in school, but, like most common men, they hadn't practiced it since then. They fell into an exaggerated heavy breathing.

Only Belinda and Salistar remained standing.

"Momama!" Baput ordered his tether, "Come. Sit down with us and meditate. You too, Belinda."

"But I have to check the oven and stir the stew." Salistar dared argue with her Akash. "You can't have a Mitten Feast without us women doing what we do." She turned away and started trudging up the hill to the quarters.

"Belinda?" Baput pleaded with his soft, powerful eyes.

"Come on, Bel!" Patrick tried once more.

"Belinda!" Salistar's voice rang out from the trail above them.

Belinda's eyes darted between Baput and Patrick before she whirled and fled up the hill to join her mentor.

Patrick shook his head.

Baput just shrugged, used to such things. "Are you ready?" he asked his army of meditators.

"Do not look at Shavarandu.

He will burn your eyes—"

Felsic and Valko began the chant they'd memorized at three years old.

"No!" Baput roared, his longstick thudding on the soft orchard soil. "No Kakeeche chant. That is the chant they used to blind us, to brainwash us against Shavarandu. Against technology. I told you of the vision I had: The Old Ones built the weapon and used it on the Vishnians, the Blue People. It vaporized them into the blue mist we still see and fear today. But that was a thousand years ago, or a thousand cycles. Even the old Akash didn't know when our world 'began', according to his own lore. Nor do I. But it doesn't matter. It was long, long ago. It is time we come out of that shadow, and live in the light of Shavarandu instead of the ignorance of a cold rock in space. Perhaps that is another reason we have come to Earth. To escape the lie and relearn our true place in the universe. I have made up a new chant to bring us to the Plane. Say it after me:

The Akashic Plane is there to guide us,
If we only try
To witness an eternity
And let it all go by
The power is within us
Patience is the key
Just inhale the boundless wisdom
And allow it all to be."

He placed a large, brass bowl on his open palm and struck the edge with a padded wooden mallet. Then, he ran the mallet around the edge. A resonant tone emerged, as if from the bottom of the bowl, and spilled out to cover the seated mediators like a heavy mist.

He switched the chant to Nauvian while Patrick continued in English, as they had practiced. Valko and Felsic lapsed into their native language. The staccato rhythm of their short syllables punctuated the English rhyme and the round, swelling tone of the bowl. Soon a deep rumble at the bottom of the audible range added a resounding baseline. Valko was snoring.

Colors played across Baput's third eye, swirling in spirals before shooting off in a straight line into an endless distance.

A familiar denim-blue aura appeared on his left. "DNA for Nauve" Patrick's spirit crooned.

Baput was startled by a new presence on his right. Felsic had never joined him in meditation before! But there he was, in a shimmering olive-green aura that resembled his skin color. Baput sent him an ethereal thumbs up and saw a flash of his own aura, full-spectrum white since he had embraced Shavarandu last Mitten, exactly three years ago.

While the others continued the chant in two languages, Baput cast his question into the never-ending River of Sight.

"How can we return to Nauve?
And bring the DNA we need, to save the People?
This is why we are here on Earth
This is our chance to save the People
We are ready now, and open
To receive your instructions, to save the People
Our future depends on this
I am Akash
I must bring the Holy Seed into the future
To save the People!"

The swirling colors faded to a dull grey mist. Baput inhaled a deep Akashic breath and exhaled slowly into the fog. The mist organized itself into an image of the same dull grey color. Grey cinderblock walls, a grey plastic table with grey folding chairs on a featureless grey concrete floor. The back of a bulky man in a green uniform took shape before his eyes, the words, US BORDER PATROL blazoned in yellow across the broad back.

"Who's that boy?" Felsic's unfamiliar spirit-voice almost shattered Baput's concentration. The vision waivered, then recovered, sharply focused on a seven-year-old boy with coffee brown skin and thick black hair who sat across the table from the big man. His young face was contorted and wet with tears, and although he spoke no English, Baput, Patrick and Felsic understood every word.

"Where's my popa?" the boy squeaked in almost a whisper.

"He's been arrested," the burly man informed him, none too gently. "He's been to the United States before, hasn't he?"

"Si," the boy nodded.

"Well, we kicked him out, told him not to come back, and he came back anyway, so we arrested him."

"Are you arresting me, too?" the boy asked, almost eagerly. "I can share a cell with my popa. I won't be any trouble, mister, I promise."

The blocky head with the close-cropped hair shook side to side. "I can't put you in there. You're not arrested. And, you're a kid. Now, do you have any relatives in the United States? Someone who can take care of you?"

"I don't know," the kid whispered to the tabletop, just inches from his lips.

"You don't know? Who were you going to stay with when you got here with your dad? He's been here before. There must be someone."

"Mi Tio, Jose. Except he's not really my uncle."

"Well, does not-your-uncle Jose have a last name? Where does he live?" The border agent fired questions too fast for the terrified child to answer.

"He lives in San Dago!" he suddenly remembered.

"Jose in San *Dago*," the agent leaned back in his chair, closed his file folder.

"Yes!" the boy brightened. "Do you know him?"

A chuckle escaped from the border agent's flabby cheeks. "No, but I bet these guys do." He turned to his left, where rows of similar tables stretched all the way to the back of the vast grey room. He bellowed, "Hey! Anybody know Jose? He's from right here in San Dago!" He leaned back further, balancing on the two back legs of his chair, and roared with laughter.

The men and women at the other tables all repeated the routine, "Jose from San Dago, yeah, I know that guy! Ha ha ha!"

When the laughter died down and the little boy's heart had run the gamut from fear to hope to humiliation, the man resumed his questioning a bit more gently.

"Do you know where in San Diego?"

"In a trailer. In his partner, Jim's backyard."

"Does Jim have a last name?"

"I don't know."

"He's a partner, eh? What do they do together? Sell drugs? Make speed?"

"I don't know."

"What's Jim's phone number?"

"I don't know," the kid whispered, squirming in the hard chair.

"Didn't your dad give you anything? A full name? An address? A phone number for you to call if you got separated?"

The kid sat up as tall as he could, but he still looked smaller than he had before the questioning began. Looking right into the agent's face, he spoke out loud for the whole, vast room to hear. "We were supposed to stay together!"

Anniversary

On an unseasonably warm Saturday morning at the end of March, the Musiks arrived at the community hall in their new pickup truck. Kramer waited in the nondescript white van with the tinted windows, parked on the street out front. He talked into his wrist.

"You were right, Girl. She's got them all roped in. Even the kid."

"Elmer, too?" Rita asked hopefully, feeling vindicated. She didn't know how to hook up telemetry, but she knew people.

"Oh, yeah. He's not looking too happy. She's unlocking the door. They're carrying stuff, ice chests, tables, uh-oh, presents!" he jeered. "Here comes more people. Two old biddies in a pickup truck."

"Her friends," Rita mused warmly.

"They've got more stuff for good ol' Elmer to carry. Dangly paper stuff and a ladder. Oh, boy, he's fully roped in now, here for the duration, that's for sure. Get ready. I'll be right there."

The three agents entered the deserted farm the same way they had before. Boyd set the first camera on the oak tree in the west orchard that hung over the driveway. It covered the platform and the cave mouth, framed just like the photos they'd found on Jerry's friend Kate's phone. The cameras were tiny, wireless and weatherproof. All they needed was a clear view of the target and a clear path to the southern sky, where satellites orbited the Earth constantly sucking up data and spitting it out, hopefully on demand.

The houses weren't included in the warrant, Rita noted smugly. She was dreading bugging the inside of a private home, especially the home of a family that, according to months of intensive investigation, were nothing but fine, upstanding citizens. Hard working farmers. So what if they hired undocumented workers sometimes? Even green ones. She was sure the green people were gone, if there had ever been any. There was still no sign of them at the farm.

Kramer declared the shop to be OK, 'not a private residence', he said.

Boyd placed a tiny camera high up in the corner where it could watch the woodstove, mill, lathe and part of the workbench, and report what it saw to the sky just outside the open front.

Now, the part Boyd had been waiting for. All three of them went on foot this time. They crossed an open grassy place. The worn trail they had followed on their Christmas visit over a year ago was getting overgrown.

They stopped at a little stone building in the middle of the field. They had hurried past it last time. After finding that weird rock, the stone shed hadn't even caught their trained attentions. But now, they had plenty of time. Kramer led the way, pulling the swollen door open, letting a slice of spring sunshine into the dank.

"A woodstove?" Rita asked, crowding in. "Is it a drying shed?"

The older agent corrected her. "It's a sauna. You get that stove all hot and throw water on it, and steam yourself. What's this?"

He pulled a long, straight stick from a lower bench. It was carved in elaborate patterns, skillfully done, but rough, as if done by a true artisan using a crude instrument. The point was charred to a flaky, dull point. He stood it on end, twirled it thoughtfully.

Boyd pressed through the narrow door and reached for the stick. "Can I see?"

Kramer tightened his grip. "Why?"

"It might have something to do with that orb, or the aliens."

"It's just wood." Kramer reluctantly handed the stick to Boyd, who twirled it just like Kramer had. "Pretty low-tech stuff, for aliens. Take a picture and put it back," Kramer ordered. "We were never here, remember?"

"Yes, Sir." Boyd took the stick outside and laid it on the grass in the sun. He took several photos and a bunch of measurements and notes. "The

RID guy, the deputy, he said those green guys fought with sticks like this. Especially the old guy. I think this is his."

"Then he *is* dead. He wouldn't leave it," Rita speculated.

"Maybe he got a new one," Kramer answered drolly. "Come on. You gonna put a camera here or what?"

"In that shed? It's too dark." Boyd handed the stick back to Kramer. "Come on, let's go down to that orb thing."

Kramer set G-pa's longstick back in the sauna exactly the way he'd found it. As they walked the rest of the way to the alien orb that jutted from the ground beside the river, Boyd once again summarized the research he'd done over the last eighteen months.

"I can't find anything like it on the internet. I contacted two different materials science professors at University of California. They both asked for a sample. I told them it's too hard. They had some ideas. A diamond drill and a hot probe. But I think it's too hard for that, even. Anyway, when I said I couldn't get a sample, they wanted to come and see it."

"And I said 'no,'" Kramer reminded tersely. "We're keeping this quiet."

"Yeah." Boyd grunted. *Quiet?* He thought sarcastically. *From the guy that wanted to tell the townspeople we were designing video games in that empty store? We'd have the snotty noses of every kid in town pressed up against those blacked-out windows twenty-four seven if we'd gone with that story. Nice, boring accounting software development. Cheap rent, decent internet, just the kind of industry your little town needs to replace your retail, your factories, your failing farms.* That was the line they'd gone with.

The trail along the river was less worn once they'd passed the weird old willow tree, tied down with an old leather belt so the trunk grew horizontally, forming a bench overlooking the river. Still, Kramer could make out tire tracks from more than one vehicle.

They came around a bend and found a giant pile of brush stacked in the middle of the wide, flat spot where the orb had been. "Where is it?" Rita asked, immediately wishing she hadn't. *Duh! I'm an FBI Agent!*

Ignoring the stupid question, Boyd rushed to the pile and began removing the dry, bare limbs of pomegranate and willow.

"Don't change anything!" Kramer barked. "They'll know we were here."

Boyd kept on removing limbs. "I'll put them back. I've got to see it. See if it's still buzzing."

"You put them back exactly like you found them." Kramer insisted.

Boyd stopped at that. "Chief, do you really think they remember exactly where they put each stick?"

"We're here to put up your cameras. Not play with that stinking orb."

Boyd dug a tuning fork and a stethoscope from his shoulder bag. He felt like a kid on Christmas. Having to unwrap the gift only added to the thrill. He leaned into the hole he'd made in the orb's disguise and put both hands on it. He didn't feel the buzz. He brought his face down until his cheek rested on the smooth, cool surface. Then he placed the stethoscope and the tuning fork on the rock side by side, being careful not to strike the sensitive fork on the orb. He stayed like that, just his backside sticking out from what looked like a big pile of brush ready to be burned. After a long few minutes, he stood back up and stepped away from the strange object.

"No buzz," he reported.

"Did you hit the tuning fork on it?" Rita asked.

"No." Boyd spoke softly, as if reporting the death of an old friend. "I wanted to see if it was still buzzing by itself, like it was before. You know, from the event."

"What event?" Kramer and Goldsmith asked in unison.

"The day the flying things showed up at the fairgrounds. They came from here. I've got the parts to prove it. They set this orb thing off, or it set them off, and the green people came after them. Or maybe they came first, running from those things, those predators. They ran straight into a whole different world!"

"Ran from where?" Kramer snarled impatiently.

"Who knows?" Boyd gushed. "Another planet?"

Kramer shook his head slowly. Rita eyed them both curiously, not sure who's side to take.

"I wonder when it stopped buzzing. It's been, let's see" He counted the months on his fingers again, as if he hadn't been counting them every day of his frustrating wait for the paperwork and the opportunity to visit this wonderful orb again, this genuine space portal, he was sure. "It buzzed for all of October, November and December. Three months! Then I hit it again. How many months did it buzz after that? I wish I knew."

"Drop it, Agent!" Kramer barked. "We've got work to do."

Reluctantly, Boyd packed the sound measuring equipment away and brought out a boxed set of tiny cameras. He'd been at the top of his Surveillance Tech class at the Academy. With the help of his team, he soon had cameras in the trees and in the vines of the cliff, watching the orb and the river. He jogged down the narrow part of the trail and rode the solar winch up to the platform, where he set a camera on the rail, facing right into the little cave hole through the mangled rebar grate, and another facing the river below.

"I love Tech!" he declared as he pulled up the feed on his laptop. Six frames opened, displaying crystal clear images of the orb, the river, the cave, the platform, the shop and Kate's spot, where she had recorded all the action at the cave eighteen months ago. "We'll see this on my screen at the office. All live, real time."

"And we're gonna sit there and watch all the time?" Rita asked, not intrigued enough to relish that assignment.

Chief Kramer agreed. "I'm not getting up in the middle of the night to watch some deer come through here eating grass."

Boyd rolled his eyes. "Of course not, Boss. It records constantly. If it detects any movement or sound, it sets off an alarm and marks that spot on the recording. It won't erase it until you tell it to. We'll have a permanent record of everything that goes on at the Look 'N Up Ranch until the portal opens again. Then, we'll see that!"

Nauve, Mitten

Tamaya's 22nd Birthday

It was a rainy winter. The misty, gloomy nights, all the same. Kakeeche hid themselves behind the leaden clouds until Bazu lost track of their cycle. "Let them keep the monthly ceremony in their huts, like they did all last cycle," he declared to his Guard and Tether. "They will stay warm and dry, and so will I. Why should I turn my face up to the sky in the pouring rain, shouting words no one can hear, that they have all heard a thousand times before? They know the ceremony better than I do. They can do it for themselves." So, Bazu and his tether remained in the Holy Cave all winter.

It was almost Mitten before the weather was perfect enough for the Holy Akash to resume his longstick practice. He didn't seem to know or care that it was Tamaya's birthday, and she didn't mention it. *Let him go*! She thought. After a long winter cooped up in a cold, damp cave with those two men, she was ready for them both to be gone. She wanted to go for a walk in the sun, but she had to wait for Rakta. *Will he show up this time?* She wondered.

If Bazu was going to claim leadership of the longstick line, Rakta would have to stick around for that. The thought angered her unexpectedly. Wasn't that what they wanted? For Bazu to assert himself, become more aggressive? But he was so obnoxious now! Even more than before, and such a fool! He never used his one strength, his brains, to try to impress. He always picked something he was especially weak at, like this longstick business.

Bupple had been sparring with him, with the longstick and with his words, trying to teach him how to interact with the men. Tamaya had been sharing the tricks in Baram's book with Bupple, whenever they had a private moment. He was getting quite skilled at making the suggestions without letting the Wise One see their true nature.

At times, Bupple had managed to talk the glorified boy out of assuming leadership of the longstick line. Sometimes he got Bazu to agree it was too soon. Not because *he* wasn't ready, but because *they* weren't, an argument

Bupple had cleverly made Bazu think was his own. But on those rare occasions when the young Akash actually accomplished one of his longstick tricks without a hitch, he was determined to declare his supremacy, ready or not. So maybe Rakta would have to put down an uprising, maybe he wouldn't.

Tamaya sighed, scanned the blue sky wishfully. Bazu and Bupple had been gone for almost an hour. Rakta wasn't coming. She wrapped her precious silver gown around her shoulders to ward off the morning chill and headed down the stairs. The willows rustled, catching her eye. Rakta emerged in his dress battle garb, carrying a basket of fat, red berries and a handful of wildflowers.

Is that why he's late? she wondered ungratefully. She could have done without the berries and flowers and the extra stress. After four months of thinking about this moment, worrying about it by day and dreaming of it at night, she still had only a vague notion of what *it* was, hadn't decided if she wanted *it* or not, and had no idea how to stop it if she didn't.

At the foot of the stairs, Rakta extended his gifts. "I brought you these."

She accepted them without thanks, in her people's way. "Is my husband master of the longstick line?" she asked earnestly with a perfectly straight face, like an eager, loving tether. He threw his head back and laughed too loud, then suddenly quieted and looked around.

"He performed a most spectacular feat on arrival," he announced more quietly, grabbing her elbow gently and guiding her slowly up the stairs. "I must admit, it took a kind of courage I don't possess. He got right up there in front of everyone and twirled that fancy, fake longstick around, had it going, too. Then he got it too close to himself and hit his own foot. That stopped it short, and the other end struck him in the head. He's got a shiner now, like a real warrior! Heh, heh. The men loved it. You know, they would have reacted the same way if Bupple had done that, or Buppan, or even me. He could have done a lot worse. I was proud of him, and Bupple, for his teaching. But after he failed, he turned back into the same old Bazu. Whining, blaming people. He even blamed Bupple, after all that good work."

"Poor Bupple," Tamaya sympathized. "He is so good with him. So loyal. Yet he treats him so badly. Such a sweet man."

"He is good to you? Respectful?" Rakta asked pointedly, as if it was his business.

"He is like a good friend. I don't know what I would do without him to talk to, or what I would do alone with Bazu." She found herself more excited talking about Bupple than her husband, the Akash. But neither interested her like the subject right in front of her.

They had reached the porch at the top of the stairs. She looked him up and down. "You're all dressed up," she noted coolly.

"First practice day of spring. I was expecting some grand ceremony in the longstick line." He looked her up and down, too. "So are you. Is that the gown you wore to your wedding?" He reached down and picked up a corner that hung down in the back, where a hard little box, about an inch square, had been strangely woven into it. Two small prongs stuck out of it, made of a shiny material, strange, but now familiar. He stared at it, ignoring Tamaya.

"I don't know what that is for." She found herself talking about her gown, for Kakeeche's sake! Yet, she went on. "I think it's a clasp, but I can't figure out how it works."

He finally looked at her. "Where did you get this?" he asked, flowers and berries forgotten.

Why did the War Chief care about her gown? She found herself rushing to answer, desperate to keep his attention. "Bazu says his momama made it, but I don't believe him. I think he found it in the cave."

"In the tunnel," Rakta stated, nodding as if he was sure of it.

Tamaya noticed he did not say "Death Tunnel", and he didn't sound scared when he said it. She caught the drift and pushed. "Yes, the tunnel," she whispered intimately. "Let's go."

Tamaya plugged the comforting lamp into its socket in the door jam and walked boldly into the space Rakta had once sworn never to enter again. She removed her robe and spread it in the air. It floated slowly to the floor in a perfect square.

Rakta grabbed the coiled cord he had examined last time from the wall. "Ah ha! Look!" he exclaimed, reminding her of Bazu for a sickening second. He brought the cord over to the strange little square in the corner of her cape. Tamaya was on her hands and knees on top of the garment.

Rakta babbled excitedly as he brought the end of the cord together with the clasp of her gown. "Watch!" He pushed the two prongs into the slots. Her knuckles and knees tingled, sending shivers up her arms and legs. He pulled it out, and the sensation stopped abruptly. He shoved it in again, giggling like a schoolboy. "What does that remind you of, eh? Heh, heh."

Tamaya sat up, facing him, her hair standing on end. "The lamp," she replied. "That's how I light it. But the other end of that rope has to go into the holes by the door, where the lamp's rope is now."

Rakta pulled the plug again. He looked back toward the door, shrugged, and turned back to Tamaya. Her tousled hair lay flat on her slightly sweaty brow. She no longer tingled. "What else?" he asked.

"What else what?" she replied impatiently. She was starting to wonder again what he was here for. Did he just want to play with the weapons, too?

He set the cord down and crawled to her. He bowled her over gently and kept crawling until she was on her back with him on his hands and knees on top of her. "In and out of the slot, in and out, don't you see?" he giggled. He lowered himself onto her, fully clothed. He rubbed the part of her that ached with something hard and bulging inside his pants. She moaned softly. It felt so good!

He sat up and wrestled with his belt and all the tools and weapons that hung there. She took the time to smoothly remove her tunic. He gasped when he spied her young, pert breasts. They finished undressing awkwardly. Rakta kept hearing noises, but it always turned out to be that trickle behind the wall.

He kissed her all over, and rubbed her gently. She felt obliged to return his favors, and found it far more enjoyable than she had expected. The biggest surprise was how much she wanted it. "I'm ready," she whispered at last when she could wait no longer.

"Oh, Tamaya, I have waited so long!" he moaned. She felt him enter, finally! Oh, how she wanted him to push, but, ow! A stab of pain, then another, threatened to topple her from her peak. Then *his* cry. Did it hurt him, too? He withdrew abruptly.

"You are intact!" he squeaked his shock in a voice more like Bazu's than the mighty War Chief's.

Tamaya slammed her legs shut, insulted, confused, mortified, rejected. "I told you he doesn't..."

"Not at all? Never?" Rakta sputtered helplessly against the evidence. "How is that possible?" He searched Tamaya's eyes with warm concern and deep confusion. "The most beautiful woman in the village is his tether, and he, never?"

"I told you," Tamaya said, almost inaudible. The complement helped a lot, but she still felt like she had failed in yet another of her duties. She had tried. What was she supposed to do? Rakta didn't need to be coaxed and begged. Until now. Now, he was pulling his trousers back on, babbling as he struggled with his belt like a first-cycle clubber.

"I would be the first. I would be the one to defrock the Holy Tether. I cannot. I must not. Surely, I would be cursed forever."

She didn't want him to leave now. "No one will know, Rakta. You said so yourself. They won't say anything."

"He will know, Tamaya."

"When I bear a strong son—"

"Before that, Tamaya. Don't you understand? You show with babbet, he will know it is not his. All those months, before they sing the praises of his strong son, he will know. He will live with you, look at you, all those months knowing, wondering who... He might kill you, Tamaya!"

Tamaya hissed a scoff, certain the Akashic weaponry ranged from whining to tantrums. "That may be. I will bear it. Still, when the child is born, he will claim it. Maybe he won't even care. He doesn't want me. If he can have sons without doing the deed he hates so much, maybe he will accept that."

Rakta shook his head "I can't imagine a man who wouldn't care about that. I can't imagine a man who wouldn't want *you*."

"Why?" Tamaya asked innocently, reluctantly gathering her clothes. "Because I am Tether to Akash, and you want to be the true Popa of the Akashic Heir?"

"That is part of it," Rakta grumbled, making his way out the Death Door.

"What's the other part?" She got up, half dressed, and rushed to his side.

He searched her face deliberately. His eyes looked hurt. Tamaya couldn't see why. She hadn't rebuffed him. She'd actually wanted it. And as soon as she did, the offer had been rudely withdrawn.

Suddenly, he brought his mouth to hers and kissed her deeply, rekindling the fire in her loins. "The making of it, Tamaya," he whispered tenderly when he'd finished. He held her cheeks in his palms. "The sheer pleasure of pleasuring you, Your Highness. That is what I desired. But I am afraid it cannot be. I cannot be the first."

He was gone in a flash, through the arch and down the stairs. Tamaya remained in the Death Tunnel, staring at her robe on the floor with the cord lying beside it. Her head was spinning with shock and frustration, anger and shame, and that feeling that came over her sometimes, like when she was a small, motherless girl wanting to smash her way out of the kitchen with her momama's rolling pin.

Dream

That night, Tamaya lay beside her husband, coldly apart. She hadn't been able to bring herself to try him again. She doubted she ever would. She slept fitfully, troubling images swirling. She was in the Death Tunnel lying on her robe. It tingled wherever it touched her. It felt good, but irritating. She wanted to get off of it, but Rakta lay on top of her. He turned into Bupple! She felt the weight increase, then drop to almost nothing as Bupple morphed into Bazu. He pressed something hard against her, like Rakta had. She looked to the side and saw Akira watching, wrapped in the same gown that still tingled beneath her.

"No," Tamaya squeaked like a child, "I don't want to! Please don't make me, Akira. Please let me go."

Akira spread her arms and opened the shimmering gown so she looked like a great bird hovering over the couple. Then, she brought her arms down, spun around on her heel like Rakta did, but in a full circle. She looked down at the magnificent fabric that swaddled her, glowing like Kakeeche.

"Wear this when you go," Akira ordered. Tamaya felt a déjà vu. Had she had this dream before?

"Go where?" she asked, just like before. "To the Great Hall?" She still couldn't imagine where else she would go in her fancy gown.

"Wear it like this when you go." Akira was suddenly on the Holy Rock with her back to Tamaya. She turned just her head around to face her. The corner of the fabric with the strange clasp hung low in back, nearly touching the Rock. The cord Rakta had found was plugged into it. It ran toward Tamaya where she now stood, at the entrance of the Death Tunnel. It was dark, the lamp was off. The slots were occupied by the cord from her gown.

"Wear it just like this. When you go." Akira stated once more. She looked taller standing on the crest of the smooth, round surface. Then she disappeared, as completely as the old Akash and his family.

Tamaya sat up in bed with a throaty gasp.

"Quiet! I'm thinking," Bazu murmured his usual good morning.

"Take it when you go, Tamaya," her momama's voice rang from a past dream.

"Wear it when you go, Tamaya," Akira's voice echoed from the empty Rock.

Meetings

With only a week until Mitten, Bazu and Bupple went to the practice field every day. All the warriors were collaborating to perfect the spectacular ceremony Bazu would perform. Every afternoon he would come home so excited about his progress, he had to share it with Tamaya, who wore her best fake smile.

"Even Rakta is helping now! He was always too busy before. Wait until you see this routine. I'm sure to win the awe and respect of the entire village."

Or their laughter and ridicule and complete loss of faith. Tamaya kept her doubts to herself.

Now, it was time to find out. Mitten. Halfway through the cycle, eighteen Kakeeche cycles until the Season of the Nimblies and Bumblies. The Ceremony would begin right after the Council meetings.

While the common women bustled about the Great Hall preparing the feast, Tamaya sat before Akira in the meeting room. Deaf Ogala was there to tend to the babbet and two toddlers who occupied cradles and cribs in the nursery while their momamas worked. She couldn't hear the intimate meeting between the Akashic Tether and Akira, but even she had a pretty good idea of the subject. Everyone had noticed. It was Mitten, eighteen months since the Holy Wedding, and still no Akashic babbets.

"No more examinations." Tamaya put her foot down. "It isn't me, Akira." She knew Rakta wouldn't have shared her secret. Still, now that someone else knew, it was easier to let it out. "It's him. He won't do it. Ever. He won't even try." She remembered what Rakta had called her, in his shock. "Wed for half a cycle, and I am still intact, Akira!"

Even Ogala could hear the stunned silence that followed. Tamaya turned her face away from the deaf woman, just in case. "Is there someone else Akira? Someone who could come in secret?" She felt that warm feeling between her legs when she said it. "We could say it's the Akash's—"

"He will know!" Akira snapped.

Tamaya jumped back, suddenly realizing how close she'd been, whispering in front of a deaf woman. "If you command it, he will have to accept it. I see no other way, Ma'am. I have tried and tried. He has no interest."

"In you?" Akira sounded as incredulous as Rakta had. "I will speak to him. Perhaps a male companion could teach him. He might be more comfortable."

"I suggested that." Tamaya had, after her Popa and Rakta had both suggested it. It was not a good memory. She mocked her husband's squeaky voice. "Do you think I would let a man touch me where I won't even let a weak woman?"

Akira allowed herself a half-smile, then a deep sigh. "Perhaps if I spoke to him. Explained the importance of carrying on the Holy Seed..."

"I have explained it a thousand times. Rakta has, too."

"Rakta?" Akira's face zoomed in on Tamaya's like a hawk on a dracna.

Tamaya froze, just like that mouse. She had to think fast, or give herself away. "Bazu says so. He comes back from practice saying Rakta says this, Rakta says that."

Akira nodded, said nothing.

Does she know I'm lying? Tamaya wondered in horror. The War Chief's comings and goings were "man stuff", of no concern to Akira. How would she know? *Because she has spies everywhere, knows everything...*

"The child would not be of the Akashic line." Akira concluded suddenly, breaking Tamaya from her spin. "What good to impregnate the Tether with a non-Akashic babbet? He is the only one left of the Akashic Line, unfortunately. You are going to have to make do."

"Make do?" Tamaya replied slowly, temples throbbing.

"I will find a counselor. A woman who can teach him."

"An Unmarriageable?" Tamaya snapped, surprised by a stab of jealousy. "What would an Unmarriageable know?"

"No, of course not," Akira replied. "An older, more experienced woman who has already had children. Just to teach him, mind you." She grinned broadly, unnerving Tamaya to the core. "Perhaps Azuray, Rakta's tether, would be suitable." She studied her prey carefully.

The chill in her spine froze Tamaya in place, guilt waving like a flag above her head.

Akira took it all in, calculating. "Perhaps someone of lower stature. Someone discreet, of course, sworn to secrecy. I will find someone."

"And Bazu will know I told you," Tamaya whispered as she stood to leave.

The old lady looked up at her blankly and nodded once. "Yes. I will tell him. Summon him now. Tell Rakta the Council Meeting will start when I send for him. I must speak to our young Akash alone first, don't you think?" She raised her eyebrows playfully, then waved her hand as if swatting Tamaya away, concluding their meeting.

Council

Tamaya rushed from the room, avoiding any prying eyes that might be following her to where Bazu stood with Rakta and Bupple. "Akira wishes to see the Akash alone before the Council meeting," she reported breathlessly, without looking at anyone. The men exchanged curious glances, then

Bupple escorted the Akash across the crowded hall. Tamaya remained a respectful distance from Rakta, her arms folded in front of her.

"What is that about?" Rakta hissed in his battle whisper.

"I told her." Tamaya hissed back between her teeth.

He glanced around the hall. "About us?" he asked, barely audible.

"About him. She is going to get him a counselor." Tamaya had a hard time saying it quietly. She felt like screaming in his face. "He'll be furious with me. It will never work." She finally focused on Rakta's face. He was smiling!

"Maybe it will, Tamaya. And when it does," he leaned closer, "as soon as he penetrates you, you let me know. I will finish the job."

"If he can, why would I need you?" As soon as she said it, she knew the answer. She knew she would never be satisfied with that sniveling stick. Maybe before, but not now. And she knew Rakta would never be satisfied either. Not without completing his conquest.

Kaysee

When he was finally summoned to the Council Meeting, Rakta entered the room cautiously, ears ablaze. He knew they wouldn't discuss such a matter in front of him, but he searched for signals in his trained way, his keen senses seeing, feeling, even smelling the tension in the air. It looked as he'd expected. Bazu sat across the table from Akira, arms crossed, legs clenched together, feet intertwined, face more red than green. He wouldn't look at Rakta. That made sense, but it still made Rakta nervous. He checked out the old lady. She was looking at Bazu like a dog who had finished playing with its prey and was now deciding whether or not to eat it.

Rakta said nothing. He took his seat quietly and waited.

"There is the matter of the Orchard Keeper's son, Kaysee." Akira brought up the next subject on her agenda.

"What about him?" Rakta snapped, as jumpy as he'd ever been in the trenches.

"He claims he has new knowledge from the Plane. It's about the body and how it works. He goes on and on about systems and diet and health.

That's bad enough, but he professes to teach his secrets to any peasant who will listen."

"Is it Shavarandu?" Bazu asked, a little too eagerly. His color was returning to normal.

Akira paused to think, not about the hairline distinction, but about how to elicit the reaction she wanted. "Not exactly," she waffled. "No spooky actions. He offered to teach you, Akash..."

"Does he know how to fire the weapon?"

"No, of course not. He knows how the body works inside, how to heal and prevent diseases. You should let him teach you," suggested Akira, "and then forbid him from doing it. Only you can. People must come to the Akash for their healing. You will be the Healing Akash."

Bazu's eyes wandered to the hefty ceiling, then the cribs along the walls, clearly not interested. When she finished, he turned baleful eyes on her. "My tether, a woman, teaches me to read, and other things, or she tries. Now another peasant would..." he trailed off. His eyes flashed to Rakta, then wandered again. At last, he leveled them at the old woman and rapped his frail fist on the heavy table. He had learned not to pound. Ogala jumped anyway, as if she could hear the thump and the angry tone. "Now a mere tender will teach me to get on the Plane *his* way and learn all about *his* musings? I will not. I refuse. Not unless he wants to teach me how to sit and watch a tree grow."

Rakta saw the problem and chimed in. "We can't have him running around saying he knows things the Akash doesn't know, and that he can teach everyone. He's a Tender, for Kakeeche's sake! Soon everyone will think they can just go around doing what they want," he watched Akira closely, "marry who they want." She turned to look sharply at him, just as he'd calculated. "He must be stopped," he concluded.

"I will not share my power with a peasant." The young Akash agreed, nodding. "Shut him down."

Two votes sealed the deal. "How?" Akira asked the only remaining question.

"I'll make a warrior of him. No more sitting around the orchard thinking too much. I will have the men whip him into shape, make a man out of him. His little brother can ascend to Tender."

Akira rolled her eyes. "That is your answer to everything!"

Bazu objected, too. "I will not share the practice field with someone who wishes to usurp me. Why would you train him to fight?"

"Good point," Akira agreed, nodding. "If he is so ambitious, maybe a simple threat will work. If he does not stop his practice, he will never ascend to Tender. He will become apprentice to his younger brother when *he* ascends. And even then, he must stop this business, or the punishment will be even more severe."

"Like what?" Bazu asked, his mouth watering.

Akira winked. "Let him wonder. He'll make up his own. His worst fears, whatever they are, will haunt him. They don't have to be named." She whispered her dry breath into the Akash's face. "It's an Akashic trick, my Boy. You're learning."

Mitten Ceremony

When their business was concluded, the Council emerged from the meeting room. The crowd parted and hushed as the three leaders filed toward the platform for the ceremony. Tamaya tried to study Bazu's averted face as he marched past her. He didn't seem as humiliated as she had expected. Rakta must have found a way to build him up. That wouldn't be possible if he knew about her and Rakta. She breathed a little easier, but still dreaded her next hours.

Bazu's Mitten Ceremony surprised them all, repeatedly. He twirled his longstick flawlessly for several minutes. Then he balanced it lengthwise on his palm and ran around the stage chasing its swaying. When it finally fell, he caught it deftly, as if it were part of the act. He wore a maniacal smile that reminded Tamaya of the Old Akash. His little chest puffed out like a male kiko bird's. Then he made his grand announcement.

"My people, I have been to the Plane and been touched by a miracle! I am now blessed in a way no other Akash has been blessed, not even the great Badon who disappeared."

Murmurs spread through the crowd, including Tamaya, Rakta and Akira. They didn't seem to know about this announcement, either.

"I know you are all asking, 'why no Akashic babbets?'"

Tamaya's heart sank. She exchanged glances with Rakta and Akira.

"It is because I don't need babbets," Bazu reported scornfully. "I am the last of the Akashic Line. It can stand no more dilution."

Faces turned to Akira, standing behind the Akash. She shook her head and openly shrugged.

"I alone must carry on the Holy Seed, the Akashic Line. So, I shall live forever as the Last Akash. The Immortal Akash. The One Who Lives Forever!" He raised both arms above his head, longstick in his right hand. With his left, he beckoned the crowd to provide a refrain.

"The Immortal Akash. The One Who Lives Forever," they complied in a monotone.

"I will not grow old and die like you peasants do." He scanned the silent crowd. "I cannot be killed. Not by nimbly or bumbly, not by dog or ganeesh." His gaze fixed on the young warriors who stood together. "Not by man. No one can kill me."

He nodded once and flowed off the stage like a specter. He popped up next to Tamaya, beaming. "You no longer need to worry, my tether. I no longer need babbets, or a guard, though perhaps I will keep Bupple. He is useful and far better company than you are. I suppose you can stay as well, although you don't cook or clean or anything. Maybe I don't need you at all."

"You still can't read." Tamaya snarled loud enough for the passersby to stop and turn, privileged to witness the rare spectacle. She was keenly aware of their eyes. Bazu seemed oblivious.

"I don't need to read. The Plane speaks directly to me. I don't need those foolish Old Ones. They knew nothing."

"But, the weapon..." Tamaya whispered. "Don't you want to�"

"There is nothing in those stupid books about the weapon. Just the babbling opinions of old men who knew they were about to die. I have no need for such things. Reading and writing. Why should I write down my thoughts? For whom? I will have my thoughts with me forever. Over the years I shall accumulate more knowledge than all the Akashes before me. I will be second only to Kakeeche in greatness. By the end of time, I will shine more brightly than Shavarandu, and I shall smite him from the sky with my longstick."

He brandished the toy weapon at the onlookers who had gathered around, drawn by his swelling voice. Bazu took in his audience, as raptly as when he'd made his initial announcement. They were eating it up! Even Akira and Rakta stood staring helplessly. He turned to his tether, widely considered the most beautiful woman in the village, and sneered, "So, no, my tether. I have no use for your books or your reading. I don't need your babbets. You don't even cook. You are useless! I don't need you. Perhaps you should be put in the Lair with the Unmarriageables."

A collective gasp circled the couple. Akira stepped forward.

Bazu wrapped his arm around his tether's shoulders and squeezed hard. He felt the unique softness of the special gown he had given to her, the only thing she seemed to appreciate. "But for now, come, Woman. Let's eat. I have an appetite for some fresh food for once."

Numb, Tamaya obeyed without resistance.

Forever

The three residents of the Holy Cave walked home together in silence. Tamaya trailed behind the men like a tether should, according to Akira's school. She stopped to use the outdoor boor before climbing the stairs.

When she climbed the stairs, she met Bupple on the porch. He was carrying his sleeping mat and woven blanket. "Good night, Ma'am," he whispered politely. He gave her a warm, concerned look. "I will be right outside." Then he rushed down the steep stairs, leaving Tamaya to face her mad husband alone.

He greeted her haughtily, still wearing his Akashic robe. "I sent Bupple out for the night. We have some Akashic business to conduct."

Confused for a second, Tamaya asked, "Do you mean you want to�"

"That?" he snapped. "No! I told you. I don't need that. I don't need anyone to teach me. Why did you tell Akira?" He screamed, shaking his fist in her face. He dropped it abruptly, and turned away. "I don't need babbets."

"You need an apprentice." Tamaya countered, feet planted firmly in reality.

"I do not! I told you. If you want babbets, that's not my problem!"

"It *is* your problem. You are my husband. And I don't want babbets, but I will do my duty."

Bazu scoffed. "Your duty? You don't cook or clean or write down my thoughts."

"What thoughts? Your ridiculous rantings? You're worse than Badon! At least he didn't think he could live forever."

"He couldn't. I can. I will live forever."

"How do you know?" she demanded. "You can't meditate. I've seen you trying, twitching and fidgeting. When my popa meditates, he sits totally still and breathes very low. He doesn't scratch and twiddle and open his eyes and look around." She exaggerated an imitation, looking around the cave, eyes wide, scratching her nose. "Why, the only time you ever had a vision was when the Cave Shavarandu bit you, when you were messing with that light. I wish it had killed you, like it did my Batuk."

"I told you. I cannot die," Bazu insisted. "And Batuk was never yours. He was Badon's. He did what he was told."

"He was my betrothed."

"Yes, yes, and you would have lived in a hut in the village with babbets hanging from those precious breasts everybody likes so much. They would cry all night and keep you awake, like your brother's babbets do."

"And I would have a strong, handsome husband who would make love to me. You're making all this crazy stuff up just so you don't have to. What is the matter with you? Didn't your momama teach you what to do?"

"No!" Bazu yelped. "That would be wrong!"

The pitch of his voice was even higher than usual. He clenched his legs together. She knew she'd struck a nerve.

"Did your momama teach you?" he countered sulkily.

"I didn't have a momama then."

"Well, I didn't have a popa, *then,*" Bazu jeered, mocking her.

"I thought men just knew what to do," she ventured, based on experience she wasn't supposed to have.

"Why would you think that?"

Trapped, she shrugged. "They talk about it, as boys. My brother did."

"I didn't have a brother, either. There was no one to teach me. It is because I don't need an apprentice. My whole life has shaped me for this greatness. The Old Akash disappearing, my place at the end of the Akashic Line, my freedom from that base obsession you people all suffer from. The more I think about it, the more it all fits together. This is my destiny."

"So, what about me?" Tamaya asked, with no idea what answer she hoped for.

"I don't care. I don't need you. Ask Akira. She'll find a place for you." He rocked his oversized head back on his scrawny neck and laughed a hearty, fake laugh.

Tamaya dared to imitate Rakta's warrior turn. Bazu wouldn't notice. He didn't care. But doing it made her feel Rakta for a second, and that lifted her spirits just enough. "Then I'm going to my popa's house, where the babbets only cry for half the night." She floated down the stairs, her gown billowing around her.

Tamaya and Jenevan

"Ma'am!" Bupple's voice came from under an overhang in the massive cave wall. He pushed his damp blanket aside and struggled to his feet.

"Don't say anything you may regret, My Lady," he whispered as he fell into step beside her. He escorted her down the worn trail through the deepening darkness. The only sounds were their light footsteps and the willows along the river swaying in the breeze. Bupple watched her enter the hut where she had grown up, bathed in the warm lamplight that spilled out the open door. Then he disappeared into the village, toward his son's hut.

The silence couldn't last through dinner. There were too many questions in the air. Too many for four-year old Pindren to hold inside his little skull. The pressure was just too much. Something had to come out.

"Did you and the Akash have a fight?" the perceptive child asked honestly, simply repeating what his parents had whispered upon her arrival.

His aunt looked at him dourly, then nodded.

Now the boy's momama picked up the line. "Really? Do Akashes and their tethers fight like regular people?"

Tamaya wasn't sure if Jenevan's concern was genuine or sarcastic. She looked at her popa's face. She knew what she saw there was real. True concern, tempered by hopeless resignation. Whatever the problem was, he knew he could do nothing to help his daughter.

After dinner, Tamaya surprised Jenevan by showing up in the kitchen to help with the dishes. Jenevan looked her up and down, wondering what she was doing there, then handed her a plate and a mullein wipe. Jenevan washed, and Tamaya dried. About halfway through, Tamaya suddenly asked, "Did your momama teach you what to do, you know, on your wedding night?"

Surprised, Jenevan eyed her strangely. "Not really. I saw the dogs doing it, and she told me what it meant. Sure enough, a few months later, there were puppies."

"What about my brother? Did my popa teach Pindrad?"

Jenevan shrugged uncomfortably. "I don't know. He didn't talk about it. He just grunted, went right to it and did it. He's slowed down since. You know what I mean." She looked expectantly at her guest. Then her eyes bugged out. Her hands rushed to her round cheeks. "By Kakeeche! Are you saying? After half a cycle? That's why no babbets?"

Tamaya hushed her desperately. Pindrad was passing by the kitchen. To Tamaya's chagrin, Jenevan called to him.

"Pindrad, when you were a boy, before we were married, did your popa teach you," she lowered her voice a bit, "to, you know." She made an obscene gesture with her fingers.

Pindrad blushed a muddy red-green, gave the same puzzled look Jenevan had worn, and answered very quietly. "He drew pictures for me. The other boys talked about it all the time, so I knew it was real. Then I started having feelings." He grinned lecherously. "On that Passascenday night, when I saw my whole, naked Jenevan for the first time, I needed no instruction. My body told me what to do."

"Animals just know. Why wouldn't people?" Jenevan figured.

Pindrad put his hand on her belly. "We've done it again, we think."

Jenevan swatted his hand away playfully. "We don't know yet. It's too early." She looked at Tamaya earnestly. "Don't tell anyone yet. It's bad luck."

"Who would I tell?" Tamaya asked sourly, glad for the change of subject.

Tamaya lay awake in the bedroom that now belonged to Pindren. Her four-year-old nephew shared the room, stuffed into his old crib.

Bazu was right about one thing. The babbets *did* cry all night. The wet winter had left little Wendolyn with the croup. Just when Tamaya would manage to drift off and escape her tortured thoughts, the babbet would wail. Then the boy would wake up and start in with his questions. "Aunt Tamaya, do you have a dog? Don't you like dogs? What's it like in the Holy Cave? Can I see? Will the Akash really live forever? Is that why you don't have any babbets?"

Tears squeezed onto her cheeks every time she blinked her tired eyes. She started smashing things with her mental rolling pin again. It just made her feel worse. Her thoughts swirled endlessly without conclusion, like the writings of the old Akash. By the time Shavarandu shined His first pink light through the lattice of her east window, she had come to only one conclusion, but that one was certain. She didn't want babbets.

Akira and Edijay

Akira and Edijay conducted their most sensitive and secret discussions in the depth of Akira's lair. The venerated woman would sit cross-legged on the cushion below her breeding matrix, her apprentice kneeling before her.

This time, they were discussing the ancient practice of sending the Downudara Children, the ones with mental disabilities who couldn't learn a skill, into the caves with poison gas to kill the nimblies and bumblies while they hibernated. The child would die too, but it was considered, in those days, to be their highest and best use. Besides, if they lived, they would carry the Curse out of the cave and spread it to their loved ones as they died.

"We discontinued the practice years ago." Akira assured the grimacing young woman. "It is too upsetting to the people. Funny. Parents would rather be burdened for the rest of their lives than to see their child go into that cave. It does little good, anyway. The nimblies and bumblies kept coming, just as many, more or less. No difference. No matter. We mustn't kill all the nimblies and bumblies anyway. It would be our end."

"Our end?" Edijay sat up, suddenly paying attention. "Haven't we all dreamed of wiping out the nimblies and bumblies since the beginning of time?"

"Yes, yes of course," Akira hurried dismissively. "But I want you to picture it with me, Edijay. After all the dancing and singing and celebration. A year after? A cycle after? Two cycles? Use your imagination, Girl. What would it be like?"

"Young men will live to marry their betrotheds so they don't have to take the Long Walk." Edijay started the virtual tour from her own perspective. "No more lowering of bones into the pit. The women will no longer mourn their husbands and sons after battle each cycle. The men won't have to fight."

Akira snorted rudely. "Did Gibled and Dubley have to fight yesterday?"

No! Of course not. Squabbling over who won a silly game. To come to blows! I thought Dubley was going to stab Gibled with his spear."

Akira snorted again, a laugh this time. "If Buppan hadn't stopped him, he surely would have. So, tell me, did they have to fight?"

"No, I already said. It was foolish men's business," the young unmarried woman said with certainty.

Akira agreed. "That is what men do."

"Foolish business?"

"Yes," another snort of indulgent humor. "And fighting. They fought because there is no battle. It is Mitten. Last cycle's battles are too far gone for them to feel anymore. Next cycle is but a dream of future glory. For now, there is nothing but their games and their practices, so they play and spar and lose themselves in that, until they feel like they are in battle. Then they strike. If no nimblies or bumblies, then they strike one another. Now, what if that future glory never came? No next season? No more nimblies, no more bumblies..."

"Not ever, no more." Edijay finished the chant that would be sung on that great day, so far only a fantasy.

"And then what? Look forward, my apprentice, the future Akira! Breathe deep with me and see." They both drew a long breath, filling their abdomens, their chests with air, then exhaling it slowly, feeling it leave their chests first, then their bellies. They ascended into the colorful flow of the River of Sight. Edijay looked down through the mist. She could see the future village clearly.

Peace. A feast at the Great Hall, to celebrate the harvest. The women would still have to prepare food, but not three days' worth. It was like Easy Harvest, the harvests between the deadly Seasons. Everyone was busy bringing in the kips, pressing the oil, filling the dryers, making the wine. No time for a three-day celebration.

The men picked kips all day, and at night they drank wine and laughed and sang and drank more wine. "They drink too much." Edijay remarked to her mentor's spirit, bobbing in the ether beside her.

A fight broke out among the men around the fire. Edijay gasped. "They fight, just like yesterday, at Mitten. They fight with each other. They go home and fight with their tethers, their children. That one's had way too much to drink. Why is he so angry? He's going to strike her! The boy! His little son!"

The shared image disappeared in a flash of red light. The two women found themselves back in the depths of Akira's Lair. The breeding matrix drooped its loops above their heads, some strings shooting off the walls, all alone, the rest hanging in a tangled clump. Akira stood, burying her head among the hanging threads. She closed her eyes and traced a pair upward toward the ceiling.

"Don't you worry, my Apprentice." She offered an unexpected comfort. "We will never defeat the nimblies and bumblies. And they will not defeat us."

"But�" Edijay groped in the dark for the hope Akira claimed to offer.

"We will succumb to the wasting before that. I can see it, right here among these tangled threads."

Edijay suppressed an eye roll. Here she went again, the old madwoman pawing at the mess she revered, spouting her doom and gloom. Edijay could work the incomprehensible system mechanically. She knew how to search the lines for pairings that weren't too close. But she had never understood her master's obsession, the importance she assigned to her silly game.

"Is it possible? Can the Akash live forever?" Edijay asked.

"Of course not! Don't be a fool!" the old woman snapped. "He lies, because he is ashamed. He can't do it, Edijay! Or he doesn't want to. He doesn't have the desire, even for Tamaya."

"Perhaps a man�" Edijay came up with the same answer as everyone else.

"No. I tried that. He wants none of it. It is a function of the wasting. No babbets, bad babbets, now this. No drive." She turned doleful eyes on her apprentice. There was an infinite sadness in them that left Edijay speechless. "We are running out of something. Each generation has less of it. I don't know what it is, or how to replenish it, or stop it from running out."

"What is it, Akira?" Edijay sounded like a very young girl when she asked. "What are we running out of?"

"Time." Akira answered. "We're running out of time."

Lies

Tamaya returned to the Holy Cave in the morning, escorted by her brother, Pindrad. They brought a morning meal to the Akash, carefully carried on a covered plate. Pindrad handed it to his sister and watched her climb the long staircase. Then he turned and headed home, keeping his thoughts carefully controlled. *He is Akash. She is his Tether. Her fate is in his hands. I can do nothing for her but give her shelter in my hut if he decides to send her away. My poor sister! The most beautiful woman in the village. She was always destined to be Tether to Akash, but she's already lost two betrotheds. Now this unheard-of state of affairs. No babbets, no sex, a husband who will live forever...*

"I will let you stay on one condition." Bazu informed his tether coldly when she appeared at the arched doorway. He wore his grand Akashic Robe and clenched his ceremonial longstick. There was no sign of Bupple. He must still be in the village. The smooth rock shined dully in the indirect morning light. It reminded Tamaya of her dream, the one where Akira disappeared.

Beyond it, the Death Tunnel loomed darkly, hiding its amazing contents. The books! The books only she could read. The wisdom of the ages, that Bazu said he didn't need. That he would never read. No one would, if she didn't stay. Then, even if the Akash lived forever, and she knew very well he wouldn't, the knowledge would be lost. She couldn't cook or weave. She would never have babbets. But she, and only she, and Akira, could read the holy books and pass the knowledge on to *someone* in the future. Teach *someone* to read them. But who?

She had to stay. Where else would she go? To a noisy bedroom that was no longer hers, in a home where she no longer fit? To Akira's Lair? An Unmarriageable? She shivered. Maybe she could be Akira's apprentice! She had Edijay now, but her apprentices never lasted. They never ascended. None of them understood her rantings well enough to satisfy her. *But I can.* Tamaya told herself. *I have the books. I will read them all, and keep feeding Akira the parts I decide to share, when it suits me. But I will keep some of it to myself. I will have something she wants, something she can't have without me. Then, if the time comes when I must leave here and go to the Lair, she will make me her apprentice. I will be the next Akira. I will decide who marries, who has babbets with whom. That ultimate power will be mine!*

Having made her decision, she finally answered the Akash. "What condition?"

"Akira still thinks she will send me to some old lady for counseling, because of your big mouth. I won't have it. You must fix it."

"How?" Tamaya wondered. "I already told her you don't..."

"Un-tell her!" the Akash demanded, pointing his dull longstick at her. "Tell her you lied."

"That would be a lie."

"Well, lie then. I'm sure it's not your first time. Tell her I'm better now. Now that I have found my true power, I am unstoppable!" He reached for her. She stilled, forcing herself to let him grab her up in his arms. He stopped, dropped his hands and turned away, a cruel smile stretching across his porcelain face. "Beg her to forget the councilor. Tell her you can take no more of my lovemaking. That I have satisfied you beyond your wildest dreams and you no longer pine for your precious Batuk or your little spare, Baput. Tell her the Immortal Akash is the best sex maker in the thousand years since the Old Ones."

"There will still be no babbets," she reminded him.

"Like I tried to explain," he said slowly. "I don't need babbets because I will live forever."

"You know that's not true," she stated coldly.

"Do I? Do you? Did anyone know the Old Akash was going to disappear with his apprentice? No! That is the way with Akashes, you never know what they can do until they do it. And those old people, Akira," he sneered, "and Rakta," Tamaya clenched her muscles defensively. "Even Bupple, my only friend. They are old. They will be long dead before they find out if I live forever or not."

"What about the young people, who believed their Akash would live forever, when you finally die and leave them without an Akash, or even an apprentice?"

"Ha!" he threw his head back, showing off the errant hairs poking from his nostrils. "Why would I care? I'll be dead then, if I really can die."

"You don't really believe�"

"I am the Immortal Akash. I shall have no son, no apprentice. I shall not die. And if I *do* die someday in the far future, it serves them right. Let them fret and worry and tear their hair out, Samard and Maffoon and all those boys and girls who laughed at me before I was Akash. They will have to tell their children they were wrong when they promised them their Akash would live forever. Let them suffer. I will be watching, and laughing, from my place as the brightest star in the sky."

So, Tamaya lied to Akira. She told her the Akash was better now. Perhaps he thought the pressure was off, now that he didn't need babbets. Perhaps his new identity had emboldened him, given him the confidence he needed. Whatever the reason, no counseling needed. Everything was fine now.

She did not tell Rakta the same story. If she did, he would come around again and soon find out she was lying. He would be angry and frustrated and he wouldn't stop like before. Tamaya somehow knew it. Then she would get a babbet. And if she *didn't* get a babbet, Akira would know she lied.

Bupple came and went. No longer needed as a constant guard, he was more of a friend and trainer. He slept at his son's hut at night, and most of his time with the Akash occurred on the practice field. The Akash still worked with the men, learning tricks and sometimes presuming to teach. Tamaya settled into a lonely routine, reading the books whenever Bazu went to the practice field, which was almost every day.

Earth, Summer 2019

Battle of the Bugs

Belinda headed straight to her locker, not looking at anyone. Kyla stared at her, chewing thoughtfully, surrounded by her minions, a bevy of girls who followed her everywhere. The kids had all grown used to Belinda's odd look, or at least tired of making fun of her. Now, right when junior high school was about to release its cruel grip, this new girl from L.A. had shown up with fresh, new ideas to torment her. She said Belinda looked even more like a bug than Old Bug-eye, Mrs. Pearson, a frustrated entomologist who harbored a menagerie of insects in the middle school Biology lab. Soon everybody was calling Belinda 'The Bug', 'Buggy Belinda', or 'Bug-eye 2.0'. She focused on the lock, dialed the combination. *Just two more days this week, then finals next week, then sweet summertime, and after that, high school. Mom says kids act more grown up in high school, but what does she know? She's pretty.*

She opened the locker door, just a crack. Not even wide enough to pull out her American History book and peek at the secret photo of Baput she kept hidden in there. When things got bad, just seeing his face usually kept her from crashing. But not today.

A plump beetle stepped out of the cracked door into thin air. It tried to unfold its jet-black wings, but, too late. It hit the floor with a light ticking sound, spun on its side, rolled to its feet and hurried off, just as a second scarab emerged from the locker, then another. Belinda held the grey metal door, her knuckles white, while insects poured out of the crack in a steady stream, dropping to the floor, finding their feet and scurrying away down the hall. Belinda screamed.

Kyla and her gang advanced, pointing and laughing.

Belinda pried her fingers from the door and ran past them to the girl's room, where she hid in a stall until the bell rang. She showed up at History class late and bookless.

Her locker stayed open as she wandered silently through her morning classes, never looking up or raising her hand. The teachers left her alone, didn't call on her. Her grades were excellent. She always did her homework. They didn't need to call the class's cruel attention to her. But time passed, and lunchtime came, too soon.

She took her lunchbox from the coat area in back of the classroom and went the long way to the cafeteria, avoiding the crowd, avoiding her locker. So what if they ravaged it? What if they found Baput? They'd just think he wasn't real. Some little kid's fantasy character they were too old to remember, but that little weirdo, Belinda, she didn't have any friends. She probably still plays with stuffed animals and dolls and watches little kid TV. *Who cares what they think?* She resolved. She found a seat alone at a corner table, still not looking at anybody.

She opened her lunchbox and unwrapped the primitive vegan delicacy Salistar had prepared. Rice and fresh greens and peas wrapped in broad grape leaves tied together with tender, edible grass. Centering herself above a napkin, she lifted the first one to her mouth and bit down. The veined, gray-green surface rippled in front of her eyes. A bulge appeared. It was moving! She pulled the stuffed leaf away from her face. Rice escaped the hole she had bitten, pushed out by a round black stink beetle who waved hello with his long antennae from his cozy place inside her lunch. He turned back inside, apparently to greet his mate who joined him, pushing eagerly through the tattered leaf until they both fell on Belinda's waiting napkin.

Another embarrassing scream brought the whole cafeteria to attention. All eyes found Belinda on her feet, furiously gathering up her ruined lunch and its soiled wrappings and shoving it, lunchbox and all, into the trash. She finally looked at them, scanning the whole cafeteria with both eyes shooting in different directions. There were the cheerleaders, all perfectly dressed, perfectly pretty. Mom used to be one of them. There were the nerds, with their glasses and conservative clothes, cool in their un-coolness. The Hispanic kids sat together, whispering in their own language, probably glad it wasn't them getting the business for once. And the "freaks", so called. They didn't all dress the same or talk the same, but they were somehow the same in their differentness. And she, the true freak, didn't belong with any of them. She didn't want to. Didn't need to. Suddenly, she was hungry. She held her head high so they couldn't see her eyes, and got into the lunch line.

She accepted the grilled ham and cheese sandwich, the instant mashed potatoes, the canned peas and the two store-bought cookies. She carried the un-vegan fare back to her corner seat, wondering if she could keep it down, or if she would puke all over the place, in front of everyone. She didn't see the big white tennis shoe that jumped into the aisle to trip her.

She could see the culprit with her awkward left eye. That clumsy bully, Scott Black. *He likes Kyla. He wants to impress her* she thought as she descended to the cement floor, where her face planted into her grease-charred sandwich.

A bubble of hoots and brays rose all around her. She lay motionless for an instant and the crowd quieted. "Is she alright?" one of the kinder ones thought to ask, in a whisper.

She was okay. Maybe it would be better if she wasn't. How could she ever pull her face out of her lunch and stand up with all of them looking at her? Something tickled her hair.

"Aw, come on!" somebody said. Sounded like Clarence. He was a nice boy.

The tickling was getting worse. Encouraged by Clarence's voice, she raised her head, but she didn't look up, not yet. She saw what was tickling her. More bugs! Big black ants marched in a line from where Scott had tripped her. Two by two, they climbed right over her, to her lunch. Belinda shrieked again. She hated doing it, but she couldn't help it. She clawed at her hair. Ants struggled to hang on to her thick, wavy locks until they fell to her tray, where they happily discovered her food.

She couldn't look up. She had to crawl to avoid their eyes. She crawled on her hands and knees across the cold, hard floor, her tunic riding up, exposing her behind, clad in bright purple leggings. A purple-ended Belly Bug.

After another long session in the girl's room stall, it was time for Biology class. Mrs. Pierson was her favorite teacher. Not because she was a bug-eye, too. Well, maybe. Maybe that's why she treated Belinda like an adult, like the smartest kid in the class, which she was. However, when she arrived in class, her face washed and the gaa wiped from her knees, she found her friendly Mrs. P. in a knot as tight as her own.

She stood in the lab, surrounded by deserted aquariums full of mud carved into elaborate networks of tunnels. "Where are my *podisus maculiventris*?"

"Your what?" Kyla asked, far more attentive than usual.

"My stink bugs, as you would cruelly call them! Where are my *orytes beas,* and my, my..." She ran her fingers through her frizzy hair, "My big, black ants!" she sputtered, lapsing into simple English.

Belinda stood up beside her chair, the only kid with the answer, as usual. "The scarabs, I mean, the *orytes beas* are in my locker."

"She took them!" Donald claimed.

"She rescued them." Brittney said, looking at Kyla the whole time. "She thinks they're her babies."

"Buggy Bel's babies!"

"She had to save them."

"They're her family." The kids carried the theme away.

"I didn't..." Belinda protested weakly.

Mrs. Pearson wasn't listening. "And my *podisus*?"

"Your stink beetles are in my lunch." Bel retorted.

"She ate them!" the comments swerved collectively, like a school of fish.

"She ate her own babies!"

"Were they bad, Belinda?"

"Did they taste good?"

Belinda could take no more. She folded her arms, stamped her foot. "I didn't take them! They put them in my locker, in my lunch!" she bellowed, an ugly sob.

"Belinda Musik, I never thought I'd have to say this, but go to the Principal's Office! Now!"

Belinda dashed from the room and ran down the hall to the Principal's Office. *No running*, she recalled. *What can they do to me, send me to the Principal's Office? Take my lunch*? She ran the whole way.

"Why, you're never in trouble." Principal Watkins greeted her, her painted eyebrows raised like the Golden Arches. "Mrs. Pierson says you turned her insects loose." Her look softened as her eyebrows lowered. "Were you rescuing them, Honey?" she cooed, "I understand." Belinda burst into tears.

When the whole story had been blubbered out in gory detail from the school's most skewed perspective, Mrs. Watkins picked up her phone. Belinda tensed. She dialed only four numbers. Belinda relaxed, but was she calling Mrs. Pierson? *Will she believe me this time?* Bel let go of that last thread of tension while Mrs. Watkins calmly directed the custodian to round up the bugs. "Catch what you can. Bring them to the biology lab. Try not to kill any more than you have to."

She pushed the button on the receiver cradle, hanging up while still holding the mouthpiece. She consulted a file on her desk and dialed a nine and seven other digits. Belinda tensed again, and held it for an hour until her parents showed up. Both of them.

The principal couldn't stop looking at Patrick's eye. She had grown uncomfortably used to Belinda, but seeing it on a man, a grownup, seemed to hold a morbid fascination for her. Had she thought the girl would grow out of it? She cleared her throat and began, awkwardly.

"Belinda has been subjected to some harassment because of her, um, physical appearance." She turned her gaze deliberately away from Patrick.

"What did they do to her? Are they being punished?" Lorraine grilled.

"Perhaps later. That's not why I called you here. I want to make a suggestion, if I may."

Lorraine could arch her eyebrows pretty high, too, and hers were real. If there was actually a contest going on, she had won, hands down.

"We have a virtual high school. The kids attend on line, by Zoom. Perhaps next year, Belinda could attend high school that way."

Lorraine grumbled something, then lashed out at the principal. "I don't like home schooling. We're educated, but we're not experts in every subject. Kids need real, qualified teachers."

"It's not like that," the principal reassured her. "It's part of the school system. Real teachers, the same ones that teach the in-person classes. We call it Virtual Academy. It's a complete high school, grades nine through twelve."

"She needs to know kids with different opinions, opposing viewpoints," Lorraine argued.

"Is that what this is?" Patrick muttered.

The principal continued her pitch. "There will be lots of other kids online with her. Lots of opposing viewpoints. But they can't hit you. On line classes are supervised by the teacher the whole time, and your URL will not be disclosed, so the kids can't contact her outside of class. Now, there's always cyber bullying, but it won't happen through our system, I assure you."

Lorraine looked cynical, but interested. Patrick's expression was unreadable.

"She can attend all her classes on line, or just some of them. In her second year she can even take online college classes, if her grades are good enough. And she can attend all the school events," her excited eyebrows wrinkled a bit, "If she wants to."

"Halloween," Patrick grinned suddenly. "I used to love Halloween parties. The only time I could be myself."

"Dad!" Belinda hissed through clenched teeth.

"Why sure! We have a Halloween party" the principle crowed. Her face fell again. "But it's a dance. Most of them bring a date."

"In fall of first year?" Lorraine complained.

"It's for the whole high school. All years," the principal informed her.

Patrick was grinning weirdly. He locked his odd eye with Bel's. "I think we can handle that," he drawled.

Lorraine growled and rolled her eyes.

Belinda's smile broke through her tears for the first time that day.

The principal came from behind her desk. "School is almost done, and Belinda's attendance has been nearly perfect. Her grades are excellent. I'm afraid she's learned all she's going to from this barbaric institution. I am going to excuse her for what's left of the school year. I'm afraid this unrest will only get worse as the time approaches. It happens every year. Hormones, you know. It's like trying to keep worms in a jar." She looked at Bel, then Patrick. "Sorry," she mumbled, took a breath, and plunged on.

"Finals are next week. I have your schedule right here. You'll come in Tuesday at nine for History, stay for Math at ten, come back on Wednesday for Biology and Social Studies. Between tests, you need to go to the Councilor and tell him your decision. He'll sign you up for Virtual Academy, full time or part time. He'll explain the options."

The three sat silently before her like errant students waiting to be dismissed. "You can go. See you Tuesday, Dear." They dispersed in a flash, just like those naughty schoolchildren.

Lorraine looked at her watch as they rushed down the corridor. "I can still make it back to work in time to finish that proposal."

"Where's your lunchbox, Babe?" Patrick asked.

"Thrown out." Belinda mumbled.

Lorraine sprinted away to her car without a word. Patrick drove Belinda home in Little Truck, now painted with the same goofy logo as the Look 'N Up Plumbing van.

As they pulled out of the parking lot, away from the chamber of horrors that is Middle School, Patrick's thoughts ran in a circle. *Are we giving up? Running away? Will she learn as well? She has the discipline. She won't mess around. She's so serious! Maybe she can concentrate better without all this crap. She needs socialization. They say it's important. But, does she need* this?

Visit

Jerry drove the Falcon up Interstate 5, chatting with Elmer in a language that consisted largely of motor noises. When they arrived, Patrick rushed out to greet them. "Come on up to the shop! I've got something to show you."

After four hours of cringing in the back seat, Francine wasn't about to ride on to the shop for more motor talk with the green guys. She spilled out of the back door.

Patrick embraced her. "Where are the dogs?" he asked, peering through Falcon's foggy windows.

"My brother is staying at the farm," she answered. "He and his wife need a few days apart, again. I worry about those two."

"What did you tell him about the purple one, Lassen?"

"Like I told you. Champagne. That's what you get when you breed a golden lab with a white German shepherd. He 'tsk tsked' me for not fixing Brodey, but he's happy to take care of them. I'm going up to the quarters to see Salistar."

Salistar and Belinda greeted Fran on the porch with excited squeals and eager hugs. Shastina and the two girl pups circled around them, sniffing and panting and yipping for joy. Pulling back from her embrace, Fran had to ask Belinda, "Does your mother know you're hanging around here?"

Belinda just shrugged. "We're drying strawberries. We planted lots, and they're all coming ripe at once. Star's showing me how they dry them, so we can have them all year. She calls them zazu berries. Come on!" She urged her aunt inside.

Iron

The familiar roar had brought Felsic out from underneath the Mustang. "She's off a touch!" he lamented, cocking his head.

"Who?" Baput wondered as he turned another screw, affixing another strand of wrought iron ivy leaves to the ornate metal frame. "Who's here?" he repeated.

Falcon appeared, red and dusty, with a tiny wrinkle in the front left fender where Jerry had slightly wrapped it around one of the posts that guarded the propane tank in the high school parking lot.

"Jerry!" Baput answered his own question. He hastily collected his tiny screws and poured them from his wide palm into a pint mason jar.

"I drove the whole way all by myself." Jerry bragged as he emerged from the driver's seat. "I've got my license, and an awesome ride, I'm free for the summer, and next year, I'm a senior! Hey, B!" he finally greeted his eager best friend.

Elmer struggled stiffly from the passenger seat, pumped Valko's hand vigorously, then high-fived Felsic in their special way. Patrick emerged casually from the back.

Jerry headed straight for Mustang. "Is this done?" He ran a finger along the contours, tracing the fine black lines that set off her shape. "Looks hot."

Felsic fired it up. Its throaty music filled the shop. Even Jerry backed up a step when Felsic revved it.

"Might be too much for you, Jerry," Patrick suggested.

"Hell no!" Jerry disagreed. "Can we trade?"

Patrick rolled his eyes. "Check this out!" he changed the subject. They're rebuilding a new luxury hotel in Lake Tahoe. They want handmade wrought-iron rails for all the porch decks. Six hundred panels! These guys have been cranking, see? The hummingbird goes in the middle, and on each side of the deck. The rest of the panels are just this ivy design. We're cutting the shapes out of sheet metal, this fake copper-looking stuff. Then we twist the iron tubes on the lathe, weld them to the rails, and screw the decorations on. We've got thirty done already."

"Only 570 left, huh?" Elmer asked, fingering the hammered effigy of a hummingbird nectaring on a lily. "By when?"

"We have a whole year, maybe more. Construction hasn't even started yet, and we go on near the end. Plenty of time."

"That's good, cause these guys will be gone in a little over a year, you know," Jerry reminded them.

"Not without the Net, we won't." Baput was sure.

"Well, maybe you can get back to the Look 'N Up for next year's harvest," Elmer hoped vainly. "Do some real work, if I can get rid of those RID guys."

"My momama would like that," Baput said quietly, picking up his screwdriver.

Elmer produced a six pack of beer from the trunk, and he and Felsic settled in the folding chairs, slowly savoring, like in the good old days at the Look 'N Up.

Valko returned to the lathe. Patrick found a couple of screwdrivers, and he and Jerry sat down beside Baput, joining the assembly line.

Dinner

The families dined separately, as usual. Fran prepared pasta and two sauces, one with meat and one vegetarian. While the bowls were passing around the table, Patrick asked Jerry, "You're a senior next year. Have you started looking at colleges? What do you think you'll major in? Physics, astrophysics? Lorraine and I can write you recommendations for Cal Tech, where we went. They have a great program..." He trailed off as Jerry's eyes began to wander.

Returning to Earth with a heavy sign, Jerry eventually replied, "I always figured I'd go. I dreamed of having access to some mega telescope or an electron microscope, maybe even a particle accelerator, but now, I don't know."

"What don't you know?" Patrick's voice tightened.

"It's just not exciting anymore. Not when I could go to another planet, see a world no human has ever seen. Who wants to stare into a dusty microscope when I can do that?"

"Over my dead body!" Fran declared, slamming the plate of garlic bread on the table in front of him. She diverted the family's attention from that ongoing debate to another: Belinda's schooling. "So, Belinda, you're going to high school next year!"

Belinda took a chunk of garlic bread from the plate and shook her head. "No, I'm not. I'm staying home."

"What are you talking about?" Fran demanded, her gaze lighting on Lorraine, who had finally put down the book she was reading and tucked into her plate of spaghetti with meat sauce.

Lorraine held her finger up while she swallowed. "It's been a rough year," she explained. "The kids were really piling on at the end. Junior high is the pits!"

"There's a super mean new girl from L.A., Kyla." Belinda told the story of 'Buggy Belinda', to her extended family's growing dismay.

"What did they do to the kids who did it?" Elmer demanded with a snarl.

"Detention," Lorraine answered, rolling her eyes. "For the rest of the year, which was less than a week."

Fran grasped Bel's hand, tilted her head with an exaggerated frown. "It'll get better in high school," she promised.

That's what I told her," Patrick admitted. "But it's not the same. I had you guys looking after me. Elmer, beating up the kids who made fun of me, until I told him to stop it. But still, the fear lasted even after you graduated, Bro." He turned to Fran with a childlike smile. "And I had you looking after me, after Elmer graduated. Hell, Mom was even there. She started the Science Club just so I could have fellow nerds to hang out with, under her watchful eye. Bel won't have any of that. She doesn't even have any friends, not really."

Bel squeaked a protest, then lowered her head in admission, while her dad went on, still trying to justify the decision. She held her breath, hoping her extended family wouldn't talk him out of it.

"She'll be all on her own out there in an even bigger shark tank." Patrick went on. "Best we can hope for is a good friend, or maybe an especially caring teacher who'll protect and nurture her, but they're the ones who are telling her she should school online from home, with Zoom. It's a real school, part of the public high school system."

"Nah!" was Elmer's knee-jerk reaction.

Fran objected more eloquently. "Home-schooled kids only hear their parent's opinions. They don't get exposed to opposing viewpoints."

"That's exactly what I said," Lorraine agreed. "They need to get to know people from different backgrounds, different cultures..."

"I think we've got that covered, Mom," Belinda quipped.

Francine turned to face Belinda, the actual subject. "Is this what you want, Honey? She asked tenderly.

"Yes," Belinda replied. She had that dreamy smile on her face, the one she wore when she thought about you-know-who. "Baput can hide behind my screen and listen. That way, he can go to school, too. And in my second year, I'm gonna take college courses in genetics, so I can solve his problem, and our problem, too."

Elmer cackled. "She's got it all figured out."

Fran wasn't satisfied. "What if your dad has a job or something? You'll be here all day by yourself?"

Belinda didn't skip a beat. "Star will be home. All the Nauvians are home all the time. I'm never alone. I'll be here, safe and sound, with people who love me."

"But you'll miss a lot of important stuff. Dances, graduation, the prom..." Jerry pointed out.

"She can go to all the school events," Patrick informed them. "There's a Halloween Party! I used to love Halloween. I'd wear a mask and, for one night, it was like being a regular kid. After a while, I started incorporating my specialness into my costume. I embraced it. Dad helped. He was great at it. I was an alien in junior year. Senior year, I was, guess what? A bug!"

"Dad! No way. You never told me that."

"Embrace the bug, Babe. It suits you. Make it yours. What's wrong with being a bug?"

"Will you help me make a bug costume?"

"Sure, Baby."

"Can I really bring Baput, Dad?"

"No!" Fran, Elmer, Jerry and Lorraine all cried at once.

"Why not?" Patrick asked. "His costume is already made. He's the Alanakash of Nauve. Now why don't you kids go visit Baput, Okay? I know he's dying to see Jerry." His eyes cut to Lorraine. "Okay, Mom?"

Lorraine caught the somber look in his straight eye. "Oh. Yeah, run along kids, have fun."

Belinda and Jerry bolted for the door.

Patrick's Idea

As soon as the kids left, Patrick leaned forward in his chair. His eyes darted around the room as if looking for secret watchers, or listeners. He reminded Elmer of their dad, back in the eighties, when he had pot plants in the back of the orchard and the helicopters came over, throbbing the air.

"I've had a vision," the wild-eyed apparition declared.

Elmer hissed a scoff. "Too much of the wacky weed, eh?"

"No," Patrick insisted. "It was real. Baput saw it, too. Even Felsic saw it. It was Mitten and we meditated together, and we all saw the same thing. A kid getting separated from his dad at the border. I heard about this last year. It happened a lot."

"Yes, I heard it, too," Fran replied grimly. "I saw the big Walmart where they kept them in cages. They looked like dog kennels! But I thought they put a stop to that. Do you think what you saw might have happened a year or two ago?"

"I don't know," Patrick replied. "I did some digging. It happened a lot during 2017 and 2018, but once the world found out about it, they supposedly stopped it. According to my research, it's still happening, and there are still at least 2,700 kids in those cages. And, get this! They've lost track of the parents! They've all been arrested and deported without their kids. Some kids are, like, three years old, even younger. Babies! They didn't give them ID tags, bracelets, or even written records of where, or even who, their parents are. Babies! They can't even tell you their name, or where they're from. How are they ever going to reunite them? They don't even know if there are relatives in the U.S. who could sponsor them. And if there are, they're afraid to come get them, because if they're illegal, they might get thrown in jail, too.

"The kid we saw, he looked to be about seven. He knew he had an Uncle Jose in San Diego. But that's all he knew. No address, no phone number. They just laughed at him."

Fran wrinkled like a raisin. "Well, are they just going to keep them forever, in those cages?"

"I don't know. I dug all through the internet. Baput did, too, and he's limitless."

"He don't really know is way around, though," Elmer snapped. "He's got no idea of the deviosity people can reach. Especially in this administration."

"The whole idea is horrible," Fran fretted. "They did it on purpose, just to scare people out of trying to come here. It's terrorism."

"Hey, now, Fran," Elmer objected. "They're coming here. It ain't terrorism if we're not going down there and scaring them in their homes. They don't have to come here."

"But they *do* have to come," Fran argued. "We're not scaring them, but somebody is. Most of them are refugees seeking asylum from warring factions, drug lords, cartels, and drought. We don't know what they're going through, or what their reasoning is. But we know they're human. They have the same needs as everyone else. And kids need their parents. Parents need their kids. I can't imagine what they're going through!" Her eyebrows peaked into a question mark. She turned to Patrick. "So, what are you saying, Patrick? Did you and Baput find a way to help them?"

Lorraine coughed abruptly and buried her face in her book.

Patrick took both of Fran's hands into his. "I'm ashamed to admit it, but I was thinking more about how they can help us. The Nauvians, anyway."

Fran drew her hand from Patrick's and brought it to her mouth. "You mean, we would take them, the babies, and send them to another planet? What about their mothers? They'll never find them! They'll never, ever see their kids again. Never know where they are, how they are..."

Elmer jumped to his feet. "She's right, Bro. These are real people you're messing with. People with feelings! You gotta think about everybody. You know that. It's the Look 'N Up Way!" He swelled with rage and pride.

Patrick laid his hand lightly on Fran's arm, focused his straight eye on her tearful blue ones, and whispered, "Those mothers are never going to find their kids anyway. The government made sure of that, either intentionally or by gross negligence. It's the 21st Century, and they can't record whose kid is whose, and track them through the system? It's ridiculous, but true. Those kids will never be reunited with their folks. At least we can give them new families, a new life, not in a cage."

Lorraine closed her book and spoke over her glasses. "A miserable life in a dreary, backward world with no freedom. No girls. Just send boys. Their lives are slightly less miserable."

"Tell that to Felsic." Elmer grumbled. "Boys from Earth will fight back, disrupt everything. We should send girls."

Lorraine slammed the book down. "You put an Earth girl in that culture and you'll see some disruption!"

"I don't know about that," Patrick countered. "Most rural South American cultures are like Nauve, for the women, anyway. They take care of their families, their kids. They're tethers, just like Salistar. But we should try to get young ones who don't remember what life was like before the cages."

Fran shuddered. "There's no place for them in this world. Just like our Nauvian friends."

"Nauve needs them," Patrick answered. "The survival of their whole population depends on them. They'll be adopted, have families, grow up as part of the village."

Fran recited the customary caveat, "If they live."

Elmer was pacing around the table, the way Patrick often did. "So, we're gonna kidnap someone else's kids from some government, ah, prison camp? How the hell do you think you're gonna pull that off? We can't send anyone to Nauve, anyway. We don't have the Net, remember?"

Patrick sighed, "I know. We'll have to figure that out first. But I'm going to keep digging. It's all very secretive. We might need to find someone on the inside to pull it off. It will be hard, maybe even dangerous."

"We're all going to jail." Elmer surmised.

Lorraine smiled, nodding vigorously.

Mustang

On Sunday morning, after long embraces and tearful goodbyes, Mustang rumbled its way down the driveway in perfect tune. Patrick, Lorraine and Belinda stood in the driveway, waving goodbye.

Without breaking her fake smile, Lorraine mumbled, "You won't make any money if you keep giving the cars to Jerry!"

"Jerry traded for Mustang," Patrick explained. "Now we're going to sell Falcon. You can help, Babe."

She looked up from her phone, eyebrows up with piqued interest, eyes dull with resignation. "Me," she replied, not a question.

"Put a sign on it and park in at your office. Put your cell number on it. If anyone wants to check it out, you'll have the keys, let them drive it, whatever. If they have mechanical questions, just say, 'I'll let you talk to my husband', and call me. I'll give it to Felsic."

"I'm not going to say that."

"Why? Because it's not true?" Patrick asked to no response. "Because Felsic's not your husband?"

"It's not that. I'm just not going to say that. 'I have to ask my husband'. It sounds weak! I'll lose autonomy."

"What do you know about cars?" Patrick wondered.

"More than you!" Lorraine retorted.

"That's not much."

"I'm not going to say that, alright?" Lorraine insisted. "I'm not taking time away from work to give test drives and call mechanics. I have a real job. I'm the only one bringing in serious money around here."

"You're on salary. You work sixty hours a week. You can take a few minutes to deal with the car. You'll make your salary, plus a couple thousand for the Look 'N Up, all in a few short minutes."

"I'm an engineer, not a used car salesman!"

Nauve, Summer

Jenevan and Akira

Jenevan bowed as she entered the meeting room in the Great Hall. Akira was holding audiences there, in front of her deaf chaperone. Only women could enter, but still, Akira had come to enjoy her silent company, and had kept her on even after Bazu's ascension had brought the awkward two-person Council back to the customary trio.

"I have lost my unborn babbet," Jenevan reported shamefully, her head down.

The old woman's tone lacked the expected judgement. "Nemaray told me. You needn't feel ashamed. You have already met my expectations."

"But I have to, Ma'am." Jenevan replied humbly, still standing. "That is what I've come about. Partly..."

"What is it, Dear?" Akira had a fondness for this one. A good producer, gifted with animals. She spoke in kinder tones than she used with most, yet the girl still cowered.

"If I can have another babbet, and it is a boy�" Akira's eyebrows reminded her. Had she just cursed her future child? "If my next babbet lives," she corrected, "and if it is a boy, can he be apprentice to my Popa, the Animal Keeper?" She finally raised her eyes to her ruler's, blinking hopefully.

"Well of course. In that case, I will see that the Akash makes it so, as soon as he is born. If he lives." Even Akira almost forgot the morbid custom, for an instant.

"Yes Ma'am," the pious girl uttered her thanks but did not give the customary bow and turn away, as expected. Akira gazed at her silently, waiting for her to make the next move.

"Ma'am," Jenevan squeaked like a mouse in a trap. "There's one more thing."

Akira's face fell into its habitual wrinkles. "Surely not a problem with Pindrad."

"No Ma'am. It isn't him, or me. It's, well, I mean no disrespect." The words came tumbling out now, out of Jenevan's control. Akira listened calmly, at first.

"Nemaray told me you weren't concerned with the animals, but sometimes they have bad babbets." Now that she had said it out loud, her fear was gone. She looked straight into the ancient eyes with her desperate ones. "They say you keep the lines apart. Do animals have lines? How can I keep them apart? The ganeesh have only Momama Heffala and Popa Mangu, and all the rest are brothers and sisters. How can I keep their lines apart? There is only one line. They won't breed. It's like they know."

Akira replied with Popa's mantra. "Always listen to ganeesh, for they are wise beyond our knowing."

She looked smaller, somehow. Jeneven could no longer see the power she had feared just a moment ago. She just saw a frail old woman with an infinite sadness etched indelibly into her face. After what seemed an eternity, Akira spoke.

"I will say something I rarely say, My Dear. If anyone deserves the truth, it is you, my faithful girl. However, I must swear you to secrecy."

Jenevan nodded helplessly.

"I let you down. Do you remember when you were just a girl and the um, special ganeesh was born?" she asked, as if speaking to a child.

"Of course, Akira. There were twins. The first one, Dambu, was perfect. The second one had two trunks, but couldn't breathe through either one. He died minutes after birth."

Akira seemed to be shrinking before Jenevan's eyes. She made up for it by jumping to her feet and interrupting, pacing and gesturing. "By then the Akash had all the people gathered around, gawking at the hibudara ganeesh. They all saw it!"

"Hibudara?" Jenevan asked, showing the appropriate ignorance.

"Yes, it is what I call it when a babbet – an animal babbet – is born with some kind of deformity. It happens sometimes, with animals. You must know that."

"I do." Jenevan stiffened and stood up taller than the ancient woman before her. "That is what I came to ask you. How do you stop it, in people?"

Akira didn't answer. She just went on with her story. "Back then, with the two-trunk ganeesh, I should have come and looked for myself." She looked at the frustrated girl then, as if it were her turn to speak.

"Why didn't you, Akira?" Jenevan only dared to ask because her ruler seemed to want her to.

"My strength failed me. I couldn't bear it." Akira unloaded a sigh like a hot breeze coming down a flaming mountain. "I couldn't set my eyes on that sight, though I have been expecting it all my days as Akira."

"A ganeesh with two trunks?" Jenevan asked eagerly, hoping it had meant something after all, besides a cycle of misery for her family.

"The last ganeesh." Akira's voice seemed to shake the walls.

"What do you mean, Akira?" Jenevan heard herself ask from a distant, foggy place. Akira's ancient eyes met hers and almost bowled her over with their soft sadness. Akira knew things. Things no one else knew. *Not even our new Akash*, Jenevan was certain. The expression didn't change, as if Akira was frozen, giving Jenevan plenty of time to study it, to feel that expression. To let the realization sink in. Then the frown cracked open and the old woman spoke once more.

"You're a good girl." Akira appraised, bringing Jenevan back from the brink of that dark place she had shown her. "Go take care of the animals, just like you always have." She studied Jenevan's face, making sure she understood. Her hand was unusually warm when she grasped Jenevan's. "Do the best you can. And make your Popa an apprentice!" She ordered and nodded her head, signaling the end of the meeting.

Trillella and Kaysee

Peratha's moans rasped with a little scream at the edges of them, until they stopped, which vexed Trillella even more. She'd used the herbs, and done the massage, just like Kaysee had shown her, but Rodan had never used his battle clubs before.

Kaysee hadn't been around in over a Kakeeche cycle. Why? They had been good, of course. No one would think of breaking the rules, like Romey and Jakima had so many generations ago. They were all told the ancient tale in school during their fourth cycle, nine to twelve years old, before their 'horns were out'. The tale of the grizzly consequences of mating with anyone other than your betrothed and risking a *hibudara,* a forbidden offspring.

No, they had been good. Kaysee came only to help Peratha and teach Trillella to help, and more and more it was the latter because Kaysee's Popa, and Rakta and Akira, and even the Akash, were all trying to stop him from helping people in his mysterious and suspect way.

So, he came less and less often. Trillella thought about him more and more, and The New Thing inside her grew strong, and steeled her with its resolve. She knew the poor Thing was doomed from the start, but still it gave her something to live for, and a way to escape this life.

She was only thirteen, and The New Thing was also very young. It would be called a puppy in an easier world, a mere crush. It waited around the edges of everything she did, like a timid zebkin watching her from the bushes, waiting until the end of the long day when she locked her bedroom door and lay in her bed all alone and let it out. Let Him in. But only in her dreams. Anything else would be literally unthinkable.

Peratha's hoarse moan ripped through Trillella's reverie like a bumbly's horn ripping through green flesh. Momama had never been this bad. She needed Kaysee, now. Trill dabbed her with a mullein leaf and drew the thin sheet of woven grass around her trembling shoulders. "I'll be right back, Momama," she promised, knowing her only parent was long past hearing her.

She slung the strap of an empty woven bag across her shoulder and stepped out into the garden. First she looked east, upriver, toward the Holy Cave, where Popa had vanished, toward the nimbly bumbly caves and beyond, to wherever the kiko birds went when they weren't putting on their spectacular mating show in the orchard. She looked that way every time she came out into the garden, a ritual she kept to herself. Continuing her private rite, she turned toward the orchard, gazing across the meadow, sighting along the narrow foot trail used by only one person, now filling in with fresh, untrodden grass. Resolutely, she set out on that trail.

She found Kaysee performing his stereotypical duties as Orchard Tender, sitting cross-legged under a pomegranate tree, eyes closed, breathing in long, soft breaths. Was he sleeping? Trill cleared her throat timidly. One dark eye opened a doorway to another reality for far less than a second, before the familiar Kaysee returned to that eye. Trillella swooned.

Kaysee unfolded his legs and stood in a single, smooth motion that seemed impossible. He grasped her elbow politely before she fell, staring intently into her worn face. "Trillella! What's wrong? Is it your Momama?" he asked, almost hopefully, as he scanned the girl up and down for breaks and bruises.

"Yes, she is bad. You haven't come."

"Have you tried..."

"I've tried it all!" Trillella snapped. She tried to pull her arm away. He squeezed her elbow tighter. "It helps a little, but..." She closed her eyes and inhaled. "He used his battle club. One of the little throwing ones!"

"Where? How many times?" Kaysee let go of her and produced a woven bag from the tree he'd been sitting under. It bulged with an odd assortment of implements, oils and plant parts.

"Hurry," he said, shooing Trillella ahead of him along the trail. His eyes shifted furtively between the practice field, the village huts, the Great Hall and back toward the orchard. He rushed right through the garden without stopping to pick any of the herbs Trillella had planted.

Trillella opened the door to a nauseating odor of old wine, urine and vomit. Peratha lay on her back, snoring noisily. Her eyes darted back and forth behind closed eyelids that seemed too thin and too blue. Kaysee forced one eye open, then the other.

"Her head is swollen inside. Around the part that makes us think. Cold, wet leaves from the garden, or that mullein there, do you have any clean?"

Trillella searched her supply of wide, dry leaves, and dipped one into a bowl of water that had pomegranate seeds and mint steeping in it, and the leaves of those yellow flowers. She brought him the leaf and the bowl, and Kaysee went to work.

"You haven't come around at all," Trill complained, now that he was here and real.

"I am supposed to be shut down completely. No more, my Popa says. The wise Council," he sneered, uncharacteristically, "Rakta, Akira and the

Akash," he snorted a bitter laugh. "They say I can't ascend to Tender if I keep doing this. Like I care! But, my Popa does. He wants to retire."

"Retire from sitting�" Trillella bit her tongue. That cruel village talk just rolled off it so easily, without even a thought. "I'm sorry," She whispered

"I know," the boy agreed, "but it's what he wants, and he's Popa. He'll tell the Council on me, if he catches me, even though it means I won't ascend and he'll have to slave away in the orchard for another two cycles, waiting for my little brother! But I will be punished. Severely, by the Council and by Popa. I can't image what they will do. If anybody in the village sees me, they'll tell, except the people I'm helping, of course." He rummaged through his bag for something. Trillella hoped it was a miracle.

"Your hut is at the edge of the village, closest to the orchard. I can come here without being seen. But only if it's urgent, like now. Not if you just want to see me. I want to see you, too, but I can't be caught. Maybe after Passascenday..." His eyes turned to the lumpy bag.

"You'll be married then." Trillella whispered. She had to say it, but she said it as softly as she possibly could, with her eyes squeezed shut and her fingers crossed on both hands. "If you live."

Kaysee cupped Trill's chin with his right hand, gently forcing her eyes toward his. With his left hand, he pulled a tiny, hollow bone from his bag.

Her rapt face fell, then turned to stone. She jerked her chin from his hand. "That's a kiko bone!" she accused. "Kiko birds are my friends." She turned away.

Kaysee's eyes followed hers and they met over Peratha's eerily motionless slumber.

"I found it lying under a kiko bird tree, so, freely given."

"Someone died in battle." Trillella mused, taking the bone reverently.

"It happens. I've found a lot of these bones under the trees the kiko birds choose for their contests. Gifts for the Orchard Tender, I suppose."

"For your Popa, then."

"Ha!" Kaysee laughed awkwardly. "He cares not for kiko birds. He used to shoo them out of the trees, before I took over. 'Too messy', he'd say. As if a little bird boo could hurt anything! Even that holds something the plants need, I believe. It's all connected. Blow on it."

Trillella blew. Peratha stirred and moaned, pleasantly this time.

"It sounds like a kiko bird." Trillella was mystified by the idea. *A bird sounds like air blowing through its leg bone?*

"Yes," Kaysee replied. "If you need urgent help like this again, go out to your garden, face my way, and blow that whistle. I'll hear it, and no matter what, Trillella, I will come. If anybody else hears, they'll just think it's a kiko bird."

Earth, Harvest 2019

School Days

The busy summer passed too quickly. The crew kept working on the wrought iron rail panels for the Silver Slopes Hotel that would someday net $25,000 for Look 'N Up Industries. They received their salary as shares in the unofficial book. Lorraine managed to sell Falcon at work, to a senior engineer with a midlife crisis. She spent more time talking to him about it than she would have to a stranger, but he spent at-work time, too, on a very long test-drive, so somehow that made it alright. She even had a little fun, listening as her co-worker held a highly technical conversation with a 'very knowledgeable mechanic' without ever knowing he was talking to an olive-skinned alien who had never even dreamed of a car until five years ago.

At harvest time, the Look 'N Up hired Jerry's classmates again, but the knuckleheads were even more distractible than last year, being that much more mature. Elmer led the inspectors through the east and west orchard. They didn't bother to go down and look at the burn pile again. Nothing to see there, as Agent Myron Boyd would gladly attest, and often did, to his bored co-agents behind the blackened downtown storefront.

Every morning, Belinda joined her freshman classes via Zoom. She used a filter that made her look like a googly-eyed praying mantis. Her handle was 'Bel the Bug". The teacher allowed it, out of sympathy, but that meant she had to let all the kids use filters. It was an eclectic class of two cats, four dogs, a frog, a lizard, Darth Vader, Spiderman, a purple velociraptor and Bel the Bug. Baput, the avocado-skinned Alanakash, hid behind the screen and learned whatever the Earth kids learned.

During the break after Spanish class, Belinda and Baput would go to the kitchen together and eat the lunch Salistar prepared, fresh, hot and home cooked with no meat, no cheese, no bugs. While they ate, they practiced their third language.

"You are very pretty, muy linda�" Baput tried, then stopped. "Hey, *linda*, like Belinda, right?"

"Right." Bel nodded. "My name means pretty-pretty. Belle is Italian for good looking. Linda is Spanish for cute. So, they named me pretty twice, I guess to make up for the fact that I will never be pretty. They should have named me Melinda. Mal means bad. Bad Pretty."

"You're not bad!"

"My pretty is bad. It doesn't follow the rules. Bad Pretty."

"You *are* pretty." Baput insisted. "Muy bonita," he found yet another word for pretty. He didn't care what she looked like, except, she didn't look happy.

"You don't get it!" she snapped. "You're like my mom!"

"No, I'm not!"

"Yeah, you are. On Nauve, you were Apprentice Akash. You were highborn, the highest family, all your life. You're big and strong and you have nice hair and beautiful eyes..."

She trailed to silence, brought her nose to his until he had only one big eye. Then she stepped back and looked away. "I'm Sorry. You're not like my mom. Not at all. You just don't get what it's like to be me."

"I don't know what it's like to go to your school, where other kids make fun of you. But if I went to school, they'd pick on me, too, because I'm green. Yes?"

"Yeah, maybe." Belinda sniffed. "Or they might like you, because you're different.

"But people hate people who are different."

"But you're *way* different. They've never seen or even heard of someone like you before."

"Same with you, right?" Baput asked.

Bel turned and walked to the window.

Baput was afraid to follow. "Belinda..."

"Don't you see?" she asked the window in thick sobs. "The difference is, you're pretty, and I'm�" She turned her eyes to him, tears glistening.

Baput to rushed across the room, lifted her face to his and hushed her lips with his own.

Halloween Dance

Lorraine looked up from her work and raised her eyebrows at Baput, who suddenly stood before her in his fancy robe, holding his showy longstick with the fake gold point.

"Meet the Alanakash of Nauve," Belinda presented, explaining the obvious to her mother.

"Do they know that's even a thing?" Lorraine asked drolly, refusing to be impressed. Another of Patrick's awful ideas. She would not be held responsible for the horror that would inevitably result.

Undeterred by her mother's aloofness, Belinda answered brightly. "Everyone will go 'oh, yeah!' and walk away wondering how they missed that movie." She lifted a green pillowcase with a paper towel roll attached to form a proboscis, and two toilet paper rolls made into googly eye stems. "And I'm me, Bel the Bug, see?" she modelled, her voice muted.

Patrick stood silently behind Lorraine, his thoughts racing. This was starting to look like a first date. The ridiculous looking couple stood close together, Baput a little bit behind and a lot bigger. Patrick snapped a picture he had never thought he would take. Belinda's first date. "I'll drive you. If you need me to pick you up early, just call. I'll be there in a flash, Baby."

Belinda opened the passenger door of the Subaru and stepped out onto the asphalt of the gymnasium parking lot. She pulled her unwieldy costume over her head.

Baput emerged from the back seat in his Akashic robe, a little queasy from the long ride. He leaned back in and wrestled his longstick out. He'd had to wedge it crosswise between the floor and the ceiling to get it to fit.

Patrick came around the front of the car and carefully straightened Bel's costume it so it looked just right. "They might not let you take that inside," he told Baput, a bit late.

"Why, Dad? It's his costume," Bel objected.

"It's a weapon," Patrick answered, wishing he'd thought about it sooner.

Belinda took in her impressive date. The effect wouldn't be the same without the long, carved Holy Akashic Staff. "He's got to have his longstick. How can he protect me? Come on, Baput." They hurried away toward the gym, Baput clinging to his staff so tightly his knuckles glowed white against his green fingers as Patrick watched them disappear.

"Belinda Musik, Bel the Bug, Virtual Academy." Belinda introduced herself proudly through her cardboard snout. "And this is my date, Baput, Alanakash of Nauve."

"You can't bring that stick in here, kid." The pock-marked junior at the desk informed her through his gum, not impressed in the least.

"My Dad's already left with the car," the bug whined through her tube. "Where can he put it?"

The upperclassman reached his open hand toward the kid with the crappy homemade costume and the green face paint. What was he supposed to be, anyway? "Give it here. I'll hold it for you. Pick it up on your way out."

With an anxious look toward Belinda, the Alanakash meekly allowed himself to be disarmed. Only then did they make their grand entrance. Two steps in, and Belinda's proboscis fell to the floor. She picked it up and folded it, threw it in the trash, took Baput in her arms and led him in a lively slow-dance, the pillowcase hanging limply below her chin, her bug eyes bouncing, threatening to join their proboscis.

Nobody asked who Baput was supposed to be. Nobody seemed to think it strange that the kid was green, or that they'd never seen him before. Nobody recognized Bel the Bug from the Academy, either. The kid with the sack over her head could have been anyone. Maybe that weird looking girl from middle school, but no one could be sure.

Belinda stood on Baput's feet and leaned her face on his chest, crushing the toilet paper tunnel over her wayward left eye. His stubbly, green chin was all she could see. She could feel his chest heave, deep and slow, as he breathed his Akashic breath and danced the ritual slow dance Patrick had taught them.

Baput couldn't take his eyes off of the sacred staff his popa had made for him when he ascended to Akash, lying on the floor under that front table. When the band took its first break, he wrapped his arm around Belinda's waist and rushed her that way. The pimply kid was still there, his white shirt now stained with punch. When he saw the green kid and the sack-head girl, he reached under the table, pulled out the precious longstick and handed it to Baput without looking at him. "Have a nice night," he remarked with no apparent thought.

"Was that fun?" Baput asked as they stepped out into the dark evening. A soft drizzle hovered in the air around them, quickly digesting what was left of Bel's cardboard body parts.

"I don't know," Belinda asked honestly. "I'll call Dad. Oh, look, he's still here." She waved at the car, took Baput's hand, and dragged him through the fog toward the Subaru's yellowish headlights.

Nauve, Harvest Clean-up

It was harvest, the busiest time of year for everyone. Even Easy Harvest, the two harvests out of three that were not plagued by nimblies and bumblies. If only there was a way to keep part of this bountiful harvest for next year, when the kips would over-ripen in the trees while the battle raged in the trenches, night and day. But juice kept only a short time. Wine kept longer, but surely not two seasons. The oil was vital. Salistar's oil kept for over a year, fueling the human war machine through the battle. Azuray's oil always spoiled before the next harvest.

Such thoughts were far too global for Trillella, a nobody girl child of almost thirteen, but they were easier to think about than *nauve*, home. Home where her Momama lay marinated in the last of the rank desperation wine, on the busiest day of the women's menial year.

She approached the Great Hall. The Grand Doors were open. A ganeesh entered through them, carrying a bulging basket of fresh picked pomegranates on his back. His sister passed him on the way out, her carrier empty, and headed back to the orchard.

Azuray and Banova stood in front of the pedestrian entrance beside the Grand Doors. They exchanged a beaked glance, then looked down at her. "Where is your Momama?" Azuray demanded.

"She's sick," Trillella squeaked her reply to the ground, "again."

No condolences were offered. Banova handed Trill a straw broom and a bundle of mullein leaves. "You are cleanup. Start in the back there, where the older Unmarriageables are working."

"Yes, Ma'am." Trill muttered, scurrying in the indicated direction.

"You'll be joining them next Passascenday" Azuray muttered cruelly to the girl's back.

"If she lives." Banova replied automatically.

Rows of tables were set up on either side of the ganeesh path. Women separated the dark purple skins from the white honeycomb-like husks, then picked out the seeds, one by one. Every part had a use. Every part was vital.

But none more than the oil trapped inside those thousands and thousands of seeds. The very stuff of life, Kaysee had said. Trillella believed him.

"Girl!" Yilnetar, the puffy-faced wife of the pot maker, Cottar, tapped harshly on the table as Trill hurried to her assigned post. She stopped dutifully. Yilnetar tapped the table again. "You. Wipe here."

Trillella approached the crowded table with her mullein rag. She leaned over an empty chair and began to wipe the table.

"What were you saying, Feleza, about the wine?" Yilnetar invited.

Feleza, wife of Buppan, smirked and seemed to continue a story. "As I walked here, I noticed, almost every dooryard has a still now. Every house with a drinking man, anyway. It's scandalous! It's like saying 'a drinking man lives here' to all who walk by. Not that there's anything wrong with having a drinking man. Girl, come on, get this gaa right in front of me!" She banged on the table with her calloused finger.

Hiding her blushing face behind her hair, Trillella bent over the table and wiped so hard, the mullein leaf broke into little rolls.

"You're making an even bigger mess!" Yilnetar accused to hoots and cackles of laughter.

"What do you expect of Felsic's child?" Feleza cried.

Trillella backed away from the table. Mersilla, the quiet, intelligent wife of Keplar, the Miller, summoned her by tapping her table softly. Trillella pulled a fresh leaf from her bundle. Mersilla addressed her in a soft voice the other tables couldn't hear. "It's the waste of it that concerns me. Everyone having a still, instead of one big still for all. It's like if everyone had their own mill, and milled their own rice. It doesn't make sense." She leaned in closer and Trillella made as if her wiping brought her ear to Mersilla's mouth. "I am afraid we will each be making our own oil, too, after next Passascenday."

Trillella drew back and met her thoughtful eyes. "If we live," she replied, and withdrew to the back of the room where the Unmarriageables worked in pairs.

Trill started at the last table, where the two oldest crones sat. Passed over all their long lives for Apprentice to Akira, they had both eventually attained the rank of Councilor. Nemaray worked with the tethers of the high-born families, including the former Akashic tether, Salistar, but not Tamaya. Ophilite had been Counselor to the low-borns, like Trillela's family, until last cycle when she retired and Aoti took over. Dried and barren, they reminded Trill of two old trees. Nemaray resembled a towering pine in the forest, lush green with sharp edges and sharp needles, who whispered and threatened to fall on people. And Ophilite, shorter, rounder, was like a grandmother pomegranate tree. Her face even resembled a kip, wide and round, but dry and wrinkled, in a dull sage tone.

They seemed to be in deep conversation, so Trill hesitated. At last, Nemaray turned her beak toward her, as if she had just noticed her. "Ah yes," she croaked. "Felsic's poor daughter, on cleanup. Well, come on over here, Honey, I've made a mess." She deliberately dumped her glass of pomegranate juice on the table. "Ooooh, look! Gaa, gaa, gaa! Hurry, girl!" she crowed like a raven.

Trillella drew two more leaves from her pack as she rushed to clean the deliberate spill. She knew it was a trap, but she had no choice. She bent over the table to wipe, and Nemaray began. "So, what were you telling me, Ophilite? About the boy?"

"Well, he must have been in love, I suppose." Ophilite concluded flatly.

"With who?"

"Not his betrothed, obviously." Ophilite speculated. "Why else would a boy like that run and jump off a cliff? He would have ascended and married on Passascenday."

"If he'd lived." Nemaray replied.

The customary caveat sounded so much worse in the past tense. Trillella kept wiping, rudely pushing between the two old women, her pounding heart resounding in her ears. Who were they talking about?

Ophilite took a deep breath, puffing herself up like a bullfrog. "But that's what I'm saying. A Tender!"

Trill froze in mid wipe, a hiss escaping from the side of her clenched teeth. The two old ladies exchanged a suspicious glance and a hiss of their own.

The two old trees continued to mutter their conversation over the frozen cleaner. "Such an easy job. Barely a care. Tend the kip trees, raise your children in the peace and quiet of the orchard." Ophilite could only dream.

"And Galena is a perfectly lovely girl," Nemaray added. "A great cook. What more could any young man wish for?"

The whispering trees swayed away as Lazera's voice chimed in from the last table in the widows' row. Trillella and Peratha had sat at that table last year during the harvest. Now Lazera and bitter old Bitanda had taken their places, after losing their husbands in last Season's battle. Bitanda had also lost the last of her four sons. Her fourth-cycle daughter sat quietly next to her, her big, black eyes taking in all the gossip.

Lazera had the scoop. "My son, Zellack, is Galena's brother's closemate. He was one of the men who chased him. He saw it all." Work ceased as green faces turned toward Lazera to hear her fresh, second-hand story. "The boy's Popa went, of course, but his brother is too young. He will be Tender now, when he comes of age, if he lives."

"Yes, go on!" begged Bitanda.

Trillella backed away from the tables and began polishing the floor with her broom, dropping brooms straws everywhere. No one noticed her.

"And Rodan went, too."

Trillella seized. No one thought to look at her.

"Why? What had he to do with it?"

"Nothing, just his natural meanness I suppose."

"The boy is probably lucky he fell off that cliff."

Trillella stopped polishing and stood like a statue of a cleaning lady while the Great Hall filled with the caws of greedy buzzards calling for a story, a person, to devour. Kaysee. She wanted to run but she had to hear the rest of the story and she couldn't move her muscles anyway.

"No matter!" Lazera stood to hold the floor for her fifteen minutes of fame. "No matter, because Rodan couldn't keep up anyway! He didn't even make it to the Holy Cave, much less into the mists beyond."

A rumble passed through the Great Hall, part stifled chuckle at Rodan, part awed oohs and ahhhs about the mist. Even Azuray and Banova were listening, letting the women sit idle.

"Yes! The mists beyond!" Lazera thundered in full drama, writing the legend as it would be told to young people for generations, as a lesson, like Romey and Jakima. "They chased him upriver, past the Holy Cave into the mists where the nimblies and bumblies lie dormant in their caves. Where no sensible person ever goes! Kaysee, the Apprentice Orchard Tender, who was to ascend to Orchard Tender and marry the lovely Galena, ran into the mists!"

"If he'd lived," responded the rapt crowd in unison, followed by scattered remarks such as "What of Galena, now?"

"Only Akira knows."

"She's a very good cook!"

Trillella didn't feel sorry for Galena. She stood perfectly still, apparently invisible.

Lazera cleared her throat obnoxiously and resumed her tale. "He ran into the mists and they chased him. My boy, Zellack, was in the lead, of course. But when he heard the boy's footsteps abruptly cease, a stifled scream, he slowed to a walk, thank Kakeeche! He tried to part the mist with his hands, but it did little good. The others caught up, Galena's brother, Canam, and the poor old Tender, Kaysen. He made it all the way. Who would think, with the exercise he gets!"

A perfect wave of laughter rippled through the crowd, followed by someone's voice saying, "He was motivated. He wants to retire." An even louder roar of laughter echoed off the great walls.

Again, that ugly throat-clearing sound from Lazera. She strutted in place on tiptoes, acting. "Together, they crept forward through the mist. They heard nothing ahead of them. My son said it was the nothingest nothing he had ever heard." She paused for another round of oohs and aahs.

"Then Kaysen the Tender cried out. He was rocking back and forth on his feet, ready to fall. My son grabbed his arm, and pulled him back, just in time. Arms linked, they peered forward over the cliff, into the mist. A wind blew, just then, sent by Dear Kakeeche, no doubt, to clear the mist so they could see him.

"He was far below, but they could see well enough. He lay motionless on the rocks, still as a stone. He had hit so hard his leg bone had tried to leap from his flesh, and his leg bent back crazily so that his foot almost touched his head. His head was broken, too. It leaked blood right here." She pointed to her left temple, "and here, too." She touched the side of her mouth.

"Did they bring the body nauve?" asked Mersilla, the thoughtful one.

Lazera scoffed at the idea. "It was way down there. They could see it for a long time. He didn't move. My son doesn't lie. So, they left him."

Still standing, she took the opportunity to look down her nose at the thoroughly bereaved Bitanda, and concluded, "After all, not every momama raises fools!"

Bitanda hissed at the implied insult.

"Well, Kaysen apparently did." Azuray added her endorsement to the official version, making it part of the curriculum forevermore.

Do what you're told and don't try to help people or we'll chase you off a cliff, and then call you a fool. Trillella raged silently. She watched the broom dangle between her bare feet as she slinked, unnoticed, toward the Grand Doors, right down the middle of the busy ganeesh path. She didn't hear the brief hoot behind her, but she felt the trunk that snuck gently between her legs and lifted her out of the way, placing her forcefully among the tables, where she was quite visible and enjoyed another round of derisive laughter from the village women.

Ignoring them, she struggled along the edge of the path until she was clear of the doors. Outside, the cool, crisp fall air was scented with kips and ganeesh boo. There was no one outside. No one watched her.

She broke into a run, toward the battle trenches that lay in a rectangular pattern in front of the Great Hall. Dropping the broom and the two remaining leaves, she ran blindly, like Kaysee had. And like Kaysee, she fell, but not nearly as far.

She landed on bruised knees in the rear battle trench, closest to the Great Hall. She lifted her eyes to a wall smeared with the terminal gaa of a thousand of her ancestors. She squinted as a fossilized arm bone resolved itself in her eyes, then her mind. A forearm, and part of a hand, the thumb and forefinger, had been smeared by the wide, wooden paddles the Unmarriageables used to clean the trenches, and embedded into the clay walls. Trillella gasped at the sobering site. She was already sober enough.

Who was it? She found herself wondering. She stood and began to run up the west trench, toward the intersecting north trench. *I know it's not my Popa. He vanished at the Holy Cave. His bones were never found.* She turned east and ran toward the east trench, the forward trench. *I know it's not Kaysee. His bones lie broken, somewhere in the mist.*

At the intersection with the east trench, she stopped cold. A large leg bone seemed to bend around the corner, imbedded in both walls. It was too much, but still she turned the corner and entered the foreword battle trench, where only the best warriors had ever been. And there it was, the Rock of Yanzoo, or rather, the Rock of Jakima, in the woman's version. Yanzoo, the ancient Akash, may have slain the nimblies by sitting on that rock before the trenches and playing a special tone on his music bowl, but before he could get the thing started, his Tether, Jakima, standing in front of the rock as bait, had knocked all four out of the sky with her heavy, marble rolling pin, protecting her children.

Trillella leapt out of the trench like a seasoned warrior. There were no nimblies and bumblies to fear. Not this year. She stood before the Rock of Yanzoo, where Jakima had so bravely stood. She reached under her tunic, between her budding breasts, for the kiko bone that always hung there, tethered around her neck with a strand of woven grass.

She raised the whistle to her cold, tight lips and blew a long, low tone that would have passed for a kiko in mourning. She blew to the east, toward the Holy Cave where her Popa had disappeared. She blew into the sunrise, the way the kiko birds had flown away together so happily. She blew upriver, the way Kaysee had run. She blew into the mists, where the nimbly-bumbly caves went on forever and nobody ever went.

Earth, 2020

Diversity

Bel popped out of the music room where she had her school computer, all excited, Baput at her heels. "They accepted me!"

Lorraine looked over her glasses. "The Advanced Ed Class?"

Patrick rushed in from the kitchen. "The Genetics one?"

"Yup." Belinda nodded, beaming. "Next semester. I'm too young for it, but they let me in special, because of my eye. They want to study it."

"I don't know if I like that!" Lorraine objected. "It's exploitive."

"But, Mom, that's why I want to take it. We talked about this, remember? With the lady from the college, and the high school psychologist."

"I remember." Lorraine quoted the college rep in mocking tones. "She seems very bright for her age, especially for someone with a, an, um...' It's a superficial facial deformity! Nothing wrong with your brain! Yeah, Baby, you go for it." Lorraine agreed through her teeth.

Baput piped up shyly from behind Belinda. "We are going to learn about our problem, too. The Navian problem." He blushed a muddy mauve. "Not enough DNA. Jerry says we should be having bad babbets by now, but I've never seen one."

"That's probably because your Akira gets rid of them." Lorraine drew her fingers across her throat, knifelike.

"Mom!" Baput squealed, grasping Baput's hand.

Baput drew an Akashic breath. "The only deformed people I've ever seen are you two." He looked at Belinda, then Patrick. "You say you have millions of people, from thousands of places. Lots of DNA. So, why are you deformed?"

Lorraine buried her face back in her book, leaving Patrick to answer the hard questions. It was his family's thing, after all.

Patrick was ready. "We're not inbred. Our family carries this gene. Every generation has one, no matter who we marry. I suppose it would be even more prevalent if we inbred with each other, but we couldn't, even if we wanted to, because all the Look 'N Up offspring are boys, until Belinda came along.

"My Dad's folks are from Oklahoma and Arkansas, close, but that's a big area with lots of people. They didn't even know each other until they met here in California. My mom and her folks are from Boston, way back east on the other end of the continent, and Lorraine's folks are all from France, across the ocean.

"Clara St. Clair. That's my mom." Lorraine chimed in. "Both words are French for clear, or white, so it essentially means 'Whitey McWhite'. She met my dad at a prep school in Marin in the sixties, her in her poodle skirt and saddle shoes, him with his strawberry pompadour. He was the son of a rich banker who got his money out of Europe ahead of the Nazis. Mom's family brought their pinot and merlot roots from France. They were both from the Lorraine region." Lorraine smiled, embarrassed. "That's where my name came from. That's why their parents approved of their union. See, they weren't looking for diversity. They wanted someone as much like them as possible."

"But you're not inbred?" Baput asked.

"Of course not!" Lor snapped. "My grandparents didn't even know each other back there. It's a big place, lots of people, just like Patrick said. We're not inbred. We're not the freaks�" She regretted saying it before it was out. The stunned silence allowed her to escape to the window, where she didn't have to face her disfigured family. Her eyes melted the fog of her breath as soon as it formed on the pane.

"I've never met them." Belinda revealed behind her.

"Why?" Baput asked, "Are they dead?"

"No." Belinda muttered at the floor. "They, um, live somewhere else."

"Otherwhere?" Baput asked brightly, "Can't you just go there, to their place?

"No." Belinda shook her head. "It's not like that. They hate us. Me and Dad."

Lorraine whirled to face them, but didn't make eye contact. "They don't *hate* you! They just don't understand!" She turned away again and flew up the stairs to her room.

Abomination

Lorraine lay on her bed, staring at the ceiling. Mascara and eyeliner streamed down her cheeks, staining the pure white linen below. She forced herself to go through the memory again, live it once more, as a penance for detonating in front of her poor, dear family.

Belinda had been two months old before Lorraine scraped up the courage to tell her parents about their granddaughter. Those pure specimens of French perfection, the stuff of films and beauty pageants, like the ones Lorraine had been forced to parade in as a heavily made-up six-year-old. How would they react? Marrying Patrick had put a final nail in the coffin of her relationship with Mom, surely an act of rebellion that wouldn't last. But Lorraine had made a five-year plan and stuck to it, out of stubbornness, if nothing else. Having a child was part of it. Just one. Patrick had promised her, the messed-up eye always appeared on the second child. And it was always a boy. So here she was with a hideous little girl. She eventually realized she couldn't keep her "blessing" to herself forever, even though all she would get was an "I told you so," at best. At worst, complete annihilation of what was left of her relationship with her folks.

Poor Patrick hadn't understood why she wouldn't show her parents their granddaughter. The eye wasn't that bad, just a superficial physical deformity. Of course, he had to think that. *But superficial is all my mom cares about. Dad will want to see her. He's always been on my side. He'll be nice. Not Mom though. Maybe never*, she had resolved. She had told Patrick she was going shopping, just in case she lost her nerve or it got ugly. Ugly. She winced at the word.

She had bundled the pink, freckled baby with the shock of red hair like the crest of a cardinal and the left eye that was too high and too far left and surrounded by hideous wrinkles that made it look like it could telescope, like a chameleon's eye, into the car seat. For the first time in years, she crossed the Golden Gate into downtown San Francisco.

The traffic shocked her at first, but she soon got used to it again. Dad had worked at the towering office building in the business district for as long as Lorraine had been alive. He was the Founder and Chief Financial

Officer of a well-known firm that played with other people's money. Luck and timing landed her a parking place on the street right out front.

She sat motionless, staring at the edifice where the family fortune was made. She looked at the weird eye peeking at her from beneath the pink blanket. She pulled a pink knit hat from the baby bag and jammed it over her daughter's wayward eye. Sighing deeply, she opened the driver's door and came around to the passenger side, fed the meter, then opened the door. She pulled Belinda's blanket up, covering her face completely. Then she picked up the pink bundle and cradled it tightly against her shoulder.

The doorman was new. Not the handsome Winston that had greeted the boss's pretty young daughter with a smile and a lollipop, and later, with a different kind of smile. This guy was younger, stout and doughy with close-cropped blonde hair, barely visible under his oversized uniform hat, and dull grey eyes that stared at the bundle Lorraine held.

"Where's Winston?" Lorraine asked.

"Who?" the young man asked, "The old guy? Retired, I guess." He shrugged. "What can I do for you, Ma'am?"

Lorraine was not used to having to explain herself. "I'm William Deveraux's daughter, and this is his granddaughter."

The doorman reached for Belinda's blanket, removing it from her face. "Whaa...?" he exclaimed, stepping back.

Lorraine stepped back, too, into the busy sidewalk.

"I don't think so," the young doorman shook his head. He looked her up and down, searching her, as if she was some kind of terrorist, or worse, a street beggar! A homeless person looking for a handout! "Not here," he concluded. "Take your panhandling down the road."

Lorrain bristled. "My father owns that top floor. I'll have you fired!" she ranted. She held Belinda tightly, her face fully exposed.

The stranger's eyes fixed on that freakish face in the arms of the raving woman. He reached for a phone mounted just inside the door. "I'm calling security," He informed her coldly, looking down his nose. The doorman. The *help*, looking down his pig-like snout at William Deveraux's daughter! Lorraine turned and dashed to her car, Belinda's blanket flying like a pink flag of surrender.

Cars honked rudely as she opened the driver's door and leaned in to put Bel in her seat. She struggled inside to finish the job roughly. She jammed her hand into the pocket of her tight jeans and wrested her keys out, then stabbed them into the ignition. She shoved the Civic in gear and pulled out. A horn blared. She jammed on the brakes. Belinda whimpered, just a bit. "Sorry, Baby." Lorraine uttered. Another horn blared. She worked her way out carefully this time, merging with the hectic flow. Her mind fixated on survival as she battled their way to the US 1 on-ramp and through the toll booth and back onto the Golden Gate Bridge, northbound.

The other side of the bridge was a different world. Steep slopes, green trees, and good old Mount Tam, site of so many moonlit teenage memories. Lorraine relaxed a little at the sight of her childhood home. That's when she felt it; the difference. The weight, inescapable and permanent. It would always be there now, forever. She glanced down at its source, such a tiny thing, to carry so much weight.

Glad the infant couldn't understand, she spoke her thoughts to Belinda more honestly than she ever would again. "Most grandpas would proudly display a photo of their granddaughter on their desk, maybe whip out their phone and show all their pictures at the first scent of an invitation. But your grandpa won't be doing that for you, I'm afraid, Little Monster Girl." She knew, because when she started her new job in a couple months, she wasn't going to put up any pictures of Belinda, or Patrick either. "We won't ask him to, Baby," she decided for them both.

She took an off-ramp and entered a neighborhood of spacious homes and elegant yards. She turned into a long driveway and stopped at an ornate gate of black wrought iron, spotted with a badly flaking coat of gold paint. She typed in the old combination, vaguely surprised they hadn't changed it on her. She drove slowly up the flower-lined path, slowing as she approached the ridiculously large home where she had grown up as a single child.

Carmella, the maid, answered the door. Lorraine pulled Bel's hat down, her blanket up. Not again! Not another servant looking at her like�. But this one she knew. *Carmella, who took care of me, cooked my food, cleaned up my messes, took my tantrums when I barked orders at her like the servant she was! Raging at her, telling her I'd have her fired if I didn't get my way. Well, she's still here and I'm long gone. But I can't have her looking at me with that, that, pity!* She pulled Belinda closer.

"I will see my mother privately, in the library," Lorraine ordered coldly, in her best princess voice.

Carmella humbly withdrew her probing look and her grasping hand and hurried to the library to announce Lorraine's arrival.

Lorraine scanned the living room, remembering it was not the living room but the *parlor.* The annoying old clock still ticked too loudly on the mantle. The sofa and chairs were still covered with plastic. *Not for sitting,* she'd been taught. She wandered along the walls, looking at the same old pictures. Her as a kid, mostly in beauty pageants. None of her shooting competitions, no wedding pictures, no pictures of Patrick at all. She pulled the hat back and stared at her daughter's twisted face.

She heard a soft cough. She held Belinda close, hiding her face. Her mother stood in the doorway. She looked older. The makeup was thicker. And she wasn't as tall as before. Lorrane was sure. The wrinkled old woman looked at the pink bundle with the hidden face, then her eyes darted to Lorraine's, accusingly. "In the library," she ordered, just like she used to when she was going to deliver one of her long, private scoldings.

"Yes, Ma'am." Lorraine humbly obeyed. At least Carmella wouldn't see.

Claire closed the door softly and glared at the pink bundle clutched to her daughter's chest. In a surge of defiance, Lorraine stripped the hat off and lowered the blanket. Claire grasped the back of a nearby armchair, her mouth a big, round vacuum that seemed to suck all the air out of the stuffy room with one gigantic gasp.

Lorraine extended the child toward her grandmother. "This is Belinda, your granddaughter, Mom."

Claire turned her head away, refusing to look. "You said it would only happen with the second child."

"That's how it's been in the past, but..."

"So, he has been unfaithful." Claire accused prudishly.

"No!" Lorraine was pretty sure. *Who would want him?*

"Then maybe there was someone before, and he didn't tell you. I hear young men are quite wild in college these days."

"No! Well maybe one time, he was pretty drunk at that one party. He might not even remember. It was before we were together."

"Well, how could you marry a man like that?"

"You mean Dad never got drunk at a party in college? Maybe got a little randy?"

"Never. William was never *randy.*" Claire spit the word daintily, like a prune pit.

"Maybe it's because his older brother had the straight eyed kid. That's never happened before. They usually get drafted and die."

Another soft snort. "As I recall, he promised you could have one without, that." She looked at Belinda's face for the first time.

"He never promised! You can't promise something like that. You can't assume, just because of what happened before. I knew that."

"You knew it could happen."

"She's not an *it*, Mom. She's my daughter. Your granddaughter." Gulping, she again handed Belinda forward toward her mom.

Clair looked at the baby the way she'd looked at the dead bass Lorraine had so proudly brought home from an unfeminine fishing trip with Dad. Then she turned away, preferring to face a rare spot on the wall void of photos or paintings.

"Then you have deliberately created an abomination," she declared.

"My daughter is not an abomination!" Lorraine shrieked. She ran out, holding Bel close to her chest again. Belinda's hat fell to the floor as she passed Carmella on her way to the door. The maid got a good look, Lorraine was sure. That was it, for Lorraine. She had never again shown her daughter to her parents, not even a picture. And she could never, ever tell Belinda about her first and only meeting with her grandparents.

Marooned awkwardly around the kitchen table, Patrick kissed the top of Belinda's head. "Come on, kids." He headed for the music room where Bel's computer still sat. The kids followed, stunned.

Patrick sat down at the terminal and opened up his email account. "Your G-pa doesn't hate you, Bel." He opened a file marked Wm. D. "I'm going to show you something. Mom doesn't know about this yet."

"Why not?" Belinda asked as a string of emails from William Deveraux appeared on the screen.

"Well, she's just not ready yet. Someday. Soon, I think. You see, your mom took you to see your grandparents when you were just a baby. She didn't tell me she was going to. I'd been bugging her to give them a chance, so you could know your whole family, but, well, she's kind of stubborn, you know."

Belinda nodded, reading the subject lines while Patrick continued the story.

"I was a bit surprised when the land line rang. I still had it written on the truck, so I was hoping it was a new client. I didn't know his voice, but he asked for me by my first name. He said, 'This is Mr. Deveraux calling. I understand congratulations are in order.' I still didn't know who he was, until I remembered Lorraine's maiden name. It was her dad! So, I said, 'Hello, Sir,' real politely. He knew about you!"

"'So, she told you?'" I asked him. I was stoked!

"But he said, 'Not exactly. She brought the baby to see my wife. It didn't go well, according to the maid. I understand she resembles her father.'

"It sounded kind of like an accusation, but I answered proudly, 'Yes, she's a spitting image of the old block.'

"He laughed. Then he started talking fast, desperately, as if he was scared of getting caught. He said he wished she had come to his office. He would have loved to see you. He asked if I had any pictures. 'Of course you do! She's your baby daughter.' He sounded so excited! 'Can you send me some pictures? Here's my email address.'

"So, I've been sending him pictures of you ever since. He still keeps the little pink hat your mom left behind at the house, right there in his desk drawer. And he always has a current photo of his beautiful granddaughter on his desk. He says he never hesitates to break out his phone and show off right along with the other grandparents. If anyone thinks less of him for having you for a granddaughter, they won't dare show it, because then Mr. Deveraux might just think less of them, too, and in Mr. D's world, that is never a good thing.

"So, let's send him a message right now and tell him you want to meet him. We can set up a Zoom call, sometime when Mom's not home."

"Because she's not ready." Belinda repeated.

Nauve, Last Year of the Cycle

Ancestry

It had been a dismal, lonely year for Tamaya, but oddly exhilarating. She had moved across the cave to where Bupple had kept his bed. She served the food the dog brought in the ration containers. Bazu complained with his mouth full, or he didn't speak at all. He stared at the plans all day, or spent the day on the practice field with the men. Then he would speak, when he returned. He would brag of feats Tamaya couldn't even begin to imagine. Her limitation, he said. She could not comprehend the greatness of her Immortal Warrior Akash.

The best times were when he was gone. She would read the books, or take a walk, all by herself, with no guard. A babbetless, essentially single woman turning twenty-three this fine spring day. What was she, but bumbly bait anyway? But the nimblies and bumblies would not appear for another half-year, six Kakeeche cycles, so what had she to fear?

She spent a lot of time moving the ancient books, without asking Bazu for help, because it was his fault. She would rather relocate the books herself than to hear a single minute of his high-pitched defense. Besides, he didn't treat them with the proper respect. She had been relieved to find he hadn't used them for boor wipes, yet.

She had thought Akira would have heart failure right there in the meeting room when she'd told her about Bazu's discoveries. The light intrigued her, but the boor horrified her, especially when Tamaya told her where he'd put it, amid the shelves of ancient books.

At Akira's command, Tamaya brought them out volume by volume and stacked them on the floor near the front of the tunnel, pushing the pipes and wires and other strange objects, so fascinating to men, carelessly to the side. She placed them along the drier wall, opposite the running water, below the hanging cords and weapons. She arranged them by author, one stack per Akash.

She had read all of Badon's work aloud to Bazu, nearly gagging at his rampant egoism. She was surprised he hadn't come up with this immortality business. But she had learned something from the old man. Something so powerful that she was able to condense what she thought would be a lifetime of reading into a single year. She learned how to read an Akash.

Her first discovery; the shorter the stack, the more worthwhile the read. There were pearls of wisdom she had to agree with, cagey tricks she could use, history they didn't teach in school. Things no one else knew. She shared none of this with Bazu or Akira, or anyone. And Rakta? He was a memory, a worn-out fantasy she used to help herself fall asleep alone in the Bupple -scented alcove, as far from her husband as she could get.

For the larger stacks, she used the trick she had learned from the last Akash. Read their first book, then their middle book, then the last. If they're still running around and around in the same old circle, like Badon was, you could pretty much skip all the rest, and that was usually a lot. These, and only these, she shared with Akira. She told her all the Akashes were the same, like this. There were some Badon-like tomes Bazu would have liked, but she didn't have time to read that junk twice, out loud to him while he criticized it and tried to outdo it and then cry for more. She left him to squint at his plans and didn't try to teach him anything.

And that is how, one year after her erstwhile divorce, she arrived at the last book. She had started it the night before. It was like no other. First of all, the Akash who wrote it didn't even put his name on the front, like all the rest did. She couldn't find a name on it anywhere. She knew it was the last, because she found it way in the back of the middle set of shelves, precariously close to Bazu's boor, nestled slimly against that strangely smooth back wall. Also, it had a different kind of binding, not dog skin, freely given, like most of the sacred texts. She didn't know what the strange material was, but it was very old. It crinkled when she picked it up, making her wince.

She had arisen early, eager to finish the book. Bazu still slept, wheezing with apnea. She greeted Hebert at the door and unpacked the dog quietly. She placed the food on the counter, easily available, and even remembered to pack the dog with the empties, all on tiptoes.

Now to the book. The morning sun sent a shaft across the Rock and lit a patch on the floor where she sat. But the writing was so faded! She squinted, wondering if this is how Bazu must feel. She couldn't turn on the light. That would surely wake him up, demanding to know what she was doing in his tunnel, messing with his stuff, and she better not be using his boor!

She wasn't supposed to take the books out of the cave. Except Akira ordered her to bring her the books, always hidden under her special gown, for secrecy, she supposed. Akira loved knowing things others didn't as much as Tamaya, or anybody, did.

She carried the brittle volume carefully out to the porch, into the morning sun. She looked over the edge where the stairs weren't, firmly noting that it was *not* where her first betrothed had perished, as the Old Akash had said. Oh yes, lying. Another Akashic trick. The things she had thought! The things everyone thought! So many of them were lies made up by one Akash or another, usually for selfish purposes.

She sat stubbornly close to the edge where the ledge narrowed to almost nothing, her legs folded, her back against the wall of the cave, feeling its ultra-low vibrations in her spine. She propped the ancient book on her thighs and opened it to her place, half expecting the pages to burst into flame as soon as the sun hit them. When they didn't, she relaxed, little knowing the damage would be slower, more insidious. She breathed the musty odor in, relishing it like a spinster librarian. The last book. A thousand years old. Or a thousand cycles, three thousand years. Even she still didn't know which, and she knew more than anyone. The Last Book. The First Book.

It told the tale of an Akashic Family who experimented with Shavarandu. They used the sacred power of the Holy Rock to kill the nimblies on First Pomegranate Day. Just the Akash, his tether, their son, the apprentice Akash, who was born on First Pomegranate Day and would be Alanakash.

Tamaya shook her head. *How did the Old Akash write his story after he disappeared?* She wondered. *And why does this book seem so old? It's not Badon's handwriting.*

Soon the story diverged, just enough. The Akash's tether was his wife, not his daughter. His brother was Guard of Akash, not his Son-in-Law. This guard, this Brother to Akash, stood on the ground outside the cave and watched for nimblies while his brother and nephew used the strange, heavy tubes to direct the beam to kill them.

> "I leaned back against the wall as the light poured out of the Holy Cave and struck the nimblies. They fell from the sky with lethal holes poked clear through. So many were killed in such a short time! A whole phalanx, then another.
>
> "Then it happened. The blinding flash! Even I, outside the cave, saw spots before my eyes for minutes after. The next wave of nimblies came, but there were no more flashes from the cave. All the nimblies flew on by on their way to the Great Hall to devour the people I know and love, as always. They paid no mind to this place, as if no one was here, even though their dead lay all about.
>
> "When they had passed, I scrambled up the steps on my hands and knees like a dog, lest I be seen by any lingering nimblies, or shot with that beam by my own dear nephew, by mistake of course, but still, I feared that the most.
>
> "I had no need to fear. When I entered the Holy Cave there was no one there! Nothing but the heavy tubes that lay on the floor, and that beautifully woven blanket that lay draped over the rock. So soft and silvery and light!"

Tamaya nodded knowingly. She knew the feather-light warmth across her shoulders, the hem tickling her calves as she walked. She read on eagerly. Only two pages left.

> "They were all gone. Pindrale, the Akash, gone."

Tamaya breathed in sharply. Bazu stirred.

> "Pindrod, the pompous apprentice, gone. Even Laramay, the tether, and their dog. And only I, Pindjon, remained to tell the tale, after taking refuge in the Holy Cave for the entire Season."

Bazu was up. Tamaya heard him muttering about something, stumbling to his precious boor. He turned the light on. Tamaya's eyes darted crosswise to the cave entrance, then out over the landscape, far and wide. *Pind? Akash?* She tried to put the two words together in her mind. Bazu yelled, or sang, or preached to no one. Who knew? Who cared? *The food is right there on the table. What else can he want from me?*

Book clutched tightly to her chest, she scooched on her bottom down the stairs to the point where she knew she couldn't be seen from the cave if she lay flush against the hard steps. In that awkward position, she read the end of the ancient Book of Pindjon, brother to the Akash, Pindrale.

> "I emerged on Passascenday and returned to the Great Hall all alone. I told the tale, just as I have told you. They did not believe me. They accused me of treachery. I somehow killed them or let the nimblies and bumblies get them and then cleverly disposed of their bones. So cleverly that they searched for a full cycle and never found a trace, for there was none. I tell you; I saw this.
>
> "I was next in line to be Akash, so of course they thought the worst. But I had no such desires. Especially not after that happened."

"Woman! Where are you?" The Helpless Akash bellowed from what sounded to Tamaya like the table where the prepared food sat waiting. She tried to flatten herself lower to the steps. Just a couple more lines...

> "They removed me from the Akashic Line. Me and all my descendants, forever. The Akira cut my thread from the Holy Line and tied it to my momama's popa's line. The Pinds are no longer Akashic. We are rasta makers now. Perhaps that is better for us. Simple, merry artists. But for the people? With that idiot, Barad, as Akash?
>
> "They are burying all the Shavarandu again. I will bury this book at the bottom of the pile of forbidden stuff, right in front of the Ancient Door."

Tamaya heard footsteps on the narrow stone steps above. She tensed, belly glued to the stairs, the book pressed between them.

"There you are!" her husband squawked. "What did you do, fall?" It sounded more like criticism than concern.

Tamaya pressed flatter against the stairs, covering the open book, her belly pressing on it in heaving breaths. He probably thought her back was broken. If he cared. She wondered, but it was merely a timid flash in a torrent of information that scrambled to find purchase in her spinning head.

Pinds are Akashic. I am a Pind. I am Akashic. That rude, scrawny kid coming down the stairs is Akashic and I shouldn't be, I can't *be, married to him!* He touched her shoulder, tried to turn her over. He'd see the book! He mustn't. Not before Akira saw it.

"Akira!" she cried without thinking. That gave her an idea, and she went with it. "Akira!" she cried again, trying to sound helpless. "Bazu, something is broken inside. I can't move. Go get Akira, and quickly! It must be Akira herself, and only her."

"I suppose," her dear husband committed vaguely. "Afterwards, I'm going to the practice field."

She sighed with relief, hoping he would think it was due to his heroism. He finished his trip down the stairs, clutching his fake longstick and his bedraggled robe, leaving her splayed there like a crashed bumbly, just as she'd hoped.

As soon as he was out of sight, she gingerly reassembled her cold and aching limbs and realigned her poor spine, extracted her belly from the book and the stairs. She stood, dizzy, as a single thought rose above all the others. Above all the thoughts of lines and Pinds and Akashic ancestors, and all their staggering implications. She snuck a peek at that last line again.

Before the ancient door. The book had been in the very back of the bookshelf, right in front of that smooth, straight wall. *Behind* the Death Door that Batuk had opened. *Behind* the Death Door. *Before* the Ancient Door. They are burying Shavarandu *again*.

She clutched the book to her chest and scurried up the stairs, not at all the helpless wreck Bazu had left behind him. She headed right to the Death Door and plugged in the lamp. Her gown hung there. She grabbed it, wrapped herself in its soft glory, barely noticing its tingle. She carried the book and bulb through the narrow corridor like an electrified Statue of Liberty. Past the pipes, the stationary bike, the coiled wires, the rolled plans on the shelves and the stacked books on the floor. She headed straight back between the bookshelves to the Akashic Boor. It tinkled invitingly, but it stank of stale male urine. She heard Akira's warbling trill at the bottom of the stairs.

She brought the glaring bulb up to the wall at the end of the corridor, right in front of her face. She traced the smooth wall with her fingers. It wasn't all smooth. There was a rough patch, a raised rectangle, like the one at the entrance to the Death Door. She traced the ancient letters with her long, elegant finger.

"Tamaya?" Edijay's anxious voice cried out.

Tamaya winced. "I said Akira only!" she hissed to herself. She traced the letters again. They were different, less ornate. Squared and plain, with no curves or swirls or squiggles. All blocky right angles. But she recognized them. They were the same letters. The last two words were the same. That was the key. Only the first word was different. "Learn" it said, "Learn to Open," she whispered. Her right eyebrow twitched. *Learn what? I've read all the books, what have I learned?*

"Tamaya!" Edijay was charging up the stairs, leaving Akira at the bottom, for now. Cursing Akira's apprentice, Tamaya left the book on the shelf where she had first found it, leaning against the back wall of the Death Tunnel, which she now knew wasn't a wall, but a second door. A door to a place that held the wisdom of two thousand more years, back to a thousand cycles ago. Back to the very beginning.

She shook her loose hair so it feathered over her cape. She raised the lamp above her head. It made her gown dazzle blindingly, more like Shavarandu than Kakeeche. She looked away, so she wouldn't squint, held her head high and perfectly level, as if the precious book rested there, on top of her head instead of indelibly etched inside of it. In this regal way, she sauntered slowly through the Death Door, the *second* door, to where Edijay waited by the Holy Rock.

Transfixed by the impossibly bright light that the Akashic Tether bore out of the darkness, Edijay shifted uncomfortably from one foot to another.

Tamaya felt like a spider with a helpless insect caught in its web. A surge of power flowed through her. She imagined it was her Akashikness, but she knew where her power truly came from. Superior knowledge.

"I will speak only to Akira," she declared from her high place.

"Bazu said you were hurt. I came to assist," Edijay squeaked, more diffident than usual.

"Bazu lies, like any Akash. Now leave us. Go down the stairs and out of our sight. Go all the way back to your Lair. I will escort Akira back when we have finished our business."

"Akira's business is my business." Edijay's spine stiffened. "I shall be Akira someday. You know she ascended me." She recited her resume, as if sensing it was in jeopardy. Tamaya laughed inside, playing with her prey, knowing she could take it all away, if she wanted to.

"If Akira wants to tell you, that is up to her." Tamaya granted from behind the dazzling light. "But I will tell only Akira. Be gone!"

With something to defend, Edijay's mettle kicked in. She stood tall, adopting a sort of fighting stance that made her look more amusing than awesome. Tamaya decided not to laugh. It was beneath her.

"I will go to where I can't hear," the mouse negotiated, "but I must watch Akira."

"I will give her something you must not see," Tamaya countered flatly. Edijay's intrigued expression made her regret revealing even that much. "I will stand on the porch and watch Akira. And I will watch you. When I can no longer see you, I will come down, and not before. The longer you dally, the longer Akira will have to wait. You know how she hates that. Now go!"

Edijay flew down the stairs like a dracna escaping a dog's jaws. She huddled with Akira in a hushed conference. They both looked up at Tamaya. She had left the lamp behind, but she still wore her awesome gown. Eventually, Edijay sulked off, looking over her shoulder repeatedly until she was out of sight.

When she was at last convinced that the apprentice was really gone, Tamaya strode down the steep staircase in her gown. She had a meditation cushion in one hand, and a frail-looking book in the other.

Akira gave a double take when Tamaya set the cushion on the second stair, and offered the padded perch to her. "How considerate," she remarked with unconcealed surprise.

Tamaya didn't waste any more time. "I found this book at the very back of the tunnel behind the door, except it's not�" She stopped abruptly and shoved the book into the knotty hands. "You must read this. It's not long. It's very old and, um, important."

Akira studied the beautiful face. *Oh, to have more like her!* She thought wistfully. She had never seen the young woman so excited. "Alright," she agreed. She looked down at the book, deliberately turned it out of the direct sunlight, and began to read.

Tamaya stood on the staircase, a couple steps above, scanning the distance savagely for intruders as Akira murmured; "It happened before..." "the same thing..." She inhaled sharply and looked over her shoulder at Tamaya. "Get down from there, girl!" she snapped. "You're like a nimbly hovering over me."

She doesn't know yet. Tamaya calculated. *She won't talk to me that way when she knows.* She obeyed by leaping gracefully from the fourth step to the rough ground below, feeling invincible. After that, Akira didn't look at her again, and she began to pace, forgetting to watch out for intruders.

Akira's mouth opened and closed wordlessly with only an occasional squeak to mark her progress. All else was silent. The trees didn't stir. The birds didn't sing. No rodents rustled in the brush. The only sound was the rushing of the river and the ringing in Tamaya's ears, which was getting worse, of late, especially when she wore her gown.

At last, the old prune snapped the book closed. Still holding it tightly, she gazed up at Tamaya with an unfathomable expression. Eventually, she raised her eyebrows, her way of inviting her audience to speak.

Tamaya spoke her mind. "So, I am Akashic. And you have to dissolve my marriage to Bazu."

"You selfish girl! That is what you got from this? Only the small part that affects you? Did you read the rest? It all happened before! The Akashic family disappeared, and they never reappeared. And there is another door to a deeper chamber with even older knowledge and even more deadly

Shavarandu. And all you say is, 'I' and 'me' and 'my'. You are right. You are in for some changes. You had better grow up and be ready."

"Ready for what?"

"You have already been using your imagination, I see. Exploring the implications, the possibilities. I must do the same. But first, I must check the breeding matrix, follow your line all the way up," she mimicked the job, empty hands straining above her head, "for a thousand years, fifty generations, until I find this cut. Then I will have to re-weave it from there through all those," she lost her voice for a second, all air but no sound. She recovered in a wheeze. "All those wrong pairings! The true Akashic line blended like any other! Oh, My Dear, what a mess."

The wise woman's miserable gaze met Tamaya's eager one.

"Maybe you can mate me with someone else?" Not her favorite hope, but better than this life, surely. As sure as the fact that this marriage could not go on.

"Things will stay as they are, for now," Akira answered, dashing Tamaya's hopes. "First I must check the matrix, see if this is even true." She gave Tamaya an accusing look. How could she have faked that ancient crispness or that faded, archaic penmanship?

"You will say nothing to Bazu, or anyone. Is he still, um, pleasuring you?"

Tamaya's mind ran in a circle. *No? I'd have to explain my lie, but she won't worry about babbets. Yes? She'll worry about babbets. She'll have to separate us!* "Oh, yes, Akira. Every night. He is most aggressive."

"But still no babbets," Akira reminded.

Tamaya shrugged. "Any time now."

"Tell him you're ill. You already said so. Tell him it was a woman's problem and he must stop, for now." She drew back to take in Tamaya's face. "Will he respect that?" she asked with sudden concern.

"He respects nothing!" Tamaya lashed, unable to resist, although she knew it would not be an issue. "I'll handle it."

"Good. Keep it that way until I tell you otherwise. You will report to me in one Kakeeche cycle at the Lair. I will re-examine your, um, condition." Clutching the book tightly to her chest, she struggled to stand, finding ground level with her strangely tiny feet.

Tamaya came to her side, supporting her, but staring at the book. The wrinkled face, too close for comfort, spoke right into her ear as the old woman leaned on the younger. "I will keep the book, of course. I need to authenticate it. If it's real, I must read it again, search it for clues."

"Clues to what?" Tamaya asked as she walked the old lady down the trail.

"To how to fix the Matrix!" she snapped, stumbling on a root. Tamaya supported her, wondering if this was what Salistar's life was like. What her life would be someday, with the Akash who would live forever, if she didn't get out of this marriage.

Akira didn't miss a beat. "How to retrace your messed-up line. Figure out who you're supposed to be with, so you can bear Bazu a truly Akashic hear." She looked around at the empty trail and the unknown bushes and lowered her voice. "You will say nothing, of course. You will stay with the Akash."

Tamaya's heart sank out of her feet to lie abandoned on the trail behind them. "But I mustn't bear his child!" she argued, as if Akira wasn't aware.

"I will find the right one," she whispered. "You will meet in secret, under heavy guard every Kakeeche cycle, at the best time in your cycle. But you will still be Tether to Akash. You will let him think the children are his."

Without thinking, Tamaya blurted her last hope into the dismal future. "If Rakta�"

"Shhh!" Akira ordered, stopping suddenly. Tamaya, leaning close to hear her whispers, almost bowled her over.

Edijay appeared, flanked by two wiry young women with short hair and war-painted faces. "I will take her from here," she barked dryly.

Akira nodded to the taller of the painted women. "Follow the Tether back to the Holy Cave. Make sure she gets there," she ordered, glaring at Tamaya.

Pindross and Akira

"Leave us." Akira ordered Jenevan. "Take your babbets. I will speak with Pindross alone."

"But Akira!" Jenevan objected. "No man can see you alone!"

Akira lunged at the young mother who held the door open. "Can he see me?"

"No ma'am." Jenevan muttered demurely. She quickly packed up her children and left for the central garden.

Akira watched until they were well out of earshot. Then she turned back to Pindross' sightless, questioning eyes. "I have come to discuss your line, Pindross. Your daughter will not be bearing the Akash a son."

"I will have no heir?"

"Jenevan has borne you a g-son and a g-daughter."

"Then she failed, after that."

"She had the same luck you did. Two very quickly, one of each, then a spot of trouble. Not to worry, it is common."

"Yes, it happened to Kalanan twice. Then, worse happened, Akira! That is why I worry." He turned, as if to look at the painting of his dead tether that hung on the wall. "You are right. I should be satisfied. I have two g-babbets, an heir for my son, another rasta-maker. But I had hoped for an Akashic heir. The son of an Akash. Tamaya's son."

"That's why I'm here, in this unprecedented position, alone with a man. To tell you, and only you, that you *have* borne an Akashic son. You *are* an Akashic son."

Pindross wore the look of a man who sees, but does not understand what he sees. Akira poured out the last book of the old ones for his sole benefit, the third person to know *It* had happened before, a thousand years ago. The third to know the Pinds were the true Akashic line, and that their line had been cut, literally, and re-tied to the line furthest away from the Akashic line. It had been kept apart as the last line to be crossed with the premier line, saved throughout the millennium for a single purpose: to save the Akashic line from the wasting. The old Akash had shown signs of it. The weakness, the coughing fits, but he had lived a long life. Did he live now? Akira couldn't imagine how.

"So, you see, your line is misplaced. Tamaya and Bazu are both Akashic. They cannot produce an heir."

"How have you stopped them?"

"I have not, yet. I have examined Tamaya. The problem must be Bazu. Perhaps a function of the wasting. Bazu has all the symptoms already, at his young age. His Popa died of it, you know."

"Yes," Pindross recalled painting the memorial portrait for his family. "Bazed was young, in his thirties. Bazu was just a little boy. I could see he was sick, too. What is it, Akira?"

"I call it the wasting. It happens more and more each generation. Many babbets... well, they don't live."

Pindross rose and strode confidently to a smaller room off the living room, his path memorized and kept clear of obstructions. Akira followed him to the doorway and gazed into a mess only a mad genius could produce. Paintings hung on the walls. More were stacked on the floor, propped up against the wall, in stacks of five or ten.

The blind man found his way through the clutter with some kind of radar. He flipped through a stack of paintings on the floor, searching sightlessly for a particular piece. Akira stepped closer, her wrinkled brow furrowed. They were all the same! The same spiral pattern he had carved onto Tamaya's rolling pin. Two wavy lines that crossed one another, forming cells that had straight lines crossing them in pairs. It had spiraled pleasingly around the round stone surface of the rolling pin when you spun it.

Akira had seen that shape before, too, in her dreams. That's why she'd painted it on the girl's nails for her wedding. "I dream of this shape," she whispered breathlessly, glad she had found the loophole that let her leave Ogala in the Lair. The girl may be deaf, but she still had eyes. This was for Akira's eyes only. Pindross flipped through the stacks of paintings, and Akira realized they weren't quite the same. Sometimes a cell was open, or the lines that crossed it were broken, or missing.

"Sukia, Feleza, Mersilla." Pindross recited the names of momamas who had borne deformed, "hibudara" children in the last two cycles, since he had lost his sight. "Lowie and Doremos!" He opened the stack to a spiral with a missing cell wall.

"Downudara." Akira pronounced the affliction she had missed at the birth of the unfortunate child. At four, he still couldn't speak or take care of his personal needs.

"Gibled and Sukia's babbet, who didn't live. Do you see why?" Pindross asked, studying the painting as if he could see it. The tattered spiral had a section missing from every third cell.

Akira shuddered when she remembered the babbet it represented. It had skin where its nose and mouth should be. It had begged her for air with eyes that haunted her to this day. She had wanted to cut the skin over its tiny mouth and let it breath, but that was a ridiculous thought. She would have choked it anyway. She had felt unusually merciful when she had snapped that one's tiny neck while Sukia lay drugged and helpless, like so many momamas before her. And Pindross had documented them all.

"Feleza's child." Pindross displayed another flawed matrix.

"No eyes." Akira disclosed.

"Mersilla," Pindross named the next twisted spiral.

"Misshapen head, caved in on one side," Akira described grimly.

"Yilnetar, the potter's wife."

"Twins that didn't separate properly. Two heads, four arms, three legs, they seemed to share a spinal cord!" Akira shuddered at the double helix whose flaws overlapped, compounded. "I hate twins," she declared, then covered her mouth. Did he know?

He moved to an older stack, more spirals, some perfect, some defective. More momamas names, some living, some dead. He reached the last painting in the second stack. The seven canvasses in front of it rested heavily against his thin legs. "And here is your Akashic heir, Akira," he shouted in a bitter voice that didn't sound like the gentle artist at all. "Pindryl."

It was an explosion of a painting. A ruptured double-helix, far worse than any other, occupied the foreground in bold, angry colors. Behind it, an explosion of twins. A hideous pair of naked babbets with body parts thrusting through each other and coming out in all the wrong places. And behind that hideous monster, faded in dim pastels and barely noticeable, was a face. A young man's face, or was it a woman's? It was flawless, perfect. More beautiful than any living person Akira had ever seen. She touched the gently pointed cheekbone tenderly.

"My vision of what he should have been, I suppose. Poor Pindryl. We dared to name him ahead of time. Maybe we shouldn't have. But Kalanan..."

Pindross' knees buckled behind the stack of paintings. Akira rushed to his side, thinking he might collapse. She grasped his shoulder, got a handful of loose tunic. Her hand was shaking. Had she ever touched a man before? She pushed against him, propping him up. She found his unseeing eyes, flooded with tears.

"I hate twins," she repeated, swallowing a lump in her throat. "I'm sorry, Pindross, they couldn't live. And poor Kalanan, they tore her so. I couldn't save her, Pindross. I failed. Maybe this is why. Your line is in the wrong place, mixed with the wrong people. You were lucky to have two beautiful children. You never should have been betrothed."

"But now? What of my son? He is Akashic! Will you make him Akash?"

"Jenevan would be an excellent tether," Akira stated playfully.

Pindross rolled his eyes and snorted his agreement. "But what of Tamaya? You wouldn't put her in the Lair, would you? She can live with me, take care of me while Pindrad and Jenevan live in the Holy Cave."

"They won't," Akira stated flatly. That one thing was decided. She swept the hut with her eyes. "They will live here. Tamaya doesn't wish to live here."

The blind eyes fell to the floor like a dropped spoon. "Does she prefer the Lair?" he whispered, hurt.

"She doesn't know what she wants" Akira replied, exasperated. "What does it matter? Since when does a woman get to choose the life she wants? Why is she so special?"

Pindross was glad to answer. "She is wiser than she seems. Her will is too strong for a woman. It makes her act foolishly. Will you make her your apprentice? To succeed you as Akira? She is Akashic, and I am sure you've noticed, she is not like other girls."

"Perhaps. I haven't decided. Maybe there is another match for her, with this new line. I must recalculate. It will take time. Things will stay as they are for the remainder of this cycle. Meanwhile, you have shown extraordinary wisdom with your spiral paintings. You have seen the wasting and found a way to depict it. You understand far more than any of my apprentices. If you were a woman, I would make you�" She abandoned the ridiculous proposition. "But of course. You are Akashic. You carry the wisdom, the strength, the looks. But you must bear your pride in secret, I'm afraid. Your son will remain the rasta-maker, and his son will succeed him. But your next g-son, Tamaya's son, will be the One True Akash."

"Yes, my Akira!" the sightless artist bowed to her as if he was a mere woman, not the True Akash. Akira knew his ingrained modesty would guarantee his silence. Not even his son, Pindrad, would ever know his true lineage.

Akira walked the trail to the Lair all by herself. Edijay would be there, waiting anxiously, pacing back and forth, no doubt furious at her master's breach of protocol. Akira slowed her pace deliberately. She looked all around, stretched her pupils at the distant clouds. So rarely did she get outside, and never alone. Time to gaze at the amazingly endless sky and think.

But the bright sky darkened as her thoughts went straight to one of her deepest regrets.

One twin had been a hideous hibudara, like the painting. Parts sticking out randomly in all the wrong places. Again, she shuddered at the memory. But the second one, the twin, he was as close to perfect as Akira had ever seen. Like that perfect face in the background of Pindross's painting, if the child had survived to manhood.

Such a beautiful child! A twin of the most hideous hibudara Akira had ever seen. And, he had seemed responsive, of at least normal intelligence, in the brief instant she'd had to examine him. *I would have let him live. And Kalanan was fine. Too fine, actually. Too alert, too wide awake, like she didn't take her medicine. Like she didn't trust me, after two flawless births. She knew it was twins. She knew I hate twins, she must have thought... but, why? Why did she do what she did? Such a waste!*

Edijay could wait no longer and closed the remaining distance, rudely interrupting Akira's dismal reverie.

The Herb

For the next month, everything stayed the same. Tamaya and Bazu slept worlds apart, sharing nothing but the stone walls of the Holy Cave and the cold, jostled meals Hebert faithfully brought. Even the contents of the

Death Tunnel were divided, he with his plans and parts, she with her books, and she had already finished all the good ones.

The only time Bazu ever spoke was to complain, and his silence was the best thing in Tamaya's life. He hadn't touched her, of course. She didn't need to tell him any lies about her medical condition. He didn't ask.

Tamaya walked to the village unescorted and reported to the Lair for her appointment. Akira met her in the antechamber, where she met most women. She was sitting, as usual. That meant the meeting would be here. Tamaya sighed. She had hoped to see the deeper chamber, the one with the Breeding Matrix.

"It is true." The ancient woman's voice came from the dark, stinging her with its directness. "The Pind Line was cut, way at the top, a thousand years ago. Before that, it was the Premier Line. The purest! The most directly Akashic of all. But in the years hence, you Pinds have been bred as if you were common craftsmen. There is one shining light, however, my beautiful girl."

Tamaya drew in a breath and held it, unable to speak. *Rakta?* She hoped in tight-lipped silence.

"I have always admired your line. Sensitive and intelligent, yet strong and handsome. For my whole, long tenure as Akira, I been saving your line, keeping it apart, so at last I can breed you with a strong Akashic son. That would have been Batuk, or Baput. Now all that is left is another weak, sniveling, selfish Akash, as bad as the rest. But you are Akashic! Your Popa! Your brother!"

"Will you make my brother Akash?"

"If I must. But imagine the disruption, when this error is made known. All of our fates have been tainted by this lie. Their faith in the Old Ones will be shaken! Their faith in the Matrix!"

Tamaya nodded numbly. *So that's what this is about.*

"I would rather do it more subtly. You carry the true Akashic line. Everyone will think it's Bazu's Akashic Heir, but instead, it will be yours, mixed with someone else who is big and strong and pretty, as I always hoped."

"Rak�" Tamaya burbled, stopped herself. "What if Bazu doesn't believe the child is his?"

"Why wouldn't he? You said any time now. That is why, until I find your Mr. Wonderful, I will put you on the preventive herb. Now what were you saying about Rakta?"

Suddenly, Rakta was the furthest thing from Tamaya's mind. "The what?" she asked her master. "The preventive herb? You have an herb that prevents what, babbets?"

Akira nodded. "That's right. No babbets. Until you stop taking it. So, you and the Akash can't make a babbet. I never thought I'd say it, but now I'm glad you haven't had one already."

An herb that stops babbets! The idea sunk in quickly. Tamaya had it all examined and explored in an instant. *I could be with any man in this village and nothing will happen, if I don't get caught.* She stood there, mouth open, trying to imagine it. *Yuk!* She decided swiftly. *One man, two men is too many. Too much and not enough*. But Rakta, yes. It didn't matter if he was a match or not, as long as Akira kept sending the herb. And even after, it could still be Rakta. Who would know?

"I stay married to Bazu?" she spoke in a monotone. She already knew the answer, she just wanted to deflect Akira's stare.

"Of course."

"In the cave?" she asked, actually hoping so, for once. It was easier to meet with Rakta in secret there.

"Until you have a babbet, then you can move into the village," Akira granted.

Tamaya felt a surge of power. She was more important than ever, she realized, even if it was still just to have babbets. When it was *her* blood that needed preserving, it felt different. But they would still be babbets. "Will I have help?" she asked, tossing her head.

"Help?"

"Yes, cooking and cleaning and caring for my babbet, so I can keep reading, and teaching the Akash."

"The books cannot leave the Holy Cave."

"I bring them to you."

"The Lair is part of the Holy Cave. I know how to keep the ancient books. Have you moved them away from that boor?"

"Yes, all by myself. No help from the Akash. He complained when I moved them. He would have used them for boor wipes, if I had left them there."

Akira groaned a long, low growl. "No books in a village hut with your children and your dogs."

"There will be no dogs in my house. I won't live with Jenevan."

"That is too bad, on both counts. But no hut in the village yet. Things will stay the same until I find a suitable true Popa for the Akashic heir. You will take the herb I provide every day, and you will speak of this to no one. Here is your first week's supply. Dissolve one packet in a cup of tea every morning. If he asks, say it's for your condition, whatever you told him."

"He won't," Tamaya answered, staring at the seven tiny, tightly woven sacks in her hand. Herbs that stopped babbets from happening. She bundled them together reverently and headed for the door. Akira stopped her with a final bark.

"What was that about Rakta?"

"Nothing, Akira," Tamaya answered quickly. "I was confused." She hurried away before Akira could ask any more questions.

Earth, Spring 2020
Council

"Good morning, Momama." Baput sat down at the breakfast table, a strange smile on his face.

Salistar stroked his thick, shiny hair. "You are happy today!" she commented as Felsic and Valko sat down at their places. She headed into the kitchen.

"What is it, Son?" Valko asked.

"Belinda starts her sixth cycle tomorrow. Her fifteenth year. She will be a woman."

Felsic giggled. "You could wed her on Passascenday. Couldn't he, Valko? If he lives, I mean."

Valko snorted his disapproval. "You are betrothed to Tamaya."

"Tamaya's not here," Felsic stated the obvious, still giggling.

Salistar returned with a heavy iron skillet of fried potatoes and vegetables. "No," she agreed, "She is not. But Baput, you will be 18 on Passascenday. The Akash must marry. He needs a tether. What would Akira do?" she wondered as she scooped a large helping onto Baput's plate.

"Akira's not here, either." Valko chuckled. "And you are Akash, my boy. I would say, you can do whatever you wish. A strange situation indeed."

The laughter stopped. Salistar stood perfectly still, her spoon poised over Valko's plate.

"Then I shall marry Belinda on Passascenday." Baput resolved, digging in.

Valko laughed out loud, Felsic whooped.

The pan sagged in Star's hand as her tension melted. "I will make her a beautiful gown."

"I will make a rolling pin for her. Solid steel." Valko promised.

"Could you make a ring, instead, Popa?" Baput asked. He raised his right hand, stroking his ring finger. "To go around her finger? With a diamond on it."

"Diamond?" Valko queried, clueless.

"No rolling pin?" Salistar asked, "Why no?"

The young Akash scanned his simple disciples, then shrugged. "It is Earth tradition."

"Should there be music?" Felsic asked, hurriedly scraping the last of his breakfast onto his fork. "I can finish the bell I'm making for Patrick by tomorrow, for sure." He pushed his chair back, slapped his open hand on the table. "We must get to work, Brother."

Coming of Age

The next morning, Patrick and Lorraine watched their favorite Sunday talk show. There had been another SARS outbreak in China. Everyone over there was wearing surgical masks, like they had a couple years before. President Trump assured them that China was on top of the situation. "It looks like they're getting it under control more and more. So, I think that's a problem that's going to go away."

"Well, that makes me feel better," Patrick blew on his coffee to cool it. "Not."

"A pathogen," whispered Lorraine. She grabbed her laptop and started searching.

"Clang! Clang! Clang"

"What the hell is that?" Lorraine slammed the laptop closed and sprang to her feet.

"Mom! Dad! Look!" Belinda called from her room upstairs. Her feet fluttered down the stairs, providing an upbeat counterpoint to the slow, steady ringing outside. She ran right past her stunned parents and flung the door open.

Lorraine and Patrick followed her onto the porch.

A solemn procession materialized out of the morning mist and filed down the trail from the quarters. Baput led, in his Akashic robe, carrying his longstick in his right hand, his left hand clenched, white-knuckled. Behind him, Salistar and Valko walked side by side dressed in freshly woven traditional garments, the kind Lorraine had banned from the house for shedding bits of dried grass all over the place. Behind them, the source of the noise: Felsic, in a new, but humbly traditional outfit, hammered on an oversized cowbell and hooted a melody that hauntingly resembled "Here Comes the Bride."

Belinda slipped out of Lorraine's grasp and dashed down the stairs to greet them.

Lorraine started after her, but Patrick clamped his hand on her shoulder. "Wait, Babe. Just watch."

Lorraine growled, folded her arms. "This better not be what I think it is!"

Baput stopped in the middle of the driveway, right in front of Belinda. Felsic's clanging and hooting ceased abruptly.

"Bwell..." Baput sounded like he'd just had a shot of Novocain.

Salistar shoved him from behind, hissing something in Nauvian.

"Belinda," Baput managed to say. He dropped to one knee and raised his right hand, opening it slowly.

Belinda peered inside and gasped.

"Belinda," Baput tried once more. "You are a woman today."

"She's fifteen!" Lorraine corrected loudly from the porch.

Baput ignored her. Still on one knee, he spoke only to Belinda, saw only Belinda. "My Popa has made you a diamond ring, in the Earth way, so you will marry me on Passascenday."

"My ass!" Lorraine fought her way down the stairs. Patrick followed on her heels, grasping at her, trying to stop her.

Baput still knelt, his back to Bel's agitated parents. He looked only at Belinda, felt only the gentle touch of her fingers on his open palm as she took the ring and turned it slowly in her hands.

It was a thin slice of half-inch diameter steel conduit. A diamond shape had been etched in the center, with hearts on either side. Simple, playing card shapes engraved in the plain metal band. Unfamiliar shapes decked the other side.

Baput rose to his feet and took it from her. "These are the common symbols for 'Akash' and 'Tether'." He pointed to each shape in turn. Then he took her right hand and slid the ring onto her finger. It slipped down loosely.

She raised her hand to her heart, clutching it with the other hand to keep the ring on.

Baput smiled. "You like? So, is yes, then?"

Patrick and Lorraine reached the couple as a squirming, discordant unit. Patrick was calmer, and while Lorraine sputtered, searching for her words, he took the floor.

"Baput, folks, friends, look. As much as I'd like to play a part in weaving a green thread into the human tapestry, it's going to have to wait. She's only fifteen."

Baput finally took his eyes off his intended bride. He faced Patrick, looking at the top of his frizzy head. "I thought Earth people were free to choose who they marry."

"She's still too young," Patrick countered.

Lorraine nodded vigorously.

"But she is free!" Baput repeated.

Pushing Patrick aside, Lorraine moved in for the blitz. "She's a minor. She needs our permission before she can marry, until she's 21. See, it's more complicated here on Earth. Choosing is really hard. You're choosing the first girl you ever met on Earth. In your case, she's probably your only option, but�"

"Mom!" Belinda protested.

Baput's family pressed around them.

Patrick took over, far more gently. "If you grew up here, you'd go to school. You'd meet lots of girls. It's hard to choose. Young people make mistakes. Maybe you pick someone you kinda like, and then next year you fall head over heels in love with someone else. It happens all the time. You've gotta wait for the right one. You've gotta be mature."

"Mature?" Belinda interrupted. "You married the first women you could get, even though you knew she was just marrying you to piss her mom off. She doesn't even love you!"

"Bella!" Lorrain shrieked.

Still clutching her engagement ring to her heart, Belinda stood in front of Baput, facing her parents. She drew a trembling breath. "Even if I liked one of those jerks at school, they wouldn't ever love me. Baput does. He loves me, and I love him, forever. No one else. So, I'm saying 'yes'!"

She turned her back on the crowd and fell into Baput's arms, clenching her right hand in a fist, to keep the ring on.

Felsic resumed his hooting and clanging. Valko and Salistar joined hands and started humming the tune, wrapping Felsic's tenor in a sweet soprano and a resounding bass. They surrounded their Akash and his Tether-to-be, pushing Bel's fuming parents out of the circle.

"Have your fun now, little miss. Enjoy your sick fantasy! It's not happening! Not even over my dead body..." Lorraine raved as Patrick escorted her into the house.

Everything Changes

A month later, the world shut down. No restaurants, no shopping, no school.

Belinda was lucky. Her online classes continued, but they were suddenly stuffed beyond capacity. Images of kids she hadn't seen since middle school flashed and glitched and faded. No filters were allowed anymore. Too hard to keep track of who was there. Bel dreaded being exposed to the ridicule of her old "friends" again, even though they couldn't touch her. Happily, the feed couldn't handle all the bits and bytes generated by the antics of so many squirming kids, so after check-in, they were allowed to turn their cameras off. Baput could sit right beside Belinda and watch the teacher give her lessons.

Only the genetics class from the college was suspended. The college wasn't set up to be fully on-line yet.

So, Bel's life didn't change much. Lorraine worked at home, but she stayed upstairs in her office all day. Sometimes she would appear in time for the six o'clock news, where she would tolerate Baput's presence, but not his constant questions. Most days, she just kept working until seven or so, just like she'd done at the office.

When concurrent zoom meetings proved too much for their delicate satellite connection, rather than disrupt Belinda's schooling, Lorraine would go into the near-empty office in her mask to attend long-distance meetings. The company saved a ton on travel expenses, but Lorraine knew they were expecting their workers to sluff off with so much freedom, and she was determined to prove them wrong. Besides, she missed her co-workers, and her little office.

Jerry's senior year in high school sputtered to an unsatisfying close. His school wasn't ready for remote learning, like Belinda's was. They handed out laptops with cameras and speakers built in, and set up "hot spot" connections for rural and low-income kids who lacked money or infrastructure. The process was slow. So were the connection speeds. So, no live Zoom classes. Lessons were emailed, or snail-mailed when all else failed. Homework was sent back the same way.

Already well equipped, Jerry pursued his diploma as earnestly as he could, between levels of Mortal Kombat. He'd been accepted to the University of California at Davis, but who knew when, or if, that would happen?

George Floyd

The album ended. Patrick put down his cow bell and took a final toke. The soft, breathless moaning seeped gently into his consciousness. Uh-oh! *What are those kids doing?*

"Momma!" a voice whispered weakly, "Momma!"

Patrick slammed his bong down hard on the desk. Black water splashed out, flecking the already stained blotter. He rushed into the living room where Belinda and Baput were watching TV. "What are you watching?" he demanded. He saw the screen and fell silent.

He was a big man. Big and dark, like Valko. He lay in the gutter alongside a police car outside of a corner grocery store in Minneapolis. A city cop knelt with all his weight on the man's neck. A trickle of dark liquid flowed out from under the car. Two more cops flanked the scene on the street side of the car, while another kept chasing spectators back up onto the sidewalk whenever they tried to intervene.

"It's on every channel, Dad. It's real. Those girls on the sidewalk, they recorded the whole thing. His name is George Floyd."

The calls for Momma stopped. The soft moaning faded. George Floyd was silent and still. The cop still kneeled on his neck, staring boldly into the camera.

"Is he dead?" Patrick said, barely audible.

The picture disappeared abruptly and gave away to the CNN news desk, who finished the story, quickly confirming Patrick's fears.

"All he did was pass a counterfeit bill!" he mused when the commercial came on.

"What does that mean?" Baput asked. He hadn't spoken until now, and he looked as if he'd just witnessed the apocalypse, which perhaps he had.

"He used fake money. That's illegal," Belinda informed him numbly.

"It's not the death penalty!" Patrick snapped. "He might not have even known it was fake. Did he fight with the officers? He's pretty big. Did he threaten anyone?"

"No, Dad. Look, they're showing the whole thing again." Belinda pointed to the screen. Patrick watched Mr. Floyd get out of the car when the cops asked him. He sat against a wall while they questioned him. They made him get up and he walked with them across the street to their patrol car. He said he didn't want to get in, because he was claustrophobic. He thrashed unsuccessfully as four cops stuffed his bulk into the back of the patrol car. He came right out the other side, into the street in handcuffs and leg restraints. He lay there, his face in the pavement, Derek Chauvin's knee on his neck, until he could no longer breathe and his body shut down.

The show ended once more. Patrick turned the set off with trembling fingers that were as numb as his guts. "I told you kids not to watch the news without adult supervision."

"It was on every channel, Dad," Bel defended. "I turned to CNN to get the real story."

Patrick wanted to roll his eyes, but he didn't have the strength. "It's OK, Baby. This is important. Baput should know about this. So should you, Sweetheart, unfortunately." He grabbed Belinda and hugged her tight.

"It's because he's black, isn't it?" The young Alanakash of Nauve asked quietly.

"It is." Patrick mimicked the detached tone.

"It's hate," Baput recited. "Jerry told me all about hate. The white people hate the black people and all the other races, and the other religions, too. I've seen it for myself. Well, you know that." He turned his soft brown eyes on Patrick. "Jerry tried to explain it, but I still don't understand..."

Patrick let go of Belinda and wrapped his arm firmly around Baput's shoulders, giving him an affectionate shake. "That's good," he quipped.

Baput pulled away enough to face Patrick's straight eye. "Good?" he asked.

Patrick came around to face him, keeping one hand on the broad shoulder. "Yes, good. I'm glad you don't understand. Because this is something a good, rational, righteous man who is any friend of mine would *never* understand." He squeezed Baput's shoulder, then let go.

Baput squirmed. "But I have to try..." Patrick turned and walked toward the front door. Baput followed him. "I must empathize with every point of view, so I can understand..."

Patrick whirled back to face him. "Not that!" he snapped, "That's evil!"

"But I see it all over the iPlane. Millions of people believe�"

Patrick raised a finger. "You stay away from those people, you hear? Or stay away from my daughter!"

Turning to Belinda, he added, "You keep him off the hate sites, you hear me?" He stormed out of the house.

"You sound like my G-Pa," Baput muttered to his back. Defiantly, he turned the TV back on and sat firmly on the couch, patting the seat beside him. Belinda took it. They joined hands and watched the horrible story once more.

"I'm scared," Belinda breathed.

Baput squeezed her hand, gestured toward the screen. "Don't be scared, Bel. It's just on TV, far away in some otherwhere. We're safe here. It's not something for you and me to be afraid of."

Belinda wriggled her hand from his and looked at him, her straight eye probing deeply. "Yeah, Baput," she said, "I think maybe it is."

Nauve, Summer before the Season

June Garden

The women straightened their backs and looked up from their work for just a moment, as the Tether to Akash entered the communal garden. They dropped back down to their tasks as soon as she had passed, like a wave at a baseball game. The train of her magnificent gown and a trail of whispers followed in her wake.

"What is she doing here?"

"Will she help us pick?"

"Are you kidding? In that gown?"

"She never works. She doesn't even cook." The women grumbled, rough hands buried in the dirt, using sharp stones to dig the precious root crops from the tired soil.

The Tether didn't stop to talk or help. She strode all the way down the aisle between the rows to where Rakta directed a group of young men who were loading a ganeesh cart with heavy sacks and baskets of potatoes, beets and carrots. She smiled in a way she hadn't at her wedding, or at her husband's ascension. She walked right up to the War Chief, then past him. He barked at the young men to keep loading, and disappeared after her. The Akash was nowhere in sight. It must be important business, for him to send his tether with a message for the War Chief!

"It is time," Tamaya told Rakta in a whisper, her eyes burning into his confused ones. She saw the flame reignite deep inside them. The hope, the passion. It took her breath away. "In half a moon's time. Not this coming practice, but the next." She would allow two weeks for the herb to surely kick in.

He studied her. There was hurt behind the hope, and a fear no one else had ever seen in the mighty War Chief. "Are you sure?" he asked in his battle whisper. "He has opened you? He will think it's his now?"

She looked into his anxious eyes and lied with sweet sincerity. "Oh, yes! Your brilliant plan is working. His prowess with the longstick, the respect and admiration of the young warriors, has made a man of him. But he's not you. I need you, my War Chief!"

She blinked in slow motion, then turned and sprinted back to the garden on her long legs, her gown dancing in the air all around her. The young men had already departed with their load for the cool communal storage cellar below the Great Hall. Rakta trotted off to join them, re-assembling his demeanor as he ran.

The women watched from their knees as the Tether re-entered the garden. Would she just saunter through without a word, again? To their surprise, she stopped and actually got down on her knees in the dirt. She picked up a stone someone had left and started digging with her fine, delicate hands. She wrestled a long tuber from the ground, ripped the frilly greens off the top, and stashed the thick, sturdy carrot under her elaborate gown. Then she dusted the soil from her hands, stood, and strolled off in her elegant way, back to the Holy Cave.

The Breeding Matrix

The stool tottered beneath Akira as she stretched. Holding the thin, temporary thread that represented the Pind Line in her right hand, she reached for a thicker line from the matrix, the one furthest away, the one that she hadn't touched with her temporary thread even once in this whole long, agonizing exercise.

Her arms and shoulders ached from working overhead every day for two solid months. Her old bones were brittle, and if she fell, there was no one to spot her. No one had been here, in the Matrix Chamber, since Akira had gotten the news and started trying to retrace the Pind Line through all its pairings, but from a different point of origin.

No one could see what she was doing. Not even Edijay. Especially not Edijay. She already doubted the Matrix, just like all the rest of her apprentices had. Even if they understood how to do it, they just thought it was about the Power of Akira. As if telling people who they could marry was somehow glorious, done purely for her own aggrandizement. *And this one, this Edijay, craves that power, without understanding the reason for it. I need an apprentice who hates this power as much as I do. Who understands why it is necessary, who does it for the good of all of us, so we can survive the wasting!*

The stool stopped swaying. She held the desired line in her left hand, then brought her right hand up, holding Tamaya's thin, temporary thread next to it. She followed it up with her eyes, looking for the pairing it came from, its identity. "Rakta!" she gasped.

Spy

Datali's skin was the dusty green of the willows by the river, but she still wore a weave of grass and leaves to distort her shape. She dropped her camouflage and wiped the black and white streaks of magnesium and zinc powders from her face before reporting to Akira's antechamber. Once cleaned up, she looked like a delicate wisp of timidity. Short and slender, she had the petite features of a child, without the baby fat. She could have been a cleaner, or a kitchen assistant. She showed none of the strength, endurance and cunning that made her Akira's most trusted spy.

She entered the dim antechamber boldly, without the diffident hesitation most women displayed. Akira was seated, lurking at the edge of the lamplight. "I have done as you asked, Ma'am," she began. Akira nodded.

"Last week, Bupple came for the Akash in the early morning. He no longer sleeps there!" She looked up questioningly, got an unsurprised nod. "The Tether stood on the porch and watched them go. Then she went back inside and I saw her no more, until they returned at noon, and she greeted them."

"And this week?"

Datali inhaled deeply. What she had to report was so hot she couldn't hold it much longer. She was glad her appointment was so soon. As skilled and disciplined as she was, she doubted if she could have spent much time in the Lair without blurting to the first curious face that caught her expression. It was as if she really had to pee, and she was just glad she'd made it to the boor before she let fly.

"This week was the same. But an hour after the Akash left with Bupple, someone came. Not on the trail. They snuck through the bushes by the river, like I did. I didn't move. He didn't see me. He went right to the stairs and climbed up to the top. She greeted him. She wasn't at all surprised. It was like she expected him. He stayed for two hours. I couldn't see or hear anything. I didn't dare climb the stairs. Finally, they came back out to the porch. They were standing so close together, Akira, like a man and his tether. They spoke quietly. She nodded. Then they kissed! For a long time! I saw it!"

Datali's voice had risen to a shrill pitch. She had never seen such blatant misbehavior in all her years of watching people's secrets play out in what they thought was privacy. She thought she had seen it all, but a tryst like this among two of the highest-ranking citizens in the village? *Even they are not happy with their lots*, she had realized on the thoughtful trip home.

Akira countered her unprecedented excitement with an icy calm. Did nothing surprise this old woman? They said she could see the future. Datali wasn't sure about that, but she knew Akira had probably seen everything before, in her uncounted years.

"And who is this man who visits the Holy Tether?"

Datali dropped the bomb on ground that looked like it had already been razed. "Rakta."

Akira just nodded again, with no sign of surprise. "You will watch all week, and the week after. Whenever the Akash leaves the Holy Cave without the Tether, you watch those stairs. See if anyone else comes. Report to me every week." She looked Datali up and down. She had never slipped, but she had never been privy to a secret like this. "You remember your oath."

"Of course, Akira. No words to anyone, ever. Yes, Ma'am." She hurried out. She would take a long run around the perimeter of the village before she re-entered the Lair full of the prying eyes and probing ears of crowded, frustrated females.

Apothecary

Akira let two more weeks go by. Two more reports from Datali. She marveled at how quickly the young woman adjusted to the situation. What she had spewed so breathlessly just two weeks ago was now just the same old thing. Nothing new to report. The Tether seemed to never leave the

Holy Cave. No one came to her but Rakta, and he came faithfully whenever the Akash went to practice with the men all morning, a situation the War Chief himself had created.

"You have seen no one else? Only Rakta?"

"Correct, Ma'am. Rakta is the only one. He stays longer each time. They kiss longer on the porch. They are getting careless. I was almost afraid the Akash would return and catch them!"

Akira had to chuckle at her spy's emotional involvement. The woman couldn't help but root for the secret lovers, even though they were snooty high-borns.

Right after Datali left, Akira made a rare trip to the back of the Lair's kitchen where Contina the Apothecary mixed the herbs Akira and her counselors ordered for various woman's ailments. She ordered a new formula for the Akashic Tether. The Apothecary dared object.

"Akira, surely, that can't be right! It's just a sweetener. You left out the—"

Akira nodded. "Mix it, wrap it in usual willow bark and have Nemaray bring it to Jenevan to deliver to the Holy Cave with their meal, as always."

"But, Ma'am, it will not be effective!" Contina tried once again. Akira had been especially addled of late.

"Let nature take its course," the woman's ruler muttered as she waddled away.

Tamaya braced herself for that first sip of her breakfast tea. Its bitterness always shocked her. It made her taste buds clench so she couldn't enjoy her breakfast. It was worth it, though. She would drink mud if it meant she could continue her delightful meetings with Rakta every week without worrying about a babbet coming along and ruining everything.

With that resolve, she drank deeply, and was pleasantly surprised. It tasted good! The bitterness was gone! *Good old Akira!* she thought in a rare moment of gratitude. *She treats me much better now that she knows I'm Akashic. I complained about the bitterness, and she found a sweetener that covers it completely!*

Earth, Summer 2020

Graduation

The principal's muffled voice crackled through the ancient radio speaker affixed to the Mustang's slightly lowered passenger window. Jerry, Fran and Elmer stared through the windshield at the pudgy, balding official on the big screen, orating through a three-ply cloth mask blazoned with a blue and white Husky logo.

The principal apologized for the rough year and the valedictorian cheered her classmates for being "troopers" and never giving up, as if they'd had a choice in the matter.

When the speeches were over, the spectators pulled their cars from their assigned places and headed toward the exit in precise order, one row following another. Jerry put on his Husky mask and latex gloves and maneuvered the Mustang into his place in line. His lopsided grin hidden under his mask, he shoved the car into neutral and tapped the gas, treating his class to a Husky graduation roar.

Fran grabbed the back of the seat and squealed, "Careful, Hon!"

Elmer cackled.

A giant blue and white husky that stood on two legs handed Jerry's diploma through the driver's window with a blue-gloved hand that protruded from its immense, blue paw pad. Jerry's name was announced over the speakers to the half of the class that remained hooked up. If there was any cheering, he couldn't hear it. No choice but to stay in line and drive out of there, and then, well, home.

"I wish my folks and Patrick's family could be here," Fran mourned.

"We're only allowed one car!" Elmer snapped. "They couldn't all fit in here with us, now could they? It wouldn't be socially distant," he grumbled as the Mustang loped through a shuttered downtown. "It's not like we could go out to dinner after, anyway."

"No parties, either," Jerry concurred. He hit the gas and accelerated out of the desolate town, headed home to the Look 'N Up.

Photo Degradation

The alarm beeped on the Look 'N Up camera. Boyd's coffee slopped out of his mug as he whirled his chair to face the console. He set it down carefully on a side table, away from the sensitive equipment. He clicked a knob, and the screen with the flashing light blossomed into a live action movie, complete with sound.

"What if they come down and see it?" It was the kid, Jerry's voice. He and his dad, Elmer worked on either side of the brush pile, removing the covering branches and setting them aside so they blocked the trail.

"I won't let 'em." Elmer sounded determined, but helpless. "I kept them out of here the last time."

"Maybe we should wait." Jerry wasn't working as fast as his dad.

Now Elmer stopped working, fully addressing his son. "Wait for what? It's only a month until First Pomegranate Day. It'll be the first day of harvest, right when the inspectors get here," he sneered. "After this one, it'll be all over. They'll be gone. Back to Nauve, or whatever they call that place."

"Not without the Net, Dad," was the boy's cryptic reply.

The agents watched the uncovering of the rock in silence, wondering about the upcoming First Pomegranate Day, and the Net. Was Boyd right? He wasn't gloating. In fact, he looked a little disappointed.

"I guess sunshine isn't considered weather," he finally remarked.

Ripped from their thoughts, the other agents grunted, "what?"

"The video. It's faded, blurry." He scrolled through the images from the other cameras. His forehead creased deeply. "Some of them, anyway. See, here's the shop."

"Looks fine," Kramer barked after the briefest of glances. He was still focused on Elmer's promise. *It will be all over soon.* Kramer had been counting the months until this nowhere assignment was over. He'd been ready to call it off months ago. Nothing to tie the Musik family to Manuel Guzman's death. They'd found some animal parts that matched, but nothing to tie the people, or verify the alleged aliens. But Boyd kept reporting progress that Kramer wasn't seeing. He said it was an "X-File". Kramer had tried to tell the boy there was no such thing. In his opinion, people who wanted to grow up to be FBI Agents shouldn't watch TV. But then, they wouldn't want to be FBI Agents, he supposed. *Point is,* Kramer resolved in his head, *this job isn't near as exciting as they make it out to be.*

Boyd was rattling on. "Yeah, that one's fine. It's pointing into the shop. And the one up in the orchard, I call it Kate's spot, that one's in the shade of the tree, pointing down. But look at these others, down by the river in the sun. They're all blurry. They've gotten worse over the summer. I think the lenses are photodegrading."

Kramer leaned over Boyd's shoulder, peering at the screen. "Looks OK to me," he repeated.

"But they're fading. We need to replace them," Boyd urged.

"It's only one more month! We ain't going through that again just so you can have your 5G. I grew up watching TV that didn't look anywhere near that good. You can see that just fine. Suck it up!"

Get Your Knee Off My Neck

Fifty-seven years after Martin Luther King, Jr's March on Washington, the world turned its eyes to the Capitol Mall once again to watch his descendants, and a host of relatives of other slain black people, speak at the "Get Your Knee Off Our Necks" rally.

Lorraine had a meeting at work. She seemed to have a lot of those lately. She went into the office almost every day, now that she had a matching mask for every outfit. Patrick had a plumbing job, but he told the kids it was OK to watch the march. So, as the time approached, Baput and Belinda sat down on the couch together. Belinda turned on the set.

A strangely familiar sight appeared. A line of light-colored men in uniforms and helmets advanced on a line of people whose skins were various shades of brown. The pale ones carried shields, clubs and guns. The darker skinned folks were not as well equipped for battle. Even so, they threw something at the armored ones, and the scene ignited. In seconds, they were all beating each other with clubs and fists. Something like smoke billowed around the ones that ran away.

Baput leaned forward, extending his arm at the TV. "I saw that! On the iPlane, when we first arrived at the Look 'N Up. Jerry called it 'Ferguson'. It was about a man named Michael Brown. I was so confused. His name was brown, his skin was brown, and why was he killed?"

The scene changed, the action didn't. Same thing. Sheilds, helmets and tear gas. But there seemed to be more white people among the ones without armor. "That's last month. After George Floyd. Remember?" Belinda prompted.

"Of course I do!" Baput snapped. "He was as big as my Popa, but he let that little guy kneel on his neck until he died. Too afraid to fight back, like the guy was Akash or something. My dad could have smashed my G-Pa. I know he wanted to sometimes, but he never did. He was afraid, because G-Pa was Akash. But Earth has no Akash. People are free here. So why do they still have to be so afraid?"

"He thought if he cooperated, he'd have a chance to survive. But he didn't. He..." Belinda's attempt at an explanation faded into thoughtful silence as a montage of demonstrations and riots played across the screen. Rallies for Eric Garner, Trayvon Martin, Breonna Taylor, Jacob Blake, Ahmaud Arbery, Emmett Till...

Baput's mouth felt like it was stuck closed. He struggled to speak. "All those people killed, by men like the ones who came to the Look 'N Up wanting to kill us. Why, Belinda? Jerry tried to explain. He said people came from otherwhere, and the people were afraid of them because they were different, and they might take what they have or ruin it somehow."

Belinda took Baput's oversized hand in her petite one. She examined the creases that had appeared so suddenly on his dear face. She caught herself imagining what he would look like as an old man. Would she see it? Would she still be with him, somehow? She couldn't imagine how, any more than she could imagine life without him.

"Do you know why the black people came here?" she asked gently.

"A better life?" Baput guessed.

Belinda gasped. "Didn't Jerry tell you about slavery?" She glanced at the TV. They were still showing past footage. A box in the lower right corner counted down the time until live coverage of the Commitment March would begin. Six minutes to explain the roots of systemic racism to an alien who had never seen a stranger until he arrived on Earth six years ago. She put her other hand on top of his and looked deeply into his eyes.

"They came from Africa. It was primitive there, like your village. No guns, just spears and arrows."

"Like we have," Baput replied.

Belinda nodded. "White people came with guns and forced them into ships and brought them across the ocean all stuffed in a hold like cargo! When they got here, they were sold to plantation owners and stuff. They had to work in the fields. They lived there, and they got food, but no money. No freedom. They couldn't leave, couldn't quit. If they ran away and got caught, they'd get hanged by their necks from a tree. The owner could even sell the momama and popas away from the family. Or sell the kids!"

Baput's look told her he didn't believe her. "How could they sell a person?"

"They were slaves," Belinda replied earnestly. "People owned them, like we own..." she looked around the room. "Well, like Falcon and Mustang. We bought them. Felsic fixed them up, and we sold them for more money. Well, Jerry took them, but we sold the Falcon, eventually. Now we'll use that money to buy another car. It was like that, but with people."

"Falcon and Mustang are not alive," Baput countered numbly.

"Ok, it's like Shastina, then. She's your dog. You own her."

More wrinkles creased Baput's young face. "We don't own Shastina. She's a part of our family."

"Where did you get her?"

"From the Animal Keeper. They are born in the stalls with the ganeesh and Maylar takes care of them until they're old enough to go to a family. Any family can have a dog join them, if they ask. My G-Pa wanted one, and he got Shastina. But anybody can have one, not just the Akash."

"Do they give the Keeper something in return? That's like buying."

"No. We don't do that. No buying or selling. Not even giving. Everything in the village belongs to all of us."

"I guess that's why Jerry didn't tell you about slavery. You don't even get owning a dog, or a car!" Bel's green eyes shined with admiration, but Baput's were clouded and far away. Was he trying to imagine being a slave? White people coming through the portal to Nauve with guns, rounding up his people and forcing them to come here and...

"Are we slaves?" Baput rasped without looking at her.

"No!" Belinda cried, slapping his chest playfully.

He turned his wet eyes to her. "We live in the worker's quarters, and we work for you. We get food, but we don't get paid."

"You do so!" Bel insisted. "You just can't use your money, because you're not in our system. So, we use the money you earn to buy you whatever you want."

Baput nodded. "That's what Jerry said. But we were slaves on the Look 'N Up, too. We couldn't leave there. We can't leave here. Did they sell us? Did your Popa buy us?" He choked on a lump in his throat. *His best friend Jerry, and dear, sweet Francina, slave owners?*

Belinda stretched her arms around him. He stiffened.

"You're not slaves, silly! You're our friends, our family! We're helping you, protecting you. We love you. No matter what." She rolled off of his chest to face the TV. "Look, it's starting."

Reverand Sharpton gave a stirring introduction. Then, Martin Luther King III spoke from the steps of the Lincoln Memorial, the same spot where his father had spoken 57 years before. Then Dr. King's twelve-year-old granddaughter, Yolanda Renee King said, "We are going to be the generation that dismantles systemic racism once and for all, now and forever."

"She's a little younger than me," Belinda whispered. "That's my generation she's talking about!"

After the families of George Floyd and Breonna Taylor spoke, another young woman, Letetra Wideman took the stage. Her brother, Jacob Blake, had just been paralyzed by seven bullets shot by a cop, right in front of his kids. She addressed 'Black America', telling them, "You must stand. You must fight, but not with violence and chaos. With self-love. Read, learn, grow and live, and question everything."

"We don't do that on Nauve. We don't question anything," Baput muttered under his breath.

When her compelling speech ended, Belinda addressed Baput again. "I like how she speaks up. Her and Yolanda King. Young women, like me. See how important it is for women to speak up? They don't just grunt about fighting, like the men. They think into the future, because they have kids, or expect to. And they talk about positive solutions people can do for themselves. I think everybody should speak up about this. With the iPlane, anybody can speak and reach the whole world."

"We can?" Baput asked.

"Well, maybe not us." Bel's face fell. She turned away.

"But, why not?" Baput reached for her. "You said anybody can."

"But you're green. And I'm, well, different."

"So? Different people aren't allowed to speak up?"

"Oh, they're allowed. But nobody listens to people who are different. They're just thinking about how you're different. That's all they see."

Bored

Valko hurled the twisted metal rod across the workshop. It penetrated the sheet metal wall and stuck there, like that first dart fired from Felsic's spring gun. "I tire of doing the same design over and over."

Felsic stopped the lathe and removed his goggles.

Valko put his cutting shears on the workbench and sat heavily in the oversized folding chair. "I tire of peace," he muttered.

"What?" Felsic asked.

"Peace!" Valko replied, his mumble building into a roar. "This peace Patrick values so much. No more nimblies, no more bumblies..."

"Not ever, no more." Felsic completed the familiar chant.

Valko broke into a smile. He raised a finger at Felsic. "The RID Men! We should seek out those RID Men and fight them. You and me, Brother, we'll�"

Felsic stood beside him and clasped his tense shoulder, as hard as the steel rod he'd been twisting on the lathe. "I feel it, too, Brother. The Season. It's almost here. Only one more Kakeeche cycle! I used to dread the Season. The fear, the pain, the death... Now, when I think of it *not* happening, well, that scares me even more. Because there is nothing," he ran his fingers through his thinning hair, a habit he'd picked up from Elmer. "I can do," his mouth worked noiselessly as he tried to swallow, "about that."

Nauve, Last Kakeeche Cycle
Caught

Rakta took his time, teaching Tamaya all the tricks he had learned in his ten cycles of marriage. Tamaya didn't know how lucky she was. The taking and giving of such pleasure occurred rarely, only among the few couples fortunate enough to find one another attractive and care for each other deeply. Rakta and Azuray must be such a couple. But now it was Rakta and Tamaya, while Azuray cleaned their hut and waited for her War Chief to return from his business.

They were in the Death Tunnel with the light off, lying on Tamaya's silvery cape. Rakta liked the way it tingled on his skin when he spread out on it, flat and naked, his tender parts fully exposed. The tingling felt good, but it bothered Tamaya. She still thought it was bugs from that ganeesh ride last Passascenday. They had gone dormant or something for most of the cycle. Eggs, maybe, that had hatched last spring. Since then, the gown had grown more prickly each day.

She stroked and kissed Rakta's exposed body gently. His manhood rose. She straddled him. He opened his mouth as if to speak. An airy moan escaped, then a squeaky voice. Not Rakta's.

"I tell you, Bupple, I made that shot!" Bazu squealed from the steps.

"You would have, if Samard hadn't blocked it."

"Yes. He should be flogged. See to it." Bazu went straight to the Death Door and turned on the lamp.

Bupple followed him. "But Sir, it's part of the game�"

Bazu's scream pierced the depths of the Death Tunnel and rattled the high, domed ceiling of the Holy Cave. It excited the sensitive molecules of the Rock, making it glow and hum, barely enough to notice, unless you were sitting on it. The gown beneath the guilty couple tingled more than ever. Tamaya could feel the vibration coming right through her lover and into her depths. They were both motionless, still she felt him course through her while she straddled him and looked at her husband, the Holy Akash. His eyes were slits and his mouth was pulled back in a tight grimace that looked like it hurt. Tamaya stayed where she was. She didn't dare get up and leave Rakta so exposed.

She searched behind the screaming Akash for Bupple. Had he seen? There he was, covering his face with his hands, trying to unsee it. He wasn't leaving, though, Tamaya was relieved to see.

Rakta grabbed an edge of the gown and rolled away from the Akash, taking Tamaya with him, wrapping them together in the tingling fabric. The itching died down as the scream faded to a hoarse burble that wrenched at Tamaya's heart, or at least her conscience. Rakta reached for his pants and war belt, packed with weapons. He managed to get into his pants and extract himself from the gown, leaving it all to Tamaya. She wrapped herself in it, ignoring the itch and the assumed insect bites, and struggled to stand beside her coconspirator.

Bazu faced them in the doorway, Bupple towering behind him, looking big, but totally helpless.

Bazu's scream and murmur had descended into an absolute a silence that itself made the Rock ring. Tamaya looked at Rakta. Still shirtless, he stood battle ready, but restrained. Muscles taught, but not moving. He stared at his adversary until he felt Tamaya's eyes on him. He turned her way for just an instant, and she gasped at the depth, the intelligence, the tenderness he'd shown her, the selflessness he showed every Season, risking his life as War Chief.

Then she looked at the Immortal Akash, as cold and calm as the Old Akash, as any old, dried up, loveless Akash in history. Tamaya knew them all. She had read their innermost thoughts. Now she saw every one of them in this skinny, wheezing, impotent, self-centered little boy! The so-called Akashic Line. They had always been this way! Time for the true Akashic Line to emerge. She would name her son Pind, and he would contain not one drop of this weak, stupid line. He would ascend to Akash and correct this terrible error, if he lived. If he was ever born.

When the Akash found his voice, his calmness frightened Tamaya more than any fit he'd ever thrown. "So, you have decided, My Tether," he sneered her title, "to go ahead and have a babbet without me. You said you didn't want any. I don't need any, for I will live forever. So, I granted your wish, freed you from the burden you always dreaded. I never touch you." He looked at Rakta, who looked at Tamaya. She shook her head and shrugged. The Akash took it all in. "Though my loins ache for you every night, I leave you alone, as you wish."

"I didn't... You didn't ever want..." Tamaya sputtered under Rakta's troubled gaze.

Bazu dropped her like a peach pit and turned to Rakta. "And you, War Chief! You come in here, to the Holy Cave, to defrock the Akashic Tether? To plant a usurper in *it* that you think will someday receive the Sacred Longstick and the Holy Seed? You presume to *be* the Holy Seed?" Bazu stepped forward, forcing Rakta further back into the Death Tunnel, Tamaya glued to his side.

Bazu folded his arms and adopted a less aggressive stance. "Very well. Easily remedied. Let me tell you how it will be. Rakta, you will enjoy your last Season as War Chief. If you live, I will announce your transgression on Passascenday, as well as yours, My Tether, if you live. You will be staked out, clothed only in the thin, sheer silk of the lin spider, just like Romey and Jakima, only a bit closer together, I think. I shall make Bupple my new War Chief."

Bupple grunted uncomfortably.

"For you, Rakta, I think I will reinstate the position of wine maker and put you in it. I'll get that little girl, Felsic's daughter, to teach you. You can see how it feels to be taught by an idiot female."

He walked forward and cupped Tamaya's cheek. Rakta tensed, ready. The Akash just kept his hand on that tender, moss-colored cheek as he explained his vision for Tamaya. "As for you, My Dear, after a staking like that, the woman goes to the waiting hole, if she lives."

"The waiting hole?" Tamaya rasped.

Bazu laughed delightedly. "You don't know? My Momama's sister is an Unmarriageable, you know. She tells my Momama things. She should probably be killed for telling. Perhaps I will tell Akira on her. But, anyway, it is a dark cell in the depths of the Lair where Akira keeps the Unmarriageables when they get caught like this."

"But I'm not Unmarriageable!" Tamaya replied haughtily.

"You will be, after this!" Bazu leaned his head back and laughed wickedly. "If you are with babbet, you stay in the hole the whole nine

Kakeeche Cycles. When your time comes and you emerge, blinking and half starved, Akira will birth your babbet. When she sees its face, its fat cheeks and dark complexion, that bald head, ha ha!" He pointed derisively at Rakta's head. "She will know. She will hold him up above her head," he demonstrated with clenched, empty hands. "She will say, 'this babbet is not Akashic. He is an imposter!' She will raise him up by his fat feet, and swing him," he demonstrated further, to his spectators' horror. "She will bash his big, ugly head on the cold, stone floor of her Lair, where it will burst open like a perfectly ripe kip."

Tamaya knew none of this would happen, but Rakta didn't. He shoved Tamaya behind him and lurched forward in battle mode, in defense of his unborn son and his mate, if feelings counted. He was way too far outside the lines to know what counted and what didn't. He acted on pure instinct. He punched the Akash in the face.

Bazu's pasty hands flew to his nose, which gushed blood. He fell back. Bupple caught him, held him tightly.

Rakta grabbed his shirt and wrapped his arm around Tamaya's shoulders, still tingling from the gown draped across them. He put his hand next to her face, protectively, and the joined pair scurried past the whimpering, bloody mess, out the entrance, and down the long staircase.

They hurried down the trail toward the village, their voices hushed. "It won't happen you know," Tamaya told him. "All that stuff he said Akira would do. She won't. I know it."

"How do you know that? You know the story of Romey and Jakima. That is what always happens when someone makes a hibudara, a forbidden child, not of their betrothed. You are no different, My Lady, Akashic Tether or not."

"But I *am* different, War Chief. You don't know all of it. Akira will let my babbet live, no matter who it comes from."

"You are a naïve child." Rakta informed her hopelessly. "Akira lies, just like an Akash."

The path to the Lair departed from the main one, heading past the entrances to the extensive cave system that housed the Unmarriageables and their kitchens, meeting rooms, classrooms, laboratories and prison cells, to the front entrance with its elaborate façade, and Akira's Antechamber.

"Leave me," Tamaya ordered her still-shaking lover.

"I won't."

"You must. Go on to the village. I go to Akira."

"No!"

"Yes, she will protect me, I tell you. Now go, before we're seen together. Akira's spies are everywhere."

As she spoke, Datali backed silently from a nearby willow thicket and ducked into an underground passage that would get her to the antechamber unseen, ahead of the AkashicTether.

Tamaya hadn't shaken like this upon reaching the huge wooden door since before she was Tether. Now she was not only Tether, but Akashic herself, yet she shook like the eleven-year-old who had been called to prepare for her upcoming wedding to Batuk, her first betrothed, four cycles ago. The guards hurried to open the door for Her Majesty, the Akashic Tether. Akira was waiting, as if expecting her.

Love

"Did you dally too long, My Dear?" Akira's cool, droll voice came from a silhouette seated in the darkness. Tamaya could just make out the outline of her round face and tousled hair.

"The Akash has caught me with another man," Tamaya confessed, as she had practiced. It was easier than she'd expected. The old lady seemed to know anyway. Did she know *who*?

"Who is this man who dares to make hibudara with the Holy Tether?"

So, she *didn't* know everything. Tamaya was relieved, then worried. What would she say? She looked at the floor and spoke quietly.

"It is Rakta." Saying his name bore her up like wind under a pair of weary wings. "He loves me. And I love him."

"Love?" Akira laughed cruelly. "The alpha male sniffs his way to the alpha female, like a couple of dogs! That's your love." She sneered the word, never to know its true meaning. "No matter. Done is done."

"No matter?" Tamaya's numbness wore off all at once. "He will tell everyone on Passascenday. Stake us out like Romey and Jakima. He will make Bupple War Chief and Rakta will be winemaker."

Akira hissed a laugh at that, riling Tamaya even further.

"He said you would kill our babbet. But you won't, because there is no babbet. Right? Akira?"

Akira's silence sent cold chills down Tamaya's spine. "He said you would put me in the Waiting Hole. In the dark, for nine months."

Now Akira leaned forward. "How does he know about the Waiting Hole?"

"His aunt, Ritamay's sister told him."

"I will have to take care of that." The voice in the dark dripped with venom, but not for Tamaya, or Rakta. Tamaya waited, not breathing.

Akira spoke at last, but not to Tamaya. Tamaya could barely make out the words as the old woman ranted, as only the most senior Unmarriageables had seen her rant of late, and they were worried.

"So, the sickly Ka Line ends itself. The egomaniacal Ba Line, my own, mind you, managed to," she clicked her tongue, made the pop sign with her hand, "disappear itself."

She looked at Tamaya, her eyes shining through the darkness, and suddenly her voice was clear, as if she'd come to a decision. "Now the Line of Pind will re-emerge to its rightful place. Strong and beautiful," she reached across the table to touch Tamaya's face like the treasure it was. "And wise. Your Popa has the wisdom of a great Akash, Tamaya! Did you know that? Yes, the Pinds will take their rightful place as the true rulers. But quietly. In secret. Through you, my precious girl."

A numbness stole through Tamaya, starting at her toes and spreading to the top of her head, where her hair stood on end.

"He is the one," Akira declared. "The matrix says so. His babbet will be the next Akash. The babbet you now carry."

The bubble that had formed around Tamaya burst. "But, the herb..."

Akira stamped her feet on the floor and pounded the table, cackling insanely. Tamaya stepped back, glanced toward the door, shut tight, the guards outside. "Ah, My Dear! I have known of your lover for months now. I knew he was the right one, so I gave you a placebo, these last three

Kakeeche cycles! At the rate you two busy yourselves, you surely bear his child by now."

Tamaya put her hand on her belly. It didn't feel any different. How long before...? A babbet! Anger surged. Rakta's babbet! Tenderness flooded her, completely foreign, yet already a part of her.

"You will need protection," Akira was saying, "Perhaps Bupple can resume living with you, as your guard, since the Immortal Akash doesn't need one?"

"Bupple saw us."

"What did he do?"

"Nothing. Cuddled the Akash after Rakta punched him."

Akira rose at that news. "He struck the Akash?"

"Yes, when he said all the horrible things you would do to the babbet, his babbet, our babbet..."

"Will Bupple protect you?"

"He would, but Bazu will make him War Chief, and Rakta..."

"Yes, yes. A tactical disaster, surely. Bupple is a good man, but he's no war chief! I will speak to the Akash about all that. Will you be safe in the Holy Cave if Bupple is there, or do you have to stay here in the Lair?"

Tamaya squeezed her eyes at the shorter woman. "In the Waiting Hole?"

"No, of course not. Your child is not hibudara. He is authorized by the Breeding Matrix. But still, we must keep this all secret. The village has seen too much disruption already, these last cycles. Babbet or not, you will continue to see Rakta in secret, until there is a son. I will say he is the Akashic Son, and the people will believe it, even if he looks nothing like Bazu."

"He will tell everyone on Passascenday. They will all know."

"That would make it much more difficult for people to believe it's his. I must point that out to him. He can have a strong, healthy Akashic son and gain the people's respect. They will hide their doubts beneath the blankets of their nighttime conversations. Or he can have his fun humiliating Rakta. But in the end, his Tether will bear a child, and by all indications, it won't be his."

"It won't be," Tamaya agreed through clenched teeth.

"But you will still be his. You will meet with Rakta in utmost secrecy. No sloppy kissing on the porch of the Holy Cave. You will come here, perhaps to the Waiting Hole, since you know of it already. You will have your trysts in the dark under heavy guard, and no contact outside of that. Never. No flirting at the Great Hall, making plans in the garden. Do you think people are fools? Or just blind?

"When the babbets come, you will have a hut in the village. The Old Akash's family's hut is still empty. Plenty of room for babbets; an heir, a spare, and a daughter, all strong and healthy, just like Salistar had."

Tamaya squirmed more now than she had during her confession. "You said I would have help."

"We'll see, My Dear, we'll see. Now, can you go to your popa's? Datali will escort you. Or you can stay here until I speak with the Akash. You might have to stay with us until Passascenday."

"Can I see the Breeding Matrix?"

"No. You are not my apprentice. You have another path."

"Making babbets for the Akash." Tamaya sighed. Even the fun part had turned ugly.

"Hasn't it always been so?" Akira answered gently, raising her eyebrows. "Or, you could just *go*."

Tamaya froze. There was that word again. The word from her dreams. *Go where? What did she mean?* "What did you say?" she heard herself ask through a raspy throat.

"Are you staying here or going home to Popa?" Akira asked again. "Stay out of the Holy Cave until I investigate. I will bring Rashetta to tend to the Akash's wound." She glared at Tamaya, waiting for an answer.

Tamaya's response was clear and direct. She bolted through the heavy door and sprinted swiftly toward her popa's hut in the village with Datali at her flank, struggling to keep up.

Back in the Cave

"I only allow you to return so I can keep my eye on you." Bazu informed Tamaya and Bupple when they appeared at the Holy Cave three days later, as ordered by Akira, or asked, in the case of Bupple. He served at the will of

Rakta, and the Akash. But Rakta had been scarce these past days, and the Akash was unapproachable. Bupple had agreed to move back into the Holy Cave, ostensibly as Guard of Akash, but really to protect Tamaya.

Bazu stuck his crooked finger in his tether's pretty face. "I obviously can't trust you," he looked up at Bupple, raised the finger higher. "And you know too much. I can't have you babbling the news to your son and his gossipy tether, now can I?" He stretched up and leaned forward, trying futilely to get in the big man's face, as he had Tamaya's. Failing that, he backed off and began to pace in front of the Rock, blocking their entry. Bupple set their luggage down.

"You will keep your filthy secret until after the Season, on Passascenday, when I will announce it."

"Akira says you should not —" Tamaya attempted.

"Akira does not command me! Nor Rakta! They are my subordinates. You all are! I am Akash!" Bazu grabbed his longstick and leapt onto the Holy Rock, as if to prove it. He tried to boom from on high, but his treble voice couldn't make the Rock ring, no matter how loud he roared, and his swollen shiner made him look too pathetic to fear. "You will both stay with me always. Never out of my sight for an instant, from now until the Season. On First Pomegranate Day, you, my Tether, will go early to the Great Hall to work in the kitchen, like the previous tether, Salistar used to do. No more sitting around in your pretty gown taking compliments. You will ready the weak ones for my spectacular arrival. Bupple, you will accompany me, if you serve me well until then. Rakta will bring a ganeesh and my chair and a full escort of all the best warriors, and I will arrive in grandiose fashion, *Granulara*, The Great Entrance of the Immortal Akash."

"What about the weapon?" Tamaya popped the fantasy cruelly. "Won't you stay here to shoot the nimblies with the weapon? Haven't you figured out how yet, oh Immortal Akash?" she sneered joyfully.

"That is right, Woman, Immortal. I have until the end of time to figure it out. What's the rush?"

"Tell that to the momamas and tethers of the men who die in the cycles between!" she shrieked, daring to step up on the rock with him. He retreated to the high point in the center, trying to stay taller than her. He still looked puny.

"You will both maintain your silence, under penalty of death, through the entire Season in the Great Hall. I am sorry, Bupple. I know you must be excited to tell of your ascension to War Chief. You haven't told anyone, have you?

"No, Sir," Bupple muttered to the floor. "Sir, I'm not trained to be a war chief."

"Ha!" Bazu swatted the idea away with his hand. "That's what Akira said. The old hag insulted you. She said many would die if you were War Chief. She said you were too stupid."

"No, she didn't!" Tamaya objected.

"You weren't there, what do you know?" Bazu snapped back.

Bupple looked up, more in defense of Tamaya than himself. "It is true. I am not trained. I don't know battle tactics. It would be like you, Sir, trying to be Akash with no training." Bupple's meaty paw flew to his fleshy jowls. His eyes bulged in horror as his words echoed from the Holy Rock.

"Trying?" Bazu squealed from on high. "Trying? Have I not succeeded? I am the Immortal Akash, proof we don't need to listen to the Old Ones and all their windy babble. Isn't that right, Woman? You've read their so-called wisdom. Is there anything in all those books that I don't already know?"

Tamaya had to think fast. There was only one thing, really, and he was going to keep on not knowing that. "The books in the Death Tunnel?" she asked dumbly.

Bazu rolled his eyes. "Well of course the books in the tunnel! What other books would I be talking about?"

"Well then, no, there's nothing but a bunch of lying egomaniacs making up stories about how great they are. You've mastered that already, in just one cycle." Flashing her most brilliant smile, she gathered up her things and carried them into her new sleeping spot, inside the Death Tunnel where she felt most comfortable.

Earth, September 2020

Did we cause this?

Lorraine stared idly out the kitchen window at the unseasonably early rainstorm. She had been going into work almost every day lately. She felt she did better work there, despite her private home office, her high-speed internet connection and the fact that only a few "stalwarts" were usually present. There were fewer Zoom meetings lately. Most of the clients and subconsultants were shut down even tighter than the engineering company she worked for. Until now, that is. Now, three of the "stalwarts" had tested positive. One was in the hospital on a respirator.

Lorraine had tested negative, but the outbreak had shuttered the place. "Don't come in," her boss said unequivocally, in spite of his earlier concerns about productivity. There was, at present, little to produce. Pay was no problem; she had an insane amount of comp time on the books that she never thought she'd take.

With nowhere to go and nothing to do, she watched the rain. It was pouring down hard now, running down the driveway, puddling on the lawn, percolating slowly into the rich topsoil. Not like the soil along the river at the Look 'N Up. That wasn't really soil. It was river alluvium. Sand and gravel, no clay, no organics. Nothing to absorb the water that seeped through it. Nothing to chemically grab any contaminants, or microbes. Nothing to stop them from sinking right through to the water table, the river, the bay, the ocean.

Lifting her eyes to the damp horizon, she relived the day on the riverbank of the Look 'N Up, when she had sprayed grout over the mess that had been the Akash of Nauve and the Queen of the Nimbumblyborg. In her full protection suit, N95 mask and nitrile gloves, she had covered that alien bat-borne pathogen. Out of sight, out of mind. But, underneath?

She shuddered, turned away from the window, and opened her laptop to Google. She'd heard that the first known cases of Covid in the U.S. were detected in California. And, she'd just seen a special on TV that suggested bats were the source. It talked about how common bat-borne pathogens were, and how sometimes those relationships can evolve in completely separate environments, if they find a similar niche. A cave in China, a tiny cave in California, a network of caves in a tiny world in another dimension that harbored the vicious bumbly bats...

Upstairs, Belinda and Baput were Zooming with Jerry. They'd seen that TV special too.

"I guess a lot of bats have germs, not just yours," Belinda comforted Baput. "It started in China. On their bats, not your bumblies. It's not the same as The Curse."

The screen flicked as Baput's mind raced. A window opened up to the site Lorraine was looking at, the one about bats and Corona Virus. "But maybe it spread from here, somehow, to China, to their bats, and then came back to us�"

"Aww, that's crazy!" Jerry interrupted. "All the way to China, then back? If it was from here, we would have got it first. There's no way."

"Are you sure, Jerry?" Baput asked softly, eyes glistening. "Are you sure we didn't cause this?"

"Don't say that, Baput!" Belinda cried, horrified.

"Yeah!" Jerry agreed. "You just shut up about that, you hear?"

Meanwhile, at the Look 'N Up, Fran sat at her kitchen table, sipping coffee and reading a weekly news magazine. Elmer's footsteps rumbled down the stairs. He tromped through the kitchen in his boots, headed for the dripping orchard, where the pomegranates swelled in anticipation of the upcoming harvest.

"It ain't supposed to rain yet!" he griped. "They're almost ripe! They'll mold. I've gotta check..."

"Elmer, look." Fran interrupted his grousing. "They say Covid was detected in California much earlier than we thought."

"Yeah?" Elmer wrestled his raincoat from the crowded closet. "So what?"

Fran reached for him, touched his arm before he slipped it into his jacket. "Elmer. The Curse. Did we cause this?"

"Cause what?"

"The pandemic," Fran answered breathlessly.

"Of course not!" Elmer snapped without hesitation. "It started in Wuhan, China, on the whole other side of the world, in a lab, or some animal market or something." He turned to face Francine squarely. "And don't you ever say that again!"

He stormed out the door without looking back.

"OK" Fran whispered to herself, "I won't tell him."

Water sheeted down the window as Fran watched Elmer disappear around the corner to the shop. The shop with the shower in the back room, where Lorraine had washed after she sprayed concrete all over the remains of the Queen of the Nimbumblyborg and Baput's grandpa, the Akash.

Frozen to crystals by the liquid nitrogen Patrick had pumped into the cave hole, they had dropped together to the ground when the bottom fell out of the cave, cracked off by the sudden cold. There, they had melted into a black slime that Lorraine had buried under a spray of runny grout. When she had finished spraying, she had run to that back room of the shop to shower and wash her clothes. She was so worried about that "Curse", that pathogen, that she had used way too much bleach, and killed the septic.

He was such a nice man, Mr. Emery. He came with his pumper truck and sucked the septic while Elmer was in town. "We had some foreign workers here," Fran had explained. "They didn't know how to use the washer properly. It's interesting, you never know what familiar thing is going to be an obstacle for someone from somewhere else." Fran showed her empathy.

"Yeah, I know," Mr. Emery agreed. "They're not ignorant. Some things are just different. My wife and I have an exchange student at home. She's from China."

"It's just wonderful to see how people from a more primitive place react to our modern gadgets, isn't it?" Fran recalled her friends and workers fondly.

"Not this girl!" Mr. Emery laughed. "She thinks *we're* Podunk. She's from a big city. Wuhan, it's called. And her folks are more educated than me and the Mrs. They're both scientists. They work in a big medical lab over there," he had informed her proudly as he removed his thick rubber gloves and wiped his hands. A blue-gray globule clung to his sleeve, just above where the gloves ended. Fran remembered seeing it there, remembered wondering if she should say something, choosing to be polite instead, to not interrupt what the nice man was saying. After all, he was a professional, right? He knew what he was doing.

"She's going home tomorrow." Mr. Emery had continued. "I'm pretty sure we learned more from her than she did from us. We're sure gonna miss her." Mr. Emery threw the wipe in with the soiled hose.

"Well, Mrs. Musik, you're all set. Sign here. Have a nice day." Mr. Emery climbed into his truck and headed home to his wife and the Chinese exchange student, and that globule went with him.

Fran put her hand on her forehead and shuddered. *Elmer's right*, she realized. *No good deed goes unpunished.* But Elmer didn't want to hear about it, so she bore her guilt alone.

Asian Hate

"Go home and take your disease with you!" an angry female voice woke Baput from a dream, a meditation, *what?* He thought it was a dream. A nightmare, really. He thought he was awake, but was he? *Where* was he? Not in his bed in the quarters at Patrick's place, or at the Look 'N Up. And this was certainly not Nauve!

The whole world shook, rattled and screeched. It was moving! It was a moving box, like Patrick's van. Streaks of light and dark sped past the windows. There were people sitting along the sides of the rocking box. Some had masks on their faces, covering their noses and mouths. They seemed tired and resigned, like the warriors did in the middle of the three-day battle. No one looked at him.

"Yeah, get the hell out of here, Kung Flu!" Baput turned toward the voice behind him. A tall woman with straight blond hair removed the cap from her steaming drink and threw it on a short, elderly woman who Baput recognized as someone Earth people would call "Asian."

The Asian woman looked down on her soiled jacket, and a shorthaired man in a red cap shoved her from behind. She collapsed onto the filthy floor of the subway car. "It's all your fault we're dying!" he yelled. "I lost my job!"

Now the tired, seated people came to life, but not to the aid of the victim. They lined up in the aisle to assault her, one after the other, spitting on her, kicking her, and blaming her for the pandemic that had killed their mother, their brother, their child...

They blame these Asian people! Baput's eyes snapped open. He was back in his bedroom at Patrick's place. He wished he was at the Look 'N Up, so he could talk to Jerry, like he used to. *But Jerry said not to talk about it, ever. To* never *admit it was us! And I agreed, because I didn't want to put the others in danger. I had to protect my family, and my Earth family, too. But that was before I realized they're blaming the Asian people, and hurting them instead of us!*

I need to talk to Popa. Popa always knows the right thing to do. I guess that's why he could never be Akash. His new cynicism brought a smile to his face, despite the guilt. *Yeah, ask Popa.*

Baput stayed silent through breakfast, watching Popa's every move. A couple of times Valko caught him staring and leaned into him, his eyes wide.

Felsic looked from one to the other, but decided to keep his mouth shut. He left for the shop as soon as Salistar cleared the table and carried the dishes into the kitchen.

When they were finally alone, and Baput still didn't speak, Valko prompted roughly, "What? Or should I say, 'what troubles you, my Akash?'" He got out of his chair and knelt on one knee, his head bowed.

"Get up, Popa! I need to talk to you. It's, well, it's Earth stuff."

Valko got back in his chair and leaned in again, grinning. "What do I know of Earth stuff? I stay here and make something called railings for some building I'll never see, and can't even imagine. I don't go on the iPlane or watch your teevee. How I am supposed to know about Earth stuff?"

"You know right and wrong, Popa. Right and wrong are the same everywhere, in all the 'wheres'".

Valko nodded.

Baput took a deep, Akashic breath and began. "The Nimbumblyborg is gone, but the Curse is still here. It has spread beyond the cave to the people of Earth. I didn't tell you because we're safe. We stay here all the time, like you said. But the Earth people are dying. Lots of them, in all the otherwheres, all the places on Earth. Not all of them yet, but, Popa, it's the Curse! It was released somehow when the Queen and, um, G-pa, fell through the bottom of the cave onto the ground, and Lorraine tried to bury them in that goop she sprayed�"

"Yes, Son, I remember," Valko interrupted. "So, the Curse, *our* Curse, is killing the people of Earth?"

"Yes. I am sure it's our Curse. I have evidence."

"Evidence," Valko murmured. "What does Jerry say?"

Baput leveled his eyes at his popa. "He says we shouldn't ever tell anyone it's from us. The people will come and kill us. Like those RID men, only a hundred times more, Popa!" His dream flashed through his head, the never-ending line of people...

"So, I was afraid to tell anyone. But now, they are blaming the people called Asians because they think it came from their place. They hate them. They are hurting old women because they look like they're from where they think the disease comes from. Beating them up, or worse, just because of how they look, when they didn't have anything to do with it at all!"

"And we did!" Valko rose from his chair. "And now, they hate these people in our stead." He started pacing the floor, his hands clasped behind his back. "They should be hating *us*. You should tell the people it's us, not these other people."

"But, Popa, they will come for us! For Patrick and Lorraine! For Belinda! They might go after the Look 'N Up, too!"

"Let them come!" Valko roared. "We will fight! Like we fought the nimblies and bumblies at Nauve."

"They are men, Popa! Not bugs and bats. There are too many of them. They have guns. They will wipe us out, Popa! They will kill us all!"

"You are Akash. Akash tells only the truth. Or will you bend the rules like the old Akash?" he sneered cruelly.

"Popa! I speak only the truth! But do I have to speak *all* of the truth? If we don't speak of this at all, to anyone..."

"And leave these other people to take the blame? It is the same as lying."

"But Popa, what can we do? There are millions of people, all over the world. We are only us four. They'll kill us all! Even Momama!"

The deep eyes above the dark beard were broken in a way that shattered the young ruler. "You are the Akash."

Burdened with Earth stuff for the first time, Valko turned his broad back and slouched from the room, looking about six inches shorter than he used to.

Baput returned to his bedroom to meditate. He wouldn't be present for the morning session of Belinda's school. He hoped she wouldn't miss him too much. She would be seeing him soon enough, if his plan worked. He placed his meditation cushion in the middle of the floor and sat down cross-legged, his hands on his knees, cupped upwards with the thumbs and forefingers barely touching. He inhaled a slow, deep breath and held it briefly, then exhaled, long and slow. Again and again, as the room fell away. The whole crazy Earth disappeared and he rose above the sky to the Akashic Plane. He hovered there for a while; he couldn't tell how long. He was outside of time. Time was the river flowing by with all the thoughts and feelings of Earth and Nauve, past and present. He was outside of it, watching it from some invisible bank. When he had gathered his thoughts, and his courage, he inhaled sharply and sank through a cloud to a lower level; Earth's iPlane.

On the iPlane, time was *very* present. It pushed him from behind, pressing him toward the rushing stream. He braced himself against the rush, that surge of energy that coursed through his cells. Everything streaked by at accelerated speed, like the dark world outside the window of the train car in his dream. A cacophony of voices, some angry, some singing, some whining. He heard them all, in all their languages. He understood all the words, but their meaning escaped him. He breathed faster. He couldn't do it. He could never break into that racket and be heard!

Deliberately, he slowed his breathing again. "Silence," he whispered into the roar. "Silence!" He held his breath. A window opened up in the streaking mist.

Belinda settled down at her computer and tried to concentrate on Algebra. The kids' cameras were all off. Who knew if they were even there? Once in a while, a teacher would call on you, un-mute you, and you'd have to turn on your camera and answer. You could raise your hand or ask questions in the chat box.

Formulas appeared on the screen, a cursor pointing to 'x', 'y' and 'z', while the math teacher's voice explained what they stood for. The feed buffered as it switched back to the instructor's face. His bushy auburn hair seemed to dance as his image rocked from light to dark, sharp to blurry.

Baput caused that sometimes, when he was watching a lesson and got excited about something and tried to look it up on the "iPlane". *But Baput isn't here. Where* is *he?*

"Hey, what?" the instructor reacted. His feed was messing up, too. Baput didn't usually mess up the teacher's feed, just her own reception.

The instructor disappeared, his image melting into a blue mist with a green core that slowly focused into a green face. Baput's face.

"Dad!" Belinda yelled.

Patrick dropped the dish back into the sink and ran to her, wiping his wet hands on his pants. "What is it, Baby?" His eyes fell on Belinda's computer screen. Baput's face was as clear as if he were standing right there. Belenda rushed to Patrick's side and clung to him.

"Can everyone see it?" he asked her.

"What's going on?" her teacher's voice blared, then silence.

"I think so," Belinda whispered.

"People of Earth," the green stranger boomed into the silence. "I am Baput. My family and I came here by accident, six years ago. We were fighting our predators with a weapon we didn't understand, and it blew us through a portal to your world.

"The predators followed us," he simplified. "Some of them are bats. They carry a disease, a pathogen," he used Lorraine's word. "We call it The Curse."

Patrick gasped. Belinda buried her face in his side.

"I am the Akash, the leader, of my people. It is my duty to tell you the truth. Our Curse is your Covid 19, Coronavirus."

"You aren't!" Patrick took a step toward the green young man on the screen. Belinda followed, still clinging.

"The people you call 'Asian' did not cause this. It did not come from them. It came from us, the green people. There are only four of us on Earth, and we hope to be leaving soon. We are very sorry. We didn't mean to come here and bring your people harm. It was all an accident." The image flickered, blurred, and returned.

"Stop hating Asians. They are not responsible for this. It was us, the Green People from Nauve. We didn't mean to. Please stop hating. If you must, you can hate us, but you will never find us."

He vanished, and a baffled science teacher gradually took shape, alongside a chat box full of questions he couldn't answer.

Patrick turned to Belinda, "If you must, you can hate us?" he mocked, "You'll never find us? They've been here before, and to the Look 'N Up!" He grabbed Belinda's shoulders, shook her a little. "Where is he?"

"He meditates best in his bedroom."

Patrick didn't even stop for his coat. He dashed from the house into the crisp September morning.

Belinda's phone rang. It was Jerry. "Did you see that?"

"Yes," Belinda replied in a whimper. "I was Zooming for school, and�"

"Yeah, me too," Jerry barged in. "But get this. My Mom was using her online accounting software, and he popped up on there, too. You should have heard her scream! He's popping up everywhere, Bel. He's gone viral!"

Patrick hammered his fist on the quarter's door in a way that didn't sound at all like the mellow pacifist they'd come to know. Salistar started for the door, but Valko sent her into the kitchen with a gesture. He knew what this was about. Glad Felsic was in the shop, he flung the door open wide. "Come in, my friend," he welcomed.

"Where is he?" this new Patrick demanded.

Valko gestured to Baput's bedroom. Baput appeared in the doorway. Valko let Patrick past, but followed on his heels.

Patrick rushed at Baput, wagging his finger at the young Akash. "How could you?" He wailed. "You've endangered us all! Don't you know that?"

"I have no URL address," Baput replied calmly, as if still in a trance. "I am untraceable."

"You're not. You know they've been here before. They've been to the Look 'N Up."

"That was only a few. We just call the Sheriff, and he makes them go away."

"That was before you went online and told the world you started the pandemic that's killing their loved ones! Now there will be thousands of people after you, after us. And those RID guys will make sure everyone knows where we are. Oh, Baput! After all you've seen, you still don't get how brutal this world can be."

Salistar stared at them from the kitchen door like a zebkin doe caught in the garden.

Baput looked at Patrick, his eyes an oily pool of misery. "I know they will hate us. But it's better than letting them beat up innocent people."

"They shouldn't be hating and beating up anyone!" Patrick protested.

"But we caused this. They're right to hate us."

"Hate is never right!" Patrick snapped.

The room went silent. Baput inflated himself on a deep, Akashic breath. He was almost as tall as Valko, and much taller than Patrick. He still wore his Akashic robe. He spread his arms, to show it off and make himself look even bigger, like the old Akash, his G-pa, used to do.

"I am Akash," he declared in a smooth, resonant voice. "I told the truth. It was the right thing to do, so I did it."

Patrick shook his head. "You didn't look up, Baput! Well, you stuck up for the Asian people, that's great. But you didn't think about us! We're all in danger now. What about Belinda?" Patrick wailed, "You jeopardized her. An innocent kid! *My* kid. Your, um, betrothed!"

Salistar squeaked from the doorway.

Patrick went on, wagging his knotty finger. "You know, we're aliens too, as far as they're concerned. We're as different as you are, except we're from here. And we hosted you. So did Elmer and Fran and Jerry. You remember when they came to the Look 'N Up and attacked your Momama?"

Valko stepped in front of his wife. "Salistar has nothing to do with this. I will never let them near her!" His right hand twitched to the hip that usually held his machete, like Elmer would sometimes twitch for his pistol. "We need guns, Patrick. Why don't you have any guns?"

"Guns aren't the answer, Valko. We can't take them all on. They'll wipe us out for sure if we pull guns on them." Patrick withdrew his finger. His eyes darted around the room in different directions. Then he lowered his chin into his clenched fist and muttered, "what to do...." He looked up at their rapt, green faces. "I'll call Elmer."

"He will say, 'guns'" Valko predicted.

FBI

"What the —" Boyd shouted at his desktop.

Agents Kramer and Goldsmith gathered around him. "It's him!" Rita breathed.

Baput's avocado-green face filled the screen, his resonant voice calmly explaining that yes, he was an alien who had come through a space portal, pursued by man-eating monsters.

"It's all true!" Boyd muttered. He hovered the cursor over another tab, FBI's Surveillance Center.

"Don't!" Rita touched his arm.

"Yeah, wait!" Kramer agreed. "Listen! Did you hear what he just said?"

Boyd clicked to the other site anyway. It didn't matter. The green kid was there too, confessing his people's involvement in the global pandemic.

"Hey!" Kramer objected, "That's a secure site!"

Boyd's fingers clattered over the keyboard. A black box appeared in the lower left corner of the screen. Seemingly random letters, numbers, colons and backslashes scrolled up and out of sight until they ended with an error code: "Address not found".

"That's impossible," Boyd muttered, clicking more keys. "He's untraceable. There's no IP address. No URL!"

RID Headquarters

"Hey, Otto! Is this your buddy?" Fred Brice was checking in with the online RID Headquarters when the green kid showed up on the screen.

Rod Otto, ex deputy, and Dirk Milch, Squad Leader of LA RID gathered around Fred's screen as Baput aired his confession.

"It is!" Otto spoke over the droning voice. "That's the kid!"

"He says they started the pandemic!" Dirk remarked.

Otto snapped his fingers. "The bats! I stepped in some of them, but I didn't get sick."

"Are you sure?" the others asked. Dirk stepped back. Fred wheeled his desk chair away.

"It was three years ago!" Otto argued. "I haven't been sick a day."

"Did you take the test?"

"Why, no, I, like I said, I ain't sick."

"You'd better get tested," Dirk replied, putting more distance between them. "Well, go on, now!" he swatted at Otto from across the room. "We don't want you hanging around here!"

"But you said it's all bullshit!"

"Get out!" the Squad Leader ordered.

Otto turned obediently toward the door, then whirled back to face his boss. "Bullshit or not, it's killing our country. Everything's shut down. You can't even get toilet paper, for shit's sake! Look:" He counted on his long, thin fingers. "We know they started it. The kid just said so himself. We know exactly where they are. We know their schedule. Harvest time is coming up in about a week. Those farmers, Ian's guys, they'll do their inspection. That will keep the sheriff and the Look 'N Up people occupied. And the aliens will know they're coming, so no way they'll be there. They'll be holed up at the cockeyed brother's place. Where else can they go? That's where we'll get 'em."

"The place with the scary little girl?" Fred giggled. He hadn't been there, but he'd heard some pretty amusing stories.

"That's right Fred. But this time I'll duct tape her mouth shut and stuff her into the trunk of my car. Her stoner dad, too. You know what? He says he don't believe in guns." He grinned, "He doesn't have a single one. And we'll be there with the whole damn RID army! Real men! Not guys who are gonna woos out over a little cockeyed girl," he jeered. "Wipe the diseased aliens off the planet. Ain't that what we're here for?"

Dirk nodded abruptly. "When you come back with a clean test, we'll talk. Now get outta here!"

"Don't you do it without me, Dirk. Please?" Otto lowered himself to beg. "I've been after these guys for a long time. I'm the one who tipped you off, remember?"

"I do," Dirk nodded. "And I won't forget it, when this puts RID on the map. This is huge, guys! But I need you all to swear you won't tell anyone we know where they are. Not even your wife, Fred, or the other members. Not yet. I'll coordinate with HQ. We have to plan this. It will be small, but epic! We want lots of coverage. But that means some of us might go to jail, or even die. This is war! Now, promise. RID honor!" He raised his fist in a vaguely Nazi salute. They all saluted back and clicked their heels, tacitly promising their silent obedience.

First Pomegranate Day
Earth, The Ripening

"Yes, Son, just like that." Valko nodded at Baput, finally satisfied.

By stretching his fingers, his palm, as far as he could, Baput was finally able to encircle a whole pomegranate without touching it. But could he tell if the fruit was ripe? Popa always could.

"What now, Popa? What should I feel?" Stretched above his head, his hand started to shake. It touched the pomegranate. He let go and lowed his aching hand.

Valko shook his head, rumbling softly below his beard.

"What difference does it make, Popa?" Baput asked, rubbing his palm with his other hand.

"What's the difference?" Valko asked incredulously, drawing his head back to stare at his son. "Last First Pomegranate Day, when the kips on the Look 'N Up trees were ripe, the nimblies and bumblies awakened and the Rock rang out, just like on Nauve."

"But, Popa, the nimblies and bumblies are all dead. We don't have the Net, so the portal won't open. And the RID people know we were at the Look 'N Up last First Pomegranate Day, so they'll come looking for us. There will be more of them, and they're much angrier now because of the Curse. We should just stay here."

Valko grunted, shook his head. "No! We must go there and fight them! Protect Elmer and his family. This is our fault, and our fight. We have to wipe the RID men out, as we did the nimblies and bumblies. Then we can stay there. Your momama and Uncle Felsic *must* return to Look 'N Up. They are miserable here. They miss Francina and Elmer so much! So, when, Son? When will the battle begin?"

"Popa, it's not the same..."

"Nothing is the same!" Valko roared. He seized his son's hand and held it above a smaller fruit on a lower branch.

Baput surrounded it completely with his large hand and held it there, not shaking, not touching. Could he feel the gas seeping from the ripening fruit, or was it just his imagination?

"What do you say, my Akash?" Valko prompted, more gently.

"Tomorrow?" Baput guessed.

A broad smile lit Valko's face. He nodded.

Baput grinned triumphantly. He'd finally done it! "Tomorrow," he repeated, swallowing his proud smile. "I'll tell Patrick."

Cleanup

Valko went straight to the shop to tell Felsic the news, while Baput sprinted to the quarters to tell his momama. He threw open the door to an empty, windswept space. There was no clutter. The floor was spotless.

"Momama?" Baput squeaked. A metallic clanging came from the kitchen. He peeked through the doorway. The floor was littered with boxes and backpacks stuffed with pots, pans, plates and silverware. Once again, he found Salistar standing on that rocky stool, reaching into the back of that same high cupboard.

"Momama!" Baput cried, daring to enter room he, the Akash, like any other man, was not supposed to enter. "What are you doing?" He stabilized the stool. Salistar lowered herself and, leaning on his shoulder, climbed down with a cake mold in her hand.

"Are the kips ripe? When?" she asked, resting both hands on his shoulders, the light pan squeezed between two fingers. She smiled up at him, her eyes shining.

"Tomorrow, I think," Baput replied. Had an Akash ever predicted the arrival of First Pomegranate Day with so much doubt?

"We go Nauve tomorrow," she sang happily.

It wrenched Baput's gut to have to tell her. "Momama, we can't. We don't have the Net. I have searched the iPlane for two cycles, and I have never found anything like it. Nothing looks quite like it, and it's so light! Nothing on Earth has such a low specific gravity."

Star looked at him blankly, then she backed away and waved the cake mold at him. "It won't matter. I made a mold and cast it on the Plane, like you taught me. We go Nauve on First Pomegranate Day. Or, to the Look 'N Up. Back to Francina."

Baput beckoned to her. Stuffing the cake pan into a backpack, she came to him, let him put his arms around her. He could almost make her disappear, like Popa did. "You are not happy here, Momama. I'm sorry." He rocked her back and forth.

She leaned her head back, so she could see his face. "First Pomegranate Day is always time for change. A new cycle, a new, um, *place*. But we must leave no trace of us here."

"Why, Momama?"

"Because that's how places work," she explained. "You leave no trace. You were never there. If that's how you want it."

What does Momama knew about places? Baput wondered. He didn't even quite understand them, after six years on Earth. But what mattered now was that sadness in her eyes. It tore at Baput's heart. He knew this crazy mess wasn't his fault, but he was Akash. He was responsible. "You really want to leave here?" he asked.

The wounded look seemed to freeze on her face. "I don't know 'leave'," she sniffed, "but I am not happy here, my Akash. I am removing us from this place. You must do the same, all of you. Pack everything up for Nauve, or destroy it. Don't leave a trace of us. That way, we can go Nauve on First Pomegranate Day, tomorrow."

"If it was Francina's place we were leaving, would you leave something behind?"

"If it was Francina's place, I wouldn't want to leave," she replied as if it were obvious.

"But, Momama?" Baput had to ask, "what about Belinda?"

Star's smile reappeared like the sun from behind a fleeting cloud. "She will be with us, of course. She'll be your Tether."

That Night

Long after the sun set on the Look 'N Up, Elmer drove the four-wheeler to the point where they had barricaded the trail to the Rock with the wood from the "burn pile". Fran and Jerry rode in the trailer, hanging onto the clattering load of Earth goodies their friends would take home to Nauve, in the off-chance that the portal opened.

"We're packing from here," Elmer grunted as he hefted a heavy box of axe heads, hammers, scythe blades and sharpening files. Fran rushed to slip his headlamp over his bill cap and switched it on. She and Jerry put theirs on, too, and lifted cases of wine bottles with reuseable corks for Felsic and canning jars for Salistar. The jars were scarce, but Fran would send Salistar off with the best she had, hoping the supply chains would be repaired by next harvest season.

Elmer came back for the bellows. Fran and Jerry carried the old-time two-handled tree saw together and laid it across the crest of the Rock. They all made several more trips back and forth carrying enough weapons for all the men of Nauve: Machetes, broadswords and compound bows.

"Too bad about the toilet paper," Fran voiced her regret as she placed a box of steel-tipped arrows and darts on the growing pile next to the Rock. "Valko wanted that more than anything, except maybe all these blades and the guns we won't let him take."

"Well, 'no guns' was your idea, Fran," Elmer reminded her, setting the last box of blades down on the ground. "And we couldn't have supplied them with TP for long. These days, we can barely get enough for ourselves. We'll be using leaves, like they do, soon enough." He tried to wipe his brow, skewing his hat and headlamp. "Get up there, Son. I'll hand you this stuff."

Jerry had been itching to get on the Rock since they'd arrived. He could feel it buzzing below the audible range. He put his left foot on it, and jerked back. "Wow!" He was expecting the buzz, he'd felt it before, three years ago, but, "Wow!" Putting his weight on a leg that felt like it was evaporating, he brought his other leg up and stood at the peak of the smooth orb. "It's really buzzing up here!" he declared, his voice shaking.

Boyd adjusted his headphones and turned on the screen when the alarm beeped. It was almost midnight. The other agents were in their makeshift bedrooms in the back of the store. The active camera was the one that showed the orb, the space portal. It was pitch dark, and foggy, or the lenses were. All he could see was three beams flashing around, once in a while picking up a blurred image of the orb, or a box of something, but he couldn't tell what. Was that a bellows? A tree saw?

He could hear voices, though. The Musiks. Elmer, Francine, and the kid, Jerry, who said the orb was buzzing. He knew how the kid felt, from his first visit to the orb. It hadn't buzzed the last time he'd checked it, eighteen months ago. Half of three years. The date that was furthest from the triennial event. Now, it was time. Tomorrow would be three years since the alien monsters had appeared at the county fairgrounds. The orb was resonating. That resonance would open a portal to another dimension. Of that, Boyd had no doubt.

Jerry took the last box from Elmer and searched the Rock for an empty spot. The highest point, in the middle, was empty except for the tree saw he had draped across it. He didn't want to put a box there. It might disrupt the energy or something. Besides, he wanted to see what would happen when that long, flexible strip of metal got to vibrating, when the time came. He set the box of steel arrows on top of a heavy crate of hammer and axe heads, files and chisels. "Those guys are going to have to sit on the boxes or something," he remarked. "There's so much stuff, there's no room for the people." His voice shook. "Seems like it's buzzing even more. Come check it out!"

"No thanks," Fran declined.

"Get down offa there, Boy!" Elmer commanded. "That thing gives me the willies. Let's go."

Jerry jumped off the Rock in a single leap. He went to his knees when he landed, unable to engage his shaky legs. Fran helped him up.

"Do you hear that?" Elmer asked.

Boyd heard it. The buzzing of the orb was quite audible now. It sounded like music. A harmony of keening tones, a throbbing base line, percussion and a sparkly tinkling sound.

"It's all that steel!" the kid said. "All those blades are vibrating. The swords, the tree saw..."

"The jars and bottles are rattling," said Francine.

"And the hammers," Elmer's voice added. "You know how those set it off."

Boyd did. He couldn't forget how that strange object resonated when he'd struck it with that hammer. *Hammers, saws, bottles, swords? And what was that about toilet paper? They're getting ready to go back to the home planet! Taking all the stuff they don't have at home. Stuff to fight the monsters with.*

"Are we setting it off?" Elmer's voice interrupted Boyd's thoughts. The music was putting him into a reverie, trying to take him to wherever he'd gone when he'd hammered on the thing almost three years ago.

"There's no Net, Dad," he heard Jerry answer. "Uncle Patrick hit it with the hammer lots of times, last cycle, and it didn't go off early. I don't think it can, until tomorrow morning, First Pomegranate Day."

"Maybe we should take the stuff off until morning, just in case," Fran suggested.

"Nah." Elmer overrode her. "It's gotta be ready first thing in the morning, and I won't be here to help. I've gotta stand guard."

Boyd strained to make out the distorted voices until the eerie music drowned them out completely. Boyd turned up the volume, but that just made the music louder, blasting through his cell walls. Fighting to stay conscious, he listened analytically, dissecting the sound, analyzing it: A choir of steel blades of various shapes. Behind it, the tinkling of glass bells and the weighty percussion of hammers that seemed to multiply the sound, *extending* it. And beneath it all, the low-frequency warble of the long, flexible saw...

Nauve, Preparation

It had been a long, boring month in the Holy Cave. Bazu never left for the first two weeks, until his black eye faded. Then, he occasionally ventured out to the practice field with Bupple, but he refused to go to the Great Hall to meet with the Council and help prepare his people for First Pomegranate Day and the attack of the nimblies and bumblies, as the Akash was expected to do.

Tamaya spent her nights exploring the back wall of the death tunnel with the dim oil lamp. She avoided the boor, and left the Shavarandu Lamp off. Bazu seemed to sleep with one eye open, always guarding his precious, if limited, domain.

Tamaya groped the smooth back wall of the tunnel between the bookshelves. She explored every inch she could reach with sore fingertips, finding nothing but that infinite smoothness, until she checked the very last slim, dark column between the final bookshelf and the wall. Her fingers roamed in their systematic routine until they found it.

It was a long, thin line of raised bumps. They clicked softly and gave a bit when she ran her fingers over them. They were square, about the size of her fingertip. She counted them. Twenty-five. The number of letters in the Akashic Alphabet. She brought the dim light closer and squinted. Were they letters? She pressed a square. It clicked, and she felt something move behind that wall, that door. *Learn to Open*. She recalled the message on the plate in the middle of the blank wall, by Bazu's precious indoor boor.

She spent her days avoiding her cohabitants and pretending to read while she thought up different passwords to try that night, and waited for her bleeding cycle to begin. It was late.

First Pomegranate Day arrived at last. The Orchard Keeper declared it so the evening before. It should have been his son, Kaysee, just before his ascension, to prove he was ready. But Kaysee was no more.

At first light, Tamaya dressed in her wedding outfit, her precious robe wrapped around her skimpy pomegranate-skin bra and panties, and stepped out of the Death Tunnel. The robe tingled so fiercely she could barely stand it.

"You're wearing that?" Bazu demanded as he untangled his foot from his covers and struggled to stand. Bupple dressed quickly in his niche in the corner. "You're going there to work, you know, like Salistar did." The previous Tether of Akash, Salistar, had been in charge of the entire women's operation of feeding and supplying the troops and caring for the wounded during the three-day battle to come.

Ignoring the sarcasm implied in her husband's comment, Tamaya picked up the elaborately carved, and still unused, rolling pin. "Akira told me to wear it," she uttered softly, but clearly. She walked past the Holy Rock toward the wide arch at the top of the stairs. She stepped outside. "When I *go*." She tasted the word, now flavored with a new, mysterious meaning. She seemed to float down the steep stairs, her gossamer gown, pink with reflected dawn, billowing up all around her.

Earth, Goodbyes

The Look 'N Up Plumbing van was loaded with just about everything from the quarters and the shop that wasn't too big to carry. All except the porch rail project, which had been neatly put away, unfinished. Valko had assured Patrick that the portal would not open without the Net, and that the crew would all be back to complete the tedious undertaking on time, if they lived. What he didn't tell Patrick was that the project was driving him out of his mind with boredom. It grew worse each day. He needed a release. He needed to fight. It was the Season, and he was a warrior. He wasn't going to the Look 'N Up to return to Nauve through the portal. He wasn't going to fight nimblies and bumblies either, although he gladly would, in the off chance any survivors emerged from the cave. He was going to the Look 'N Up fully expecting to do battle with Earth Men.

The families gathered at the van in the pre-dawn darkness to say their goodbyes, not knowing if they were temporary or permanent, a few hours or forever. Lorraine stood back, her arms folded, while Belinda hugged Felsic first, then Valko. She didn't even look at Baput. Instead, she engaged Salistar in an intense conversation in Nauvian. Salistar smiled through her tears and nodded. Belinda broke away, gurgled a sob and ran to the house.

Baput craned his neck after her. "Goodbye, Bel," he called, "maybe."

Lorraine broke his longing gaze, grabbed his hand and shook it roughly. She let go abruptly and addressed the gloomy, green-skinned crowd. "Well, guys, it's been real. Have a nice, um, trip. I've got to go check..." She gestured toward the house, then sprinted that way. Patrick made his way to the driver's door while the Nauvians slowly filed into the back of the van. Salistar hung back, just a bit.

Belinda's sobs rattled the walls and ceiling.

"Are you okay, Honey?" Lorraine called up the stairs.

"Leave me alone!" Belinda wailed from her bedroom.

"I'm making some toast," Lorrain offered. "You want some?"

"Just leave me alone!" Belinda screeched. She erupted into a warbly, drawn-out bawl.

"Okay, Babe," Lorraine answered, as gently as she could. "Come on out when you feel like it."

The Look 'N Up

Fran shook as she hugged Elmer goodbye. "Don't you want to come, Hon, see them off? Felsic?"

"Of course I want to!" Elmer replied. "But it's the first day of harvest. You know those inspectors won't tell us they're coming until they're right there at the gate. I have to catch 'em and keep them away from there."

"The trail to the river is blocked. They don't seem too interested in walking." Fran squeezed his arm.

Elmer pulled away. "Today of all days, I can't trust them. Fran, if they see that portal open, we'll have the Feds crawling all over this place. What if those guys went through the portal to Nauve?"

"The feds or the RID guys?"

"It don't matter!" Elmer wailed. "Either way, they'd have guns. And those green guys have sticks and spears. And they're so, well, you know."

"Naïve." Fran filled in. "Naïve Nauvians. I guess we've got a lot more to protect than just us. But, if they don't get here soon, it'll all be over. The Nauvians will be gone," she sniffed.

"Gotta go, Mom!" Jerry called from the driveway. He whistled for the dogs. Lassen and Tobey ran to him from two different directions. Brodey stayed on the couch. Just as well. He had already done his duty, providing his doggie DNA to Nauve in the form of four healthy pups.

"I'll be in the west orchard, at the overlook." Elmer told her, and brushed her cheek with the lightest of kisses. "Go on, now." He swatted her butt gently.

"Be careful, Elmer."

He looked past her to Jerry. "You be careful. You, too, Son. No catching a ride to another planet. I need you here on the farm!"

Fran, Jerry and the dogs headed down the trail to the river. Elmer watched their backs until they were out of sight. Then he took his rifle from the rack and loaded it. *After today, it'll all be over. They'll be gone,* he told himself as he drove the 4-wheeler into the west orchard, but he knew that probably wasn't true.

The plump, red pomegranates screamed to be picked. The Pom King of three years ago, he was now the lowest-grossing farmer in the county. *Either way, I'll never have helpers like them again. Never.*

He parked the 4-wheeler under the oak tree that leaned over the driveway. He settled back in his seat, sipped his coffee and watched the gate at the bottom of the driveway for the inspectors, and the tiny cave mouth with the tattered grate for surviving nimblies. In the unlikely event of the latter, he would fire his rifle into the air to warn the others. Valko and Felsic would come running, ready for battle, and the whole thing would play out all over again. Elmer found himself hoping the flying predators would eat the inspectors, but nimblies didn't seem to care for white meat.

Lorrain

Lorrain glanced at the time in the lower right corner of her screen. Four hours had passed! She cocked her ear up at the ceiling. She hadn't heard of peep out of Belinda. *She probably cried herself to sleep. Poor thing.* She closed the laptop and stood up, glancing out the window at the empty driveway. *I'd better check.*

She tiptoed up the stairs, her mind racing. Patrick had surely arrived at the Look 'N Up by now with his illicit cargo. She hoped the portal was, at this moment, whisking those greenies back to the miserable little world they came from. But she knew the portal wouldn't open without the Net. The physics made sense. The Net hovered above the Rock when it was activated, collecting the energy, concentrating it.

But, what about those RID freaks? There's a pretty good chance they'll show up down there today. That was where they last saw our aliens, three years ago at harvest time. And that idiot, Felsic, told that skinhead deputy that the nimblies and bumblies appear every three years. Then that even bigger idiot, the 'smart' one, Baput, had to tell the world that their Curse was actually Covid. What is Patrick walking into down there?

She tapped lightly on Belinda's door. No answer. She turned the knob quietly, opened the door just a crack, and peeked in. The bed was empty. She pushed the door open wider. A light breeze stroked her face. The curtains billowed around the open window. A rope of bedsheets, tied together and knotted every few feet, cascaded over the sill to the ground.

"Belinda!" she yelled out the window. Cussing though her teeth, she untied the end of the sheet rope from the leg of the bed, tossed it to the ground outside and slammed the window shut. She bounded down the stairs and threw the front door open. "Belinda!"

Shaking, she pulled out her phone and dialed Patrick. It rang, then beeped. She looked at the screen. It said, "customer out of range".

"Out of range?" she fumed out loud, "who's ever out of range these days?" Then she remembered. *The Rock! It messes with our signals. No phone, no internet, not even remote control. Especially now, on First Pomegranate Day, when it goes off. They must be right there! And it's happening right now!*

She ducked back into the house, grabbed a jacket, a mask, her phone and her keys and peeled down the driveway in her Subaru.

River Bar

The Look 'N Up Plumbing van hopped and slowed abruptly when the pavement turned to bridge deck. Patrick squinted through the thick mist that shrouded the river. The Look 'N Up mailbox loomed ahead on the right, but Patrick turned left at the end of the bridge. He inched the van down a pair of rutted tire tracks to where it dead-ended. He exhaled in relief when he saw no one was camping in the unofficial river access, his grandpa's old fishing spot. He killed the engine and stepped out, closing the door as quietly as he could. "Here we are," he whispered to himself.

The van rocked beside him and the back door swung open. He'd rigged an interior latch, so his human cargo could escape in an emergency. Shastina and her two grown puppies piled out, nearly knocking him over. In their wake, brown eyes in green faces blinked at him from the dark. He put his finger up to his lips and hissed, "Shhhh!"

Felsic came out first, stamping his feet and rubbing his hands on his forearms to get things circulating. "Whoo�"

"Shhh," Valko repeated, ducking out of the door and unfolding his bulk into a standing position. He leaned in to give Salistar a hand. She was struggling with the straps of her backpack, laden with clanking kitchenware.

Baput was right behind her, holding his hand on the back of the pack to stifle the rattling.

While his various passengers were stretching, sniffing, or relieving themselves, Patrick leaned into the van to begin unloading all the stuff his green friends wanted to take home to Nauve. Everything but the furniture, it seemed. *As if the rock would work without the Net. I guess hope springs eternal,* he mused, reaching for a heavy box of woodworking tools, hand-powered, but made of metal. Valko wouldn't go back to Nauve without some of his beloved steel. *And he can carry it, too,* Patrick resolved when he hefted it.

As if he'd read his mind, Valko appeared and shouldered the heavy load.

Patrick heard a scraping sound. He looked back into the van, where a suitcase had suddenly appeared. *That wasn't there a minute ago!* Patrick looked around at the green folks. They were just now starting to gather around to collect their assigned burdens. Next, a backpack appeared from the depths of the van, as if on its own.

"What the�?"

"Hi, Dad." Belinda appeared, pushing a second backpack ahead of her with her foot, a bulging drawstring bag over her shoulder.

Patrick's hands flew to his face. He took a step back. "What are you doing here? I told you to stay home!"

"Dad! Shhhh!" she replied, climbing out of the van and handing the suitcase to Felsic. "Here's your razors and underwear and stuff, Uncle Felsic", she told him softly.

"My spring guns?" Felsic asked, a bit too loud.

Bel nodded. She shouldered another clanky backpack full of more of Salistar's treasures; seeds, fabrics, plasticware and her special marital rolling pin she'd brought with her from Nauve on that fateful day, exactly six years ago. Bel felt especially honored to carry that for her. Without another word for Patrick, she turned and started picking her way over the rocks and through the blackberries that strayed across the trail to the riverbed.

Baput followed on her heels carrying the bulky cloth sack over his shoulder. His silver-colored meditation bowl glared from the top, encircled by the drawstring.

Felsic trotted after the kids, holding his suitcase on top of his head. The dogs bounded down the slope after him and scattered across the dry river bar, sniffing and squatting.

Valko, his sword, machete and a sheathed knife dangling from his waistband and the heavy wooden box of tools on his shoulder, grasped Salistar's hand. Her backpack clanked in response. He raised his eyebrows, gave Patrick a sympathetic smile, and headed down the bank to join the others.

"What am I going to do with that girl?" Patrick said aloud to himself. He slammed the van door, winced at the noise. Nothing to do now but follow them to the Rock and see them off. *Some* of them. He was going to be holding Belinda real tight, a safe distance away from that darned space portal! "Wave goodbye, Sweetie," he practiced as he made his way to the riverbed. "I mean, to Baput, not me," he amended quickly, glad he'd practiced. He wondered how he'd be feeling now if he thought the portal would actually work. He knew it wouldn't. Not without that mysterious Net. He was more worried about the RID guys.

Valko had to let go of Star's hand, take the box off his shoulder and bow his head in order to pass beneath the bridge. His family walked in front of him in single file along the narrow, muddy bank that hugged the concrete abutment, spray painted with symbols he didn't understand.

Once through that dark tunnel, his view widened to a grey-white expanse of gravel glowing in the dull sun. The fog was lifting, hovering above the flat black surface of the sluggish river.

Salistar rushed ahead, her backpack clanking, to join Baput and Belinda. Patrick was up ahead, too, chatting with Felsic. The dogs bounded back and forth, checking on each group in turn, herding them along on the uneven cobbles. The going was rough, but unobstructed.

Valko raised his burden to his shoulder and trudged on, lagging behind the group, deep in thought. He wanted to go home to Nauve. And he didn't. Here, he could do wonderful things with metal. But he was powerless. He couldn't even see the results of his own work. Felsic was happier here, and Salistar, too, at least when they were on the Look 'N Up. But their happiness didn't matter. His family was in danger here, and his Earth family, too, because of them, with their offensive green presence, and their Curse. They had to go. It was the only way.

Damn those cowards who hide and stalk us, watching us, trying to catch us. To take us away, *whatever that means! Why? They will attack today. On First Pomegranate Day, just like on Nauve, But, not nimblies and bumblies. Men. We fear men! Men like Elmer! His own people! Yet he fears them. He tells us we must hide from them. We sneak to the Holy Rock like dracna stealing grain from the stores.* Our *Holy Rock! When all we wish is to return home...* The last thought left him colder than the chill from his wet mukluks.

Would the portal even work? Baput said it wouldn't without the Net, like last time. Patrick was sure it wouldn't even ring without the thrumming of the nimblies and bumblies in their caves just before they attacked. He said it excited the tiny, invisible creatures he called molecules.

Valko cursed silently and spat on a stalk of mullein that sprung out of the bare gravel. Those soft, slightly fuzzy leaves would be his toilet paper again, once the precious Earth rolls ran out. Too bulky to include in the loads they carried, Francina had promised to stack some on the Rock for them. "I hope she brings lots!" he said aloud, "And lots and lots of steel." He patted the scabbard of the sword at his waist.

His eyes fell on Patrick, striding ahead in his baggy cargo jeans, Salistar's rattling backpack over his shoulder. He wondered how Earth People could mock Kakeeche, the obviously visible creatures that made up the moon, glowing in the sky every night for all to see. *Yet, they teach my son to believe in these tiny, invisible "molecules".*

He looked up and to the left just in time to catch a glimpse of the cold, grey edge of the platform. Beyond that, two figures stood on the riverbank, waving widely and silently.

The Watchers

Boyd's eyes flew open when the alarm beeped. He smelled coffee. Broad daylight streamed through the upper part of the show windows, above the shoe polish. He looked around, embarrassed, and located Kramer and Rita in the kitchen. *Did they see me here, drooling on my keyboard? Was I sleeping all that time, or what?*

The eerie music still hummed in his headphones, familiar as a lullaby. He snatched the headphones off his ears and looked at the monitor. His heart sank. It was so foggy, or blurry, he could barely make out the orb. He could tell it was still covered with an eclectic assortment of singing metals, but the others wouldn't see it, wouldn't believe him. No one would. No credible evidence. Just a grey-blue blur. He leaned forward, squinting.

"You're gonna go blind, doing that," Kramer said, looking over his shoulder and sipping from a steaming travel mug.

"You see that?" Boyd asked, pointing at the screen. "Something's moving."

A hazy specter approached the orb and leaned over the boxes, as if checking them.

"That's the kid," Boyd guessed, by the size and the shocking golden hair.

"What'cha got?" Rita joined them, swigging a cup of kava tea. "What's all that stuff stacked on the orb?"

"They put it there last night," Boyd replied, marveling at her sharp eyes. "The alarm beeped at," he consulted the log, "eleven thirty p.m. You guys were asleep. I looked, but I couldn't see shit. I could hear, though. Listen." He turned the speaker on. The musical hum swelled to fill the tiny storefront.

"It sounds different than before," Rita mused, "it's like music".

"Yeah, it's even more obnoxious. Turn it down!" the Chief ordered.

Boyd turned the sound down, muttering, "Damn these cheap plastic lenses! It's broad daylight, and I still can't see anything."

Another beep sounded. Boyd switched to the Platform Cam, that viewed the river from the metal platform the Musiks had built below the little cave hole on the cliff. That one was fuzzy, too, but not quite as bad. "See, this one's pointing down," Boyd explained. "The sun doesn't shine on it, so the lens isn't so degraded."

"What's that?" Rita asked, touching the screen. Something moved through the fog on the river bar.

"People!" Boyd counted the moving blobs. "One, two, three..."

"Really?" Kramer took another swig of his coffee.

Boyd turned to him. "Yeah, really. There are people on the river bed, walking upriver toward the portal, um, the orb."

"Are they green?" Kramer asked drolly. He could see motion in the foggy distance, but it could have been anything, the wind blowing the fog around, for all he could tell.

"That big one looks green, I think." Rita pointed again. "And that shorter one next to him. And look! That white one's eye is in the wrong place."

"Yeah," Boyd replied, "They're not aliens, just freaks." He sounded disappointed.

"The Look 'N Up Gene," Rita recited. "Eyes cocked up and to the left. Every generation has one."

"Sure," Kramer threw back his head, draining his cup. "That's what they say. But these people are all liars. Even the cops. Or haven't you noticed?"

Boyd switched back to the Orb Cam. A larger white blob had joined the first. Boyd zoomed in on their faces. "That's Francine and Jerry, I think. They're wearing masks!" The subjects turned away from the camera and faced the river, waving their arms in wide arcs.

"What are they doing?" Rita wondered. "What's all that stuff piled up on the orb?"

Boyd was pretty sure he knew the answers, but he kept his speculations to himself.

Nauve, Granulara

Bazu paced back and forth in front of the Rock, waiting nervously for his escort to the Great Hall. His new longstick was freshly stained with gaa and decked with strings of pomegranate seeds and the feathers of a Kiko Bird, brilliant red and blue and freely given, he said. This stick was heavier. A serious longstick, not meant for silly twirling tricks. He wore the old Akash's filthy but venerated robe over a freshly woven tunic and pants from his momama. A respectable enough weave, but nothing like Tamaya's magnificent gown, and only he knew why. Because Ritamay hadn't really made that gown for Tamaya, as he had claimed. He had found the swatch of fabric, alien in its eerie sheen, its feather-lightness, the tight, seamless weave of its fine fibers. It had been lying right here on that accursed Rock when he had entered the Holy Cave for the first time.

The pink had faded from the sky by the time Rakta arrived with his entourage. Tallmon and Zeltar, the two oldest surviving warriors, limped on arthritic limbs on either side of Mangu, the Senior War Ganeesh. Rakta strode before the elephant, using his notched and bloodstained longstick as a walking staff. His faithful dog, Fertek, followed at his heel.

"They're here, Sir," Bupple announced from the porch.

"I ordered all the best warriors! He brings me these geezers?" Bazu sputtered when he joined Bupple on the porch.

"The men and ganeesh must prepare for battle, Sir," Bupple dared argue.

"You are starting to sound like a war chief," Bazu said with a grin. "Now help me down."

Bupple came to his side and steadied him. He could barely descend the steps; he was shaking so! His heart was pounding in his ears. Black fog obscured the edges of his vision. He looked down at his new pomegranate-skin shoes on the steep staircase hewn of hard cave rock, and felt an unbearable vertigo. He flashed to the story of Batuk, plunging to his death from those very stairs. Tamaya had said it wasn't true, and she was right. That didn't help.

When he finally reached the ground, he raised his head and scanned the waiting group, except Rakta. He couldn't bring his gaze around to Rakta. But the others were all smiling at him! Not smirking at a secret joke about him. Actually smiling! Proudly, like he was their Akash!

All at once, his shaking stopped and his vision cleared. He allowed the old men to lift him into the elaborate seat on the great animal's back. A special seat, just for the Immortal Akash who lives in the Holy Cave. He promised himself he wouldn't be scared this time. Why should he be? He was the Immortal Akash. He could not die.

The procession started to move down the trail to the village. From above and behind, Bazu could finally stand to look at Rakta. He stared at that circle of bare green skin on the top of that balding head all the way to the Great Hall. He wished the old Akash had taught him the Evil Eye, so he could probe right through that smooth, shiny skin and boil those traitorous brains. But, no matter. He knew Rakta was marching into its last battle. As War Chief, anyway.

The men poured out of the Great Hall to witness the arrival of the new Akash. There was Samard and Maffoon and even that bully, Rodan, all cheering! Bazu's Momama keened shrilly above the rest. She was the only woman in the welcoming hoard. *Where is Tamaya?* Bazu wondered, but only for an instant. He couldn't quite picture her inside the Great Hall, leading the women in food preparation. *Just don't embarrass me,* was his last thought of his tether before he leapt onto the stage in front of the adoring crowd to conduct his first First Pomegranate Day Ceremony as Akash.

He would not break the news yet. *Let Rakta fight, maybe he'll die,* he plotted. For now, he resolved, he would just recite his prepared speech, then the Litany, and then announce the arrival of the first phalanx of nimblies.

The crowd swam before him as he searched his memory for his speech. He had to admit, in his wildest dreams he hadn't expected this jubilant greeting. He had made it! He barely dared to believe it. *I am Akash! Their Holy Man. Their Ruler! They chant my name! Not Tiny Akash, Warrior Akash! They call me Warrior Akash! Wait,* warrior*?*

He raised his hands, then lowered them, trying to quiet his adoring fans. He opened his mouth to begin his speech, but no sound came out.

"Warrior Akash, Warrior Akash!" his inferior classmates chanted. He looked down at them, then raised his head and began his carefully prepared words.

"The nimblies and bumblies are on us again. We know that Shavarandu is not the answer."

Mumbles spread through the crowd.

"The old Akash used Shavarandu, to his demise." More mumbles. "We have tried Insitucide in the past, also without success." Heads nodded in agreement. "Shavarandu and Insitucide are evil!" he continued. "They are not the way! The only way to rid ourselves of the nimblies and bumblies is to fight! Fight Hard!"

The young warriors cheered and whooped their war chants; "Fight, fight, fight!" and "You just gotta kill 'em!"

Bazu nodded like a seasoned, solemn Akash. "You just gotta kill 'em." He stated the favorite war cry of the young with an icy calm. "You say you must kill them. You *know* you must kill them. Yet, you do not. They still live. Cycle after cycle they come, and you men fight, and still they come. You have failed!" He raised his voice and turned to face Rakta and the older warriors who stood warily at the edges of the crowd. Their bony noses pointed at him sharply, deeper mumbles rumbled below the chants of the boys.

"You must fight harder! You say you are the great warriors who have trained forever!" The young Akash rolled his eyes theatrically. "I say your training is inadequate. You're lazy!" The cheers dropped abruptly. "You should have defeated those dumb animals cycles ago, by simple, brute force, just as you claim. But you don't do it! You don't fight hard enough!"

"You fight with us!" Samard's challenge rose from the silent crowd. "You say you can't be killed, so join us in the trenches with your longstick, oh Immortal Akash!" He bowed low, his straight, bowl-cut hair hanging limply. His elbow jutted out and nudged his closemate, Maffoon, another wisecracker. He bowed, too. The emptyheaded clubber joined in, then the rest of the warriors, then all the villagers bowed low, from the waist.

"I cannot. I am too important." Bazu spoke over a sea of backs.

Samard raised his impudent head. "But you cannot die. So, we won't lose you if you fight. If you are truly immortal." The crowd murmured and drew away from Samard. No one had ever doubted the Akash so openly, and on First Pomegranate Day! Samard voiced doubts they all shared, but only this impudent young warrior would speak them this way. Surely, he would get the Evil Eye. Where was Rakta? He should protect this promising youth, by shutting him up. Doesn't he value him?

Rakta was outside the door, staring to the east, watching for nimblies, they supposed, as if he didn't believe the young Akash could predict their arrival, like the old Akash had done without fail.

Samard, Maffoon, Canam and Buppan leapt up on the stage and surrounded the Akash. Buppan stripped the superfluous feathers and beads from the Akashic longstick and shoved it back at Bazu. "You'll need this. You're good. You'll kill your share. Come on, it's time."

"No, I cannot," the Akash resisted weakly.

"What have you to fear?" Canam retorted. "If I was immortal, I would charge them straight on, from the front line."

"From the Rock of Yanzoo!" Maffoon proposed to rousing cheers.

"Is that what you will do, Akash?" Rodan asked from the audience. "Will you be our front line?"

It sounded quite glorious, and Bazu actually considered it for a moment. By the time he came to his senses, the men had lifted him off his feet. He clutched his longstick with white knuckles as they carried him, squirming and whining, out the wide front doors and onto the battlefield.

Bupple ran after them. He passed Rakta at the doorway. "Rakta!" he cried, "They are carrying the Akash into battle. They really think he's immortal! They're taking him to the Rock of Yanzoo."

Rakta just stared silently upriver.

"We must stop them, Sir!" Bupple presumed to order the War Chief.

Slowly, deliberately, Rakta turned away and walked into the Great Hall.

Bupple resumed his futile chase with tears in his eyes.

Tamaya

A startled zebkin sprang away when the bushes parted. A heavy marble rolling pin appeared, then a bare green knee and thigh. The long leg straightened, and Tamaya stood, brushing the dried leaves and seeds from her delicate gown with a slightly annoyed look. Everything seemed to stick to it now. She cast her gaze east and west, upriver toward the mists and down the trail toward the village. Then she scurried up the stairs to the Holy Cave, and the Holy Rock.

She went into the Death Tunnel and found the coiled wire on the wall where Rakta had left it. With the slow, unproductive steps of a dream, she returned to the tunnel entrance and unplugged the light from the mysterious Shavarandu contraption Bazu had discovered behind the door. The cave darkened slightly. There was enough daylight to see those two slits in the wall that matched the prongs at the end of the cord that hung from her shoulder. *And these prongs*, she thought as she shoved them into the slots where she usually plugged the lamp, *are just like those two hard prongs on my gown that dig into my neck. It would be so comfortable without that, and the bugs.* She shivered. The tingling was worse than ever.

She swung the prickly gown off her shoulders. Clad only in her pomegranate-skin bikini, she squatted, holding the gown in her left hand, and the cord in the other. She ran her finger around the collar of the gown until she found those annoying prongs that Rakta had found so amusing.

Rakta had shown her. Akira, too, in her dreams. Her momama-in-law had never made this gown. This gown was not a gown. It was an instrument of Shavarandu. She shoved the prongs into the plug. The gown tingled in her hand unbearably. She dreaded putting it back on. She retrieved her rolling pin from the floor beside her, stood up, and inhaled a long, slow breath.

Earth, the Rock

"Hiiiiii!" Fran gushed quietly through her favorite mask, decorated with bulbs of garlic, sprigs of parsley, and butterflies. The dogs broke the forced silence with short, happy yaps as Lassen and Tobey greeted their sisters, Goldilocks and Tehama, and their momama, Shastina. They bounded down the short, steep river bank while Belinda and Salistar scrambled up, straight into Fran's outstretched arms. She couldn't wait for the visitors to don their masks. She just grabbed them and hugged them tight. She'd missed Star so much! Shastina sat at Star's feet, begging for her mate, Brodey.

"Hey Bel, Star." Jerry chirped as he rushed past the cooing huddle. He launched himself off the top of the bank, landing clumsily on the rocky river bed. "Hey, guys!" he greeted the men on the river bar through his midnight-blue mask decked with stars and nebulas in bright, gassy blues and reds.

The four young dogs chased each other up and down the river bar, digging their claws into the gravel, sand squirting out behind them.

"Masks." Patrick warned, slapping a green paisley print across his nose and mouth. Valko grumbled and covered his face and beard with a camouflaged fishing gaiter. Felsic donned his mask, featuring the latest Nascar winner.

"Come on, guys." Patrick started toward the bank where the women huddled too close together. No one followed. They were too busy exchanging elbow bumps and loose, awkward hugs with Jerry, and asking him where Elmer was. When he answered, Valko craned his neck downriver, toward the platform.

"Come on!" Patrick repeated. "Don't you hear it? It could go off any minute now! Round up the dogs! Get all these Earth treasures piled up on the Rock so you can bring them home to Nauve. You want to go home, right?" The sporadic progress of green flesh toward the Rock came to an abrupt halt.

Inspection

Elmer sat in the driver's seat of the four-wheeler, listening for the buzzing of the Rock, the musical rattling of the steel and glass, the subtle drone in his head as the thing tried to scramble his molecules and send him to another dimension. He couldn't hear it from here. He hadn't heard it from the house, either. Maybe he was just used to it. Maybe it was doing its work insidiously, without him even noticing. But, he reasoned, there was no Net, like last time, so maybe, probably, it would just do all that buzzing for nothing again, and the green people wouldn't go anywhere except back to Patrick's where they would struggle to find something to do, while all these pomegranates...

Something moved on the river, far below. He grabbed his binoculars. "There you are!" he whispered at a herd of green people being driven up the river by three dogs. Valko towered above the others, Salistar at his side. Patrick's white flesh glowed next to Felsic's olive tone. Elmer's little brother, out of place in any company. A similar anomaly walked ahead of him alongside Baput. Belinda! *What's* she *doing here?*

As the procession passed out of view, friendly barks erupted from the direction of the Rock. Elmer turned that way. He couldn't see the Rock from there, but he watched the sky above it for a blinding flash, or maybe giant dragonflies and bats. He listened, too, straining his ears until he heard, not the unearthly hum of a space portal opening, but a plain-old Earth pickup truck. The inspectors!

"Crap!" Elmer grumbled, "Right now? They're all here! It's almost time for�"

Ian Foster's brand-new Dodge came roaring up the road and pulled up to the locked gate. Sheriff Dave's patrol car squeezed in behind it, lights flashing, tail sticking out in the street.

Dave stepped out of the patrol car into the road. "No answer at the house. I'll try his cell."

"Don't bother!" Elmer yelled, waving from his position above the driveway in the west orchard. He didn't stick around to see if they'd heard him. Ignoring his ringing phone, he fired up the 4-wheeler and headed out of the orchard and down the driveway to where the sheriff was opening the gate. Elmer had been obliged to give him the combination, part of their agreement.

He turned the four-wheeler sideways, so it blocked the driveway, and hopped off. He left it running to cover the humming, the barking, the shouting and hooting, the screaming and crying, whatever might happen down there. He approached the visitors so that they had their backs to the Rock, while he faced it.

"Hi, Elmer," an unmasked Ted Bates jumped out of Ian's pickup and offered his hand. Elmer didn't even offer an elbow.

"Inspection time!" Ian crowed as he came around from the driver's side wearing a smug smile that raised the hair on the back of Elmer's neck.

Elmer shook his head. "I don't know what you guys still think you're gonna find. You know I ain't had no help the last three years. You're kicking my ass, Ian, economically anyway. Nice truck!"

"That's not my intention," Ian was quick to clarify. "We just want to make sure you obey the law. No harboring illegal aliens. Especially green ones. With Covid."

Elmer thrust his chin in Dave's direction. "I thought enforcing the law was *his* job."

Dave stepped onto the driveway. "Now, Elmer. You know this is the deal we made�"

"Three years ago!" Elmer cut his old friend off. "When they left. I'm telling you, they're not here. They ain't been here since then, and I haven't heard from them. I don't know where they went. Hell, I don't know where they came from, either, or how they got here. They were just here one day. And one day, they were just, gone!

"They killed off all the bugs and finished the harvest, then they left. Gone without a trace. Left me with no help, last two harvests. Just a bunch of kids from Jerry's school. I was as surprised as anyone when I saw the green kid on the iPlane, I mean, the internet." An angry lump formed in Elmer's throat. He coughed to clear it.

Fear flashed in Ted's eyes.

That fear gave Elmer an idea. He went with it. "This year, I can't even have *them* here. The wife and kid can't help, neither. They've got it!" He coughed again.

Ted backed up. "Where's your mask?"

"Where's yours?" Elmer asked, stepping toward him, closing the distance. "I wasn't expecting you guys. I was up there in the orchard, trying to harvest all by myself. You know, these days you can't just show up unannounced."

"I'm sorry, Elmer." Dave commented from the edge of the road, through a county-issued mask he had just now thought to put on. "The RID Guys have it, too. That's why they didn't come."

"Yeah!" Ian said, "it's coming from them greenies. This was their nest. Those RID guys were here."

"Yeah, like I said, three years ago," Elmer replied. "And you guys were here then, too. Do *you* have it?" Elmer advanced. Ted and Ian backed up next to Dave at the edge of the road.

"That's why your family has it," Ian insisted. "And you've got it, too!" He opened the door of his truck.

"Yeah, go on!" Elmer swatted at them. "Don't worry about me, I'm sick. I got no help at all." Another cough, another idea. "Hey, you guys know poms! Wanna help me pick? I can pay you!" He rushed at the men at the edge of the road, coughing spasmodically, spit erupting from his unmasked mouth.

"Let's go," Ted proposed, climbing into Ian's truck. He slammed the door.

"I'm sorry, Elmer," Sheriff Dave repeated through his mask. "I hope you all get better. Really, I do. Give Fran my best." He swung into the patrol car and backed into the road.

As Ian's tailgate disappeared around a bend in the county road, Elmer drew the gate closed and locked it. He felt a tingling on the back of his neck, pulsing a vibration right into the matrix of his molecules. He turned toward the Rock. A bright, white light flashed. The four-wheeler sputtered and died.

Militia

Dirk gunned his big-wheeled GMC truck for the final pitch of the steep gravel driveway. The extra weight in the bed helped the knobby, oversized tires dig in. At the top, the driveway levelled off and widened. He pulled as far ahead as he could. He'd been right. Not enough room for all those hotheads in their pickup trucks. Good thing they'd planned this. Thank God for RID. This wouldn't be like his last visit to the cockeyed hippie's place. Or the trip to that pomegranate farm three years ago.

Otto had tested positive, but he just happened to pull a negative test right after Dirk told him that RID Headquarters wouldn't wait for him. They had a lot of guys coming from all over the state, timed to coincide with the inspection at the Look 'N Up. He suppressed his persistent cough behind a mask he never thought he'd wear.

"You OK, Buddy?" Dirk asked. He never though he'd ask a good American like Otto to wear a mask in his truck, but if he was going to ride with him all the way from LA, well, he wasn't taking any chances. *Hell, the President's even got it now. Those green bastards! And we're right here in their nest.*

Dirk pulled his own mask up over his nose and stepped out of the truck as two long, black windowless vans pulled into the empty parking spots. Four armored men sprung from under the camper shell on the back of Dirk's truck while six more piled out of each van. Sixteen trained RID shoulders, plus Dirk and Otto. Not exactly uniformed, but they all wore matching hats and masks bearing the Right Identity Doctrine's logo, a boot kicking a nappy-headed stick figure over a fence. There'd been some spicy debate about the RID mask, but after all, they were going right into the source. Some of the guys would be soon be wearing full-on hazmat suits.

"Looks like no one's home." Dirk reported to the Mission Leader, offering a tight-fisted salute. Al Reich, a stiff little man in khakis, pointed to the guys from the pickup, then ran his finger in a line from the driveway up the trail to the worker's quarters. The four picked up their assault rifles and spread out so they covered both buildings.

The men from the vans were skillfully donning full protection suits. Otto and Dirk struggled into theirs.

Reich pointed to the six from the first van, then to the quarters.

Otto dared touch the commander's arm. "Let me go," he begged. "I know those green guys better than anybody."

Commander Reich stared at Otto's hand until it was humbly withdrawn. Then he looked at Otto's face, the part he could see above the mask. He was sure he had never seen this impudent ex-deputy at the RID Academy. "You're not trained for that level of confrontation," he barked. "Especially in hazmat. But, because of your contribution to the Cause, I'll let you go into the house, with your, um, handler." He acknowledged Dirk with a curt nod. "Pretty sure no one's there, but you let these guys go in first, just in case."

Dirk and Otto watched from the parking area, wearing their hazmat suits without the headpieces, while six fully suited men marched up the trail to the workers quarters.

One guy broke the door open with a single kick. Another popped the cap of a bug bomb and tossed it through the open door. They waited on the porch, guns pointed at the smoky opening. When no one came out sputtering and coughing, the squad leader nodded. Six white-suited soldiers with air tanks on their backs drew their AK-47s and marched into the quarters. They fanned out to search the kitchen, the bedrooms, the bathroom, for signs of green-skinned alien life.

The place was spotless. Not a speck on the floor, save what the troops had tracked in on their clumsy, chemical-resistant boots. Naked mattresses in the bedrooms. No food in the kitchen, no pans or plates in the cupboards, empty silverware drawers, not even a roll of toilet paper in the bathroom.

"I don't think anybody lives here." Wes Garvey's voice scratched through his internal microphone. "If there was ever anybody here, they're long gone. This place is spotless. Not a trace of any green people, not that I can see."

"Don't mean the bugs are gone," Squad Leader White replied. He leaned out of the door, looking for Reich. "Nothing here, Sir. Nothing. They're gone. It's like they were never here."

With another silent signal from Reich, two men lifted their shoulder-mounted flame throwers from the second van and jogged up the trail to the quarters.

The second team filed into the main house, where they separated into pairs to check the kitchen, the living room, and the music room. Dirk and Otto waited on the porch, discipline warring with impatience, until the squad leader beckoned. They quickly fell in line behind the last pair, who were ascending the stairs.

Gloved hand gripping the railing, Otto climbed the stairs slowly in his unwieldy suit, struggling to feel his feet on the steps. When they reached the top, they filed down a narrow hallway. Their loud, raspy breaths came through their built-in microphones, reminding Otto of Darth Vadar. The two men ahead of them peeled off into the first bedroom. Dirk and Otto kept going to the end of the hall, where they entered the last bedroom.

Frilly curtains decked the window. Unicorn posters plastered the walls and a well-loved stuffed unicorn perched in the middle of a tousled bed. Otto headed for the bedside table, where he picked up a framed photo. "That's the green kid! With the little cockeyed girl. Remember?"

Dirk took the photo from Otto, wishing he could forget that day at the pomegranate farm when that weird little girl had freaked him out so bad he'd fallen on his ass over a rock. He forced himself to look. Definitely the green kid he'd seen that day. Definitely the same one who had appeared all over the internet, claiming responsibility for the pandemic that had shut the world down. His diseased green cheek was pressed against the deformed girl's freckled one. The glass over his face was smudged with kiss-marks. Still holding the photo, Dirk turned and left the room.

Behind him, Otto raised his automatic rifle.

Dirk heard multiple shots, then breaking glass. A babble of expletives exploded through the speaker in his ear. The other two men came clomping up the hall from a room that looked like an office.

Dirk stepped back into the kid's room. The other two men looked over his shoulder from the doorway. The window was shattered outwards. A jagged line of holes ran across two walls. Bits of down floated above the holes that crossed the bed. The toy unicorn slumped on its side.

"What the hell?" Dirk's voice crackled through the com system. "You sick bastard!"

Otto grinned through his faceplate. "What difference does it make?"

"Evidence!" Dirk shouted, "bullets! What if they investigate?"

"They won't" Otto replied, shouldering his rifle. "Haven't you heard? Global warming. These mountain places burn all the time."

Otto followed the muttering troops down the hall to the stairs. When he passed the bathroom, he ducked in and plucked a plump, full roll of toilet paper from the holder. "Waste not, want not," he whispered.

As soon as he emerged from the house, Reich gestured to the flame throwers. They marched into the narrow woods between the quarters and the house, making sure the fire spread naturally, in the direction of the prevailing wind.

Nauve, The Battle

"To the trenches, men!" The instant his trained ears heard the thrumming of the approaching nimblies, Rakta broke his stubborn silence to bark the traditional, though unnecessary, order. Most of the men were already on the battlefield, carrying the beleaguered Akash to the Rock of Yanzoo in a whirlwind. Bazu's momama, Ritamay, ran after them, adding to his distress with her embarrassing shrieks.

Rakta walked slowly to his place in the forward trench, where he stood and watched the young men pin the Akash to the Rock of Yanzoo, crying, "The Immortal Warrior Akash fights with us!"

Bazu' screams drowned out their zealous cheers. They were even more piercing than the pitiful yelps from his momama, which already tore at

Rakta's sensitive ears, but not at his heart. He remained unmoved until a deeper, more resounding scream joined the horrid cacophony.

Bupple tossed the young warriors aside and spread his giant body over the rock, completely covering his Akash, just as the first nimblies arrived. The giant dragonflies sank their long proboscises through his tough hide; one, then two, then five... Bupple disappeared beneath their fluttering wings as they sucked him dry.

The screaming stopped. The young warriors ran to their positions in the other trenches. Rakta took up his longstick and went to work battling the second phalanx of ravenous flying beasts. Bupple's lifeless, desiccated body still covered the softly whimpering Akash.

Ritamay arrived at the Great Door just before the fifth-cycle boys had drawn it all the way closed. They'd been too busy watching the immortal Akash's first battle to close it when they should have. They bowed their black-haired heads as the hysterical Momama of Akash came staggering through. The door boomed woodenly behind her, and the log bolt scraped into place.

Azuray grasped Ritamay's shoulder and escorted her to a seat, like she did for so many grieving momamas each cycle. The rest of the women stared at her from a confused knot in the middle of the wide room.

"Let's get to work!" Peratha slurred loudly, a bottle of desperation wine in each hand. Aoti rushed to her side. Peratha extended a bottle toward her. She narrowed her eyes, then suddenly smiled, shrugged her shoulders, and took a long, deep draught.

Kepson, the miller's boy, tapped Larami on her shoulder, grinning wickedly. Her eyes lit up, and the couple slipped away to the privacy of the empty ganeesh pens in the back of the Great Hall, while her betrothed fought and his betrothed returned to the kitchen. No one watched them go.

Going

Tamaya swung the gown around behind her so it floated gently back onto her shoulders. The weird prongs were at the bottom now, still plugged into the chord, the way Akira had worn it her dream. *Wear this when you go*, is what she had said. "Go." Tamaya whispered, still not knowing what it meant. Did anybody? *The Old Akash and his family. Baput, my true betrothed. I guess they know.* Would she be seeing them soon?

She gripped her rolling pin more tightly than she ever had. Three years of nightmares stacked themselves in her head. Akira saying, "wear this when you go." Her Momama handing her the rolling pin Popa had made, one Momama had never seen, saying, "take this when you go."

The Holy Rock glared with a harsh, white light. She glanced at the cave entrance. Sometimes the sun hit the Rock just so, but never this early in the morning. No, the Rock was glowing from inside, on its own. Brighter, whiter, blindingly brilliant, but cool as ever. It was humming, too. Or were her ears ringing? When had that started? Her gown felt like a thousand insects dancing on her back.

"Go-ing," she croaked the strange word through chattering teeth. She lifted a numb, shaky leg and stepped onto the perfectly round, glowing surface. The light collected under her gown, making it billow wildly around her, exposing her bare, shapely legs and pomegranate panties. She pushed it down modestly with the rolling pin that suddenly felt so heavy! The handle brushed the Rock, and her gown touched the smooth, humming surface.

The brightness swallowed her. Nothing but pure whiteness, and the worst headache she could ever have imagined. She couldn't tell how long she stayed that way. At last, the mist dropped and vanished, all at once. She found herself outside, looking out over the river. Was she on the porch of the Holy Cave? Who were those people standing on the river bed? The blurred blobs slowly focused into five very strange people. Two were the wrong color, one of them had an eye in the wrong place, and none of them had noses or mouths!

Earth, the End

Video

"What the?" Boyd slammed the side of the monitor with the heel of his hand, then shook the pain away. Still, the image continued to dissolve into a blur. He turned some dials, no better. "What's with this thing?"

"I don't know." Rita sat down next to him and scrolled through the other camera feeds on another monitor. "These other images are okay; the house, the quarters..."

"Yeah, it's only blurred where the action is!" Boyd whined. "The part I need to see! Something's going on. They must have some kind of signal jammer."

Arrival

"Look!" Belinda cried, pointing to the Rock. Was it the sun, breaking through the river fog? No. The rock was glowing! A solid beam of stark, white light shot straight up into the sky.

The women on the bank backed away. The men, still on the river bar, stood perfectly still. The beam was too bright to look at, but they couldn't look away. Gradually, it dispersed into a scattered glow with a dark shape in the middle of it. A human shape.

The image sharpened as the brightness faded, resolving into a buxom young woman with long black hair, standing on the tree saw at the round peak of the Rock, muting its deep vibration. She was wrapped in a disheveled gown that now seemed to glow more brightly than the Rock. A bare, moss-green leg emerged, stepping over a crate of shuddering machetes.

"Tamaya, I presume." Jerry quipped from Baput's side on the river bar.

Picking her way around the rattling crates of weapons and cookware, Tamaya stepped off of the Rock. She thrust the rolling pin at Salistar without looking at her or the other women on the bank. Her eyes were fixed on the men below her on the river bed.

"The Akashic Rolling Pin," Star whispered reverently, turning it in her hands. She looked up at Fran, her brows knotted. "But I have the Akashic pin. It is mine, not this. Look. It is rough. Poorly carved. Never used," she meowed at the back of the magnificent young woman who stood at the edge of the bank, legs spread slightly, hands on her hips, long, dark hair stirring dramatically in the morning breeze.

"This is for you," Star declared, handing the instrument to Belinda.

Pondering the implication, Belinda slowly, reverently received the second Akashic Rolling Pin. She turned it in her hands while the women looked on. The pattern of spiraling cells seemed to climb up and disappear as it spun.

"It's beautifully carved," Fran appreciated, contradicting Star's judgement.

"It looks like DNA," Belinda mused. "Aunt Fran, I'm sure. That's a DNA spiral!"

"That," Fran replied, "is a cry for help from Akira."

Even with the strange face coverings, Tamaya recognized Valko, Felsic, and Baput. She scrambled down the bank. Her silvery wrap floated up around her, weighed down by the cord that dragged behind it and bounced over the river cobbles.

Leaving her precious new rolling pin in Fran's admiring hands, Belinda took Tamaya's place at the top of the bank. She watched Tamaya step gingerly across the uneven river cobbles in her silly pomegranate-skin sandals toward the men who had still not found their legs. She stopped right in front of Baput, her betrothed. She adopted that stance again, arms akimbo, legs apart, green flesh poking out from under that flimsy gown that wafted out of control in the rising river wind.

Baput just stood there, his jaw gaping, his eyes focused on her breasts.

"B," Jerry whispered, poking his frozen friend, "c'mon! That's gotta be rude on any planet!" He glanced up at his cousin standing on the bank, her stare launching daggers even *he* could feel.

After a silence that seemed to last forever, Baput's lips moved. Silently at first. Then a squeak. Finally, he found his words. "The Net!" he croaked, fondling the soft, silvery fabric that barely covered Tamaya's pert left breast.

Epilogue

Nicaragua, 2020

Gelupe was in her tree when the men came. She could tell they were Zitas by the patches on their shoulders and the logo on their berets. A scorpion, a deadly AK47, and a bolt of Z-shaped lighting. Mama was at a Leones meeting. The local cartel had been all but wiped out, but the Leone's legacy continued in the loosely organized groups who still resisted the brutal cartel from Mexico that had taken over the tiny villages along the border of Guatemala and El Salvador. The Zetas knew Mama was at that meeting. That's why they came now, today.

Gelupe didn't make a sound. She lay down on the branch of her tree, resting her cheek on the cool bark, and waited, her soft breaths fluttering the leaves that hid her face.

The men walked around the house to the back. They tried the back door. "It's locked," the tall one reported.

"Break the window," the shorter, rounder one ordered. The tall one must have hesitated, because the apparent commander snapped, "What's the difference? It will all be a heap of ruins in a minute."

"Tortuga!" Gelupe whispered. At eight years old, she was well acquainted with La Bomba. She helped Mama make them out of fertilizer and heating oil. She knew how they worked, and what they did. Mama had used them herself, on the Zetas. Now they would use one on her, to break her heart by killing her daughter. But they wouldn't get her. They would only get her pet turtle. There was nothing Gelupe could do but mourn.

The men broke the window, entered the house for just a minute, and left in a big hurry. They never saw the girl in the tree. Did they see the helpless turtle in his box in her room, her shabby lean-to alcove off the kitchen? They wouldn't care, Gelupe knew.

There was a bright flash, a numbing roar, and the roof of Gelupe's bedroom flew into the sky.

The next day, other men came, wearing the lion badges of the Leones. Mama was expecting them, but she wasn't glad to see them. Neither was Gelupe.

Staring blindly, Mama took Gelupe by the arm and walked her towards the men and their plain white van. "Aqui. Mi niña. Mi oro, mi preciosa. Take care of her, don't let her..." She pushed Gelupe at a kind-looking man with a lined, brown face. He took her by the arm, guided her gently to a seat in the back of the empty, windowless van and closed the door.

Mama's cries sounded so strange, muffled through the steel wall of the van. Gelupe had never heard her cry like that, not even when the Zetas killed Popa. She was angry then. Now, she was, well, something else.

The van rocked. The front doors slammed. They started rolling. Gelupe couldn't see where they were going. They stopped many times before they left the province, each time picking up more people. Five middle aged men boarded at different spots, all wearing a weary expression that made little Gelupe feel tired. Then, a lone woman in her mid-forties joined them. She had huge breasts and buttocks, and she wheezed when she breathed. At the last stop, a nervous young man came aboard. He kept looking at Gelupe, sniffing his fingers and muttering to himself. When he tried to sit next to Gelupe, the fat lady fell on her, swallowing her between fleshy breasts. She wouldn't let go, and Gelupe couldn't breathe. "I won't let him touch you," she assured her airless charge. It was very hot. Gelupe wanted her to let go, and she wanted her to keep holding her. They rode that way for a long time.

Gelupe didn't know how long it had been. They stopped occasionally. They were fed and let out to stretch and take care of their burning personal needs. The fat lady, Gelupe never learned her name, always stayed between Gelupe and that twitchy man. Wherever they stopped, it was desert for as far as her young eyes could see. Not a house in sight, in any direction. *Is this America? So much empty land! Why doesn't anybody live here? Why can't we just stay here, and build a hut, and get Mama and she can come live here with me and the fat lady and no more Zetas. No more bomba.* But they always loaded back in to the dark van that smelled like sweat and gas and misery. Until the last time.

It was midday, and the sun was blazing white-hot in a pale sky. Like the other stops, blank desert spread away forever. Nothing moved but a single lizard that skittered away from them in terror. She looked around for the food. There was none. The driver just said, "Estamos aquí" meaning, 'we're here'.

Is this America? Gelupe thought again. It looked the same as all the other stops, except, the helper man pointed past the front of the van. Following his finger, she looked to the north. A rambling line of sticks spread across the desert, a fence, of sorts, but with lots of gaps where people had removed the slats, and saggy parts where they had bent the support poles to the ground. Beyond that, a line of sluggish grey water shone like molten steel in the pitiless sun.

"Adelante!" The man told them to run. Gelupe ran, north, toward the failing fence, toward America. She was the fastest runner, and soon she was alone. She slipped easily through a missing slat on the fence and ran to the river. The grassy bank was a couple of feet above the water, which ran shallow over a perfectly flat bottom, concrete, not gravel. She stepped in.

The water was refreshingly cool against her hot skin, until the burning started. She waded across. Her legs felt like they were on fire. The burning and stinging were unbearable. She looked back. She was more than halfway across, and the weird guy was stepping into the river behind her. She didn't see any of the others. She kept going.

The opposite bank was a vertical concrete wall. How to climb it? A tree root twisted down from above the wall. She reached for it, took one more step. The river bed dropped out from beneath her. She let out a guttural squeak as she plunged neck deep in the freezing, burning water. She fumbled for that root, but it was out of reach. In its place, she found a thick, meaty hand. *One of my fellow travelers?* she hoped. She had never learned any of their names, but they were her family now, even the creepy tio. She pivoted from her dangling arm to look back for him, but he was gone.

She looked up at the man attached to the hand that hauled her straight up out of the water and onto the top of the bank. A handsome young man with black hair and light brown skin, like hers. He wore a golden badge and a patch on his sleeve. Not a lion or a scorpion, an eagle! The sign of the United States of America! Gelupe knew it, because Mama had drawn that symbol and made her memorize it. "The Americans are on our side," she had said. "They will help you. When you are in the van, you tell no one what side we're on. Say nothing about the Leones, or the Zetas. No matter what they ask you. No matter what they say about us. You're just a *niñita*. You know nothing of such things. But when you see the eagle, you tell them your Mama fights the Zetas! Tell them your Papa died fighting them! That they tried to kill you, blew up your bedroom!" Mama had grasped her hand so tightly it hurt, like this man held her hand now. "Tell them you seek asylum in the United States. Ass-sie-lem," she had pronounced slowly. "Can you say that?"

"I seek asylum in the United States," Gelupe told the man with the eagle on his uniform.

Don't miss out!

Visit the website below and you can sign up to receive emails whenever Janice Carr Smith publishes a new book. There's no charge and no obligation.

https://books2read.com/r/B-A-NTEX-PLDCJ

BOOKS 2 READ

Connecting independent readers to independent writers.

Also by Janice Carr Smith

Look 'N Up
Look 'N Up Liberation

Watch for more at https://www.looknup.us/.

About the Author

Janice Carr was raised by liberal parents in '60s in Cambridge, Massachusetts, a short hike from Harvard Square. As a kid, she liked to read, write, and act out her stories with her stuffed animals, and sometimes her brother, Charlie, while Dad's Wurlitzer Organ buzzed the corners of the ceiling, rocking the house. Mom would be out marching for some left-wing cause or candidate.

All that ended when Janice was twelve. Cancer struck, first her mom, then her dad. By fourteen, she was orphaned and living in Florida with relatives who had a very different world view. When they decided to move farther into their rural world, Jan rebelled and returned home to finish high school, living with a dear family friend to whom her first book is lovingly dedicated.

Itching to be on her own, no longer a guest, she left campus-rich Boston for a Radio-TV-Film major at Northwestern University. The college Outing Club opened her city-born eyes to the natural world with hiking, rock-climbing and spelunking trips, and she switched to a Geology major.

After years of wandering, she married John Smith and became an Environmental Consultant, shepherding public works projects through

California's rigorous environmental compliance process, first at a private engineering firm and later for a rural county public works department in Northern California.

In 2017, Janice retired in the same county with the same husband. One day, in her garden, she started hearing voices. She looked up, and the Look'N Up was born.

Read more at https://www.looknup.us/.

www.ingramcontent.com/pod-product-compliance
Lightning Source LLC
LaVergne TN
LVHW090547110826
845146LV00001B/52
9798987517925